TO CLAIM HER HEART

By Jodie Wolfe

TO CLAIM HER HEART BY JODIE WOLFE
Published by Smitten Historical Romance
an imprint of Lighthouse Publishing of the Carolinas
2333 Barton Oaks Dr., Raleigh, NC 27614

ISBN: 978-1-946016-47-8

Cover design by Elaina Lee
Interior design by AtriTex Technologies P Ltd

Available in print from your local bookstore, online, or from the publisher at: ShopLPC.com

For more information on this book and the author visit: https://www.jodiewolfe.com/

Scripture quotations are taken from the Holy Bible, King James Version (KJV)

Brought to you by the creative team at Lighthouse Publishing of the Carolinas: Eddie Jones, Shonda Savage, Karin Beery, Pegg Thomas, Brian Cross, Ann Knowles, Lucie Winborne

Library of Congress Cataloging-in-Publication Data
Wolfe, Jodie
To Claim Her Heart / Jodie Wolfe 1st ed.

Printed in the United States of America

Praise for *To Claim Her Heart*

Did you ever wonder what life was like for the pioneers? Jodie Wolfe mingles etiquette lessons with a vivid picture of the hardships the early homesteaders faced in this gentle tale of faith, friendship, and finding love where it's least expected.

~Amanda Cabot
CBA and ECPA bestselling author

Jodie Wolfe takes you on a fun ride back to the days of settling the west and land claims. Ms. Wolfe keeps you entertained while giving you tidbits of history along the way. If you like westerns, you're sure to enjoy To *Claim Her Heart*.

~Debbie Lynne Costello
Author of *Sword of Forgiveness*
Amazon's #1 seller for Historical Christian Romance

Jodie Wolfe has penned a heart-warming tale of friendship, adversity, and romance in the days following the Cherokee Strip land run. The feisty but troubled heroine will keep you smiling with her antics while the kind and patient hero will melt your heart. *To Claim Her Heart* is a charming, engaging story well worth reading.

~Vickie McDonough
Best-selling, award-winning author of 46 books and novellas
Gabriel's Atonement, book 1 in the Land Rush Dreams series.

In *To Claim Her Heart*, Jodie Wolfe's authentic faith shines through her depiction of the hardships and joys of homestead life. A place where the weak find strength they didn't know they possessed and the strong learn to trust and lean on others.

~Angel Moore
Love Inspired Historical Author

Staring a fiery heroine and a stalwart hero, *To Claim her Heart* by Jodie Wolfe offers a memorable story of determination and grit, love and faith, on the Oklahoma frontier.

~Naomi Rawlings
Bestselling author of the Eagle Harbor Series

Jodie Wolfe has created a lovely chemistry of opposites between Elsie Smith and Benjamin David as they each bring their dreams to the Cherokee Strip and fight for their right to the same piece of land. *To Claim Her Heart* is a beautiful story of perseverance, hope deferred, and reconciliation with God and fellow man. Wolfe draws the reader into the world of frontier settlers with impressive historical detail, revealing their daily struggles and battles against nature with realism. Her spirited characters, Elsie and Benjamin, have stayed with me long beyond closing the last page of the book. I highly recommend *To Claim Her Heart* to fans of inspirational historical romance!

~Kathleen Rouser
Award-winning author of *Rumors and Promises*

Dedication

My first praise goes to my Heavenly Father.
You are the reason I do what I do.

This book is in loving memory of my sweet mother-in-law,
Merrietta Jo Wolfe. You shared with me
your love of Oklahoma and the family
history of those who made the run. I'm forever
grateful. You are dearly missed, Mom.

To my beloved husband, David.
I'm blessed to be married to *my* hero.
Your support, love, and pitching in while
I worked endless hours on this project, hasn't gone unnoticed.
Thank you, Sweetheart.

To God be the glory.

"Follow peace with all men, and holiness, without which no man shall see the Lord: Looking diligently lest any man fail of the grace of God; lest any root of bitterness springing up trouble you, and therefore many be defiled."
Hebrews 12:14-15 (KJV)

CHAPTER ONE

Competition should be relegated to the male species. Proper young ladies should avoid a situation which permits rivalry, particularly involving the male species. If unavoidable, allow the gentleman to win. Be above reproach in this manner.
Mrs. Wigglesworth's Essential Guide to Proper Etiquette and Manners of Refined Society

September 15, 1893, Kiowa, Kansas—Border of the Cherokee Strip
"Elmer Smith?"

For once in all of her days, Elsie welcomed the name Pa had insisted on when her life began and Ma's had ended.

"Is that you, son?"

"Ain't your son." *Ain't no one's son.* Elsie shifted her Stetson lower to ward off the man's scrutiny.

"There's no need to get your prickles up. Do you testify you're at least twenty-one years of age and head of your household?"

Elsie nodded and bit back a retort.

"Then sign here." The man shoved a paper across the makeshift desk. Beads of moisture dotted his upper lip.

She scrawled her name on the line. The page crinkled when she folded and shoved it into her shirt pocket, along with the copy of *The Homestead Laws* and Pa's hand-drawn map.

"Get out of the way, kid." A scraggly looking fellow jabbed into her shoulder.

Elsie stepped out of line, glaring at him. He ignored her and turned his attention to the clerk.

She elbowed through a crowd of men. How had her small town swelled to so many folks? Thankfully there were few she recognized, or more so, who recognized her. The less who knew her gender, the better. She certainly didn't need no man to help her get the land she and Pa had dreamed about.

Elsie scooted her hat up and swiped at the sweat on her forehead before dropping it back into place, scrunching the thick braid she'd pinned up three days prior. Hefting her saddlebags to her opposite shoulder, she hiked the short distance to the livery and retrieved Buster. A short ride would clear her head and prepare her for what lay ahead.

Dust swirled and nearly choked Elsie as she rode in the opposite direction of the throngs to see the old farm one last time.

Acrid smoke filled her lungs. Nearby fires, to deter Sooners from entering the strip before the race began, burned in the west, but not out of control.

Elsie urged Buster, careful not to tire him. Everything hinged on finding the land tomorrow.

Everything.

September 15, 1893, Hennessey, Oklahoma Territory—Border of the Cherokee Strip

Benjamin David pocketed the certificate and patted it as if the paper provided some sort of assurance of his quest. His heart weighed like a stone in his chest. He'd thought about this day ever since President Cleveland proclaimed the strip opened for settlement. Some said it would be the last great race for land. By the folks lining the streets, Benjamin believed it.

All manner of transportation could be seen. Wagons fully loaded with goods, buggies, even a few bicycles. A train whistled in the distance. A cacophony of sounds assaulted him.

He reached into his pocket and withdrew the compass Pa had given him. Benjamin studied the inscription before dropping it back into place. Lord willing, by this time tomorrow a hundred and sixty acres would be his. He'd studied the maps of the strip enough to know Enid would be the closest place to file his claim if he didn't head too far west, otherwise he'd have to travel to Woodward.

He bent his head to ward off the gleaming sunlight. *Lord, I'm here because of Your leading. Direct me like You did Moses to the Promised Land. Help me to recognize the parcel when I see it.*

"You're a preacher, right?" A disheveled man blocked his path. Dusty clothes hung on his lean frame. The man's dull brown eyes pleaded with Benjamin.

"Yes."

"Somebody said they thought they saw you reading the Good Book, so I figured you might be a man of the cloth."

He shook the man's calloused hand. "Benjamin."

The man grasped his shoulder and tugged him forward. "This way. I need your services. You see, my friend just passed. Must be these confounded temperatures."

Benjamin allowed himself to be guided through the throng of unwashed bodies, the stench choking him. They elbowed their way to a man lying on the ground. The scent of death wafted upward. Benjamin froze as if a block of ice encased him. Not again.

The unkempt man whipped his hat off, and his bald head shimmered in the sunlight. His knuckles shone white against the black hat clamped in his fingers. "C-could you say a few words over him?"

Benjamin swallowed. A few men standing nearby bowed their heads and removed their hats. "Dear Lord, we pray for our brother. May he rest in the safety of Your arms." His throat tightened, and he couldn't go on. It brought back too many reminders.

"Amen." The men slapped their hats back in place and carried the dead man away.

Benjamin stared after them until they disappeared, then worked his way to the makeshift diner. The tent flap blew in the breeze. A swirl of dust blew grit into his eyes and nose.

He hacked as he collapsed onto a wooden bench. Maybe eating would keep his mind off the dead man.

Benjamin flicked a nickel to the waiter, and a glass of water appeared. His folks would never believe the outlandish prices businesses were getting away with on the strip. Benjamin guzzled the tepid liquid and debated eating an early supper. Yesterday he'd waited till dinnertime, then stood in line for hours only to have the food sold out by the time he'd gotten to the front.

He plunked down the price for a plate of food, and the same waiter brought a meal that couldn't be recognized. Benjamin bent his head for a brief prayer before digging in.

"Mind if I sit with you?" A black-haired man wearing an expensive suit stood by Benjamin's side balancing silverware, a glass of water, and a platter of steaming grub.

"Help yourself. I'm Benjamin David." He shifted so the gentleman would have more room on the narrow seat.

"Pleased to meet you. I'm Herbert." The fellow scraped the food back and forth across his plate and frowned at it. "What do you plan to do if you get land tomorrow?"

"We, *I* plan to set up a small farm, as well as start a church."

"I take it you're planning on a regular plot instead of a town plot?"

Benjamin nodded. "I figured the competition for a town plot might be a bit fierce." Besides, the Lord would provide in time. "What about you?"

The stranger didn't respond right away. In fact, Benjamin managed to finish his meal, and the man still hadn't answered. Benjamin swung a leg over the bench and inched back a bit so he could see the man better.

"A regular one."

Something about the way he said it made Benjamin uncomfortable. The cut of the man's clothes suggested he was from a large city, but the stranger's actions didn't coincide with his appearance. Benjamin cleared his throat. "Where you from?"

"Originally from Boston. I've done some traveling through Kansas and Oklahoma Territory. In fact, I snuck into the strip a few days ago during nightfall so I could scout out the land and know where the best plot is."

Benjamin shifted on his seat. It was illegal to slink in ahead of time.

"There's money to be had out here. I'll find a way to sell it to the highest bidder." Herbert scooped another spoonful into his mouth before shoving the plate away. "A quarter section isn't much, but I have plans. Big plans. And I won't let anybody get in my way."

Alarm shot through Benjamin, and he dropped eye contact, unsure how to respond. The stranger reminded him of folks he'd met that just couldn't keep their business to themselves. Did the man assume they'd never see each other again? The chances were slim since it was reported that close to eleven thousand folks lined the streets of Hennessey. He lifted his head and studied the man again.

Herbert's eyes darkened. "You make sure you don't follow me, you hear?" The man shifted the edge of his suit coat to reveal the glimmering handle of a six-shooter.

Kiowa, Kansas

As Elsie threaded her way through the rabble filling the streets, her spirit hadn't calmed any after seeing the farm. Tomorrow would be better, when there'd be open spaces and not so many folks wandering around. She was hard-pressed to make a single move without running into someone.

Steam from a train engine billowed as she rode past. Elsie struggled to calm Buster. All manner of conveyances and folks rambled over the prairie like ants scurrying to and fro.

Elsie nudged Buster to the starting line. She swung down from her horse, settled on the dusty ground, and rummaged through her pack. It looked like a few strips of jerky and two stale rolls would constitute her supper. She shifted on the ground and tried to get comfortable. The sun's rays blazed on their descent. It would be dark in a matter of minutes. She lowered her hat to cover her face, not remembering when she'd last slept. It had been at least three days or more.

Elsie awoke to something knocking against the side of a tin bowl. She yawned and stretched. Her stomach growled. The sun shone high overhead. Hadn't the sun been setting when she sat down? She jumped up. How long had she slept? It wasn't like her to doze so long, especially with all the noise. Three days of standing in line to register for the race must have taken its toll. Around her, folks packed up their final belongings. Mothers called out to their children.

Elsie rummaged through her pack, found the jerky, and popped it into her mouth. She patted her pocket. Pa's hand-drawn map, the certificate, and the homestead rules were there where she'd left them. She didn't have to pull out the map to remember his description. The slight hill with the stream and a sprinkling of trees with their limbs arching over it, and the rich soil. He'd included the exact mileage and landmarks to look for along the way. If she headed south and slightly east, she wouldn't have any trouble finding it.

Confident that nothing was missing, she blew out a breath. Her horse stepped closer and snorted against her cheek.

"Sorry, fella, I don't know what happened. You'll have to do with water from my canteen for now. I'm not going to risk losing my spot." She poured half the container's contents into her hat and offered it to the horse. He slurped the water, then she slapped her Stetson back in place. She'd save the stale crust of bread in her pack for later.

Folks shuffled forward, kicking up dust in the process. They stood restlessly at the line, waiting for the shot to ring out at noon to start the race. Some were on foot while others sat on horseback or atop wagons. People pressed on either side as well as behind Elsie. She glanced over her shoulder.

"Heard tell there's fifteen thousand folks here," the fella beside her said. He whistled. "Never saw so many in my life."

Ten yards away, soldiers stood near the starting line making sure nobody entered the Cherokee Strip before the time. A tremor ran through Elsie. It boggled her mind to think that, at nine different starting places along the territory, others were lined up to race as well.

One of the soldiers glanced at his pocket watch. "Fifteen minutes!"

A hush fell over the crowd.

Elsie mounted. The leather saddle creaked. Her fingers gripped the reins.

The soldiers paced back and forth, holding the line.

Minutes dragged by.

A horse stamped his foot beside her. Buster answered with a thump of his own.

Wagon harnesses jangled in the stillness.

The soldiers pointed their rifles in the air. One checked his timepiece.

A tremor ran through Elsie's body. *Help me get it, help me get it, help me get it.* Every fiber of her being tensed in anticipation. Her heart beat against her ribs.

A shot rang out.

Buster bolted and ran in the opposite direction of the strip.

September 16, 1893, Cherokee Strip

Adrenaline surged through Benjamin's body. Milly responded in kind. His little mare shot ahead of the other horses and various types of conveyances. The steady drumming of hooves pounded the ground, but he didn't dare waste time peeking backward to survey their closeness. The future lay ahead. Perhaps he could trust God to have great things in store for him after all.

Terrain whizzed past as he ran Milly hard. *Lord, show me the place You have for me.* A calm settled on Benjamin's heart.

Holding tight to the reins with one hand, he slipped the compass from his pocket to check his direction of travel. He slowed his horse to get a good read before tugging the reins slightly to the left to correct his course.

He threw a glance over his shoulder. A trio of riders crested the rise he'd just crossed over. "Good girl, Milly." He patted her sweat-soaked neck and urged her forward.

Half an hour later, Milly slowed to a trot. Benjamin continued to pray and study the land around him. Up ahead lay a small grove of trees. As Milly wandered closer, he spotted a stream trickling a path through the trees. A hill swelled on the right side.

"This is it, isn't it, Lord?" A quietness confirmed what he already knew. "Whoa, Milly."

Benjamin slipped to the ground and searched through the saddlebag. Finding the stake and a small hammer, he drove the piece of wood into the ground, claiming the land the Lord had given him.

"We're home." His heart warmed.

He picked up the reins and walked Milly to the corners of the lot, making sure there were no other stakes in sight. Benjamin jotted down the coordinates on his map. "We'll rest for a few minutes, girl, but then I'm afraid you have a few more miles ahead of you. We need to get to Enid as soon as possible." Milly snorted.

September 16, 1893, Cherokee Strip

Elsie bit her lip to keep from grumbling aloud. Not that it mattered. She'd calmed Buster enough to turn him back in the direction of the race. As they got closer to the starting line, a quick look around confirmed her suspicions—the racers were way ahead of her.

When they re-crossed the line, someone called out, “Yer a little late there, fella. Saw you headin’ the wrong direction a while ago.” A cackle followed.

She ignored the man and spurred Buster to a faster pace. “Giddyup. We need to get to Pa’s land before someone else finds it.”

Hours later Elsie reached her destination—at least she hoped so. It wasn’t like she could calculate the exact mileage while riding. The plot appeared to be the right one. There were trees and a stream. Dropping from the saddle, she glanced at the stone marker on the ground.

Yep, the rock bore the same coordinates Pa had scrawled across the bottom of his map. *This is for you, Pa.* She shoved her stake into the soil. A quarter of a square mile. Not a huge parcel by any means, but it was all hers. Well, it would be as soon as she got to Woodward and registered her claim.

The trip to Enid had been uneventful. Long, but uneventful. With nine different starting places for the race and only four land claim offices established throughout the territory, it had taken Benjamin a while to file his paperwork. The deed now rested in his shirt pocket. He couldn’t believe he owned one hundred and sixty acres.

He stepped out of the claim office. Tent after tent fluttered in the late afternoon breeze. Hammering filled the air and folks milled everywhere. The newly formed town of Enid was well on its way. Benjamin stopped by the tent marked “store,” picked up a bunch of supplies, and purchased a wagon and harness.

With the sun at his back, he turned Milly and the wagon toward his new home. He swallowed past the lump in his throat. It would have felt more like home if he had a wife to share it with him.

Elsie rolled her aching shoulders. It had taken much longer to Woodward than she'd planned on. The line to the claim office stretched and snaked beside the tents that fluttered like handkerchiefs on a clothesline. Finally, it was her turn.

Her breath hitched as she held the claim certificate in her hands a few minutes later. She smiled. *Home.* She liked the sound of it. It'd been a while since she had one.

She swooped onto Buster and traveled the distance to her new claim. The red soil spread out for miles. Dusk had descended by the time she finally reached her destination. She squinted as the pale light of the moon glimmered off a large shape on the hill.

That shouldn't be there. As she got closer, she could see something flickering—like firelight.

Withdrawing her rifle, she cocked it and took aim. "Come out from behind the wagon."

She swung her leg over Buster and dropped to the ground. A stranger eased out of the shadows. "I don't know who you are, mister, but you have sixty seconds to get off my land."

CHAPTER TWO

A proper young lady dresses appropriately according to each occasion. She should never be seen in society without gloves in place and a smile on her face.
Mrs. Wigglesworth's Essential Guide to Proper Etiquette and Manners of Refined Society

Benjamin's heart hammered against his ribcage. Was that a gun the lad held? He lifted his hands in the air and inched out from the safety of the wagon, praying with each tiny step. He squinted in the dim light but couldn't distinguish more than the form of a gangly boy beside a horse. Perhaps offering food would make the fella stop aiming the gun at him.

Benjamin cleared his throat. "Put that thing away before you hurt yourself. Are you hungry, boy? I can share my supper and fire with you tonight, but tomorrow you'll need to be on your way. I've already claimed this land."

"I don't think so. It's you who needs to be leaving *my* property."

The young fellow sounded like his voice hadn't changed yet. How well Benjamin remembered his awkward teen years when one moment he desired his mother's comfort and the other demanded to be treated like an adult. He chuckled.

"There ain't nothing funny about trespassing on a man's property." The boy ground out the words like rocks against a washboard.

"There's no reason to get your spurs a-spinning. If you put the rifle away, I believe we'll be able to get this all sorted out." Benjamin dared move closer. A full minute passed before the metallic uncocking of the rifle split the air between them and the boy slid the weapon back into the scabbard. Benjamin blew out a pent-up breath. "Why don't you come closer to the fire, and we can sort this out?"

The lad grunted. Apparently, he hadn't had the proper upbringing Benjamin had.

"The beans are about ready. You hungry?" He kept an eye on the boy in case he decided to draw his rifle again. "You can tie your horse beside Milly there."

The boy watched him for a moment, but then led his steed to the spot beside Benjamin's mare.

"What's your name?" Benjamin bent to scoop a mess of beans onto a plate.

The boy opened his mouth and closed it before he finally muttered, "Elmer."

"Pleased to meet you, Elmer. I'm Benjamin." He thrust out his hand. The fellow hesitated before offering a small, soft handshake. Benjamin passed the boy the plate of food.

The lad accepted it without a word and started shoveling beans into his mouth.

"If you don't mind, I'd like to say grace for us."

Elmer's head lifted, and his eyes flashed. "Don't believe in it."

Benjamin ignored him and bowed his head. "Dear Lord, we thank You for this food You've provided. Thank You for my new friend, Elmer. Bless us and keep us in Your care, amen." Perhaps the Lord had sent the boy so Benjamin could point him toward the Savior.

"Just 'cause you're feeding me grub don't mean you can stay on my land." Elmer scraped the last bit of beans from the plate, then licked it.

The lad could use some manners. "You keep saying this is *your* land." Benjamin hesitated before taking another bite.

"I have a deed that says so." Elmer grinned.

"You can't possibly have a deed for this lot. It's mine." Benjamin withdrew the document from his coat pocket.

"Then yours must be a fake because I've got my own." The whippersnapper waved a piece of paper under Benjamin's nose.

"We can't both have a certificate to the same place. Let me see it." His thoughts whirled, not sure what to think of the boy's bravado.

"There ain't no way I'm letting you get your grimy paws on my certificate. How do I know I can trust you?" Elmer yanked the paper back.

Benjamin studied the low-burning flame of the fire. "I'm afraid it's getting too dark to read either of them tonight. Why don't we call a truce for the evening and turn in? You can bed down here, and we'll settle it in the morning." He raked a hand through his hair, anxious for the matter to be cleared up. "What do you say?"

"How do I know you won't kill me in my sleep?"

Benjamin laughed. Could the lad tell it sounded fake? The question was, could *he* trust the boy? "I think you've been reading too many of those awful dime novels. I give you my word, as a man of God, that no harm will come to you in my camp." Hopefully, the boy would agree too. After all, what good was a man if he didn't stand by his word?

Elmer chewed on his lip. Finally, after several moments of silence, he shrugged. "I reckon I'll have to trust you for the night, but don't you try anything. I'll be sleeping with one eye open."

Benjamin wanted to laugh at the lad's bluster, but he suspected it would further rile him. Hopefully, a good night's rest would bring clarity to the situation. "You can bed down wherever you choose." He stoked the coals.

Elmer moved off into the darkness. From the sounds of it, he unsaddled his horse.

Benjamin crossed to the wagon and withdrew his bedroll and another blanket. He spread it close to the fire. "Do you need another cover?"

"No."

"You're welcome to come closer to the fire."

"No."

"Suit yourself. Good night, Elmer." Benjamin settled his long frame onto the bedding.

"Don't try anything funny. I got my rifle at the ready." The young voice cracked.

"No need to worry, son. I'm a man of my word. Put the gun away so you don't get hurt."

"I ain't yer son. Don't call me that, you hear?"

Elsie shifted her rifle closer and sank onto a blanket. Come morning she'd deal with the praying claim jumper. Grit lined her eyelids. What she wouldn't do for a few decent nights of rest in a row, but she daren't drift off and risk the snake knocking her on the head and stealing her deed. Admitting to being a man of God meant nothing. How many in Kiowa declared to be Christians, yet when times had worsened, none of them helped.

"You sure you don't need something, Elmer?" Benjamin's voice cut through the dark night.

"Never you mind." Elsie forced herself to think about other things. Anything other than the man settling down for the night.

Within a short time, the stranger's deep breathing carried across the slight distance separating them. Elsie didn't dare give in to the temptation to fall asleep. She wrapped her quilt around her body but stayed sitting up.

Quiet settled. Not even the horses stirred. Elsie yawned so wide her jaw cracked. A cool breeze blew across her cheeks. She shifted the quilt tighter around her body and lifted part of it over her hat to ward off the chill.

Elsie awoke as the sun crested the horizon. Her muscles protested. She was getting more and more like her pa. Able to fall asleep in any position.

Pins pricked her feet as she uncrossed her legs and struggled to stand.

The first rays of sunlight split the cloudless sky. Her land stretched before her, and the creek gurgled its own greeting. She sucked in the brisk morning air, relishing its sweetness.

"Morning." A deep, sleep-laced voice greeted her.

Elsie whipped around and spotted a man behind the wagon. The property stealer. How could she have forgotten about him?

When she finally got a good look at him, she sucked in a deep breath. The dim firelight from the night before hadn't done him justice. He sure didn't look like any preacher she'd ever met. Blond curls tumbled across his broad forehead as hazel eyes studied her. Stubble lined his face. She ducked her head and checked to make sure her Stetson hadn't shifted during the night.

Her heart hammered a steady cadence. Elsie couldn't resist another gawk at the handsome stranger. The quicker she got rid of him, the better. A good-looking fella would only mean trouble.

Benjamin cleared his throat. "I hope you slept well." A grin crossed his features. Had he said something else that she'd missed because of her drooling over his appearance like a lovestruck schoolgirl?

Instead of answering, she crossed the short distance to the creek and took a long drink of its coolness. Oh, to be able to scrub the dirt away. *Nope*. Best to stay dirty until she could get rid of him.

She ambled over to the campfire and took a big sniff. Something sure smelled good.

"Coffee's ready." He handed her a mug. The scent of bacon wafted on the morning air.

Elsie accepted the warm beverage and took a sip. Creamy and sweet. Her stomach sent out a loud gurgle while he continued cooking breakfast. Hotcakes bubbled in the pan.

"Thank you. Cream and sugar are a rare treat." She couldn't recall the last time she'd had the luxury of having both in her coffee.

He flipped a flapjack, slipped one onto a plate next to crisp bacon, and gave it to her. She settled on the ground with the tin plate balanced on her lap. Once the last cake finished cooking, he sat across from her. This time she waited to shovel the food in until he'd said his prayer. Silence reigned while they ate the simple meal.

She licked her fingers after finishing the last bite of bacon. "The meal's great. I appreciate your kindness."

"My pleasure." Benjamin grinned. He set his empty plate beside him and held out a piece of paper. "What do you say we get this straightened out?"

She took the deed and inspected it. Her gaze narrowed and her chin jutted. "Looks like a pretty good forgery, but you ain't the owner of this plot. I am. Not sure how you got it to look so official-like." She thrust her certificate out, so he could read it, but not actually hold it. "But as you can see, mine is legit."

He jabbed his hands through his curls, causing them to stand on end. "There has to be some type of misunderstanding. We can't both own the same piece of land. One of us has to leave."

"Well, it ain't going to be me."

A muscle in Benjamin's jaw flickered. He could be upset all he wanted, but nothing he said would make Elsie leave. Nothing.

Benjamin pocketed his document. "Your deed says you filed in Woodward. Why don't we head to Enid and get this mess cleared up? It's closer than Woodward. Surely there has been some type of filing error."

"I'm not wasting time going there when I already know I'm the rightful owner. You can go if you like. I'm staying here, on *my* land." She stood up and dusted off her backside.

"But you have to go along in order for us to settle this."

"I don't need to go nowhere with you, mister. If you'll excuse me, I got work to do, making improvements on *my* land." If she started soon, she could prove up on the plot by planting fields and building a home to show it was truly hers. Besides, the preacher looked too green to handle the demands it would take to get the tract in shape.

He scowled at her. "You don't appear old enough to have claimed land. How do I know you're twenty-one? Why, you should probably be back home with your mother."

Elsie curled her fingers into a fist and clenched it at her side. She ought to slug the low-down thief. "I happen to be a w … man of my word." Her cheeks flooded with warmth.

She strutted over to Buster, slung the saddle over the horse, and tightened the girth. The stallion tossed his head. She shoved her quilt back into her saddlebag, fastening it behind the saddle before swinging onto his back. "Be off my land by nightfall."

Benjamin watched Elmer race his horse to the other side of the property. Somehow, one hundred and sixty acres didn't seem as big as he first thought, not when the lad was only a little over four hundred yards away. *Lord, what kind of mess have You led me to?*

The scrawny boy swung down from his horse. He could imagine Elmer's blue eyes glaring at him. The lad had kept his hat clamped on his head ever since they met, and Benjamin had yet to see what color the boy's hair was. The kid's chin had been smooth like he hadn't started growing facial hair yet. He couldn't be twenty-one. But how could Benjamin find out?

He kicked at a clump of buffalo grass. Another day wasted going back to Enid. He should be plowing his land—of course, he didn't know the first thing about it, but he sure wouldn't tell Elmer that. Benjamin hesitated to leave his wagonload of belongings behind, but he'd travel faster with Milly if he did. He'd have to trust the boy not to wander off with his things.

Benjamin kicked dirt onto the coals, making sure they were out before mounting his horse. The saddle creaked as he shifted his weight and peered after Elmer. Lord willing, Benjamin would throw the trespasser out when he returned.

"What do you mean I have to wait?" Benjamin wanted to pound his fist on the makeshift table in the land claim tent.

A man with greasy hair blew out a stream of smoke and removed his cigar before answering. "You aren't the first one to claim the same property as someone else. I reckon you have a few options. You can flip a coin to see who wins the land, or you can hire a lawyer and wait for your case to be called at the land office. I heard of two fellas who started from the same place they did afore and then raced again to see who got to the property first." He cackled. "Didn't hear who won it the second time around. But if you do the lawyer route, last I heard, late November is the earliest they'll get 'round to the case."

"*November?* I can't wait until then." Benjamin rubbed his pounding temple.

"It's up to you. There's plenty of lawyers if you change your mind."

Benjamin left. He couldn't go back to his land without an answer. He wandered across the trampled-down buffalo grass. A sea of tents stretched as far as he could see. More folks were here than yesterday. He shook his head. It boggled his mind to think of how fast the town had sprung onto the strip in only two days.

The sun beat down as he wandered around searching for a tent labeled "law." Spotting it, he squeezed inside a curtained off area where a bunch of men nodded before going back to their discussions. One by one, the fellas were called back until the makeshift room completely emptied. Benjamin was finally instructed to go to the back of the tent.

"How can I help you?" A gray-haired man glanced at him over the top rim of his spectacles.

Benjamin shared his scenario. "Will you be able to assist me?"

"Of course, but it comes with a price." The man's brown eyes bore into Benjamin.

The fella quoted an exorbitant price. Benjamin plunked down a portion of the cost. "How soon will the mix-up be decided?"

"Cases keep pouring in, so I'd say mid-to-late December if you're lucky. If you write down your plot coordinates, I'll get word to you as the time gets closer."

Benjamin choked back his frustration. "You'll get the rest of the money when you get my land back."

"Sounds fair." The lawyer bit one of the coins. He smiled. "Don't you worry. I haven't lost a case yet."

He didn't have the heart to ask him how many cases he'd actually argued, or if he had a valid law license. Benjamin had a feeling he wouldn't like the answer. Best not to know and trust God to work out the situation.

Benjamin exited the tent. By the time he swung back onto Milly, the sun shone directly overhead. The day had been a waste. He had nothing to show for it, other than less money in his pocket.

The miles back to his place stretched out, making it feel longer than it took to get to town. He lifted his Stetson and wiped the sweat from his brow and neck. A smile spread across his face when his land came into sight. Something to call his own. He never dreamed owning a plot of land would elicit such pleasure. His grin changed to a frown when he spotted Elmer plowing up his land. A small pile of rocks stood off to the side. He urged Milly to a trot. The lad used a shiny, new sod plow pulled by the boy's horse. *My new plow.*

"What do you think you're doing?" He dismounted and stomped across the uneven ground. "I didn't tell you to plow up *my* land."

"I don't need your permission to do what I want to do on *my* land." Elmer's blue eyes flashed. Dirt smudged the boy's face.

"You do when you're using *my* plow." Benjamin ground out the words.

The lad actually squirmed and stared at his feet.

Elmer kicked a clod of dirt with the toe of his boot. "You weren't here to ask, and I figured you wouldn't help me anyway. Folks haven't helped me before when I needed it, so I took the harness and plow from your wagon."

The words cut through Benjamin. How could he show the lad a better way of life if he didn't offer him kindness? He glanced at the horizon. But if he showed kindness, how could he ever get Elmer to leave the land? He couldn't give up what God had led him to. Surely the Lord had shown him this Promised Land for a reason. He'd had to hold on to that. Benjamin crossed his arms and glowered at the boy. "You can't help yourself to someone's property without asking first."

"Sorry." The toe of Elmer's boot nudged deeper into the soil.

He clenched his jaw. *What do you want me to do, Lord?*

The boy studied the ground. Elmer's horse snorted. The stallion's head jerked up, and the boy's hat flew in the air, releasing waist-length blonde waves that tumbled around Elmer's shoulders.

CHAPTER THREE

A true gentleman treats a lady as a genteel weaker vessel who is precious and someone who needs to be cherished.
Mrs. Wigglesworth's Essential Guide to Proper Etiquette and Manners of Refined Society

Of all the times for Buster to knock off her hat. Elsie stooped and snagged her Stetson. She gulped. Maybe he hadn't noticed. Should she stuff her hair back in it and act like nothing happened or—

"You … you're a girl." Benjamin turned as red as a strawberry. He ran a finger between his collar and neck. "But … you said your name is Elmer."

"It is."

His eyebrows rose. "We better start over. I'm Benjamin David, and you are?"

"Which are you? Benjamin or David?" She crossed her arms and stared.

"Both, actually. David is my last name."

"Never heard such a thing. How do I know you're speaking the truth?"

"Why would I tell a falsehood about my name? You're one to talk about the oddity of names. Who would name a girl Elmer?" His hazel eyes scrutinized her.

"Believe it or not, it truly is my name. If you'll excuse me, I got work to attend." Elsie turned her back, hoping to dissuade any further questions. "I'll get the sod splitter to you once I finish cutting enough for my house.

"G'yup, Buster." She tapped the reins across the horse's back.

Another few lengths and she'd have enough ground to make a little home. Her arms trembled as she plowed the last several rows. It took all she had to finish the long, hot job. Elsie chanced a quick peek to the other side of the property, but didn't see Benjamin anywhere. Good riddance. Hopefully, he'd pack up his things and leave. Although his supplies would be most welcome.

"Whoa, boy." She released the plow handles and moved to pat Buster's dark mane. "I think you deserve a rest." Elsie placed her fist in the small of her back as she surveyed the fresh, turned-over soil.

After returning the plow and brushing down her horse, she snagged her rifle and collapsed onto the bank of the creek while her stallion slurped heartily. Her stomach rumbled. Breakfast had been a long time ago, but her eyes needed a rest.

Benjamin scrubbed a hand across his forehead. Elmer being a woman complicated things. Who in their right mind named a girl Elmer? And how blind had he been not to notice her feminine curves and face? Heat rose up his neck at the thought of her long tresses falling like waves of honey.

He'd noticed her icy blue eyes before, and somehow, they'd been different when he thought of her as a man. But seeing those thick eyelashes up close ... *Great.* Just what he needed. A distraction.

He groaned. *Lord, is this a test to see if I'll remain faithful to You?*

Benjamin coughed when dust from the plowed field coated his throat. He couldn't stop watching the strange woman. She'd handled the sod splitter and her horse with ease as if it wasn't her first homesteading experience. Nothing clumsy or hitched in her movements.

He could learn a thing or two from her.

Opening his saddlebag, he withdrew his Bible. Something in God's Word would guide him. He sank to the ground and flipped through the pages until he came across two underlined verses. "'Likewise, ye husbands, dwell with them according to knowledge, giving honour unto the wife, as unto the weaker vessel, and as being heirs together of the grace of life; that your prayers be not hindered. Finally, be ye all of one mind, having compassion one of another, love as brethren, be pitiful, be courteous.'"

Surely it didn't pertain to his situation. He had no intention of marrying any woman after what he'd been through.

Benjamin swiped at the sweat on his brow. A light breeze brought little relief from the heat. He allowed the pages to blow in the wind and glanced down. "'If ye fulfil the royal law according to the scripture, Thou shalt love thy neighbour as thyself, ye do well.'" He couldn't say he loved Elmer like himself.

He hefted a sigh and continued reading. "'Let every one of us please his neighbour for his good to edification. For even Christ pleased not himself; but, as it is written, The reproaches of them that reproached thee fell on me.'"

Lord? Surely You can't mean for the two of us to share this tiny plot? No answer came. *Am I supposed to show her Your love and her need for You before she moves on elsewhere? Perhaps it's why the delay until December. Surely I can last until then.* Benjamin stood. *It's way shorter than the Israelites faced before they reached their Promised Land. Three months. Help me last that long.*

Elsie awoke to the sun's final burst of rays dipping below the horizon. She yawned and rolled over. Every fiber of her being ached. What she wouldn't do for a soak in a warm tub.

"You're finally awake."

She jumped and grabbed her rifle.

Benjamin crested the hill where she'd dozed beside the creek. "Sorry I startled you. I thought perhaps you'd like to join me for supper."

Her stomach scraped against her ribcage, reminding her of the many hours since she'd last filled it. A meal would be nice, but she couldn't help but feel he had something else on his mind. "Why you being so nice to me?"

"Just neighborly."

"You're trying to trick me into turning my deed over, aren't you?" She stood, refusing to let him see how much she ached from plowing.

"Nope. I figured after your long day you must be hungry. Besides, I cooked too much. No need being wasteful."

"I suppose I can help you out. This once."

They tromped down the hill side-by-side toward his wagon. Both horses were tied beside it. An ember from the campfire sent up a shower of sparks as they headed toward it. When she turned her ankle on a patch of thick grass, his arm shot out and steadied her. A tingling sensation pricked her arm. Her unsettled heart raced. Maybe she'd spent too much time in the sun. She jerked away.

"You sick or something?" His right eyebrow lifted.

His manly scent tickled her nostrils. She wondered what *she* smelled like. Elsie sniffed. Spring onions more than likely. She heaved a sigh and sank to the ground beside the blazing fire. The sun must've fried her brains to leave her so addlepated that she cared about how she smelled.

He sent her a questioning look.

"I'm fine." She forced the words out and dipped her head.

"Dear Lord, we thank you for this food and your many blessings. Thank you for Elmer, and help me to be a good neighbor. Amen."

What did he mean by that?

"How did you get the name Elmer?" Benjamin handed her a heaping plate.

It couldn't hurt to share a little about herself. "Named after my Pa."

"I'm surprised your mother agreed to such a name." He chuckled.

Elsie shrugged. "She weren't around to make that choice on account of she died giving birth to me."

"I'm sorry."

"No need to be. Never knew her, so there's no reason to miss her." Elsie tore off a chunk of bread and popped it into her mouth. She wouldn't tell him there had been many years she'd cried into her pillow, missing what she'd never experienced.

"Did you have a nickname growing up? I imagine your schoolmates must've teased you from time to time." He stared at his plate but had yet to take a bite.

"Elsie's what most folks call me. My Aunt Kate insisted I get a girl's name too, so I got the Esther for my ma." She spoke around a spoonful of food.

"Esther is a beautiful name. It's in the Bible." His gaze flickered to her face.

Elsie ducked her head. Time she shut up and focused on eating. No use telling a stranger too much about herself.

They finished the meal in silence. Benjamin seemed lost in his own thoughts, which satisfied her because he no longer pelted her with questions. It wasn't like her to tell so much about herself with someone she barely knew, let alone a man. She didn't know why she had.

"You're welcome to finish my meal." He offered his plate. "I'm not very hungry this evening."

"You sure?" She didn't wait for him to change his mind but grabbed his plate and dug in. When she'd finished the meal, she wiped her mouth against the cuff of her sleeve. "Thank you kindly."

"Certainly. Settle your bedroll near the fire this evening. It feels like it might be a cooler night." He took her plate and walked the short distance to the stream. Water splashed, tinkling against the tin dishware.

The breeze had been hotter than a cookstove earlier in the day, but now she shivered and shifted closer to the flames. Rolling to her back, she studied the starlit sky. One lone star blazed a trail across the heavens. In a few minutes, she'd get up and settle close to Buster, but she needed to rest her aching body a little longer.

Benjamin returned to find Elsie softly snoring. He stored the dishware in the back of the wagon, careful not to clink them together. He turned toward Elsie and took a few steps closer. Her Stetson lay beside her. In the flickering firelight, her face looked softer, gentler somehow. The creases at the corners of her eyes had disappeared. His hand itched to brush her cheek, but he left it at his side. He had no business touching her.

He trekked back to the wagon and rummaged until he found a small stack of blankets. He rolled one into a pillow and lifted her head. She murmured something but didn't awaken. He cautiously draped two blankets across her.

Benjamin moved to the opposite side of the campfire and used the two remaining blankets for himself, though he had the feeling sleep would be slow in coming. Her steady breathing rippled across the gap that separated them. Was this what it would have been like to have Mary with him? Of course, she'd be dressed more like a lady than a cowhand. He sucked in deep and let the air out slowly. *Lord, why did You have to take her?*

He sighed and stared back at Elsie. The poor girl never had a mother's influence.

Benjamin shifted on the hard ground. What if she'd been sent here first and others in her family followed? What would he do if they all were clamoring for his plot? He couldn't give up his Promised Land.

A soft whimper interrupted his wrestling thoughts. He held his breath, waiting for another sound.

"Don't go, Pa." She rolled back and forth.

She continued to cry out in her sleep, and he continued to pray.

Elsie woke covered in a sheen of sweat. She shivered as the night breeze whispered across her wet skin, chilling her to the bone. She snuggled deeper into the blankets.

If only it had been a dream. Elsie sighed and shifted her head to watch the dying embers. Funny, she didn't recall starting a fire for the night.

Had she really eaten a meal with the preacher again, or had it been part of her dream? Her thoughts blurred as she tried to put the events from earlier into place. They remained foggy. Maybe the fellow had drugged her coffee. She jumped up, struggling to see through the darkness. Her heart pounded. She forced herself to calm her erratic breathing. What had she done with her rifle? Elsie felt naked without it.

An animal howled. Her hand trembled as she searched in vain for her rifle.

Another wail sounded in the night.

Coyotes.

Of all things, why did it have to be coyotes?

Uncontrollable shivers raced the length of Elsie's body. She wrapped her arms around herself and nestled closer to the fire.

Elsie had no idea how much time passed before the creatures stopped their howling. Slowly, she identified the other sounds in the night. The soft breathing from the preacher, at least she hoped so, the gurgling of the stream across the rocks, and the snorts from the horses.

Elsie stood and stepped around the smoldering embers, examining the man as if he could bring some sort of reassurance to her, even in his sleep. Not enough light flickered to see the features of his face, not that it mattered. His arm flopped across his head. It reminded her of the last time she and Pa had visited her sister. Elsie's nephew had done the same thing when he took his afternoon nap. The boy always covered his eyes so he could sleep. Unlike her nephew, at least the preacher was close by if the coyotes returned.

Maybe she should take advantage of the quiet. She tiptoed to the wagon and started rustling through its contents. The moon didn't shed enough light to find what she really wanted—the man's deed.

Her heart raced like a thoroughbred in the last leg of a sprint. Could she really steal from him? He'd shown her nothing but kindness. Her conscience and Pa's words echoed in her mind.

"Elmer, we don't steal. We don't lie. It's important to be a girl of integrity, especially when things are hard."

"I promise, Pa." In the morning, she'd honor Pa's advice.

CHAPTER FOUR

When seeking help from the male species, be sure to employ your feminine wiles—use of a fan and eye fluttering speaks to a man's ego.
Mrs. Wigglesworth's Essential Guide to Proper Etiquette and Manners of Refined Society

Benjamin awoke to find Elsie standing beside his head, rifle slung over her shoulder.

"It's about time. You're sleeping away the best part of the day. Get up. We need to talk."

"Why don't you put the gun away?" He hated the way his voice shook. Clearing his throat, he tried again. "There isn't any need for that thing." He stood and folded his blankets. Hopefully, the motion would help to calm his racing pulse.

She kicked a clod of dirt. "I, uh, need to ask you something."

His focus settled on her flushed cheeks. She hadn't shifted the gun away from him, so he took a huge step backward.

"What's wrong with you? Did you step on something?" Her blue eyes studied his face before glancing toward the ground.

"What did you want to inquire of me?"

She toed the dirt with her boot. "I need to ask you to forgive me," she whispered.

Definitely *not* what he'd expected. She shifted her weapon toward him. Was she going to use it on him if he didn't forgive her? He'd never been asked for a pardon at gunpoint before. "Why?" The word croaked out.

"I shouldn't have used your plow yesterday without asking … or snooped through your stuff last night."

"You rifled through my things? What were you looking for?" His heart pattered as he checked for the paper in his shirt pocket. Still there.

"Are you going to forgive me or what?" Her eyes snapped with fire. She took a step closer.

"Y-yes." He raised his arms in the air.

"What are you doing that for?" She glanced at him and then at her rifle. "Oh, sorry. Say, you never did tell me about your trip to town."

Benjamin dropped his arms and willed his breathing to calm. "Not much to say. The dispute won't be resolved until December unless you decide to leave."

She shook her head. "Nope. Not happening. I figure you'll be the first to leave."

"Not me. I'm staying. If you aren't twenty-one though, your deed is invalid."

Elsie glowered at him.

Obviously asking about her age was off limits. Maybe if he changed the subject. "I, um …" Benjamin gulped.

"Yes?" She stooped and picked up the blankets she'd used and thrust them towards him.

"You seem to have some experience with farming. I, uh, hoped we could call a truce."

Her fingers brushed his as she handed him the covers. He glanced at the slenderness of her wrists. What had he been saying?

Benjamin took the blankets and crossed to the wagon to put them away, and to get a little distance from her. "I don't know how your finances are, but I thought maybe we could work on some things together."

"Such as …"

He swallowed and plunged ahead. "I have the money and supplies, but not the know-how. Perhaps we could combine forces. If you'd be willing to show me how to do some things, I'll let you stay until December." It wasn't easy for a man to admit he needed a woman to show him how to build up and prove on a homestead, but maybe Elsie could help him get started.

She laughed. "I'm the one letting you stay. But since it seems we're stuck together until the courts tell you that you're leaving, I guess we should make the best of it."

As much as she hated to admit it, Elsie needed him too. Well, she needed his supplies and strength. It took all her gumption to extend her hand. "I'm willing to show you a thing or two." He hesitated, then his strong fingers wrapped around hers. She stared him in the eye and attempted a smile.

"Agreed. What's the first order of business?" His eyes twinkled with something she couldn't identify.

"Breakfast, then building a home."

The color drained from his face. "We've come to a truce, but it doesn't mean I'm willing to share a house with you. It isn't proper."

"No, I mean … I didn't … separate homes." Her cheeks burned. What made him think she'd consider such a thing?

She blew out a breath and tried again. "I need your assistance to lift the sod into place for *my* house. I don't know what you had in mind for *your* home."

He laughed. "Certainly, although I don't understand why you'd want a dirt house." Benjamin shuddered. "I ordered lumber while in town yesterday. They'll deliver it sometime in the next few days."

"Well, I guess you can do a fool thing as that. Don't make much sense, though. I reckon I can always tear yours down after you leave. Not sure how a board house will hold up to twisters. I'd rather be safe in a sod house. 'Course it would be better if it was built into a hill." She made her way to the remains of the campfire, then bent and blew life into the coals.

He searched through his food stores in the back of the wagon that she'd seen the night before, pulling out a slab of salt pork and a handful of eggs.

She whistled. "Where did you get those? I didn't see them."

"I managed to bring them from town without breaking any." He started cracking them in the pan as she fried the meat. They worked side-by-side like she and Pa had done. It felt right nice to have the companionship.

Benjamin arched his aching back a few hours later. The woman planned to work him to death. They worked where she had plowed yesterday, adding layer after layer of stacked sod to the walls of her home. As small as the dimensions were, it was more of a hovel than a house.

"What are you stopping for?" Elsie stood with hands on slim hips. Despite her diminutive stature, the woman was a workhorse.

"I'm coming." The muscles in his arms complained with each length of sod he lifted into place. He grunted as he hefted an eighteen-inch-long piece above his head.

"I don't think we need to go any higher." Elsie stepped back and surveyed their day's work. "I'll need to scrounge up some wood to make a door, but it's almost finished. It would've been better if we dug it into a hillside, but the only decent hill on the property is the one by the creek. I'm not willing to risk floods."

He glanced in that direction. "You think it ever happens? Sure been mighty dry. Can't remember when it last rained."

"I bet this little creek of mine raises when we get a gully washer."

"You mean *our* creek." He bit his lip. He hadn't intended to make it sound like *that*. Heat crept up his neck and face. He didn't want her to think they had any kind of future together.

"You sick or something? You're looking funny all of a sudden. Maybe you better sit down. I suppose you aren't used to working outside all day in these temperatures." She shoved her canteen into his hand. "Here."

He took a long swig, too exhausted to respond.

Someone on horseback crested a hill in the east and headed in their direction. Elsie reached for her rifle and scanned the horizon. Benjamin, however, welcomed the distraction. The approaching man smiled.

"Howdy, neighbor." The man swung off his horse and extended a hand. He was a good ten years older than Benjamin and about four inches shorter. He lifted his hat. His wispy brown hair blew on the breeze revealing the beginning of a bald spot. "Ma'am. I'm Henry Larson. The wife and I live south of here. I thought I'd ride around and meet those who live close. Saw you folks working and figured I'd say howdy. Mildred will be happy to learn there's other womenfolk nearby. I don't like being gone from her for too long since she's increasing."

"Hello, I'm Benjamin David, and this is … Elsie." He couldn't recall her last name.

"Pleased to meet you both. I see you almost have your home completed. Tell me if you need anything. I'll bring the missus and stop back in a day or so." He jumped onto his horse and trotted away before Benjamin could correct the man's misconceptions.

Elsie's gaze followed the man as he rode west. She hadn't said a word during their neighbor's brief visit. What thoughts ran through her head now?

"I'm sure you'll enjoy having another woman close by since women are pretty scarce out here."

She stared after the stranger for a minute longer before she turned toward him. "We'd better scrounge up some supper. Why don't you start the fire and a can of beans, and I'll see if I can round up some fresh meat." She didn't wait for his response but walked off in the opposite direction with the rifle across her arm.

Benjamin shook his head. With Mary, he'd been able to tell her thoughts, and she'd been quick to share them too. Not so with Elsie. Maybe he was better off not knowing.

The muscles in his lower back complained as he walked across his property. Elsie soon disappeared behind the hill. The depths of the creek called to him. He didn't know if it would help his aching muscles, but at least it would cool him. With a quick check of the area, he unbuttoned his shirt, letting the sweaty garment fall to the ground. Moments later, he eased his body into the cool, trickling water. He sucked in a breath as his muscles tightened from the coldness. Benjamin found the deepest area to sit in and let the water lap around his shoulders.

Too bad he hadn't thought to grab a bar of soap and a towel. At least the chilly water brought relief to his hot body. He bent his head backward and stared up at the sky. "You put Adam in the garden to work, and work is a good thing, but I sure am tired, Lord. Strengthen me for the days ahead."

He stayed in the creek until he had completely cooled. Splashing the water across his face, he saw the last rays of sun hovered near the horizon. He'd better get moving if he wanted to get the beans started before Elsie returned. Stepping out of the water, he shivered into his clothes.

Benjamin shoved his feet into his boots and bent to gather some sticks. He stopped when a scent tickled his nostrils. Hurrying to see where it came from, he rounded a tree and saw Elsie bending over a fire. His heart pounded. Would she be angry that he hadn't started the beans? He never expected her back so soon. How long had he been soaking in the creek? She stared at him with those frigid, blue eyes. As he stepped closer, he figured he'd earned her ire.

Elsie stirred the potatoes and beans, then shifted the prairie chicken to a hotter part of the fire. She couldn't help glancing at Benjamin again.

His damp hair curled across his forehead. A swarm of hornets took up residence in her belly as she recalled seeing him sitting in the creek. Being the youngest of four sisters, Elsie didn't have any experience when it came to men, other than Pa. She hadn't seen her sisters' husbands much after her sixth birthday when the last of her siblings had moved away. No male had ever affected her like this preacher did. Maybe if she ignored him, the peculiar feelings would go away.

Benjamin unlocked his gaze from hers. "Sorry." He settled on his haunches, stoked the fire, and added the few measly twigs he'd brought. "Smells wonderful. It reminds me of my ma's cooking." He breathed deep. "Thanks for getting things started. Sorry I took so long."

She grunted, not wanting to enter into a conversation about what he'd been doing in the creek. Instead, she stooped and picked up the tin plates.

"The Lord provided us with a fine feast this evening." He sat and sent a smile her way.

"You mean *I* did."

He chuckled. "The Lord directed you to the chicken. You may be the one cooking for us, but He's the one who provided the food."

She bit her lip to keep from arguing. Let him think what he wanted. She knew they wouldn't be enjoying this fine meal if it hadn't been for her.

While the grub cooked, Benjamin crossed to the wagon and returned with a book. He flipped open its pages and started reading. *Good.* She could think about what else she needed to do with her claim come morning.

"Since we're going to be helping each other out, I thought we could share God's Word together. I always find it to be beneficial." He glanced up, then back at the page.

Could the man not think of anything else besides his preaching?

If the food were ready, she wouldn't have to hear him reading because his mouth would be full. Perhaps she could stand it for one meal.

"I've been reading in Ecclesiastes. I'll start where I left off in chapter four." He tilted the Bible toward the light of the fire and started reading about a man needing others.

She'd heard her pa read the same passage and had believed it until they'd run into troubled times. Then she found out it'd just been words on the page. Most times folks didn't help when you needed them. They certainly hadn't helped her and Pa. Elsie shoved the thought aside.

"Supper's ready." She scooped the food onto plates and thrust one toward him. Anything to stop him from reading. She didn't need reminding of being alone.

He accepted the meal. "Thank you, Esther."

"Don't call me that!"

"Sorry, I didn't mean to upset you, but you mentioned it before." The muscle in his jaw twitched.

"Only because you asked my given name." Pa had never spoken the name after Ma died, and Elsie couldn't bear to be called it either. It felt like she dishonored Pa's memory if she let others refer to her like that. Elsie ducked her head when moisture pricked her eyes.

Benjamin must've figured she wanted him to pray again because that's what he did. She didn't listen to the words but used the few moments to compose herself.

He smacked his mouth after his first bite of the chicken. "Mmm. This is delicious. You can cook for me anytime."

"Don't get used to it. Come morning, I figure we'll start having separate meals." Too much time with the man affected her in ways she hadn't planned on. Best to set some limits.

She pushed her food back and forth across the plate. The few bites she'd managed soured in her stomach.

"But I thought we were going to work together on things. I've got plenty of supplies, and I'm willing to share." His brow puckered. "Did I say or do something to offend you? I'm sorry for not starting the fire like you asked."

Her stomach lurched. Pa had always said she wilted like a wildflower, especially when she hadn't drunk enough water throughout the day. She hadn't taken time for a single sip while they worked, and now she wished she had, and so did her gut. What little food she'd consumed found its way up.

Elsie jumped when Benjamin's arm curled around her back, supporting her when she got sick a second time. Her head pounded. The sooner she got him off her property, the better.

CHAPTER FIVE

In the area of courtship, always keep the male species guessing. This arouses interest and provides ample opportunity to deepen the relationship.
Mrs. Wigglesworth's Essential Guide to Proper Etiquette and Manners of Refined Society

Elsie awoke to a steady pounding. She rubbed her temple and realized the sound came from outdoors. Stumbling to the doorway in stocking feet, she squinted at the bright sunlight. Two days wasted while she lay sick in her new home, all because she hadn't taken breaks from working to drink like she should. Days she should've spent tilling her fields. Pa would've scolded her for her recklessness.

Benjamin had fussed over her like a mother cat caring for her young. He'd insisted on building a cedar-poled sod roof to shield her from the sun and get her out of the bright rays. She'd been too weak to protest and welcomed the time away from his side, as well as the conflicting emotions that stirred when he was in such close proximity.

Her muscles quivered as she stooped to shove on her boots. Her mouth was dry and pasty. The brilliant sunlight momentarily blinded her as she stumbled outside. When her eyes adjusted, she squinted at the scene before her.

Folks scurried everywhere like ants seeking out food at a picnic. She rubbed her eyes, but the spectacle didn't change. A group of men had already raised the end walls of what appeared to be Benjamin's new home, close to the hill, just above the creek. A couple of wagons lined up beside Benjamin's, and she counted five horses tied near Buster and Milly.

A woman heavy with child stirred a steaming pot at the spot where Elsie and Benjamin built their campfires, her blue calico dress stretched tight against her swollen middle. Elsie guessed the woman to be in her mid-thirties. A few streaks of gray marred her dark-brown hair. The woman turned and waved, wiping her hands on her apron as she waddled toward Elsie. "Howdy there. I'm Mildred Larson. Your Benjamin said you've been feeling poorly. If I'd known sooner, I would've brought you some prairie chicken soup. Are you sure you should be out of bed yet?"

"How are you feeling, Elsie?" Benjamin strode toward her from the building site. "You don't look so good."

"I'm fine." Elsie's legs wobbled like a newborn colt as she stumbled closer. How could only two days of sickness have knocked the starch right out of her? A wave of dizziness struck her. She caught herself from swaying.

He closed the remaining distance between them and steadied her. Moisture formed above her lip. Warmth crept up her limbs as he scanned her face.

"Hey, Preacher, we need your input on how long you want this wall to be."

Benjamin's gaze swung to the small group of men working, then back to her.

Mildred walked over and threaded her arm through Elsie's. "I can help her back to the sod house. Go. I'll make sure your woman's taken care of."

"Don't overdo it." He squeezed her arm and disappeared before she could respond.

Elsie waited for Benjamin to correct Mildred, but he didn't. Elsie didn't have the gumption to say anything either. She was too bone weary. It took all of her strength and concentration to walk the distance back to her sod house, even with the woman's help. Her whole body trembled as she sank to her bedroll. All she could think about was putting her head on the pillow.

"You rest, dearie, and I'll check on you in a few hours. Don't worry about the menfolk. Beatrice and I've already started on their noontime meal."

Beatrice?

Elsie would tell the lady the truth after she took a short nap, when she could string two coherent words together. Mildred needed to know Elsie'd never hitch herself to the likes of any man—definitely not a preacher man.

Benjamin gripped the handle of the hammer tighter, thankful that working hard didn't leave much energy for talking. He glanced at the three men who had agreed to help him build a home. He'd spotted them working on nearby claims a few days ago. When the lumber he'd ordered had arrived from Enid, he'd gone to each of his neighbors to see if they'd be willing to come and help.

While he worked, he kept an eye on the sod house to see if Elsie ventured out again. She'd trembled like a baby bird in the nest. He'd never anticipated seeing her weak, especially after witnessing her strength while they'd built her home. Her sudden sickness had taken him by surprise. She probably didn't remember much about the past days. He'd cooled her face with fresh creek water all night.

"You all right there, Preacher?" Henry Larson stopped hammering a board into place. "You've been sitting there doing nothing."

"What?" He swung his eyes back to the task at hand. "Sorry, fellas. You caught me woolgathering." He chuckled. "I'm afraid I'm not used to physical labor in my profession."

John Clark, a single man in his mid-twenties, halted his work. "Good thing the Lord gives us different gifts. Building things and working with my hands happen to be mine." The sandy-haired fellow grinned, and a set of pearly white teeth sparkled beneath his mustache.

"We best get working before the ladies call us to the meal." Mark Sawyer handed a sack of nails to Benjamin. "Thought you might be out. Figured you stopped your hammering because of it. Either that or you were thinking of someone." The younger man's brown eyes twinkled as he tilted his head toward the soddy.

Did John and Mark assume Benjamin was sweet on Elsie? When they stopped for the midday break, he'd have to make it clear he had no romantic interest in her. He held a concern for her because of her sickness, nothing more. It would have been no different if it had been anybody else. Well, except if it had been Mary.

He shook off memories of his deceased fiancée.

They'd just completed work on the west wall when Beatrice Sawyer called them to lunch. She stood beside the skeleton of the house, a smile lighting her face.

Blisters were forming on his hand where the hammer had rubbed, so Benjamin welcomed the break. A time to eat and visit with his neighbors, and also to check on Elsie.

While the other men washed at the bucket, Benjamin scurried across the short distance to Elsie's soddy. It took a few minutes for his eyes to focus in the dim interior. Elsie lay with her back to him. He rested a hand on her forehead, and she stirred, mumbling something.

"Elsie?"

Her eyes fluttered open. "Benjamin? What are you doing in here? What time is it?"

"Close to noon. How're you feeling?" Elsie stretched and pushed back a rose-patterned quilt. How could she be chilled on this warm day?

"Better, I think." She stood. "Are the folks here yet?"

He nodded.

"They must think something awful of me, sleeping the day away. I best get over there and help."

"I told them you've been feeling poorly, so there's no need to worry that they think you're being lazy. Are you sure you're feeling up to being outside again?" When she started to rise, he moved to assist her. "Here, why don't you take my arm?"

"Why should I?" She glanced at him like he'd gone loco.

"Do you remember this morning?"

Bright spots of color sprang to her pale cheeks. "Why didn't you correct Mildred about me being 'your woman'?"

"Huh?"

She curled her fingers into a fist. "Don't act like you don't understand."

He racked his brain but couldn't recall when Mildred had used that phrase. "If that's what has you riled, you have no reason to worry. I already planned on setting things straight. Although it seems to me you could've done the same thing."

She didn't respond as they walked side by side to the blankets spread on the buffalo grass.

"Here's the little missus." Mark Sawyer smiled.

The opportunity to set things straight with his new neighbors had arisen. Benjamin opened his mouth to speak.

"You're mistaken." Elsie's face turned as red as the roses on her quilt. "I'm Elsie *Smith*, and we ain't hitched."

"You mean you're living together?" Henry Larson stepped in front of his wife as if to shield her.

"No!" Benjamin rubbed his hand across his forehead.

"Absolutely not." Elsie wanted to slug someone.

Benjamin yanked on the collar at his throat. "I think we need to start over, folks. You see, Elsie and I both claimed the same land, but at two different offices."

"You aren't married?" Mildred stepped around her husband.

"No." They answered in unison.

A handsome, mustached man lifted his hat and winked at Elsie. She ignored him. Her knees wobbled, and Benjamin placed a warm hand on her shoulder. She took a step away from him.

"You see we are waiting for our case to be heard, but the first available time isn't until December," he said.

"We both agreed to share the land for the time being." Elsie swung her hand toward her home. "This is my place, and you're working on Benjamin's."

"But it's not proper for the two of you to be living here together, especially with him being a preacher." Henry jabbed his finger in Benjamin's direction.

"I can assure, you nothing improper has taken place. I've been sleeping outside. We are helping each other out until December." Benjamin cleared his throat. "I realize it's not an ideal arrangement. As a man of the cloth, I can assure you I wouldn't do anything unseemly."

"Don't seem right having you two live here without some sort of chaperone." Mildred sniffed.

"Believe me," Elsie's hand shook as she shifted her Stetson, "I have no romantic notions toward Benjamin."

A black-haired woman sidled up to Elsie and squeezed her arm. "I know what would solve your problem. You could have a marriage of convenience. It's what Mark and I did, and we're quite happy." She gestured toward a brown-haired man.

"Yep, she's my mail-order bride." The man grinned and tugged his wife back to his side. "We got hitched a few months before the run."

The starch drained from Elsie's body.

Benjamin's collar tightened like a noose. He unbuttoned the top fastener. "There's no need to be worried about this. We're merely neighbors. Nothing more. It's simply like living across the street from one another. We're both dealing with a filing error and are waiting for the courts to decide whose claim it is."

Elsie folded her arms across her chest and jutted her chin out.

"You have my word, folks. I'll remain a man of honor and in no way taint Miss Smith's character, so there's no need for us to get married. What do you say we eat this fine meal the ladies have prepared before it gets cold? I'm sure Miss Smith would love to get to know each of you."

Henry gave him a long stare but turned and lifted the pot of steaming food, carrying it to the back of one of the wagons.

Benjamin crossed to the creek to wash up. The chilly water slapped his skin and helped to cool his topsy-turvy thoughts. As he flung the droplets from his hands and headed toward the small gathering, he noticed Elsie had sunk to the ground on one of the blankets, her face pale.

"Would you mind saying the blessing, Preacher?" John interrupted his perusal.

Benjamin nodded. "Dear Lord, we thank You for this day. I ask You to bless the ladies who prepared the meal. Guide our conversations. May we say things which bring glory and honor to You. Help us to be instruments of Your love to those who are floundering. Bless this food. In Your name, I pray, amen."

Amens echoed across the small group. After the food had been distributed and they'd all settled on the ground in a small circle, Benjamin motioned toward John. "Why don't you tell us about yourself, and how you came to the Oklahoma Territory? El, uh, Miss Smith hasn't had the pleasure of introductions yet."

Elsie eyed Benjamin but didn't say anything, as she took miniscule bites of food.

"Well, there isn't a whole lot to tell. Name's John Clark. No wife or family. I lived in Ohio until I heard about the land being opened for settlement. Decided I needed a change, so here I am. Who knows, maybe I'll find myself a wife." He ripped off a chunk of bread and stared long and hard at Elsie. "Have a lot of experience with building, so we should get this project finished in a day or so."

Henry spoke up, "I reckon you two already met me and the missus. We came from the middle of Kansas. Land's becoming scarce where we lived, and I wanted to have a plot of my own, especially with the young'un coming."

Mildred blushed to the roots of her chestnut hair and studied the ground.

"Well, I suppose you've heard part of our story from Beatrice. We got married three months ago." Mark grinned. "We're the Sawyers. Beatrice and I came from eastern Kansas. The run took its toll on my wife, but she's perked right back up again."

Black-haired Beatrice had the glow of a newlywed wife. The couple's love for each other shone in both of their gazes. Benjamin had married enough couples to recognize it.

"It looks like our young'uns will be playmates." Mark nodded his head toward the Larsons. "Our little one should come in the beginning part of next year, although I don't know what we'll do when the time comes for our child to be born." He studied the landscape. "Living so far away from a town has its disadvantages."

Benjamin's gaze flickered to Elsie. Fire burned in her eyes. What could she be thinking?

"What about you, Preacher?" Mark looked at Benjamin. "What's your story?"

"I came from Oklahoma Territory. My family lives a bit south of here. I have a brother, Isaac, who lives at home with my folks. He's ten years younger than me.

"I, uh ..." He cleared his throat and tried again. "My betrothed and I had planned to make the run together."

"Is she coming later?" Mildred smiled.

The familiar ache burned in Benjamin's throat. "She died a week before our wedding."

"Oh, my, what happened?" Beatrice leaned forward and patted his arm.

He couldn't resist peeking at Elsie, but he couldn't read her expression. "Mary died in a flash flood. Her puppy had wandered into the stream, and she tried to save him."

"You poor dear." Mildred sniffed. "No wonder you don't want to get married yet. I'm sure the good Lord will provide someone when the time is right."

"Me too." Beatrice peered at Elsie. "You never know who God will bring."

Elsie tried to avoid her neighbors' obvious matchmaking attempts. She felt sorry for Benjamin, but not enough to consider the man as a husband.

John drained his coffee cup. "How'd you become a preacher?"

"My pa's a preacher. He expected me to take over for him when he retired, but Mary and I wanted to come on the run and find a place of our own. Before coming here, I rode the circuit and preached a fifty-mile area."

Elsie didn't want to hear any more about God. "Thanks for the food, ladies. I'll take care of the dishes."

"Wait, you haven't told us about yourself." Beatrice smiled and tucked a strand of hair behind her ear.

"Not much to tell. I came from Kiowa. My pa and I were to make the run together, but it didn't happen." Elsie refused to divulge anything else about her family. Some things were best left unsaid.

"Well, I suppose we should get back to work if we want to finish these walls before sunset." Henry stood. "Thanks for the food, ladies." He tipped his hat and sneaked a kiss from his wife.

Mildred smiled and wrapped her arms around his neck before he left. Elsie shifted away, not wanting to intrude.

"Here, let me help you with those." Beatrice reached for a stack of dishes in Elsie's arms. "Mildred said you've been feeling poorly. Why don't you grab the cooking pot and those mugs, and we can wash them together at the creek?"

Elsie trekked behind the young woman. She guessed Beatrice couldn't be a day over twenty.

"It's nice to have someone my age nearby." Beatrice giggled. "I think we'll be good friends."

Elsie didn't know how to respond. Because her sisters were so much older, she hadn't had a confidant growing up, and mothers hadn't taken too fondly to a girl in trousers.

"If you have no intent on marrying the preacher, maybe someone else will spark your interest." Beatrice bent to rinse the dishes in the flowing water. "I believe the Good Lord has a special man for you, Elsie."

CHAPTER SIX

A felicitous young man should avoid sustained interaction with a woman unless he has an invested interest and desires to enter into an agreed upon courtship.
Mrs. Wigglesworth's Essential Guide to Proper Etiquette and Manners of Refined Society

Elsie choked. She wiped her sleeve across her forehead and longed for a glass of water.

"Oh, you poor thing. Why don't you sit there and rest, and I'll take care of these?" Beatrice reached for the pot.

"I'm fine, really." She jerked the pan out of Beatrice's hands and submerged it in the flowing stream. The chill of the water helped to calm her frazzled nerves.

"There's always John if you don't like the preacher." Beatrice stooped beside her and slipped her arms around Elsie's waist. The young woman gave a quick squeeze before rinsing the plates in the stream.

"I have no desire to be hitched to *any* man. I claimed my land by myself, and I certainly don't need no man to keep it."

"Didn't the preacher say you're working together, helping each other out?"

Elsie opened her mouth to argue but realized that—for now—she needed Benjamin's generosity. Once December came, or she somehow managed to get funds of her own, she'd shoo him off her property without one single regret. "For now."

"You know, I didn't like Mark when I first met him. In fact, our first few weeks of marriage we fought like the North and the South."

"What changed things?"

"I read in the Bible that love is a choice. I could choose to be miserable in my marriage, or I could choose to love Mark."

"But you were complete strangers, weren't you? How could you choose to love someone you didn't know?" Elsie left the pot to soak for a few minutes and sat back on her haunches.

Beatrice glanced over her shoulder at her husband. "Each day I forced myself to find something good about Mark."

"What good did that do?"

The woman smiled. "God started changing my heart. I couldn't see all Mark's faults anymore, and I began to notice the ways he tried to please me."

God. Why did every conversation lead back to God? A groan escaped Elsie before she could halt it.

"Are you feeling poorly? I can help you back to your home." Beatrice's brow wrinkled.

"No. I'm tired of all this talk about God." Elsie rose and grasped the trunk of a tree to steady herself. "God may answer *your* prayers, but He sure don't answer mine."

Benjamin snuck a glance at Elsie, stalking off in the direction of her house. Hard to tell what set her off. The woman was pricklier than a porcupine. Even so, it took all he had not to chase after her. He swung his gaze back toward the men. Best to remind himself, daily if need be, this situation couldn't be anything other than temporary.

"What're you thinking, Preacher?" Henry's scrutiny shifted back and forth between Benjamin and Elsie. "Were you wanting to go check on her again?"

Mark chuckled. "You may say you aren't interested, but you sure do watch her a lot. I thought you said you didn't have any claim on her."

"I don't." Benjamin choked out the words.

"Good, 'cause if you don't have any notions toward marriage, maybe I can sway the little filly into taking a chance with me." John's gaze followed Elsie's path.

"If God's leading you in her direction, be my guest." Benjamin started hammering again. The tool echoed the thumping of his heart. He had no rights to the woman, nor did he want any. Why did the idea bother him so much?

The steady sound of nails finding their mark helped to calm him as they constructed the final wall. Benjamin concentrated on his task so as not to hammer his fingers in the process. His work engrossed him until a guffaw caused him to glance up.

Elsie stood a yard away with feet planted a foot apart and a hand on her slim hips. "Hand me some of those nails, Henry."

"Missy, you leave this work to the menfolk and go help the women with cooking our next meal. I'm sure they'd love the company." Henry held the sack away from her grasp.

John dropped a handful of his nails into her outstretched hand and grinned. The single man tilted his hat and stepped closer. "I like a woman who isn't afraid to work alongside a man."

Benjamin watched the interaction but didn't move from the spot where he'd been working. She shouldn't be out of bed, let alone hammering boards into place, but he wouldn't be the one to tell her. *Nope*. He'd not say a word.

"Don't you agree she doesn't belong here, Preacher?" Henry asked.

"It's not for me to say." He clamped his jaw tight.

Elsie ignored all of them, took the nails from John with a smile, and started hammering a board in place beside the man.

"Whew. You sure are a handy thing to have around." John waggled his eyebrows and nudged closer to her. "Any man in his right mind would realize the asset you are and swoop you up."

"There won't be any swooping," she said around a nail held between her teeth.

Benjamin couldn't stop his grin from spreading.

All the talk of marriage made Elsie antsier than a child about to be spanked. Stuff and nonsense. She ignored them, but she couldn't dismiss the words Beatrice had spoken. What did the young mother-to-be know of the pains of life? Likely her only difficulty had been marrying a stranger.

"Henry Larson! What're you doing making Elsie help when she's been so sick. Honestly, sometimes I think you men don't have any sense." Mildred stood beside her husband with arms akimbo.

"I-I tried to stop her," Henry stammered. "She wouldn't listen."

"I can hear both of you." Elsie sighed. Her arm trembled from the exertion.

"Now, honey child, there's no reason to do a man's work. Come sit by the fire. You aren't looking so well." Mildred pulled the hammer from her hands.

Elsie bit her lip and handed the remaining nails back to John. These folks were no different than the ones back in Kiowa. Nobody accepted her back home, and here these folks were already trying to change her. She'd been a fool to think things could be different.

Not wanting to suffer their judgment, she took off at a sprint to get some distance from them. After saddling Buster, she urged him into a gallop.

The hot wind whipped against her face, as she held tight on the reins. A scene from her childhood tumbled through her mind.

"Sarah Grace, I don't want to see you ever playing with the likes of her again." Sarah's mother motioned in Elsie's direction.

"Mama, she's my friend."

"We aren't friends with children like her." Sarah's mother drew her daughter close to her side as if Elsie had some sort of contagious disease. "There're plenty of other proper girls you can be friends with.

I don't ever want to see or hear you consorting with this ruffian. Do you understand?"

Sarah Grace dipped her head and kicked a stone. She'd refused to glance at Elsie.

"Sarah Grace?" Elsie's heart cried out for her friend to defy her mother, but as the two left, the girl didn't send a single glance backward.

From that day onward, none of the girls would play with Elsie, and they whispered about her whenever she got close to them.

Elsie's jaw tightened, and she wished she could erase the memory. She didn't need those girls then, and she certainly didn't need her neighbors now. With a sniff, she edged Buster toward the sparkling mountain in the distance. Now seemed as good a time as any to check out what caused it to shimmer in the sunlight.

By the time she reached the site, Buster's coat glistened with sweat. She slipped from the saddle and swayed on unsteady legs. Gripping the reins tighter, she waited for the blackness to fade from her eyes. When her head finally stopped swirling, she ground-tied Buster before starting along a narrow path up the mountain.

Dark-red soil dusted her boots as she walked. A grasshopper whirled ahead of her, landing on her pant leg. She flicked it off and glanced toward the summit. The ridge likely didn't qualify as a mountain in most areas of the country, but here on the plains it rose majestic, its crags and rocks pushing up from the earth. Elsie bent to examine a stone. It sparkled in her hands. If she remembered correctly, the range had a name. She'd have to check Pa's map when she returned, which wouldn't be soon.

Perspiration soaked through Elsie's shirt. Her limbs trembled, and she sank to the ground, ignoring the poke of pebbles into her backside. Waiting for the weakness to pass, she closed her eyes.

Nobody spoke after Elsie bolted. Benjamin wished he could've prevented whatever had caused her to leave without a word. They worked for a few more hours, but a pensive mood hung in the air. When the women called them for supper, Elsie hadn't returned yet. He couldn't help but wonder if she lay hurt somewhere and needed his aid.

"Did we say something to upset her?" Beatrice's soft voice interrupted his thoughts.

Benjamin shrugged. He didn't exactly have an understanding of any woman's mind, let alone Elsie's.

"I shouldn't have told her what to do." Mildred worried her lip. "Do you think we should go search for her?"

"Now, Mildred, you're not going anywhere." Henry patted his wife's hand. "Not in your condition."

The woman fidgeted at her husband's words. Benjamin glanced away. What would it have been like to have a wife—Mary—expecting his child? He sighed. He'd never know.

"I'll do some looking on my way back home." John glanced at the horizon. "It'll be dark before long. She'll need a strong man to protect her."

The fellow sure was in an all-fired hurry to attach himself to Elsie.

"Preacher?" Beatrice brought him back to the present again.

What exactly had she asked him? Something about Elsie being gone so long? "I'm sure she's only lost track of the time." Benjamin glanced toward the countryside, but nothing moved in any direction, though she could easily be hidden by the gentle swells in the land and the copses of trees dotting the plains.

Somehow the food on his plate didn't hold his interest anymore.

"I think we'll shove off." Henry slipped his arm around his wife. "This little lady needs to get off her feet and rest a spell."

"But—"

"Honey, you know I'm right." Henry gathered their things and secured them in their wagon. He then lifted Mildred onto the high seat. "We'll be back sometime in the next couple days to help finish your house. Tell us if Elsie doesn't return, and I'll help you find her."

"Thank you for everything." Benjamin shook the man's hand. "I appreciate all you've done."

"Glad to help." Henry slapped the reins across his horses' backs.

"I think we'll be heading out too." Mark wrapped his arms around his wife's waist.

"Don't you think we should find Elsie first?" Beatrice twisted a towel in her hands. "I hate for her to be alone in the dark."

"No need to fear, ma'am." John lifted his hat. "I'm heading out to search now. Her trail should be easy enough to follow. If you don't hear from me, know that I've found her and brought her back home."

"Thank you." Beatrice smiled. "I'm sure she'll be safe in your hands."

What did that mean? Just because John was bigger and stronger didn't mean Elsie wouldn't be safe in Benjamin's hands. Not that he wanted Elsie in his hands.

The Sawyers waved as they left. John swung onto his horse.

Benjamin threw water on the flickering flames. "If you give me a moment, I'll get my horse saddled and join you."

John nodded and glanced around. "You'd better hurry. It'll soon be dusk."

The coals smoldered as Benjamin saddled his horse. John dismounted and kicked dirt across the pit.

Didn't he think Benjamin could put out a fire? Benjamin sighed. He should be more appreciative of the man's help. The important thing was finding Elsie, so why did it seem he competed in a race he couldn't win? Weariness tugged at his back and shoulders. He couldn't think straight.

"Time's a wastin'." John clicked to his horse.

Benjamin swung onto Milly and trailed after the man on the pinto. *Lord, keep Elsie safe.*

"You think we should swing by the soddy to make sure she isn't there?" Benjamin glanced in the direction, just in case he somehow missed her return.

"Nope. I've been watching all afternoon. She hasn't returned." John kicked his filly into a gallop.

Where had Elsie gone? Benjamin's pulse hiked. He sensed an urgency to get to her as soon as possible, and he didn't think it had anything to do with not wanting John to find her first. Benjamin didn't stop to consider why that thought bothered him.

Elsie stirred from her crouched position on the shadowed mountain face. Stones jabbed into her spine. She struggled to see, as darkness had settled upon the land. An animal snorted.

Buster? She shook her head to clear the sleep from her brain. Her fingers grasped for her rifle but scraped against the jagged rock instead. Another rock bit into her hand. She caught her lip between her teeth to keep from crying out. Trembles rippled up her spine. Something caused the hair on the back of her neck to stand on end.

A pebble pinged and echoed below her. "Shh. Be quiet. I think I hear a horse." A man's voice rang out.

"You're loco," another man answered. "It's jist our horses. Why'd you want me to meet you here? You said we weren't to make contact until next week."

"As long as you weren't followed, it shouldn't matter."

Elsie couldn't place the man's accent. It was one she'd never heard before.

"I weren't followed." The man's voice lowered.

"If you can't get the claim, then shoot him. Not to kill, but to scare them off."

Elsie strained to hear more, but their voices grew fainter until only the clatter of horses' hooves echoed back to her. She didn't dare move from her hiding place since she had no idea which way they'd rode off to, or if they'd be back.

A long while later, something moved above her. Pebbles fell as the soft pads of an animal's feet sounded off to the right. How far away, she couldn't tell, but it was something big. The howl of a coyote sounded below her. She sat riveted to the spot, unable to move.

Had she imagined it, or had an animal's hot breath washed across her skin? She shivered and shrank closer to the rock wall without making a sound. Straining to hear, she forced her breathing to calm. Elsie couldn't tell if the thumping came from the creature or her throbbing heart.

Stones clattered down the wall of the mountain again.

Whatever hunted her stood directly above her head.

Did she dare run?

Even if she could make it down the craggy mountain without breaking her neck, where could she go in the darkness?

A deep-throated growl ripped through the air.

Elsie screamed.

CHAPTER SEVEN

Church attendance should be esteemed and valued as an important part of society. Not just for spiritual enrichment, but also as a way of climbing the social ladder if desired.

Mrs. Wigglesworth's Essential Guide to Proper Etiquette and Manners of Refined Society

A scream split the air, and Benjamin's heart stampeded. *Elsie.*

Crack! A shot just ahead.

"Elsie!"

If only the clouds would part, they'd have more visibility.

Milly surged forward into the darkness. He prayed they'd reach Elsie in time. *Keep her safe, Lord.*

"Over this way. I heard some kind of wild creature." John's voice guided Benjamin through the blackness. "Hopefully, my gunfire scared it off."

"Elsie!"

"I think her horse is ahead."

How could the man see *anything*? A horse nickered. He prayed it was Buster. A whole slew of scenarios fired through Benjamin's brain.

"Elsie?" John swung down as Benjamin reined his horse to a halt.

The full moon broke free of the clouds, illuminating the area. *Thank You, Lord.* He dismounted and hurried over the rocky terrain.

"Stop." John hissed and shot out an arm to stop him. "We could be walking into an ambush."

Fiddlesticks. Benjamin stumbled through the underbrush until he found Elsie slumped against a rock with her hands over her ears, her eyes squeezed tight. He touched her shoulder, and she jumped.

Her wide eyes stared at him. "B-Benjamin? What are you doing here?" Her eyes darted back and forth. "I heard voices earlier, and d-did you see an animal? I crept down the mountain to try and get away from it."

He helped her up, and she sagged against his chest. Her body trembled as she surveyed the area. She held tight to the front of his shirt. Could she hear the steady thumping of his heart? Something had scared her to make her cling to him like this. Scared him too when he'd heard her scream.

"We haven't seen a thing." He patted her hand.

"W-we?" The moonlight shimmered off her blonde tresses.

He blinked. The fatigue from the day must be affecting his eyesight.

"You found her." John stepped out of the shadow of a cedar tree and frowned. "What made you scream?" His hand rested on the butt of his rifle.

"You must have scared the creature off." Elsie glanced above them. "The men left a while ago."

"What men?" John edged closer.

"I'm not sure. I couldn't hear them very well. They said something about properties, but that wild creature …" Elsie's voice shook, and she shivered in Benjamin's arms. Her eyes widened. She tried to take a step backward but bumped into the rock wall instead.

"Why'd you run off?" John gripped his hat.

Elsie shook her head.

Benjamin rubbed her arm. "I think she needs to be taken home and not hounded with questions."

"Do you want me to see you to your soddy, Miss Smith?" John inched closer.

"Nonsense." Benjamin laced his fingers through hers, not giving her a chance to respond. "We don't want to take advantage of your kindness any longer, John. Thank you for all you've done today. I appreciate it. Besides, it's already dark, and it would be out of your way. If you'll excuse us, I'll make sure she gets home safely."

Benjamin tugged her along the path to the horses. Something was definitely wrong because she didn't make one single attempt to shrug away from his grip.

Elsie shivered and edged closer to Benjamin's side, glancing over her shoulder to make sure the animal hadn't tracked them. She couldn't tell whether it had been real, a delusion, or merely a bad dream. It had been many years since the dream had plagued her. Hopefully, it hadn't returned.

At any rate, she didn't want to take a chance of being alone again at night, away from the property. Definitely not this far from home. Buster snorted as she drew near. She checked him over, but no claw marks or scratches covered his coat.

Benjamin swept her up into his arms, and she squealed. "What are you doing?"

He deposited her on Milly's back. "I'm not risking you falling off your horse." He looped Buster's reins over his saddle horn and swung up behind her.

"Really, it isn't necessary. I'm fine."

"Good night." John's voice carried across the darkness that separated them. "You win tonight, Preacher."

"What did he mean by that?" Elsie twisted to watch the man leave.

"I have no idea." Benjamin clicked, and his horse started walking. "Let's get you home."

She wanted to protest, and she would. Later. It had been quite a while since she'd had the comfort of someone caring about what happened to her. She'd forgotten how nice it felt.

Elsie resisted the urge to snuggle close to Benjamin and seek refuge in his comfort. She breathed in his scent. It reminded her of Pa. A combination of musk and sweat. With a sigh, she forced herself to sit as straight as a post and not lean into Benjamin's solid torso.

"Relax. I'm not going to bite you." A chuckle rumbled in his chest. "You can rest against me, and sleep if you like. I'll wake you when we get home."

Home. If only she had a way of returning to her home with Pa. She cleared her throat and forced her eyes open. "Gotta stay awake." *Can't let my guard down and let Benjamin worm his way in.* She yawned again. How could her body be so tired when she'd hardly done a thing all day? She jerked awake and shook her head.

"Sleep, Elsie. You can trust me." Benjamin shifted her against his broad chest.

His heart thudded loudly in her ear. Almost as if he'd just run a race. What had gotten him stirred up? Had he seen something? Her eyelids flickered, and she tried to pry them open. Maybe it wouldn't hurt to rest them for a minute. Nothing could happen in a moment, could it?

A swooping sensation startled Elsie awake. Her arms flailed. "What?"

"Shh. Go back to sleep." Benjamin stooped as he carried her through the open doorway of her soddy, placing her on the bedroll and covering her with the quilt her ma had made. "Good night. I'm glad no harm befell you."

He left without another word. She heard him through the quietness of the night, unsaddling Buster and speaking to him just outside the house. Somehow the sounds brought peace she hadn't experienced in a long while.

She thought for sure sleep would claim her quickly. Instead, Elsie lay awake thinking about what it had felt like to be in the arms of a man. She sighed and rolled over. "You might as well get it out of your head. Falling for a man isn't part of the plan."

Benjamin concentrated on the rhythm of his strokes as he tried to regulate the erratic beat of his heart while brushing Milly. Having Elsie fall asleep in his arms brought back memories of his beloved Mary, but it also stirred new thoughts that he didn't care to consider. When he finally turned in for the night, sleep was a long time in coming.

He spent the rest of the week intentionally keeping his distance from Elsie. He helped his neighbors build their homes and invited them to attend the first church service he planned to hold near the creek. He prayed and agonized about what to preach in his first sermon, but all he could come up with were the Israelites at the Red Sea.

By Saturday, he still wasn't making any progress with his sermon. Benjamin shoved to his feet and headed toward Elsie's place to invite her to the church service the next morning. He'd delayed seeing her long enough. Might as well get the unpleasant task behind him so he could concentrate more on his sermon.

"Elsie?" He stood outside her sod house and tried to see into the dim interior. If he had leftover lumber when they finished his house, he'd give it to her so she could have a door. He shivered to think of what manner of critters could crawl in during the day or night.

Hearing no stirrings inside, he peered toward the fields. Nothing. He hadn't seen her by the creek. Where could she be?

Buster. *Nope*. The horse wasn't grazing anywhere nearby.

Retracing his steps, he found a piece of paper and a pencil in his saddlebags, wrote a brief note about the service and invited her to come. Trekking back to her house, he shoved a nail into the sod, pinning the note in place.

Elsie's stomach grumbled in complaint. Benjamin had been keeping his distance the past week, which meant they hadn't eaten together. It had been two days since her last meal. The small amount of money she had from Pa needed to be saved for seed. Not wanting to see Benjamin had kept her away from fishing in the creek. That meant she *had* to find something to eat today.

She spotted movement ahead in the swaying buffalo grass and swung from Buster's back. There. A prairie chicken stood near a mess of weeds. She closed one eye and took aim. Her shot split the air. A moment later, when collecting the game, she found two eggs as well. Pocketing each of them, she tied the hen's legs together and slung it over her back. An evening meal *and* breakfast. Her stomach growled in anticipation.

Not willing to risk jarring the eggs while riding, Elsie walked the distance back to her place. When she caught sight of her land, a sense of calm and pride soared into her heart. Why couldn't Pa have lived to see it?

Dusk had settled by the time she reached home. She had time to light a fire before the first stars of the evening twinkled. Wrapping the eggs in buffalo grass, she placed them in a corner of her house inside her saddlebag. She smiled in anticipation of eating them the next day.

Her stomach protested as the scent of roasting chicken wafted. Finally, the bird was cooked through. Elsie devoured it, burning her mouth in the process. The food settled in her stomach, and she could swear her belly purred in contentment.

The next morning, Elsie awoke to a sheen of sweat covering her body. It looked to be another blistering hot day. She stretched, stepped outside, and glanced around. No Benjamin. His horse grazed nearby. If she hurried, she might make it to the creek and back before he made an appearance.

Dipping the bucket into the cool stream, Elsie splashed some of the water onto her face and neck. One of these days, she hoped to dip into its depths. She wanted to get another field ready for planting winter wheat. If it rained soon, Elsie'd eventually have her first harvest, then some money to buy the additional things she needed.

Back at her house, she poured half of the water into a small bowl she'd borrowed from Benjamin when they'd been on regular speaking terms. She stripped her shirt and made quick work of washing the perspiration from her body. She ran a brush through her tangled hair, braided its length, and shoved it back under her Stetson. Elsie shrugged into a fresh shirt and tucked it into her britches before rolling up her sleeves.

She left the rest of the water in the corner of her house, hoping it would stay cool in the dim interior. One trip to the creek without spotting Benjamin was enough. It wasn't worth risking again. Stopping to fetch her saddlebag and frying pan from the soddy, Elsie set both outside and reached inside the pack for the eggs. Something wriggled. Pulling out the little snake, she threw it away from her house. She'd never developed a taste for the creatures, or Elsie would've eaten it too.

The next time she looked in the bag before reaching inside. *Good.* The eggs were intact. She cracked them into the pan, pleased to find they were fresh, without baby chickens growing. In no time, a small fire blazed, and the scent of fried eggs wafted. She made quick work of eating and cleaning up.

Minutes later, she harnessed Buster to the sod splitter. "Giddy up, boy." The horse plodded across the uneven ground. Elsie glanced behind as the plow broke up the soil. There weren't anything finer than seeing a fresh-plowed field. She could envision what it would look like with the winter wheat waving and whispering in the wind.

Elsie worked for a couple hours before slipping into her soddy for a water break. As she dipped a ladle into the bucket and glanced out her doorway, she paused. Wagon loads of folks were arriving. Benjamin must've invited everybody over again.

Elsie fiddled with the collar of her shirt. Pa and Aunt Kate used to tell her to confront her problems and not run from them, but she didn't want to face any questions about why she'd run away from their last gathering. Months ago, she would've, but she no longer had the gumption to fight. Elsie turned away. She could survive just fine on her own. It didn't do no good to get involved with folks. Only hurt came from it. Best if she remembered that.

"Welcome, folks." Benjamin adjusted his tie as he stepped outside and closed the door to his house. "Thanks for coming. Since it's such a warm day, I thought we'd hold service outside in the shade of the trees. I'm afraid my house is a bit warm." He led the way to the creek. A light breeze fluttered the leaves as his neighbors took their seats on the grass.

"We need to finish your roof before long, Preacher." Henry glanced at the sky. "Sure could use some rain. I can't remember when last we had some."

"Then we'll make sure to pray for rain." Benjamin smiled as he welcomed each of his neighbors. "I'm so glad you all could attend today."

"Is Miss Smith coming?" John peered at Elsie, bending to remove a rock from the field she was plowing. "You did tell her about the services, didn't you?"

Benjamin cleared his throat. "I haven't seen much of El—Miss Smith this past week. I left a note for her yesterday. I suppose she has other plans."

"Doesn't she remember it's Sunday?" Mildred rubbed her swelled abdomen. "Maybe I should go say something to her."

"Now, Mildred, if she wanted to be here, she'd have shown up like the rest of us. I say you start the service, Preacher." Henry patted his wife's arm.

They bowed their heads, and Benjamin prayed, committing the morning to the Lord. He led them in a few hymns and a time of prayer. Each of his new neighbors lifted their voices and concerns to God in regard to the lack of moisture.

When they finished, Benjamin riffled through his notes. "I've been thinking a lot about Moses when he led the Israelites toward the Promised Land. They had the promise of a land God had chosen. They left Egypt, thinking their troubles were behind them." Dust rolled across the field where Elsie had returned to plowing, coating his suit coat. He coughed but continued.

"They came to the Red Sea and had nowhere to go. Pharaoh, with his chariots and men, was behind them. They were afraid and accused Moses of leading them to certain death." He opened his Bible and read the passage from the Old Testament.

"Amen, brother." Henry nodded.

"Maybe today you feel a little bit like Moses. God brought you to the Promised Land, and things are harder than you anticipated. God is instructing us to be silent as we wait to see His salvation." Benjamin hesitated as the words penetrated his heart. He needed to take his own advice.

The service ended with a prayer. Each of his neighbors thanked him and said how much they anticipated getting together.

"Why don't we plan on a meal after each service?" Beatrice smiled as she shook Benjamin's hand. "It's hot today, but hopefully by next week it will be a little cooler, and we'll be able to enjoy our time better."

"Sounds like a great idea." Mark beamed at his wife. "What do you say, Preacher?"

"I think it's a wonderful plan."

He waved to everyone as they rode away, sighing when the last parishioner left. He really had hoped Elsie would join them. *"I guess I need to pray more for her, Lord."*

Loosening his tie and shedding his jacket, he trooped into his house and prepared a simple meal. He dozed for a short time, lulled to sleep by the hot breeze brushing across his skin. When Benjamin awoke, he stepped outside and stretched. The sun blazed in the late afternoon sky. He glanced in the direction where Elsie had been plowing.

Odd. Buster stood with his muzzle hovered above an object on the ground. He didn't remember spotting anything there before.

Benjamin surveyed the area, but there were no signs of Elsie. Unless …

He took off at a sprint.

CHAPTER EIGHT

No extenuating circumstances permit an unmarried woman to be in the company of a gentleman without a proper chaperone.
Mrs. Wigglesworth's Essential Guide to Proper Etiquette and Manners of Refined Society

Benjamin's heart squeezed in his chest when he spotted Elsie sprawled in the dirt like an abandoned sack of potatoes. A lump formed in his throat as he bent over her motionless form.

Memories of Mary's lifeless body flashed through his mind. He refused to lose another woman. He scooped Elsie into his arms and carried her to the soddy.

Her flushed skin scorched through the fabric of his shirt. He carefully set her on the bedroll. Not a single quiver rippled across her skin as he laid her on the blankets. Her breathing came in shallow, rapid bursts.

"Elsie? Can you hear me?"

She didn't stir. He wished a doctor resided close by, but he didn't dare leave her alone in this condition. Not one drop of perspiration covered her face or hands. She should be sweating with the soaring temperatures.

He had to bring her fever down. Benjamin spotted a bucket of water and a rag. Dipping the rag into the tepid water, he wrung it out and set it across her forehead.

She didn't move when a drop of water fell on her nose.

Rushing outside, he dumped the warm water and raced to the creek with the bucket. Immersing it in the cool depths, he ran back, not caring when some of it sloshed against his leg.

Benjamin cradled Elsie's head in the crook of his arm and trickled water into her mouth. Once he'd gotten some moisture in her, he grabbed a towel, dipped it in the bucket, and began to dribble liquid over her entire body, soaking her clothes. He did whatever he could to help get the fever down, praying while he worked.

Elsie didn't shift once.

After an hour, he quieted his breathing so he could check hers. It remained fast and shallow. He continued to pray and pace the tiny enclosure. Each time her body heat dried her clothes, he soaked them again with cool water, not knowing what else to do.

Hours passed, and no change occurred. How long could her body withstand the fever raging through her? He paced the room, reaching the far wall in only a few strides before going the other direction again. Shoving his hands through his hair, a pain formed in his chest. He couldn't bear to see her suffer.

Sitting beside Elsie, he glanced around the dim interior. Other than a bucket, saddle, saddlebags, and bedroll, Elsie had scant possessions. She didn't even own a lamp. Why had he never noticed it before?

He pressed his hand against her forehead, but nothing had changed. Surely it wouldn't hurt to be gone for a few minutes.

Benjamin scurried the short distance to his wagon. Finding a lamp, supplies, and his Bible, he carted them to Elsie's hovel. His conscience pricked. He had a real bed waiting to be placed in his house as soon as he finished the roof. She didn't even have a door.

As he rushed back to the soddy, Benjamin spotted poor Buster standing in the field still hitched to the plow. Setting his items down, Benjamin sprinted the short distance and unbuckled the leather straps, leaving the plow where it stood, then led the horse to the creek. He patted the steed's neck as he tethered the stallion. "Sorry, fella, I forgot all about you."

Buster whinnied and shook his head before going back to guzzling water from the stream. Benjamin would rub the sweaty animal down later, but for now, he didn't dare leave Elsie any longer than absolutely necessary.

When he returned to find no change, he continued to pray for a miracle. Benjamin drizzled water across Elsie's limbs and face again.

Lighting the lamp, Benjamin sat beside Elsie and poured his heart out to God. He couldn't lose her.

A blazing fire gripped Elsie's body and refused to loosen its hold. She moaned. Her head throbbed a steady cadence—more like hammered—while her stomach tossed, flipped, and turned like a tiny boat thrown about in a stormy ocean. Her muscles cramped.

"Elsie? Can you hear me?"

The darkness sucked at her body.

"I'm here, and I won't leave you."

"Pa?" It didn't sound like him.

She couldn't hear his response. Instead, the beady eyes of a pack of coyotes stared her down.

"No!" She twisted, covering her head to protect her face. Elsie kicked, but the hounds nipped and bit at her legs. "Dear God, help me!"

Images faded and blurred. One time she thought she saw Benjamin, but he'd kept his distance since that night when he cradled her in his arms, so why would he be here now?

When she awakened again, dampness covered her body. Had she sweated that much? Her eyelids fluttered open.

"Thank God you're awake."

A face loomed closer. She blinked, and her eyes cleared. "Benjamin?"

"You gave me quite a scare." His hand grazed her forehead. "You're burning up yet. How're you feeling?"

"I ache all over. My muscles are like a baby bird's neck—limp and weak. I couldn't stand if my life depended upon it."

"Here." He supported her shoulders and brought a cup to her mouth.

The cool water trickled down her throat. Her limbs trembled. She refused when Benjamin offered another sip, and he carefully eased her back on her bedroll. He tucked a strand of her hair behind her ear, rubbing the bottom of the lock back and forth between his fingers before he pulled his hand back.

Elsie scrutinized him. The fever had to be playing tricks on her brain for her to believe the man would have an interest in her. Must be a dream. Or nightmare. She couldn't tell which.

Her heart pattered. Best get rid of him so she could think straight. "I'll be fine. Y-you can go on home now."

His hazel eyes studied her. He didn't say a word. Maybe he wasn't really there. She touched his sleeve and squeezed. Sure enough, he was real. Elsie expected him to turn his back and leave, but he didn't. Rather, he sat beside her and opened his Bible. Benjamin read aloud.

How many times had Pa read it to her over the years? Too many to count.

She drifted in and out. His deep, assured voice putting her mind at ease.

"'Thy word is a lamp unto my feet, and a light unto my path.'" Benjamin continued to speak, but she couldn't get past those words. They reminded her of her childhood.

"Elm, always remember to seek the Lord and follow His ways. Let His Word be a light for your path and a lamp for your feet. He'll show you each step to take."

"I'll do it, Pa. You can count on me."

Elsie sighed. God had done nothing to stop the hurts of her world, no matter how much she'd begged Him. He'd allowed her and Pa to lose their home because of a bank foreclosure, church folks to turn their backs on them, and Pa to die.

God couldn't be trusted. His Word hadn't lit her way in a long time.

Benjamin prayed Elsie's heart would be open and receptive to God's Word as he searched for another scripture to read. Perhaps God had brought about this heat sickness, or whatever caused her illness, so Elsie would turn to Him.

Benjamin flipped through the pages. Her eyes had closed, but he suspected she was listening. He cleared his throat and started again.

"'Let all bitterness, and wrath, and anger, and clamour, and evil speaking, be put away from you, with all malice: And be ye kind one to another, tenderhearted, forgiving one another, even as God for Christ's sake hath forgiven you.'"

"Hogwash." Elsie snorted.

When he looked at her, her eyes were open and blazing.

"What do you mean?" He prayed God would give him the words to minister to her obvious need.

"Those verses are plain hogwash. It ain't true." Anger lined her face. "All I have is bitterness." She shifted her head to the side.

He reached over and tilted her head back so he could see her eyes. "Why the bitterness?"

A muscle in her jaw flickered. "Because folks aren't kind or tenderhearted. Oh, they may be for a while, but when things get rough, nobody stays with you. They don't come to help." She bit her lip. "N-not God either."

His heart ached for her and the obvious pain she'd suffered. "God is always with us. He promised to never leave."

She shook her head. "I can't follow a God who wasn't there when I needed Him most." Elsie's face contorted. "One who allows bad things to happen and doesn't care." Hurt shone in her eyes.

"Folks can't be trusted either. I've learned the hard way, and I won't make the same mistake again. I'm better off alone." She struggled to turn away. "Leave, Benjamin. You don't want to ruin your reputation by staying with the likes of me."

Poor thing. He longed to take her in his arms and soothe away her pain.

"Bitterness isn't the answer, Elsie." He touched her arm, but she stiffened and tried to lean her body away from him.

Benjamin didn't want to further agitate her. Heaving a sigh, he stepped outside into the moonlight and prayed. He had no intention of leaving, not until he knew her health improved. Truth be told, he doubted she really wanted him gone. Besides, the woman couldn't get rid of him so easily.

Elsie had told him to leave, so why did she have such an ache in her heart when he did? She shifted on her bedroll. Sleep took its time in claiming her.

She awoke sometime later, squinting at the light in her home. Where had it come from? Her heart hammered in her throat.

"Elsie."

Benjamin's one word soothed her battered soul. He hadn't left her after all. Peace washed over her.

He lifted her head and helped her take a drink of broth. She nodded when she had her fill.

He sat beside her bedroll and rested the back of his hand against her forehead. "Looks like your fever's going down. We don't want you to get chilled." He tucked the quilt under her chin.

"Why?" She didn't have the energy to finish her question.

His tired eyes twinkled. "Why didn't I leave?"

It took all her strength to nod.

"How could I leave when you were in obvious need? That's what we're supposed to do for each other. Be there and assist as we are able.

"I'm thankful God prompted me to help you when I saw Buster standing beside you in the field. There's a good chance you would've died if I'd found you later than I had." A muscle in his jaw flickered.

Was it possible that God had directed him? Did God really care what happened to her? Elsie shoved the questions into the back of her brain.

Weariness lined Benjamin's face. "I've also been thinking about what you said about bitterness and bad things happening. I'd love for my life to be without trials, but I find that it's during those times I grow the most. If things were always easy, I wouldn't have any reason to change and learn to do things differently."

He grasped her hand and rubbed a thumb across the back of it.

She gasped.

"You know I lost my fiancée before coming here. We'd made a great many plans. I suppose I haven't taken time to fully grieve her passing, with the run and everything." He glanced at their hands and dropped hers as if he'd been scorched. "I'm sorry."

Benjamin got up and started pacing the tiny enclosure. "I wish things had been different. God could've saved her, or prevented her dog from wandering into the swelled stream, but for some reason, He didn't." He raked his hands through his hair. "I rely on the *fact* that God is trustworthy, even when we don't understand the things happening to us. I don't have all the answers, Elsie, but I think we both need to find a way to give up the bitterness."

His admission shocked her but somehow gave her hope. Maybe things could change.

CHAPTER NINE

Help those who are in need. Be kind to those less fortunate. Don't take advantage of their depraved situations.
Mrs. Wigglesworth's Essential Guide to Proper Etiquette and Manners of Refined Society

Elsie lay on her bedroll, squinting at the light filtering through her doorway. She moaned and flipped back the quilt. Her legs wobbled as she arched her back. Something shuffled in the corner of the room. Someone leaned against the wall.

Her fingers edged toward her rifle. "Don't move a muscle. I've got a gun, and I ain't afraid to use it."

A chuckle rippled. "Except your weapon is over here with me."

"Benjamin?" Her heart slowed its rapid cadence. "What're you doing here?"

"Elsie, you in there?" A female voice filtered through the open door of the sod house.

Benjamin shoved off the shadowed wall and stepped into the light.

He grabbed Elsie's elbow. "I don't think you're ready to be up yet."

"Elsie?"

In a second, Beatrice would cross the threshold. What would she think when she found them together?

Elsie snatched up her quilt, threw it over Benjamin, and stumbled outside into the morning sunshine.

"Beatrice, what a nice surprise. Did you come by yourself?" Elsie threaded her arm through the young woman's and guided her toward the creek, hoping Beatrice wouldn't notice how much leaning she did. "I'm powerful thirsty this morning. Why don't you join me?"

"Elsie? You seem nervous." Beatrice stopped and turned. "Oh, hello, Preacher." Her brow puckered. "What were you doing in Elsie's house?"

"Good morning, Mrs. Sawyer. I stopped by to see how Miss Smith was doing. She's been ill for a few days."

A high-pitched laugh pealed from Elsie's throat as she tugged on Beatrice's arm. Elsie clapped a hand over her mouth. Had that sound really come from her? "I'm feeling much better now. Had a little too much time in the sun the other day, that's all."

Beatrice frowned. "You do look quite pale, but why are you so on edge?" She glanced back and forth between Elsie and Benjamin. "Did something happen with you two?"

"Nothing more than me caring for a sick parishioner." Benjamin twirled his hat. "As you can see, I've been sleeping there"—he indicated a bedroll about ten yards from the house—"so I'd be nearby if Elsie needed anything. I would've come and asked for help, but with how high her temperature soared, I was afraid to leave her." Fatigue lined the corners of his eyes.

"You poor thing." Beatrice hugged Elsie tight. "I would've come sooner if I'd known. What can I do to help? Oh, I can't believe I forgot. Preacher, Mark's at your place trying to find you."

Elsie glanced in that direction. Sure enough, the Sawyer wagon was parked beside Milly. Mark strolled toward them with a grin.

He tipped his hat to Elsie. "We missed you at church service, Miss Smith. Beatrice kept bugging me to come check on you today so she could see how you're faring. I figured the preacher could use some help getting the roof on before the rain comes." Mark studied the cloudless sky. "Although it doesn't appear to be anytime soon."

"Service? Is that what you folks were doing? You didn't tell me you planned to hold church services on my property." Elsie pinned Benjamin with a stare.

"The preacher mentioned he left a note for you. Didn't you find it?" Beatrice squeezed her arm.

Elsie shook her head.

Benjamin cleared his throat. "Perhaps it blew away. I tacked it to the sod beside your doorway. I'm sorry. If I had known—forgive me. I should've made a point again of coming to invite you in person."

He'd stopped by to ask her to come? She swallowed. Why did the thought affect her heart?

"We best get busy on that roof." Mark clapped Benjamin on the back. "Unless you planned on doing something else today. I figured I can only spare the morning before I need to get busy again on my place."

"Of course." Benjamin shot the women a sideways glance before the men tromped to the opposite side of the property.

"He took care of you, huh?" Beatrice turned toward Elsie, her eyes twinkling. "Are you sure you don't have feelings for each other?"

"What? Nothing like that."

"What happened?"

"I was out too long without a break." Elsie stared down at her bare feet. "I know better, I just can't seem to think straight—"

"When the preacher is around?" Beatrice's laughter rang out like a bell.

That had nothing to do with it. Did it?

Benjamin checked over his shoulder one more time before he turned away.

Mark chuckled. "You've got it bad."

"I'm merely concerned for Elsie's welfare like I'd be for any other person in my congregation." He glanced at his neighbor.

"Elsie, huh?" A grin spread across Mark's tanned face. "Sure. You keep telling yourself that. One day, you two will come to your senses and realize you care for each other."

Benjamin bit back a snort. Surely the man had been out in the sun too long. "You sure you're up to working? You seem a bit befuddled."

Mark's eyes twinkled. "What do you say we tackle that roof?"

The remainder of the morning they spent in companionable silence. The ping of hammers against nail provided the only clamor. Still, Benjamin struggled to keep his thoughts from wandering. Clearly, Elsie was on the mend and no longer needed his assistance. Why did he feel a sense of loss?

The morning with Beatrice had been a nice distraction for Elsie, at least for a little while. She'd have worked in the field and finished plowing if she'd had the strength. Her bed called to her, but she refused to go to her soddy and succumb. If she napped now, she likely wouldn't sleep at night. Stifling a yawn, she eased her body down and sat with her back against a tree. The stream gurgled across the rocks even though the water level had lowered in the past few days.

Elsie picked up a pebble and tossed it into the stream. If they didn't get rain soon, it might dry up, and then where would she be? She reached for another rock. Best to keep her mind off the things that might happen. Each day had enough trouble of its own.

Her head dipped against her chest, and her eyelids fluttered. She awoke with a start, blinking to clear her vision as Benjamin walked toward her.

A furrow creased his brow. "You feeling poorly again?"

She shook her head to clear the last bit of fuzziness. "Nope. Just relaxing for a little bit." She smiled. "I see you and Mark got your roof finished. Looks like you're about ready to move your stuff in. Where'd you get it all? Surely Milly weren't strong enough to tote all that."

"No. I ordered some things last time I was in Enid, and the store delivered it."

Elsie whistled. That must have cost a fortune. Her heart sank. He weren't likely to budge from the property if he had a whole household full of goods. The man wouldn't ever leave at this rate. There might be other plots nearby still available that she could move to, but Pa had wanted her to have *this* one. Somehow it represented the only thing she had left of him. She refused to let it go.

Benjamin plucked a blade of grass. "I've been thinking."

Her eyes narrowed. What was he up to now?

He rubbed the back of his neck. "I have leftover wood from my house. Some I'm saving for making a privy. I thought maybe we could use a few of the boards to build a door for your soddy."

"A door?"

"That way critters won't crawl into your home, or at least will be deterred."

The critters didn't bother her so much, but it'd be nice to have more privacy. She should say no and not be beholden to him, instead, she said, "I can't afford to buy it."

He smiled. "You'd be doing me a favor. I hate to see the wood lying around and doing no good to anybody."

"Well …"

"It's decided then. I'll be back in a jiffy."

"Hold up there. I'll start toting things with you." Elsie pushed to her feet and walked with him side-by-side to the stack of boards beside his new house.

They worked together measuring and building a doorframe.

Benjamin took a swig of water from his canteen and offered it to Elsie.

She accepted it and took a long draw before capping it and wiping a few drops of moisture from her lips.

"Once we get these cross-sections in place, I think we'll have the door finished." He scratched his head. "Although I guess we don't have a way to attach the door."

"I'm sure I can figure out something." Elsie squinted as she studied the doorframe. The next time she went hunting maybe she could find game big enough to dry the hide and cut leather hinges. It should last for a while at least, supposing she could find a deer. The meat would provide many meals for her. Her stomach gurgled at the thought.

"If you search inside my wagon, there's a sack of potatoes and some salt pork. Would you mind frying them up for us while I finish here?" He swung his hammer, not giving her a choice.

Strolling the short distance to Benjamin's campfire, she stirred the coals and blew on the embers. With some encouragement, they sprang to life.

She stood on the wagon wheel, leaning over the side. Finding the items, she tucked them under one arm and grabbed the frying pan and a knife.

A short time later, the pork and potatoes created a delicious scent. Benjamin sauntered over with tin plates and cutlery. He handed them to her. "Thanks for fixing the food. I hadn't realized how hungry I was."

She nodded. "Thanks for helping with the door. I, uh, appreciate it."

Her luminous blue eyes spoke something, but Benjamin couldn't decipher it. He took the last bite of the meal she'd prepared. "This is delicious. You're a good cook."

Elsie snorted. "I'm fair at best. You're just hungry."

She jumped up and grabbed his plate and the fry pan. "I'll rinse these in the stream." She took off in that direction before he could reply. He watched her as she worked, wishing he could find a way to get her to open up.

Elsie returned a few minutes later. "Thanks again for your help with the door, and for the food. I guess I best get back to work." She gave a slight wave and jogged to her place, not glancing at him once.

Images of Elsie's empty house popped into his mind. The woman was practically destitute. No extra food lined the floor. No shelves held supplies. When he'd tripped over her saddlebags this morning, the pouches had been light. He guessed she had one change of clothes since he hadn't seen her in anything else. Maybe she'd switched shirts once. Benjamin couldn't be sure. He didn't typically notice such things.

"Dear God, here I am with plenty because of the money I got from Grandpap, and she has nothing. Show me what I can do." He had to find a way to be a good neighbor and help her more.

Maybe he'd come up with an idea as he set up his household. Shoving to his feet, he flipped back the tarp on the wagon and started unloading.

Sweat poured off his body as he flopped the mattress onto the rope bed frame. He didn't need such a large one, but nothing else had been available at the time. Next, he placed a small table and lamp to one side of the room near the bed. Benjamin shoved a small chest of drawers against one wall, covered the smooth wood with a flour-sack towel, and carefully set a pitcher, bowl, and various shaving items on the top.

The tiny kitchen, open to the sitting area, already held a table, chair, and cook stove. He carted in crates of food and canned items, along with the sack of remaining potatoes. When the last item had been brought in, Benjamin glanced around the room, satisfied with his work. Seeing all his bounty, he knew what God wanted him to do.

He clapped his Stetson on his head and stepped outside. Benjamin patted Milly then threw the saddle on her back, securing it.

"Come on, girl. We've got a mission to do." He studied the sun's position in the sky. "I doubt we'll make it back this evening, but I promise it'll be worth it." Benjamin whistled. His heart felt lighter as he snapped the reins.

Elsie peered up from currying Buster to see Benjamin leave. "Wonder what he's up to." She patted her horse. "What do you think, fella?"

Pa would think her crazy if he could see her now. When had she resorted to talking to herself or her horse? Benjamin had no need to tell her his comings and goings. Best she remember that and not get too attached to having someone nearby.

She'd worked side by side with her pa all her life, never shouldering all the responsibility of their farm all by herself.

A lump formed in her throat. *Pa, why'd you have to die when I need you most?*

CHAPTER TEN

Accepting gifts from a gentleman is improper in all situations except if a promise of marriage has been ascertained.
Mrs. Wigglesworth's Essential Guide to Proper Etiquette and Manners of Refined Society

One can of beans. Elsie recounted her coins and took stock once again of her scant supplies. A few herbal remedies, clothes, bullets, Pa's neckerchiefs, Bible, and pocket watch. She sighed. No avoiding it, she *had* to make a trip to town. If her funds stretched to cover the price of a few food items after she bought seed, she'd be grateful.

She shoved her hair inside her Stetson and stepped outside. Tossing a saddle on Buster, she secured the cinch and tied her filled canteen to the saddle horn. Mounting, she shifted her hat to shield her eyes. Moisture hadn't fallen in months.

Elsie yawned and allowed Buster to set the pace. She'd tossed and turned most of the night waiting for the sound of Benjamin's return.

Since when had she started caring about his comings and goings? If her sisters could see her now, they'd laugh at her fickleness. One minute she wanted him gone, and the next she was worried because he hadn't made it home. If Benjamin had decided to call it quits and leave his home to her, she'd sleep in her new house tonight, although the man was proving to be as stubborn as she was.

When she finally entered Enid, Elsie gawked at the scurry of activity. Tent after tent had popped out of the prairie floor like flowers bursting forth overnight. The strip had been without a single building before the race. Now hammers pinged all around her as wooden structures stood in various stages of construction. All manner of men and beasts scurried across the beaten-down grass streets, although not many women. The whiff of unwashed bodies assaulted her senses. Of course, she probably didn't smell none too good neither.

She called out to the closest person. "Where can I buy seed?"

The man's bloodshot eyes studied her. He swaggered, stepped closer, and his odiferous breath wafted up to her. She sucked air in through her teeth to avoid the stench. "What did you say, boy?" He held a hand to his ear.

"Seed."

"No, I ain't seen no one." He waved a bottle. "Check out the saloon. Maybe they can help you there. Sure helped me." The man cackled like a hen.

Ignoring him, she tied Buster to a post, grabbed her rifle, and wandered into a tent with the word "store" printed on it. After her eyes adjusted to the dim interior, she noticed quite an assortment of things—plows, dishes, food items. Almost anything a body could desire heaped in disorganization.

"Can I help you, son?" A bearded man scratched his wide belly.

Why did everyone insist on calling her son? "Seed. You got any?"

"I reckon it all depends on what kind you're looking for." His dark eyes studied her. "What did yer pa send ya for? If ya have a list, I can help ya."

"It depends on your prices." Elsie surveyed his stock.

"Same prices here as you'll find anywhere else in town. Now, what can I get ya?"

Her gaze swung toward the stack of filled burlap sacks. "What's the price of winter wheat?"

He named a figure, and she winced. That amount would take everything she had, not leaving anything left over for food. "Thank you. I think I'll just look around."

His right eyebrow lifted. "Say, I forgot to ask ya, been asking all the fellas that come in. Ya wouldn't be Elmer Smith, would ya?"

She stilled. "What's it to you?" Her gaze flitted toward the exit, then back toward him. She rested a hand on her gun.

He studied her. "Don't matter to me whether ya are or not. I have an order for an Elmer Smith and wondered if it's ya or yer pa. Hoping to save myself a trip to the fella's place if need be, that's all."

"What if I say it is?" Elsie's chest rose and fell like a locomotive chugged beneath her shirt.

"Then I'd need to see yer name on yer claim to be sure ya ain't lying."

"What kind of order?"

"All sorts of things. There's a fancy brass bed and mattress, seed, a stove, lamp, food items, blankets. Ya name it, it's probably on the pile." He lifted an eyebrow. "Ya him or not?"

Elsie slipped her deed from her pocket and held it out to the man. "It's me."

He didn't take the paper but glanced back and forth between her face and signature. "Everything seems in order. Just like the fella said." He motioned toward a huge pile of goods in a corner of the tent. "It's going to take a wagon to cart all this stuff home. Sure hope yer pa sent ya with one."

Elsie squinted. "There has to be some sort of mistake. All this can't possibly be mine."

"My instructions were to deliver these goods to an Elmer Smith, and yer here. Now I can save myself a trip."

"But I can't afford this, and besides, I don't own a wagon."

"Ain't no debt. It's already paid in full." He scratched his head. "I guess I can have it delivered to ya. I hoped to avoid my boy having to make an extra trip if he didn't have to, especially since ya live a ways from here. Suppose Leroy can bring it out to ya tomorrow then. He has other deliveries today. If ya sign this receipt, I'll make sure ya get everything." He thrust paper and a stub of a pencil forward.

"What kind of seed?"

"On the pile?" He shoved the pencil behind his ear and pocketed the slip of paper. "Winter wheat and regular, although I don't think ya should plant either of them. With the dry spell we've had, it won't grow."

Elsie studied the tent flap blowing in the wind. "It's gotta rain soon." Without rain, she couldn't make a go on her claim.

"Don't know." The man laughed. "Selling seed sure is helping business. Is there anything else ya need?"

Elsie sauntered over to the pile and sorted through the jumble of items. "Guess not. There's quite a collection of canned goods, even prunes. Who paid for this?"

"Can't tell ya. The m … person who paid wished to remain anonymous. I guess ya don't turn down a gift like this one. Cost the, uh, customer a pretty large amount." He didn't meet her gaze. Instead, he watched the other folks inside the tent. "If there's nothing else I can help ya with, I got other things to do." He waddled off. "Leroy will be there tomorrow afternoon. The customer left directions, so I'd be able to find ya."

There was no way Pa could've set this up for her. More than likely it was one of her new neighbors, but none of them knew what she needed. Except Benjamin.

What would he expect from her in return?

Benjamin crouched behind a wagon when he saw Elsie at the edge of the store tent.

Once she ducked into the tent, he shoved his Stetson back on his head and strolled toward the livery.

A familiar looking man stepped into his path. "Howdy, Preacher. What're you up to? You here to purchase goods?"

The fella who'd needed Benjamin's assistance before the race began sure had a knack for finding him whenever he came to town. "Hello there. Yes, just made some purchases." Benjamin shortened his stride.

"Where you heading?"

"To the livery. My horse needs a new shoe."

The man drew up close to him. "Make sure you're careful. There's talk about a gang of men who are terrorizing the territory."

A jolt of alarm ran through Benjamin. "You don't say. Around this area?"

The man shook his head. "Most reports are north of here and a few to the west too."

"I'll be sure to be careful. Appreciate the warning."

"Did you get your land free and clear, or are you still having to wait?" The fellow glanced to where a line squirreled its way through the makeshift street. "I heard some won't be called to the claim office until next spring since they had so many who came to Enid. Hope you aren't one of them."

"Unfortunately, there's another person contesting the same piece of property." Benjamin rubbed the back of his neck.

"You don't say. Heard tell of one man who shot another who had challenged a claim. The sheriff hauled him to jail. I reckon neither of them got what they wanted." He smiled. "I guess it won't happen to you, you being a preacher and all."

"I should hope not." Benjamin cringed at the thought.

"Who's contesting your land? Anyone I know?"

"I'm sorry, my friend. I hate to leave, but I must get to the livery. Perhaps we'll see each other again soon." Benjamin left before the man could ask any more questions. He had no inclination to bring up the situation he faced. Would he have done anything differently if Elsie weren't a woman? He didn't have an answer.

Fiddlesticks. Elsie punched her fist against her hand. She'd been so sidetracked yesterday with the unexpected bounty that she'd forgotten to check the price of hinges. It'd have to wait. She had no plans of returning to town for a while.

She plunked a bucket of water just inside the door to the soddy, stepping beside her bedroll to run a hand across the appliquéd roses quilt Ma had made and passed down to the youngest daughter. She smiled. Pa said Ma had loved roses. He planted a bush by their home, long before Elsie had come along. It would've been nice to plant one beside her new home as well. Maybe she could find a wild rose blooming somewhere.

"Ma, I wish you could see me now." The words came out with a hitch.

She pulled her boots on and trekked outside to start a fire. She opened her last can of beans. Later in the day, she'd have a house full of goods. Her mouth watered at the thought. She emptied the can into Benjamin's fry pan, stirring them so they wouldn't burn.

"What a funny thing to have for breakfast."

Elsie startled and nearly dropped the pan in the dirt. She looked up to find Beatrice smiling at her. "I didn't hear you." Too much woolgathering was dulling Elsie's senses.

Her friend giggled. "You should've seen yourself jump. Is the preacher around? I already checked at his place." She glanced toward the clapboard house.

"Nope. Haven't seen hide nor tail of him in the past two days. I'm guessing he decided to leave. Good riddance, I say." Elsie set the pan to the side, waiting for her breakfast to cool.

"You can't mean it." Beatrice sank to a seated position.

"I always figured he weren't cut out for living here. Looks like I'll have me a fine home. In fact, I planned to move my things into it today, and all the items arriving this afternoon."

Elsie blew across the food, then scooped a mess of beans into her mouth.

Beatrice gasped. "You can't possibly be serious. Surely he plans to return."

Elsie shrugged and continued her breakfast.

"Maybe that's him coming now." Beatrice shielded her eyes and motioned toward a horse and rider. "Howdy, Preacher." She waved.

Great. Elsie's gut flopped like a fish out of water. Sure enough, she couldn't mistake the way he sat on his horse. She sighed. Her emotions bobbled like a top spinning on its axis.

Benjamin lifted his hat. "Hello, ladies. I see you're out early on this fine morning."

"I think Mark was getting tired of my chattering earlier. He suggested that a walk might do me good." Beatrice giggled. "Elsie was just telling me that she has a delivery coming later today."

Elsie studied Benjamin. "Apparently someone bought a whole mess of articles for me at the store in Enid. I have my suspicions of who." Was that a flicker in his eyes? She couldn't tell for sure since he'd yet to meet her gaze.

Benjamin looked at Beatrice, avoiding eye contact with Elsie. "Are those beans I smell?"

"Sure is." Beatrice winked at him before turning to Elsie. "I guess the Good Lord is supplying your needs, Elsie. You should be grateful and not question God's goodness."

Elsie snorted and stood. "I don't think God had anything to do with it."

Beatrice looped her arm through Elsie's. "God has a way of surprising you when you least suspect it, isn't it so, Preacher?"

He sputtered. "Y-yes." He resisted the urge to run his finger along his suddenly too-tight collar. Elsie didn't suspect anything, did she?

Her right brow lifted.

Please don't let her ask any more questions about it, Lord. He swung down from the saddle.

"I probably should be getting home." Beatrice peeked at the horizon. "Mark doesn't like for me to be gone too long when it's hot, or he worries. If I leave now, I'll make it back before it gets too warm." She patted Elsie's arm. "I wanted to make sure you're feeling better. Oh, I almost forgot, Preacher. Mark wanted to know if you would let him borrow your sod splitter."

"Of course. I'll bring it over later. If you ladies will excuse me, I need to take care of Milly. It's been a long ride." He patted his steed. The horse responded by sticking her nose in his hand.

Beatrice waved and walked away.

No sooner had the woman disappeared over a knoll when Elsie loudly cleared her throat.

He peeked at her.

"Where you been, Benjamin?"

"Oh, here and there." He tugged Milly forward and put a few steps between them. He glanced over his shoulder, and Elsie stayed put.

Whew. He'd managed to get out of the conversation unscathed. The storekeeper had told him the deliveries for Elsie would arrive later in the day. He'd be sure to make himself scarce.

He unloaded the few personal supplies he'd purchased, then took care of Milly. Stepping into the house, he welcomed the quiet and coolness. It wouldn't take long for the sun to warm it, but for now, he enjoyed the respite.

Benjamin didn't dare go outside and risk further discourse with Elsie. In an hour, he'd set out to deliver the plow to Mark. Maybe the man could give some pointers on how to start clearing his own land. He also needed to warn the menfolk about the robbers. It wouldn't do to say something to the women just yet. At least not until the men came up with a plan to keep them safe.

Elsie stared after the man. He looked guiltier than a student caught hiding a mess of frogs in his teacher's desk. She shook her head and turned away.

What did Beatrice know about God's goodness and surprises? If the woman had gone through what Elsie had, she wouldn't be so quick to say such tripe. God certainly had never done anything like that for Elsie. Or had He?

She traipsed back to the fire and grabbed the empty fry pan before stalking to the creek to rinse it. All the talk of God had her off her feed. The beans battled in her stomach.

With the clean pan in hand, Elsie stomped back to her soddy and placed it inside the door. She kicked dirt on the dying embers of her fire and headed out to the field.

A hot breeze stirred the dirt, causing her to cough. She stooped and grabbed a handful of soil and let it slip through her fingers. It weren't anything like the rich land back home. If only she'd been able to keep the farm.

Elsie shoved to her feet. Wishing didn't bring about nothing. She whistled for Buster, and he trotted over. In no time, she had him harnessed to the plow. Perhaps hours in the blazing sun would boil her brain. With any luck, she'd finish the field before Benjamin took the sod splitter to Mark, and it would be ready for seed once it arrived with the afternoon delivery.

Sweat ran in rivulets down Elsie's body as she leaned against the plow, watching a wagonload of goods pull onto her land. After hours of working, it was as good a time as any to take a break.

A young man jumped from the high seat. He smiled, revealing two rotted upper teeth. "You want me to unload things at the house or in your shed here?"

"Here." Elsie grimaced. *Shed indeed.*

Leaving Buster and the plow, she helped unload the items. Once the wagon was empty, and her soddy was full, the man withdrew a small package from his pocket and handed it to her. "Here. Didn't want this to get lost." He vaulted to the wagon seat and slapped the reins across the horses' backs.

The weight of the package surprised her. As he left, she untied the paper-wrapped bundle. When the strings fell away she knew beyond a shadow of a doubt who had bought the items.

Two metal hinges weighed heavy in her hand. Somehow, she'd find a way to repay Benjamin.

CHAPTER ELEVEN

Any type of manly interest is to be avoided. When such a topic arises in conversation, be sensitive to listen, but quick to guide the discussion to different subject matters.

Mrs. Wigglesworth's Essential Guide to Proper Etiquette and Manners of Refined Society

Benjamin took a swig of coffee as a knock sounded. The sun hadn't risen yet. He set his mug on the table and crossed to the door.

"Good morning." Elsie cleared her throat. "I'm going hunting and thought maybe you'd care to join me. It's a way to repay—" She shook her head. "Thought maybe I could show you how to bag some meat for your table. Hopefully, we'll spot something, though the last few times I've gone, I haven't seen anything."

"I suppose we could."

"You've said before that you don't have experience with"—her hand swept to encompass the area— "well, you get the idea. You've been kind enough to me, and I thought maybe I could teach you how to hunt." She twisted her hands.

Benjamin pinched the bridge of his nose. He didn't have the heart to tell her he knew how to hunt. Not when she was reaching out, trying to make amends.

"Never mind. I'm sure you're busy." She turned away.

"No, wait." He grabbed her arm. "I'd enjoy the lesson, and spending time together."

"This ain't no courting." Elsie studied his fingers still wrapped around her slim arm.

He dropped his hold. "I'm honored you considered asking me. Give me a minute to gather a pack, and I'll be ready." While Elsie waited in the doorway, Benjamin threw a few things into his saddlebag. He grabbed his rifle and slung it over his shoulder. One large swig downed the remainder of his coffee.

"I'm surprised you own a weapon. I figured I'd have to loan you my rifle," Elsie said as he closed the door. "Ain't preachers supposed to be men of peace?"

"Yes, of course, but sometimes a weapon is necessary." He clapped his Stetson on, traipsed the short distance to the stream, and dipped his canteen into it.

"You ever shot it before?" Elsie kicked a pebble into the water.

He nodded.

"You feeling poorly today?" Elsie knelt beside him and filled her canteen.

"I'm fine, really. Overly contemplative, I suppose." He capped the container and stood.

She studied him but didn't say a word. A few silent minutes later, they sat atop Milly and Buster. "Lead the way," he said. He clicked, and his horse surged forward. "Do you have anything particular in mind for hunting?"

She shrugged. "Depends on what we come across. Sure would love to bag a whitetail deer, but jackrabbits are good too. You might have a harder time shooting a bird on your first try. We'll aim for something bigger to give you a better chance. That way we'll be even." Her voice dwindled off.

Benjamin had been mighty quiet for the past hour. He acted like her nephews when they'd been caught doing something naughty. The man wouldn't make eye contact. He was cagier than a dog tied to a rope with a cat crossing just out of its reach. Yep, something was up. What, she didn't know.

Might as well let him have his peace for a while. Didn't the Good Book say something about the truth coming to light? Elsie frowned. She had no desire to think about such things.

She shifted on the saddle and patted Buster. He snorted and threw his head back. Why couldn't a man be as easy to read as a horse? She'd take Buster over Benjamin any day. She dragged her focus back to the task at hand.

Benjamin whispered and pointed. "I think there's something in the grove of trees."

Elsie tightened the reins, and Buster obeyed her quiet command. She slid from the saddle and unsheathed her rifle. Benjamin did likewise.

They made quick work of tying their horses to a nearby bush. She put a finger to her lips and led the way, checking the ground before she placed each foot, trying to make as little sound as possible. "You'll want to aim to kill when we catch up to it." Her words were barely audible. "You ain't afraid of killing, are you?"

They crept closer, and Benjamin followed Elsie's steps. A deer grazed with his back end toward them. The buck's ears perked as they took another step.

"You take the shot." Elsie kept her voice quiet as they knelt side-by-side.

Benjamin cocked the rifle and brought the gun up to his shoulder until the barrel leveled on the deer.

"Nice and steady. Try and aim for the heart so he won't suffer and get too far away from us."

Elsie's breath tickled his ear.

His heart vaulted at her nearness. His thumb jerked against the trigger.

The buck scampered away.

"Good try. You almost grazed him." She stood. "You'll get the next game we see." Elsie patted his shoulder, and a string of tingles jolted down to his fingertips.

He needed some distance from her so he could think. He shifted away. "Let's eat. I'm half starved." Maybe food would get his thoughts on something other than Elsie.

They strolled back to the horses.

"I guess this is as good a place as any to eat. At least we'll get a break from the sun." She lifted her hat and fanned herself with it. Her hair shimmered as a strand whipped across her face.

Benjamin patted Milly instead of tucking the stray wisps behind Elsie's ear. He bit back a growl. He'd been hunting since he was seven. There was no reason for his missing the deer, but when Elsie's breath had fanned against his cheek, he hadn't been able to think straight. It should've been insignificant. He swallowed. The sooner they returned home, the better.

He blew out a steadying breath then rifled through his saddlebag. He drew out a piece of jerky from his pack and said a silent prayer before biting into it. They settled on the ground.

Elsie stared at him before gnawing on a roll.

His mouth watered. It had been quite a while since he'd had some bread.

She glanced at him then at her roll. "You want one?"

He nodded, and she tossed him one. "Thank you." He bit into the airy goodness.

"You don't seem yourself." Elsie leaned closer to him and stared into his eyes.

He could say the same about her.

She scowled. "Did you miss that shot on purpose?"

A piece of bread lodged in his throat.

Benjamin's face turned beet red. He coughed and reached for his canteen. Elsie pounded his back.

His spasm passed, but he didn't answer her question. He shifted his Stetson, and she couldn't see his eyes. Something was up, but for now, she'd let it go.

They finished their lunch without another word. Elsie brushed the crumbs from her shirt and stood. Game might be scarcer after having heard his shot. It looked to be a long afternoon wandering through the prairie. They could always go back home and try again come dusk, but she wanted her debt to Benjamin paid. Pa had never liked feeling indebted to any man and had taught her to compensate neighborliness whenever possible. The quicker she could do it, the better.

Benjamin trailed after her. Hours passed without spotting a thing. They'd need to head home soon before darkness settled.

A soft hissing followed by a high-pitched whinny caused Elsie to glance behind her. Milly reared on her hind legs, throwing Benjamin to the ground with a sickening thud. Elsie vaulted from Buster and sprinted the short distance between them. Milly reared again before galloping away.

"Benjamin?" Her heart pinched.

He knelt, then stood, but his face went chalk white before his legs gave way. He sank to the ground like a sack of potatoes. A garter snake slithered across Elsie's path.

Benjamin couldn't have broken anything. He'd gotten to his feet after being bucked off. In fact, he'd been fine until he'd seen the snake. If she had to wager a guess, the man had fainted. She let out a chuckle and bent over him.

Just to be sure, she checked his limbs. *Nope.* Nothing broken, as she'd suspected. She removed his hat and cradled his head in her lap. An examination didn't reveal any bumps. He ought to be coming around soon. Certainly, a swoon couldn't last long.

Elsie smoothed the thick, golden hair from his forehead, her fingers lingering on a curl. Her heart dipped. He mumbled and stirred. She yanked her hand away from him and gulped. "Benjamin?"

His hazel eyes flickered in his tanned face. Her pulse fluttered.

"Elsie?" He struggled to sit. She wrapped her arm around the taut muscles in his back.

"Is—is it gone?" Benjamin glanced around and shuddered.

"Is what gone?"

He gulped. The whites of his eyes glistened as his head swiveled, studying the ground. "The s-snake."

"You mean that little garter snake?"

His face paled again, and his arm trembled.

She laughed. "Don't tell me you're scared of a little, bitty garter snake?" She bit her lip, but a chuckle spurted out.

His back stiffened, and he pulled away. Benjamin stood and teetered for a second before steadying himself.

"You fainted." Elsie continued to laugh. "I can't believe it. I've never seen a grown man faint before." She gripped her aching sides, unable to control her amusement.

"It isn't funny." He growled, stalking away.

Benjamin's fingers curled into a fist. His heart throbbed. He prayed the snake had retreated somewhere far away.

He glanced around for Milly, but the horse probably headed home. Neither of them had ever been too partial to snakes.

He walked in the direction of his claim.

"Wait! Don't leave."

Would Elsie make fun of him like most had throughout his life? He didn't want to find out, but he didn't want to get stuck in the dark with snakes around either. His feet weighed down with each step as he walked toward her. "We'll never make it back before nightfall, especially with having to ride double."

A grin tugged at her lips. "I take it you ain't hurt."

Only his pride. Benjamin shook his head. "I'm sure I'll feel it tomorrow."

"Sorry I laughed at you." Elsie ducked her head. "I ain't never seen somebody else so scared of something."

If he hadn't seen Elsie's fear with his own eyes, he wouldn't believe she was capable. Still, he couldn't imagine her afraid of anything as small as a snake. “What do you say we call this expedition short and head home?”

She mounted and put her hand down to help him onto Buster’s back. The horse set out at a quick pace. Benjamin flailed when the animal stepped in a dip. He couldn’t figure out where to hold on so he wouldn’t go sliding off the beast.

“You can put your arm around my waist.” Her voice came out in a squeak.

He lightly rested his arm around her midsection. His thoughts bounced back to the other horse ride they’d shared together. He shoved the memory away.

They rode in companionable silence. Dusk settled and the first star twinkled in the night sky. The moon sent out enough light for Buster to pick his way across the uneven terrain.

As the silence dragged on, his conscience pricked. He’d already embarrassed himself in front of Elsie. He might as well come clean too. “I have a confession to make.”

She straightened.

He took it as a go-ahead to share his piece. “I already know how to hunt.” The lump in his throat nearly clogged his air pipe. “I should’ve told you sooner.”

Again, no response.

“I’m sorry.”

“You *did* miss the deer on purpose.” He had to lean forward to catch all her soft words.

“No, actually I didn’t.”

“Then what happened?”

CHAPTER TWELVE

Never be out with a member of the opposite gender
after dark unless a chaperone is present.
Mrs. Wigglesworth's Essential Guide to Proper Etiquette and Manners of Refined Society

The leather bit into Elsie's hands as she gripped the reins tighter. The weight of Benjamin's fingers scorched through the fabric of Pa's shirt. The scoundrel was trying to make a fool out of her. Heat soared to her cheeks. She should've known better.

She heaved a sigh, wishing they were home already. Dusk was falling, and they were some ways from home yet. She hadn't kept track of the miles they'd meandered in search for game.

"I … that is … you ..." His breath puffed against the back of her neck causing the tiny hairs to stand on end. "I'm not used to a woman whispering in my ear like you did …"

He was affected by her closeness? She wanted to shove the idea aside, but she couldn't deny the pleasure it brought. Confounded man. He had a way of getting under her skin.

Benjamin's clasp tightened when Buster stepped into another dip, pitching them both forward. Elsie whispered soothing words to the horse and patted his neck, wishing she could calm herself as easily as she did the stallion.

"I knew this hunting trip meant a lot to you. You were so intent on … well, you know." His voice faltered.

Not liking where the conversation headed, Elsie cleared her throat. "Why do you think there aren't as many folks milling around as there were the first few days after the race?"

"I heard tell that a lot of them headed back home after they staked their claims. With two years to do something with the land, I guess they figured they'd start fresh in the spring instead of trying to get a homestead built with winter coming."

"I reckon. Sure is strange not having any farms nearby, and that we're all starting out with nothing." She glanced at the countryside. "I've never been somewhere that everybody was beginning fresh."

"Me neither. Mark told me most folks don't plan to plant anything until the spring, hoping we'll have rain by then."

She peered at him over her shoulder. "Not sure if winter wheat will grow if we don't get some moisture. Hard to imagine the cold season coming soon with the insufferable heat we've been having. I don't remember it ever going this long without a break of sorts."

"I know what you mean. Back home, the drought took its toll on local farmers. Several years without a productive crop has made it hard on the area. And even though the panic from the closing of the Pennsylvania and Reading Railroad happened in the east, the whole country has been affected by it, what with a lot of the banks and businesses closing."

Her shoulders slumped. "It seems the whole country is a mess. Back in Kiowa, banks closed, and ones that didn't called in their notes on folks' property. Farmers were hit hard when grasshoppers swarmed through, and many of us lost crops. Then this awful drought. I'd hoped things would've been different here, but the soil isn't the best. Lots of rocks."

"I noticed you've been making a pile when you plowed the field. What do you plan to do with them?"

She glanced at the moon and terrain, adjusting their course. "Haven't figured it out yet. Maybe one day make a stone house."

"Never thought of that. If I ever expand, perhaps I'll consider doing that. Might help to keep things cooler in the summertime."

She snorted.

He didn't respond.

A comfortable silence settled over them.

"I suppose you think I'm a ninny being afraid of snakes."

"Never heard of a fella that was."

His arm loosened its hold on her when they reached a flat stretch of land. "I don't know why they scare me so. It didn't help that when I was six, I happened to tell a schoolmate about my fear. The next day when I opened my desk, a whole mess of snakes was wriggling and squirming." He shuddered behind her.

"They spilled out of the desk and onto the floor. One of them bit me on the ankle. It swelled and affected my breathing, so I was off school for a few days. We never could tell which type it was. The doc said I needed to be careful after that."

"That's terrible. Children can be cruel." Who was she to make fun of his fear when hers threatened whenever coyotes howled? "I shouldn't have laughed at you. I'm sorry."

His fingertips grazed her thigh as his arm wrapped around her waist again. "I forgive you. Few know of my fear. Sometimes it gets the better of me, and I lose consciousness. Not the best thing when I need to keep my wits about me to make sure the pesky critters stay far away."

"Didn't you come across them when you were riding the circuit?"

"It happened a time or two. Although I find that in most instances snakes like to be out in the hottest part of the day, so I made a point of avoiding those."

"They sometimes can be attracted to the warmth of a fire too, if the night is cool."

Benjamin shivered. He'd never thought of that. He praised the Lord it had never happened to him. In the future, he'd be more careful where he sat around a campfire.

Elsie shifted, her warmth stealing into his chest.

Benjamin stared at the horizon to distract himself.

Darkness had settled, wrapping them in a warm blanket. The moon shimmered off the rocks. In the distance, beyond a copse of trees, he saw the outline of two men on horseback. He considered waving but refrained. Something held him in check.

He kept an eye on the duo. They never came closer but traveled the same line he and Elsie were. A good while passed before the two broke off and disappeared behind the swell of a hill. Benjamin checked for quite some time, but they never appeared again. He released a breath. Hopefully, they were returning after dark like he and Elsie, and there was no reason to be alarmed.

"You're awful quiet."

Benjamin checked the horizon one more time. "Getting tired, I suppose. You and Buster must be as well." He studied the moon. "Near as I can tell, it's likely after midnight."

"Well past my bedtime. I mean, that is ..."

He chuckled. "No need to be embarrassed. It's late for both of us. I hope Milly found her way back to the claim."

"I imagine she did. Horses seem to have a knack for finding home." Elsie laughed. "Either that or they just know where the food is."

"Maybe it's a little of both."

They rode a bit further before he could make out the outline of his place. "Looks like we're almost there."

"Yep. Not soon enough. Poor Buster is laboring hard with carrying both of us." Elsie patted her horse.

A few minutes later, Buster halted beside her soddy and snorted. Benjamin swung down and stepped back. "If you don't need me for anything, I need to look for Milly. I'll bid you goodnight."

She swooped down beside him. "No, I don't need any help. It won't take me long to take care of him." She'd already started removing the bridle and bit.

"G'night." He walked a few paces away, then turned back. "Elsie."

"Yeah?"

"I had a nice time with you despite, well … you know."

She stared at him.

He turned and took a few steps away before her soft words traveled on the night air. "I did too, Benjamin."

He couldn't stop the grin from spreading.

Elsie's gaze followed Benjamin as he strolled to his place. A tune he whistled floated back to her. She smiled. Maybe having a male friend wasn't such a bad thing. He'd admitted that her closeness affected him. Did that mean he'd started to care for her? Did she want him to?

Buster nuzzled his face in the palm of her hand. "I'll get you some water in a few minutes, fella." She unbuckled the cinch and lifted the saddle from his back, carrying it inside. Elsie struck a match and lit the lamp. Snagging the bucket of water, she took it outside and held it for the stallion.

The task completed, she stripped to her long handles and settled onto the comfortable bed. Sleep took its time coming. Even though Aunt Kate had often fussed at her for doing man's work and told her no fella would ever be interested in her, it hadn't stopped her from hoping one day to find a man who would look past her crusty exterior. One who could love her for who she was.

Elsie exhaled and rolled to her side. Who was she fooling? A fella like Benjamin would never consider her. The sooner she got the silly notion out of her head, the better.

Benjamin continued to whistle as he located Milly and checked her over. *Strange.* Someone had already removed the horse's saddle and set it beside his house. He went inside and lit a lantern. Nothing was missing. More than likely, one of his neighbors had stopped by and had done a good deed.

Benjamin snagged a carrot from a bin and stepped outside again. The mare tossed her head as he combed her mane. "You had an eventful day, girl. Glad to see you didn't come to any harm when you bucked me off. I'll be the one feeling that tomorrow, not you."

He handed the horse her treat. Milly snorted and greedily accepted it. Next time he went to Enid he'd have to see if he could find some more.

Benjamin yawned as he patted the mare one last time, then stowed his equipment in the wagon. He stared up at the clear sky and the myriad of stars shimmering and twinkling. One shot across the sky, blazing a trail as it went. *The heavens definitely declare your glory, Lord.*

Back in the house, he sat on the side of the bed, kicked off his boots and set them aside. He yawned again as he stripped to his long handles and slipped beneath the sheet.

He propped his arms under his head and stared at the ceiling. Moonlight filtered through the windowpane and shone on the floor close to the bed. It was by far the best day he'd ever had with Elsie. Downright enjoyable. He chuckled.

The rugged land needed strong people to build it and make it into a habitable place. Mary had always been a slender thing. Would she have been able to make it in this harsh environment? He didn't have an answer, but thoughts of Elsie kept him tossing and turning for several hours.

CHAPTER THIRTEEN

Never allow a man to show affection without first being betrothed, and then sparingly until the wedding occurs.
Mrs. Wigglesworth's Essential Guide to Proper Etiquette and Manners of Refined Society

Benjamin chewed his last bite of flapjacks and shoved back from the table. He picked up the dirty dishes and tugged the door open.

Henry Larson leaned against his wagon with his arms crossed. "This can't keep going on, Preacher. It ain't seemly."

Mark and his wife stood off to the side looking uncomfortable.

"What's going on here?" Elsie walked over with a bucket dangling from her fingertips. Her brow puckered.

Mark stepped forward. "Glad to see no harm came to you, Preacher. Beatrice was scared when we dropped off your sod plow yesterday evening and found your horse saddled, but you and Elsie couldn't be found. Worked my wife up something awful. She insisted we stop at Henry's place on our way home to see if they'd heard from either of you."

"Gentlemen, I appreciate your concern. We merely arrived home late last evening."

Elsie's hand curled into a fist as she came to stand beside him. "Nothing happened other than we went out hunting yesterday, and Benjamin's horse got spooked by a snake and threw him. It took longer getting home with both of us riding Buster, but we got here last night and then went straight to our own places."

"Elsie, I mean Miss Smith, is correct. I remained a perfect gentleman." Benjamin studied Henry and Mark. "Mark, I assume it was you who took care of Milly for me. I appreciate it."

Mark nodded.

"I still say it ain't proper." Henry frowned.

Benjamin snuck a peek at Elsie.

Her back was as stiff as if she'd starched it. "There's no reason for you three to be concerned. I tell you, there's nothing unseemly happening." Her words came out clipped. "The quicker you get it through your thick skull, Henry Larson, that I have no need of a man, the better."

Her words stung. Benjamin didn't plan to marry her, but they still hurt.

Beatrice stepped forward and wrapped Elsie in a hug. "Well, I'm glad you're both home safe. I'd hate for anything to happen to either of you."

Mark slapped Benjamin on the back. "Good to see you, Preacher. Thanks again for letting me borrow your plow. Guess I'd better get back to planting seed. Come along, pretty missus."

Beatrice giggled.

"Bye, Elsie." She wrapped her friend in another quick embrace before the Sawyers left.

Henry grunted. "I hope we can count on you to be above reproach, Preacher, or me and the missus might need to find a church elsewhere." He swung up onto the high seat and released the brake. "We'll see how you do at service tomorrow."

Benjamin's shoulders relaxed.

Elsie turned on her heel and headed to the creek without a word.

He shoved his fingers through his hair. *Lord, I don't know how that woman keeps putting me into situations that make others question my integrity and faith. I want to be a man above reproach in all areas of my life. Help me to figure out what to do with Elsie.*

Benjamin crossed over to where Milly grazed. He gave her a pat and led her toward the creek.

Elsie stood, water sloshing in her bucket. Her chin jutted. "Why are folks so quick to think the worst?"

He exhaled. "I'm not sure. I think Henry is more bluster than bite. I wouldn't let him get to you."

She stared at him for a long moment. "I best get some breakfast going."

He watched as she crossed the property and put the bucket of water where Buster could reach it. Without a backward glance, she went into her soddy.

Benjamin sighed and scanned the area for something physical to keep his body, and hopefully mind, occupied. The sod splitter rested under the shade of a tree. It was high time he got further invested in his claim. Learning to plow couldn't be that difficult.

It took him a while to figure out how to adjust the harness and hook Milly to it, but he eventually managed to get everything in place. He smiled as he glanced across the field. Benjamin debated whether he should continue where Elsie had left off or start another section. He opted to start a new row beside Elsie's handiwork. Plowing couldn't be too difficult. She made it appear effortless.

"Giddyup." Milly plodded along as Benjamin struggled to keep a firm grip on the plow. The wood handles bit into his hands. It took steady pressure to cut through the dense buffalo grass. It was tougher than he'd imagined.

A lifetime later, Benjamin had succeeded in plowing one length. He swung around to see his workmanship. His path zigged and zagged, leaving portions of grass poking through in large patches. He'd have to fix it so Elsie could see how valuable he was to have around.

He struggled to get the plow turned and going back down the path again. He prayed he'd get the hang of it before nightfall. Benjamin snorted as the futility of the prayer washed over him. It wasn't like the Lord could make him an experienced farmer in a day.

Elsie refrained from tearing out of the house when she heard the *ting* of a rock hitting the sod splitter. It went against everything in her to not take over the job, or at least go outside and help. Instead, she lit a lamp and placed it on her tiny table.

With all the furniture Benjamin had bought for the soddy—the beautiful brass bed, pot-belly stove, table, two chairs, and a lamp—she barely had room to move around. Still, she was able to pace the small confines.

"I bet his plowing will help him see how lacking he is as a farmer." Maybe then he'd leave. Until then, she needed something to do that would keep her occupied somewhere other than near Benjamin. Spotting the door propped against the sod wall, she hefted it outside along with her tools. She should've had it hung long before, but she'd gotten distracted.

It took some doing to get the door in place, but she did it. She set her hands on her hips and studied her work, satisfied that it hung straight.

When Elsie stepped away from the entrance, she couldn't help noticing Benjamin struggling to keep the plow steady and straight. Large sections of land were unfurrowed like someone who'd done a poor job of shearing a sheep, leaving large patches of wool in one spot and shorn to the skin in others. The crazy man hadn't used enough pressure to make the point cut evenly. It would take her half a day to fix it. She blew out a breath. At least it'd keep him busy and out of the way for a while.

Knowing Benjamin wouldn't need her, she welcomed the opportunity to bathe without having to keep an eye out for him. The coolness of the creek beckoned.

Elsie kicked off her boots and grabbed a towel, fresh clothes, and a bar of soap. Behind the trunk of a tree, she stripped down to her long handles and stepped into the water's depths. The brisk stream flowed across her body, and she sucked in a breath. Underneath the water, she removed the last bit of clothes, using the soap to give them a thorough washing.

With one fling, the garment flew over a tree branch. Unbraiding her hair, Elsie ducked her head under the water before she started scrubbing the long strands. She'd wanted to cut them, but Pa had insisted she keep it long.

Memories of her childhood washed over her like the water soaking her head. Her sisters hated the way Elsie got Pa to do what she wanted, except when it came to her hair, he'd stood his ground. They'd said he spoiled her on account of her favoring their ma. She'd never been exceptionally close to them since they'd married and moved away while she was a young girl. Only Aunt Kate had stayed until Pa shipped her off.

Elsie opened her eyes. The sun shone directly overhead. Dismay gripped her when she could no longer hear the splitter breaking through the soil. She shoved the soap up and down her arms and legs quickly, making sure to keep the water up to her neck. The bar slipped from her grasp and sunk. With a growl, she dove to the bottom of the creek and searched frantically for it, coming up empty-handed. After five failed attempts, she stopped. It served her right for woolgathering. Aunt Kate would've tanned her hide at the wanton waste of a perfectly good bar of soap.

She finished wringing her hair and glanced around. No Benjamin. She stepped out of the water and dried off, ripped the dry long underwear off the branch, and yanked it on. If she hadn't lost her soap, she could've washed her clothes too. Shoving her clean shirt into the top of her pants, Elsie gathered her belongings. The ends of her hair dripped as she wrung them out again and thrust it over her shoulder. She'd have to comb it once she reached home.

Something rustled on the creek bank.

"Elsie?"

She glanced in that direction. Benjamin stood ten yards away with his back to her.

"Rest your mind. I haven't seen a thing."

Her chest heaved like a locomotive. "What do you want?" The words came out harsher than she'd intended.

"Never mind. I'll figure it out myself." His shoulders slumped.

Her conscience stung. "I'm sorry. I didn't mean to bark at you. How can I help?"

"Are you dressed?"

She smiled. "Yes, you can turn around."

He turned but didn't quite meet her gaze.

"Could you assist me?" He held out his hands. Blood rivulets ran between his fingers and dripped onto the ground.

She dropped everything and ran to his side. "Oh, Benjamin, what did you do?" She grasped his wrists. Deep blisters and open sores coated each palm.

He sank to his knees. "I don't know how you make plowing look so easy."

She chuckled and helped him to his feet. "I've had years of practice. Now let's see to these hands."

"If it wouldn't be a trouble."

Elsie had the feeling he hated asking for help as much as she did. She smiled. Maybe she wasn't the only stubborn one.

Benjamin glanced at his hands as they trekked to his place. He wished he hadn't. He stumbled as his stomach rolled.

Elsie slipped an arm around his waist. "You aren't going to get woozy like you did with the snake, are you?"

He tried to reply, but a whiff of her floral scent tickled his nostrils. *Dear Lord, what have I gotten myself into?*

Elsie clucked. "Never saw a grown man as much of a wildflower as you. When're you going to realize you ain't cut out for this life?"

"I most certainly was *not* swooning. I was merely lost in thought." The confounded woman.

"Do you think you can stand without getting lightheaded again?"

"I wasn't lightheaded in the first place."

"Uh huh. Let's get you inside. You're as pale as fresh milk."

Benjamin concentrated on putting one weary foot in front of the other, trying not to think about his bloody, painful hands, or the beautiful woman with her arm snaked around him. He swallowed. Since when had he thought Elsie beautiful?

Once inside, Elsie eased him to a chair. "Where's your wash basin and soap?"

He nodded toward the dry sink. Tiredness tugged at his frame, weighing him down.

"I could have used my own soap but ..."

Redness flared on her smooth cheeks.

"But?"

Her face grew a shade deeper, and he couldn't help but smile.

"I ... lost it in the creek." She shifted away.

Benjamin bit back a laugh. "I have an extra soap if you need it."

Elsie kept her back to him. "No thanks. I have one left from my *anonymous* donor." She spun around. Her brow lifted.

He coughed and glanced away.

"I'm afraid this is going to sting a bit." She knelt before him and placed the bowl in his lap. With a gentleness he hadn't imagined her capable of, she took one hand at a time and rinsed it thoroughly with water, gently scrubbing each wound.

He tried not to wince. Not desiring to see his torn flesh, he examined her bent head. His stomach flipped when her long, blonde hair whispered against his fingertips. He'd never witnessed such a glorious sight. No wonder God talked about long hair being a woman's crown. His heart vaulted, and his thoughts bounced to what she'd feel like in his arms.

Benjamin forced his breathing to slow.

"What's wrong? Am I hurting you?" She looked up at him, her gaze narrowed.

He swallowed again. "No, you aren't hurting me. You about finished?" He cringed when he heard the hard edge to his voice.

Hurt flickered across her face, and he hated being the cause of it.

"D-do you have any salve?" She scanned the room.

His conscience pricked. He opened his mouth to apologize—

"I have some at the soddy. I'll be right back." She scooped the bowl from his lap and disappeared before he had the chance to reply.

Elsie flung the water to the ground and set the bowl down before scurrying to her house. On the way, she snatched up her discarded clothes. Her heart thudded like she'd run across a long pasture. Being near Benjamin made her experience strange thoughts and emotions, and she couldn't figure out what to do about it.

Inside her home, she dropped the clothes into a corner and rummaged through a crate of supplies until she found what she needed. She debated taking time to do something with her hair but decided to wait. Best to take care of him so she could return to the safety of her home where she wouldn't need to see the perplexing man any longer.

Back at Benjamin's house, she rapped before entering—it didn't feel right to walk into the man's home without some kind of warning first. She knelt before him and opened the tin.

"Elsie?"

She ignored him as she coated his palms with the salve. Her hands trembled while she wrapped the strips of cloth around each hand, leaving his fingertips free. She hoped he hadn't noticed. It took a lifetime before she'd completed the task.

"Elsie. Please look at me." His words came out soft like a kitten's purr. She snuck a peek at him.

Benjamin lifted her chin with a fingertip and winced before hiding it with a smile.

She gulped while he studied her face.

"I'm sorry for being sharp with you. You're only trying to help. I didn't mean to snap at you. Can you forgive me?"

She nodded, and her heart pounded as his head lowered.

CHAPTER FOURTEEN

Never dally with two gentleman's affections by showing interest in both at once. It will only lead to trouble.
Mrs. Wigglesworth's Essential Guide to Proper Etiquette and Manners of Refined Society

Elsie closed her eyes as Benjamin's warm lips pressed against hers. She leaned closer, her heart soaring like a bird. She looped her arms around his neck and returned his kiss with fervor.

He threaded the tips of his fingers through her hair, drawing her closer. Benjamin murmured, "Oh no … Mary."

Her eyes popped open, and she stepped back.

He cleared his throat and wouldn't return eye contact. "I'm sorry. I shouldn't have done that. It was out of line. It's just that Mary, I mean … she was the one, but I'm not—"

She slapped his contrite face, enjoying the resounding whack, then she ran. Her first kiss and all he could do was think about his beloved Mary? The low-down coward.

"Elsie, wait!"

She whistled for Buster as she jogged toward her house. Elsie swooped onto her steed's back, holding tight to his mane, and kicked his sides. Once she got out of sight of her property, she allowed the tears to flow.

How humiliating. She should've never let him kiss her. Not being as good as his Mary shouldn't have bothered her, but it did. Elsie couldn't compete with the memory of a deceased fiancée—one Benjamin wished was still with him.

Buster galloped until his body glistened. She clung to him, her one faithful friend. She didn't notice how long they wandered before turning the horse toward home. He plodded his way across the buffalo grass.

Back home again, she slid from Buster's back and whispered to him as she curried his coat, then freed him to graze near the soddy. She trudged into her home and didn't bother to light a lamp. Instead, she plopped on the bed and hugged her pillow tight.

"Oh, Pa, what a fool I am." What woman wanted to be kissed and then mistaken for someone else?

Wait. Since when did she want to be kissed? She slammed her fist into the pillow, vowing to forget the whole kissing nonsense. If only her unruly heart would follow through with her brain.

Benjamin followed Elsie to the doorstep, but no further. He doubted she'd listen to him anyway. He slumped against the doorframe.

He should've never kissed her, but he couldn't deny enjoying it. His heart pinched. Benjamin hadn't meant to blurt out his guilt about Mary. He sighed and glanced at the sky. *What do I do, Lord? I've made a mess of things with Elsie. I'm starting to care about her. Show me how to make things better.*

He stepped inside and closed the door, pacing back and forth. Perhaps he'd do better to encourage John to pursue Elsie instead, but that idea didn't sit well either. Since he couldn't work, maybe a short nap would bring clarity.

Hours later, he awoke disoriented. Moonlight filtered into the room. As his eyes flickered open, he remembered Henry mentioning the service—tomorrow. Benjamin sat up in bed.

Crossing the room, he lit the lantern. He sank into the chair and flipped open his Bible. *Show me what You want me to say, Lord. Forgive me for forgetting that tomorrow is Your day. Guide me in finding something to speak to the heart of my little congregation.*

The hours passed, and his eyes grew blurry as he read portions of scripture, flipping to the book of Hebrews. No ideas came. He supposed they could sing together, but he hated to disappoint his neighbors by not being prepared.

"There has to be something You want me to share, Lord. *Please* show me." After reading the first eleven chapters again, he had yet to come up with a topic.

As he read the next chapter, Benjamin stilled. "'Looking diligently lest any man fail of the grace of God; lest any root of bitterness springing up trouble you, and thereby many be defiled.'" Had a root of bitterness sprung up in Elsie because of his thoughtless actions? The verse continued to reverberate within him. How could he teach her about letting go of the bitterness from her past when he'd likely stirred the very thing in her?

He didn't have an answer, and by now the sun was peeking above the horizon. His neighbors would arrive before too long. His conscience pricked. There was no denying it. He needed to make things right. With Elsie, and with his neighbors.

Benjamin rubbed his fingertips across his bewhiskered cheeks. He'd forgo shaving this time. Food didn't tempt him. Maybe he'd have an appetite after he cleared things up.

He changed into fresh clothes, fumbling to tighten the loops of his tie. Ripping it off, he tossed it onto the bed. He'd have to settle for his good shirt and trousers.

The squeak of wagon wheels interrupted his morning preparations. He gingerly gathered his Bible and opened the door.

Mark swung his wife to the ground, giving her a peck on the cheek before releasing her. Benjamin took a step back, feeling like he'd somehow intruded on the couple's privacy, but he couldn't drag his gaze away from their tender embrace. Beatrice giggled as she touched her husband's cheek.

Benjamin cleared his throat, and the couple turned toward him.

"Preacher. What happened to you?" She hurried forward and lightly gripped his wrist.

"Had a little difficulty with plowing yesterday. I should've put on a pair of work gloves. I'm afraid my hands suffered a bit from the process."

"Oh, my. Did Elsie help doctor your hands?" A twinkle flashed in her eyes.

"Yes. She took pity on me."

"How sweet." She smiled. "Elsie has a good heart beneath her rough exterior." Her eyebrows rose. "Had you noticed?"

"Now, Beatrice. It isn't any of your business." Mark wrapped an arm around his wife's waist.

"Nothing wrong with asking questions." Beatrice rested a hand on her husband's chest. "Can't you see, they need each other?"

The air squeezed from Benjamin's lungs. What he needed was to get away from Beatrice's desire to pair him with Elsie.

"Don't let her bother you." Mark clapped him on the back. "She means well. From what she's told me, she played matchmaker for her brothers too."

"Each one of them is happily married." Beatrice grinned. "I may be young, but I know a thing or two about what qualities make a good marriage."

John rode up, and Benjamin breathed a quiet sigh of relief. "If you'll excuse me."

Beatrice's hand on his arm halted him. "I'll leave you be for now, but mark my words, God intends for the two of you to be together."

He didn't answer as he broke free of her hold.

Elsie paced in her tiny home, smacking into the kitchen table for the fifth time. Refusing to contemplate her decision any longer, she slipped the garment over her head, pinned her hair into place, and flung the door open.

The warm air smacked her in the face and bore down like a heavy weight on her chest, despite being early morning. She hiked her skirt a smidgen and tromped across the buffalo grass. Her sisters had glided when they entered a room, but she'd never learned the art.

The words to "Shall We Gather at the River" rolled in waves over her weary body, and peace spread throughout her limbs. How well she remembered singing those very words with Pa standing beside her in their little country church. With a sniff, she held her head high. When she reached the small group, she added her soft soprano to the chorus.

When Benjamin glimpsed her way, his mouth gaped open like a fish caught on a hook.

John Clark moseyed up beside her. His eyebrows waggled. Clearly, he approved of her wearing a dress. Honestly, Elsie couldn't recall why she'd even packed the thing when she'd left home. She'd only worn it to church with Pa, so the garment had plenty of wear yet.

"You look beautiful, Miss Smith." John's soft whisper tickled her neck.

It wouldn't take much encouragement to gain John's attention, but Elsie wasn't sure she wanted to. She thrust the thought aside and sang the next verse with gusto.

After they finished singing, John spread a blanket and offered his arm as she gathered the folds of skirt beneath her to sit. Elsie had forgotten how cumbersome a dress could be. John settled beside her, sitting a little closer than she liked. She glanced up to see Benjamin watching them.

He cleared his throat. "I'm afraid you'll have to bear with me this morning." His eyes sought out Elsie's before flitting to the rest who had gathered.

John moved, and his hip grazed against hers. Elsie gulped. She hadn't intended to encourage the man by sitting with him.

If only Benjamin hadn't responded the way he had yesterday. Living without being kissed would've suited her just fine. *Really.*

She dragged her attention back to the service. Benjamin stood with his head bowed. "Open our hearts to hear this message, Lord. And forgive us when we've been the cause of bitterness. Help us to learn from Your Word. In Jesus' name, amen." Benjamin sought out her face again. "I'm afraid I have a confession to make."

Her mouth went dry. Certainly, he didn't intend to tell everyone about their kiss, did he? Her unruly heart fluttered at the remembrance. If she were still a praying woman, she'd ask the Lord to keep Benjamin's mouth shut.

The quiet stretched, and Elsie leaned forward, waiting to hear what he'd say. The trickling of the stream and an occasional snort from a horse broke the moments of silence.

"I read a verse last night, and I haven't been able to get it off my mind since." Benjamin flipped open his Bible. "It's from the book of Hebrews, and it talks about how we should live so that no bitterness springs up between us."

He stared at his Bible and didn't say anything further for a few moments.

"God showed me how I caused a root of bitterness to surface in an individual because of my careless actions. My friend had only helped me, and I did something thoughtless. Something I now regret." He stared straight at Elsie.

She wanted to run and hide. How much more obvious could the man be? Wasn't it bad enough that he regretted their kiss? Must he bring it up for all the neighbors to hear? The muscles in Elsie's neck stiffened. *Let him keep his mouth shut.*

"I realized I need to make restitution. I in no way meant to hurt this individual." Benjamin broke his steady stare.

"What did you do, Preacher?" Henry Larson folded his arms across his broad chest.

Elsie bent her head and wished she'd stayed in her soddy. She snuck a glance at Benjamin. A muscle flickered in his jaw. She refused to feel sorry for the man. Let him sweat. She'd done nothing wrong, but she didn't take kindly to his yanking out dirty bloomers for all to see.

"Confession is good for the soul." Mildred Larson nodded.

"I know they say confession is good for the soul, but I came here for preaching, not to hear you confessing, Preacher." John stood. "When're you going to get to the sermon, or should I go on home?"

"We're told to confess our sins one to another, which is why I felt God leading me to a public announcement. It's never my intent to be a stumbling block, and I'm sorry if I've done so. To any of you. Forgive me, folks, this isn't coming out the way I intended." Benjamin glanced at Elsie.

Oh, to shrivel into a tiny hole and die. She should've never come today. Elsie refused to stay another moment. She hiked up her skirts, sprinted toward her house, slamming the door behind her. Her heart stampeded as she stood against the closed door. Someone knocked. Once. Twice. Maybe Benjamin had come to apologize. Again.

"Miss Smith?" Not Benjamin. She opened the door a crack. John Clark stood with his hat in hand. "Would you do me the pleasure of going for a ride? I seem to have lost my interest in the service."

Elsie grabbed her Stetson and accepted John's arm.

Benjamin watched John and Elsie ride away, followed by the Larsons. Only Mark and Beatrice remained.

A weight settled on Benjamin's shoulders and chest.

"I reckon you had good intentions, Preacher." Mark shrugged. "Beatrice brought plenty of lunch. It's a little early for it, but we could share it together if you're hungry."

Benjamin's stomach growled.

Mark chuckled. "I'll take that as a yes."

He joined them on their blanket and set his Bible to the side, but not before he peered after Elsie. Benjamin should be happy John rode with her, but it didn't bring comfort.

"I think I'd better pray for us this time." Mark bowed his head. "Lord, we ask You to bless this food. Things don't always turn out the way we intend, and I'm guessing my brother is having some second thoughts. Comfort him as only You can. Amen."

Benjamin nodded his thanks, fearing his voice would crack if he spoke just yet. It'd been a long time since someone had prayed for him.

"I hope you like fried chicken." Beatrice opened the basket and withdrew the food. A myriad of delicious scents wafted as she placed items on a plate and handed it to him.

"Thank you."

He took a huge bite and chewed. "This is delicious, Mrs. Sawyer."

"Call me Beatrice." She smiled. "Did you want to talk about what just happened?"

Mark frowned at his wife. "You'll have to forgive her, Preacher. She has a good heart and hates to see people hurting."

"She doesn't really care for him you know." Beatrice studied Benjamin. "It's you that she sneaks a peek at when she thinks nobody's watching her."

He'd never noticed Elsie watching him. He tried to picture the way Mary had looked at him, but all he could think about was the pressure of Elsie's lips on his. He rubbed the back of his hand across his forehead.

Beatrice chuckled. "I think she only went with him because he was an escape for her."

Mark slapped him on the back. "Beatrice takes some getting used to, Preacher. Her ma wrote me a letter before Beatrice and I tied the knot. Said God must've given her daughter a gift of discernment. It's downright scary sometimes. She's especially able to tell when someone is hurting."

Benjamin stared at the young mother-to-be.

Beatrice shrugged. "I can't help it. It's just the way God made me. Getting back to what I was saying, I think Elsie's past has made her exceptionally gun shy of facing her troubles. Something tells me she wants to fight to get your attention, but she doesn't know how to."

Benjamin shook his head. "I don't know. Maybe it doesn't matter anymore. I botched things up with Elsie, and I tried to let her know I was sorry. Said something to her last night and attempted to make things right with her here, but you saw how that turned out."

"What exactly happened between you two?" Her gaze narrowed.

Benjamin's cheeks burned.

"You kissed her, didn't you?"

How could she have possibly known? Did he have it stamped on his forehead for all to see?

He hesitated but nodded.

"So, what's the problem? Didn't she like it?"

"Beatrice!" Mark glared at her.

"What? Surely he knows whether or not Elsie enjoyed his kiss."

Mark sighed.

Benjamin coughed. "I think so. At least she responded." His ears were on fire.

"Wonderful."

"Except ..." He couldn't meet her gaze. "I wasn't thinking. I blurted out ..."

"You didn't talk about Mary, did you?" Beatrice gasped.

"Not exactly, but she may think I compared her to Mary when it comes to ..." The conversation was getting much too personal for Benjamin's liking.

Beatrice huffed. "No wonder."

CHAPTER FIFTEEN

When traveling, make sure you have a companion with you of the same gender. A proper young lady should be chaperoned at all times. There are no exceptions to this rule.

Mrs. Wigglesworth's Essential Guide to Proper Etiquette and Manners of Refined Society

An uncomfortable silence fell between Elsie and John. She shielded her eyes and stared out at the dips and swells of the countryside. Buffalo grass swayed in the warm breeze.

"My spread is over here." John pointed. "I've been wanting to show it to you. Someday I plan to buy more land."

Elsie glanced in that direction. "You built a soddy too."

He nodded. "Mine is a little bigger than yours. I soon hope to have a wife and children, providing I can persuade a beautiful woman to wed."

Elsie's breathing hitched. Perhaps she could help him. "You sending for a mail-order bride?"

"Nope, I have my sights set on someone around here."

She gulped. Talk about leaping from a frying pan into the fire. "Oh? I hear tell from Beatrice that the mail-order bride route can be downright advantageous. Unless you met someone in Enid or Woodward."

"Nope." He waggled his eyebrows. "I'm waiting for you to take notice of me, and I don't give up easily."

Her pulse thudded in her neck.

"I see I surprised you. My ma always said I move too fast. I'm willing to wait for you." He reached across the short distance and squeezed her hand.

She shifted away from his reach.

"I can't imagine what the preacher did to you that he felt the need to make a public apology." John's gaze bore into hers.

Elsie lifted her chin. She had nothing to be sorry for. "Me neither."

"I realize you might have feelings for the preacher, but I'd guess he don't exactly return your affections. At least not from what I saw."

She stared off at the horizon, not needing *that* reminder.

"I'm bumbling this all up, Elsie. Forgive me." John shifted his horse closer and squeezed her shoulder. "I've had my eye on you since I first caught a glimpse of your sweet face. You're a fine woman—a real asset to any man. Some would say it's too soon, but winter will soon be here, and I'd love for us to be married by then. Take time to consider it."

Elsie gasped. Her knuckles turned white as she gripped Buster's reins and edged the horse a safe distance away from John. It wasn't like she didn't long for marriage. She did but figured it would never happen to her. Elsie desired to be loved and accepted for who she was, not as a replacement or a workmate. She felt like slugging something, or someone.

"I made lunch for us and had hoped you'd join me so we can get better acquainted. What do you say?"

Elsie didn't meet his gaze. "Thank you for the offer, but I'm afraid I'm not interested."

He hedged closer again. "I understand. You need time to think more on it. I can be a patient man when I recognize what I'm after."

"I need to be going." She shifted Buster further away.

"We haven't eaten yet."

"You can eat if you want, but I ain't hungry. Goodbye." She kicked Buster to a canter.

Once they were away, she allowed the horse to set the pace. At one point, she swiveled in the saddle to make sure John hadn't followed.

She rode toward the Glass Mountains until the sun blazed high in the sky. Buster slowed to a walk and started grazing at the foot of the jagged ridges. The range jutted out of the landscape like the sharp points had been poked through by someone. Too bad Pa's map didn't say more about it.

Elsie dropped to the ground and scratched between Buster's ears. "Rest, fella. I'm going to do a little exploring." She searched around the nearby crags to make sure the men from last time hadn't returned. Satisfied, she hitched her dress to her knees and climbed over the ragged boulders. Sun glittered off the loose stones. She stooped and picked one up. "Guess this is how the mountain got its name. The rocks sure do shimmer like a mirror in sunlight."

Buster snorted.

She laughed, and her shoulders relaxed. Her problems usually melted away when she got away from folks and enjoyed the countryside.

Elsie hiked until she reached the top, turning in all directions. A few sod houses and wooden ones poked up from the land at different spots, and cedar trees spread throughout the area. It took her a moment to spot her own home.

She sighed. What was she going to do with Benjamin? His kiss had stirred her. Of course, with it being her first kiss, perhaps her emotions were simply aroused, and it had nothing to do with Benjamin. If only she could convince herself of that.

Elsie sucked in a deep breath and stared out across the plains. This place sure would've made a great hiding place as a child. She'd have loved rambling over it. The land had a beauty all its own.

The land. Some of Pa's last words washed over her. "*Give your all to the land, and to God, and you'll be rewarded.*"

"How do I do it, Pa? I've been giving my all to the land, and all I'm experiencing is problems. What kind of advice would you give if you were here? What would you say about Benjamin?"

Am I struggling because I haven't given You my all, Lord? She couldn't remember the last time she'd prayed. Probably around the time Pa got sick. God hadn't answered the one prayer she cared the most about—healing Pa.

A rumble sounded. Dark clouds were forming in the west. She'd lingered long enough. Elsie stumbled as she descended the mountain, tripping over a rock. Something ripped, and she looked at her shredded hem. It didn't matter. She had no further use for the garment. If the unwanted reaction she received today was any indication, she'd no desire to wear it again.

Once she reached Buster, she wandered across the plains, picking her way around the base of Glass Mountain. She could go home and start plowing where Benjamin had left off, but Pa had instilled in her the importance of taking a day of rest. She'd disobeyed that when Benjamin held his first service, and look where that got her—passed out on the ground. At some point, she'd have to face him, but she had no desire to do so yet. Not until she could make some sense out of her jumbled emotions. Part of her longed to see him again, and that scared her.

Thunder boomed behind her. Buster startled at the noise. She put her hand on his neck to steady him. "Easy, boy. I know it's been a long while since you've heard it."

Rain would do them good, providing it wasn't a gully-washer. She kept her eye on the sky and clicked at Buster. He kicked up his heels and ran. Elsie laughed. It'd been a good long while since she let him gallop. It felt good to let him run free. She spread her arms wide, lifted her head, squeezing tight with her knees as Buster skirted around the base of the mountain. What would it be like to be free of the hurts from her past?

No matter how much she tried to avoid it, her brain kept bouncing back to the Bible verse Benjamin had shared and Pa's admonition to give her all to the land and to God. How could she let go and trust God again?

A crash of thunder interrupted Benjamin's conversation with the Sawyers. All their gazes swung to the sky. "What do you know? Looks like the Good Lord will be answering our prayers." He smiled up at the heavens.

"I think we best get on home." Mark stood, picked up the basket, and crossed to the wagon.

Beatrice stood and folded the blanket. "I'd hoped Elsie would make it back by now. You don't suppose something's happened to her, do you?" She twisted the fabric in her hands.

Benjamin stared again at the darkening clouds.

"I'm sure she'll be back here before long." Mark patted his wife's arm. "Come along, sweetheart. I don't want you getting caught in the rain." He shook Benjamin's hand. "We'll be praying for the two of you." He swung his wife onto the wagon seat before joining her, and they waved as they pulled away.

Benjamin watched until they were no longer visible, then turned and crossed over to his wagon. A few short trips, and he'd taken saddle, bridle, and various tack inside. He untied the oilskin cover and carted it in as well.

Back outside, he stopped and stared at the sky again. Green clouds stacked upon each other like a pile of angry pillows. The hair on his arms stood on end. Milly snorted and pranced from where he'd ground-tied her. Her eyes and nostrils flared as the wind began to pick up and blow.

Elsie still hadn't returned.

The wind tugged at his Stetson. He shoved it tight on his scalp. "Please protect Elsie, Lord. Don't let her end up like Mary."

Benjamin headed back into his house and scribbled a message to Elsie. She'd likely avoid him until she simmered down. Maybe his words of apology would help soften her heart until they could talk face-to-face.

He left the house and crossed the property, holding onto his hat as the wind whipped and kicked up dirt and debris. The door to Elsie's soddy swung back and forth on its hinges. He knocked on the frame, then poked his head inside. Benjamin propped the note on the table near the lantern where she'd be sure to see it, then secured the door behind him.

The wind increased, and the green sky darkened. Alarm shot through his body. His gaze swung toward Milly, or where he'd last seen his horse. She was nowhere to be found. He should've tied her to one of the trees by the creek instead of trusting that she'd stay put. More than likely she'd return after the storm passed. At least, he prayed so.

A gust swept the hat from his head, sending it tumbling across the dry grass. He scurried and caught it before the wind carried it away. Trotting toward his house, he made sure the door was tightly secured, then continued to watch the storm's approach.

Where's Elsie, Lord? Don't let any harm come to her. I don't know if she can take another experience where she feels You aren't there for her, but You know best. If anything is going to happen, will You let it be to me, Lord?

The sting of hail bit into his skin, pelting him from every direction.

His hands turned clammy as an eerie stillness settled over the area. In the distance, a deep gray-green funnel formed, touching the ground and rising as it moved his way. Dirt blew into his eyes. He swiped his sleeve across them, taking a moment for his vision to clear. Roaring like an approaching train rushed in. Frantic, he rushed to the lowest part of land.

CHAPTER SIXTEEN

Never be the first one to show any type of affection, except with children or a parent. Allow the male species to lead.

Mrs. Wigglesworth's Essential Guide to Proper Etiquette and Manners of Refined Society

Buster snorted and pranced, tossing his head and chomping hard against the bit. It took all of Elsie's strength and experience to keep the spirited stallion under control. He danced sideways. The reins bit into her hand as she worked to calm him. Thunder clapped overhead, and Buster rose on his back legs. Elsie sailed through the air, then hit the red dirt, jarring her bones. She shook her head until the stars cleared, then jumped up.

"Whoa!" She ran after him, but Buster was a long way off. "Great." She grumbled and kicked at a clod of grass. Ice pellets stung as they pinged against her body.

Elsie cringed with each sting to her skin. She needed a place to hunker down, and quick. Her dress tangled around her legs as she ran toward the mountain. Rain fell in sheets, soaking her as she stumbled over loose rocks in search of a hiding place. As she steadied herself, sharp stones cut into her hands and knees. There, up ahead. A place big enough for her to scrunch into to ride out the storm.

Her heart faltered as she stared at the gray-green sky, clouds billowing one on top of the other. Elsie's eyes widened, and her pulse raced. She'd seen it that wild only a few times in her life, and it always meant trouble.

The wind whipped wet hair into her face. Wadding it together, she lifted her hat and shoved it under her Stetson.

She kept an eye on the sky as she crouched tight into her hideaway. Not far off, a funnel formed and snaked its way to the ground, dipping and swooping in a strange dance. She wrapped her arms tight around her legs. Her heart hammered against her ribcage, and a tumbleweed clogged her throat.

Benjamin.

How would he fare if the twister hit their property? Surely he knew to hunker down in a safe place in a storm like this.

The funnel cloud lifted, then plunged to the earth again. As the wind blew in all directions, Pa's final admonition swept across her.

"I've been praying for God to bring a good man into your life when the time is right. Be open, and watch for him, and Elm, don't blame God for troubles. The Lord brings both good and bad into our lives, but He's always trustworthy. Always."

Elsie shook away the memory. Would she live long enough to settle down with a good man? Her gut flopped. Benjamin was the first man who had shown any true interest in her. John didn't count since she didn't care about him.

Her heart pinched as she kept an eye on the funnel cloud. She never had physically promised Pa to not blame God, but her conscience pricked knowing she hadn't honored Pa by following all he'd asked either. In fact, she hadn't honored much of what Pa had requested.

She squeezed her eyes tight, not wanting to see the tornado when it hit. She lost track of time as rain and hail pelted her, taking her breath away. Small rocks pinged against her body. Then, suddenly, the wind died. A frightening quiet invited her to open her eyes. All looked peaceful as if the twister hadn't been mere yards away moments ago.

Elsie craned her neck in all directions. There was no sign of the tornado anywhere. She hesitated, checking the sky, but nothing further developed. The rain and hail diminished, then stopped. The sky lightened.

Benjamin.

Her heart caught in her throat. The twister had come from the direction of their claim. She took off at a sprint.

Benjamin lunged for the nook of the hill by the creek bed. He shifted his hat to protect his face from the stinging hail and tried to make his body as flat as possible. His heart palpitated in anticipation of the funnel cloud hitting him. He braced himself, but it never came.

As the roaring subsided, the pings of hail lessened. He waited a few minutes before moving his Stetson so he could see the damage, settling the hat on his head as he stood and surveyed the area. Nothing out of place on this side of the hill. He crawled to the top and surveyed his claim.

Not a single thing was out of sorts.

Thank You, Lord.

Elsie. Where could she be?

He turned in every direction but didn't spot her. Wait. A horse coming at a breakneck pace.

Buster.

But where was Elsie?

Benjamin's heart plummeted.

As the horse drew closer, he spread his arms wide. "Whoa, boy."

The animal ground to a halt, his chest heaving and body lathered. Benjamin rubbed a hand across Buster's forelock. "Take it easy, fella."

He examined the horse's body and legs, talking as he checked the stallion for cuts. Once the horse had calmed and cooled down a bit, he led him to the creek for a long drink.

"Where's your owner, Buster?" Benjamin's throat tightened.

The horse lifted his head, and his ears perked before he went back to slurping water again.

He pictured Elsie injured, lying somewhere. Needing him. *Dear God, help me to find her.* He tugged on Buster's reins and patted the horse. "Sorry, fella, but I need you. Too bad you aren't a dog that can lead the way to where you last saw your master." He swung onto the saddle. "Giddyup." He nudged his heels into the horse's sides.

Buster started out at a slow trot, tossing his head, tugging at the bit.

"Come on, fella, you can do it. I know you're tired, but we've got to find her."

Elsie *had* to find Benjamin. An urgency filled her, unlike anything she'd ever experienced. She ran as long as she could before slowing to a jog. A weight pressed on her chest.

She followed the path where the tornado had touched down. In one spot, she found a cedar tree shorn off about halfway down the trunk. A short distance later, she saw where the wind had tossed the rest of the tree. It looked like a giant had shoved it tip-first into the ground until only about a foot of the trunk was showing. The soil rippled all around it.

In another spot, several pieces of wood stuck out of a tree like pegs. Elsie shook her head at the devastation. The closer she got to home, the more damage prevailed.

I have to get to Benjamin and see with my own eyes that he's unharmed.

Elsie hurried across the uneven ground. The grass was unexpectedly dry. A beam of sunlight shone through the clouds. She followed its path to the ground and saw a man riding a horse toward her.

She recognized him by the way he sat. Elsie hiked up her skirt and picked up speed, racing toward Benjamin.

Tears filled her eyes, threatening to blind her. She swiped them away with the back of her hand. Buster reared as Benjamin reined the horse hard and swung down from the saddle.

"Elsie." He held out his arms.

She didn't hesitate but ran right into them, taking comfort as he held her.

"I was so scared when Buster came back alone." His fingers ran a soothing trail between her shoulder blades.

Her tears continued to flow.

"Shh. There, there. No need to cry. God kept us both safe."

He removed her Stetson, and her hair fell around her shoulders in wet ringlets. "Why, you're soaked clear through. We didn't get any rain back at our place."

"You didn't?" Her words came out muffled against his solid chest.

"Nope, only hail."

"Had that too, then rain, and the twister." She shuddered. "It stopped right before it got to me."

"Same with me. I heard the roaring like a train, and next thing I knew, it was all over." He rested his chin on her head.

Her body went completely still. Was this what it'd be like to have a husband to care for her? One who loved her for who she was instead of trying to make her into something she could never be? She sniffed, then took a step backward—out of Benjamin's embrace. Elsie longed to shift back into it but took another step away. Hiding her face in Buster's side, she patted her horse.

Somehow living the rest of her life alone with only a horse for company no longer held an appeal. She clung to Buster's neck.

Benjamin stared dumbfounded as Elsie hugged her horse. A fire burned through him. She chose the horse instead of him? He took off his Stetson, twirled it, before jamming it back onto his head. "I'm glad nothing happened to you, Elsie."

She sniffed. "Me too. To both of us, that is."

Silence stretched between them.

“Where’s Milly?” She turned toward him.

He shrugged. “I don’t know. She took off when the winds started.”

Elsie nodded. “Buster bucked me off when a clap of thunder struck.”

Benjamin took a step closer to her. “You weren’t injured, were you?”

Her gaze swung toward his. “No. Not the first time I’ve been tossed off a horse and probably not the last. Before we head home, I’d like to check on some folks. I saw their homes when I was on the mountain, but I didn’t stop to help because, well … do you want to go with me or don’t you?”

He grinned. “Sounds like a good idea to me.”

CHAPTER SEVENTEEN

When faced with calamity, be willing to lend a helping hand. Allow the gentleman to lead. Help by serving as the lesser vessel.
Mrs. Wigglesworth's Essential Guide to Proper Etiquette and Manners of Refined Society

Benjamin felt like a little boy who'd just gotten a pony for Christmas as he watched Elsie reach out to others. He'd been praying for her to see that people could be trusted. Who knew God would use a storm to change her heart in such a way?

As they left a young couple, a frown marred Elsie's face. "Why do you keep doing that?"

"What?"

"You keep grinning like a cat who ate a whole mess of mice."

He chuckled. "I don't think I've ever been compared to a cat."

"You haven't answered my question." Her blue eyes narrowed. "Can't help but think you're keeping something from me."

He shrugged and bit back another smile. Something had changed in Elsie. Somehow the storm had gentled her. Made her softer. He'd never seen her interested in others' needs before. God was speaking to her heart. She may not recognize it yet, but Benjamin did.

Her brow quirked, but she said nothing.

As they headed home, Elsie pointed. "Ain't that the Larson's place? I've never been there before, but it sure looks like Mildred."

"It is. Appears the twister touched down here." He took off at a sprint.

Elsie whizzed past on Buster's back. By the time Benjamin reached the broken-down home, she was kneeling beside Mildred.

"You hurt, Mildred?" Elsie's gaze swung back and forth. "Where's Henry?"

Henry stepped out of what was left of the soddy.

Benjamin rested his hand on the man's shoulder. "You two injured?"

"No, thank the Good Lord. We hunkered down when we heard the twister coming. I held tight to Mildred when the air sucked part of the house away."

His wife pulled a handkerchief from her apron pocket, wiping away her tears. "It was awful. I thought we were going to die."

Elsie patted the woman's arm.

"It's a miracle you both survived." Benjamin examined their home. "Looks like you've got a lot of work ahead of you."

"What can we do to help?" Elsie's arm snaked around Mildred's waist, and she urged the woman toward the men.

Henry's head bowed. "I'm sure you have your own fixing to do."

"I was at the claim when the twister hit, and it didn't touch down there," Benjamin said.

Elsie rolled up the sleeves of her dress. "How bad is the damage? We can at least get things built enough so you have a safe place to sleep tonight, then come back and work again until the job's finished."

Benjamin stared at her, dumbfounded. Where had this new Elsie come from?

Henry scratched his bald head. "If you're sure. We'd appreciate the help. I don't like to be beholden to anyone, but I guess since we helped with your place, Preacher, we can call things even."

Benjamin stared at what remained of the sod house. Three walls and the corners stood, but the fourth was half-missing, and what stood was a crumpled mess. The roof had completely lifted off. A whinny drew his attention to the right side of the property. A team of horses was secured to a tree, a wagon sat a short distance away. "I see your team made it through the storm."

Henry nodded. "Good thing they were tied tight, or I would've lost them too. Never heard a horse shriek like that, though."

Mildred sucked in a breath and rubbed her midsection.

"You having pains, dear?" Henry crossed to his wife and reached for her hand. "You best sit down and rest a bit. We don't want the baby coming early."

Pain flickered across Mildred's face. "I'm sure the pains will go away."

Elsie rushed into the soddy. She brought out a chair and plunked it down. "Here, Mildred. You should get off your feet."

Henry eased his wife to the chair. She blew out a few short breaths as she rubbed her abdomen.

"It's easing now." She patted Henry's hand. "Don't you worry about me."

Henry hesitated before leaving her side. "I guess the first thing to do is to clear out that wall there and see what's salvageable of the sod."

"Benjamin and I can do that if you want to start cutting some new sod." Elsie strolled to the wall. "Make sure you're careful, Benjamin. You won't want to do more injury to your hands."

His heart warmed. He glanced down. Funny. He hadn't thought about them since morning.

As he reached for a strip of sod, Benjamin froze. She fussed at him like a woman who had feelings for her man. He peeked at her. He couldn't deny that he cared for her, but he didn't think he'd survive that kind of heartbreak again.

Elsie's heart skittered as Benjamin studied her. He grew quiet like she'd said something wrong. If she lived to a ripe old age, she'd never figure out what went on in the head of a man. Clearing her throat, she hefted a broken piece of sod and tossed it to the side.

Henry plowed a long strip of ground while Mildred stooped over a pot. The scent of chicken stew wafted toward them. Elsie took a deep sniff, then reached for the next piece of sod. Her hand grazed Benjamin's as he grasped the same piece. The simple touch sent their kiss scurrying across her mind.

"Something wrong?" Benjamin lifted the sod.

"What? No." She shifted so there was no chance of brushing against him again.

A couple hours later, the broken part of the wall had been cleared, and Elsie started laying sod that was still useable.

Benjamin scooped a dipper into a bucket of water. Dirt coated his bandages.

Elsie bit the inside of her cheek to keep from chiding him about his hands again.

Moisture lingered on his lips as he handed her the full ladle. She wiped her hands on the back of her dress before reaching for it, nodding her thanks, not trusting her voice. Elsie glanced away from his lips—the constant reminder of their shared kiss. She needed to change her line of thinking. Fast.

"Stew's on," Mildred called out.

Elsie welcomed the distraction.

Henry came from the field and sank to the ground. "Sure had hoped we'd have gotten more rain from that twister. You wouldn't think we had any, as dry as the sod is."

"What little you got helps hold the dirt together," Elsie said.

Henry mopped his head then said a brief prayer. "I appreciate all you two are doing to help us."

"That's what we're to do for each other—help others in their times of need." Benjamin blew across the bowl of stew.

"Glad we could too." Elsie dipped her spoon into her bowl and took a bite. "This is delicious, Mildred. Appreciate you fixing us food."

Mildred smiled. "My pleasure. Least I could do."

"I take it things have died down with … you know." Elsie motioned toward Mildred's stomach.

Mildred laughed. "Yes, my boy settled right down after I rested for a bit."

Elsie nodded, not sure what else to say.

"I think I have all the sod that I'll need." Henry glanced at the sky, "With the three of us working together, we should be able to get the wall up before nightfall. As long as you folks don't mind staying a little longer."

"Glad to help." Elsie nodded.

"I'll feel better knowing you two have your home fixed again." Benjamin smiled. "But what're you going to do about the roof?"

Henry scratched his head. "That'll take a bit more doing, but providing the Lord doesn't send any rain for a few days, I should be able to get it done by myself. Not that I don't appreciate what you two have done, but I know you've got work back at your place."

As soon as they had finished the meal, Henry used a shovel to cut the sod into strips. Then Benjamin carried the layers across the field and set them in a pile.

Elsie stacked the pieces until the wall grew high enough she could no longer reach the top. By then, Henry and Benjamin were able to finish the job.

She bit back a yawn as dusk descended.

Henry clasped Benjamin's hand and thanked him. Dirt clung to both of them.

She glanced down at her dress, hardly recognizing it. Mud smudges marred the front, as well as her arms and hands.

"Thanks, Miss Smith." Henry nodded toward her.

"Call me Elsie. We've been neighbors long enough that we can skip the Mr. and Miss."

She thrust her hand out and shook his.

Henry studied the growing darkness. "I've kept you folks too long. You best get on now."

Mildred hugged Elsie close. "Thank you." She stepped back. "You too, Preacher."

A weary smile crossed Benjamin's face. "I hope you can rest easy tonight."

Elsie meandered to the tree where she'd tied Buster. He skittered to the side as she loosened the reins. She patted his withers, but he didn't calm. She let out a sigh. His high-strung nature meant they wouldn't be riding him home. Elsie couldn't blame him. It'd been a long, trying day.

Benjamin joined her. "You planning on us riding together?"

"No. Buster's in a mood. I don't trust him to carry us both right now. With the day he's had, he might buck us both off. Looks like we'll be walking."

They waved and started toward their claim. Within minutes, darkness settled around them. Stars twinkled overhead. A howl split the air, setting Elsie's nerves on edge. Coyotes, and they sounded close. Without thinking, she grasped tight to Benjamin's arm.

CHAPTER EIGHTEEN

Avoid any type of physical touch between a lady and gentleman. The only kind of acceptable physical contact is when a gentleman assists a lady with ascending and descending conveyances.

Mrs. Wigglesworth's Essential Guide to Proper Etiquette and Manners of Refined Society

Benjamin startled when Elsie clasped his arm with a death grip. What had set her on edge? He listened to the night sounds, but nothing was out of the ordinary. A pack of coyotes yipped. A yelp split the air, and Elsie shifted even closer, her whole body shuddering.

He patted her hand. "What is it?"

The grass rustled nearby.

She squealed and wrapped her arm around his waist. "H-how close are they?" He had to lean down to catch her words.

"How close are what? The coyotes?"

The wild canines barked and called to each other. It sounded like a few of them were tussling in the grass. A growl filled the air.

Elsie gasped and vaulted into his arms. She dropped the reins, and Buster took off.

Benjamin stumbled under her weight but soon had her situated. She wrapped her arms tight around his neck. He croaked, and she loosened her grip a smidgen.

"Lord, if you're still there, please save us." Her breath was hot against his neck.

Her words stopped him in his tracks. A muffled whimper reverberated against his chest.

He patted her back. “Shh, Elsie. I’ve got you. You’ve nothing to fear. God has you too.”

The scent of honeysuckles and dirt washed over him. Mary had preferred rosewater. His heart twisted with the reminder. He swallowed past the rock in his throat.

“C-can you see my soddy? A-are we home yet?”

“Not yet. Soon.” She hadn’t removed her face from his neck since she’d hopped into his embrace. Poor thing. He thought his fear of snakes was bad. His heart ached, knowing that something scared her so fiercely. “We’ll be there in a few minutes. You think you can walk yet?”

She shook her head, her chin cracking against his collarbone as she kept her face buried.

He shifted her and kissed the top of her head. “I’ll make sure nothing happens to you. Don’t you worry.”

She settled after that, and her body relaxed against him.

A few minutes later, he stepped onto his property. He set her down when he reached the soddy’s doorstep. Her eyes were wide as her gaze swung to the right and left.

Not knowing what else to do for her, he dipped his hat. “Goodnight.”

A howl echoed through the night. Elsie jumped back into Benjamin’s arms. “Please don’t go yet.”

Benjamin must think her a dunderhead, but nothing had ever scared Elsie like coyotes. She willed her pulse to halt its thudding.

“Do you want me to start a fire?” His words rumbled in his chest, or was that the thumping of his heart?

She nodded.

“I’ll need to set you down, but I promise, I’ll be right here.” He didn’t move until she nodded again. Once she did, he set her on her feet.

Elsie followed him like a scared puppy, afraid to leave its master's side. She wrapped her arms around her body while she waited for him to stack the wood and strike the flint.

In no time, a small fire blazed. He settled on the ground and patted a spot near him. "Do you want to tell me about it now?"

She sank beside him and turned her head away from his steady gaze. What must he think of her, and why did it matter?

He chucked a curved finger under her chin until she lifted her head and looked him in the eye. "Sometimes it helps to share our fears. I know it did me."

The silence lengthened between them. Benjamin shifted so they sat face-to-face.

Elsie cleared her throat. "I've feared coyotes since I was four." She plucked a blade of grass, watching as she rubbed it between her thumb and fingers. "Our neighbor's two-year-old wandered off one day."

"What happened?"

"They found what little remained of her the next day." She shuddered. "Turned out the whole pack was infected with rabies."

He shifted and wrapped one arm around her shoulder while still gripping her hand. "How terrible."

Thickness lined her throat. Her hand trembled in his. "My Aunt Kate used to say, if I didn't behave myself, she'd put me out for the crazed coyotes to find."

"Oh my. No wonder you're so frightened by them."

"I've never been able to get past my fears." A snort burst from her before she could halt it. "Guess I never turned into the proper, young lady my aunt intended either."

Benjamin wanted to argue. He couldn't admit to her being much like a lady when he compared her to Mary, but Elsie had a strength and determination his fiancée hadn't. For some reason, it appealed to him. Benjamin longed to take her onto his lap and comfort her, and *that* scared him spitless.

Shoving to his feet, he said, "I'll be back." He needed to get away before he said or did something stupid.

With quick strides, he walked until his breathing calmed. *Dear Lord, what're You trying to do here? Elsie's getting under my skin. I'm afraid to fall in love again and risk losing someone else.*

He still desired to fulfill God's call in this place, but he'd started wanting more—a wife and children to fill his home. That meant having Elsie with him every day.

Benjamin jammed his fingers through his hair. No lightning bolt of understanding or still small voice answered him, so he traipsed back to the fire. To Elsie.

Her gaze sought him as soon as he drew near. What kind of heel was he to leave a frightened woman? He sank to the ground a couple of feet away. "Sorry. You feeling any better?" What a dumb question. She'd just bared her soul, and he'd stomped off because he didn't know how to handle his emotions.

She didn't answer. Just stared at him.

He let out a sigh. "You realize God answered your prayer tonight."

A muscle flickered in her jaw. "What prayer? I don't remember praying."

"When you were in my … that is … on our way home you asked the Lord to save us."

Elsie tucked her knees up under her skirt and propped her chin on top, wrapping her arms around her legs. "I used to pray all the time—until Pa took sick and wasn't getting any better."

"I was tempted to stop praying when Mary drowned."

"Really?"

He nodded. "It was the lowest point in my life. I felt like all my hopes and dreams were shattered. A lot of folks think that God gives us tough times because we've disobeyed Him. Sometimes that's the case. Truth is, most times He has us go through storms so we'll grow closer and more dependent on Him."

"I either was disobedient or did a lousy job of learning anything through Pa's death."

Benjamin reached out and touched her arm. "It doesn't mean you don't still have the opportunity to learn from it. That's one of the best things about God's grace and forgiveness. It's always there for us. There's nothing we've done that He can't forgive."

"You think?"

"I *know*."

Silence stretched as the fire crackled.

"I'll have to think more on that." She stood and brushed off her skirt.

"The Lord will be there, waiting for you to turn to Him." Benjamin would too.

Elsie nodded. "Good night." She strolled to her soddy, not looking back.

He sat by the fire in case she decided to make another appearance. Waiting.

CHAPTER NINETEEN

A proper young lady is demure, subdued, and quiet in nature, never giving in to anger or public expressions of displeasure.
Mrs. Wigglesworth's Essential Guide to Proper Etiquette and Manners of Refined Society

Benjamin shoved his nearly-healed hands into his stiff work gloves. Four days had passed since the tornado, and he had yet to catch a glimpse of Elsie. He had, however, convinced the neighbors to help erect a barn, so he'd spent his energy leveling the land before his help arrived. He smiled when he spotted the first wagon. The sound of hammering soon filled the air.

"How big of a barn you fixing to build?" Henry spoke around a nail clenched between his teeth.

"I want it large enough for a horse or two, and maybe a cow." Benjamin held a board in place while he hammered. "How's that roof of yours coming along? Are you sure you don't need help with it?"

Henry hammered a section in place. "I should get the roof on in a day or two. Thought it was best for the cedar poles to dry some before I lay the sod on top. Besides, you and Elsie have already done so much for me, I can't ask you to do more."

"If you need anything, be sure to let us know." Benjamin clapped the older man on the back.

Henry nodded.

"What does Elsie say about building on her land?" John asked. "Of course, if she accepts my proposal, she won't be here for long."

The hammer nearly fell from Benjamin's grasp.

"From your reaction, I gather you didn't consult her. She's going to be angrier than a wet cat if you ask me." John smirked.

Benjamin's fingers tightened around the handle. If Elsie had to choose between him and John, whom would she pick? The better question was, why did he care?

"I'm surprised Elsie isn't here helping us or the women." Mark nodded toward Mildred and Beatrice. "Have you spoken with her today?"

Benjamin glanced at Elsie's soddy, then back toward the men. "Saw her head out with her rifle early this morning."

John's eyebrows rose higher.

Benjamin cleared his throat and went back to the task at hand. They worked in silence for hours. They'd just started on the fourth wall when he studied the sky. The sun wasn't quite straight overhead. "Let's take a short break."

They headed toward the creek and splashed cold water on their faces, taking long drinks.

"Went into town the other day." Mark rubbed his hand across his jaw. "Heard more about those outlaws. They've been spotted around Enid, stealing from folks and being a general nuisance. That's a good thirty miles away, but several men said to be on the lookout. Apparently, the outlaws have been spotted to the north and south of there too."

"Do you have a description of them?" John asked.

"One's a city fella. Sounds like he's slicker than a tub of grease. Can talk his way out of anything." Mark wiped his wet hands on his pants.

Visions of the man who'd threatened him before the race slipped into Benjamin's thoughts. What was his name? *Herbert.* Whatever had happened to the man who had refused to give his last name?

"Townsfolk said one man goes in and steals whatever he can get his hands on. A week or two later, the city fella comes in and demands their deed. I'll not leave without my wife or have her going anywhere without me now." Mark glanced toward Beatrice. "I don't plan to tell her just yet because you know how women are. They get all lathered up at the littlest thing sometimes."

"My Mildred isn't going much of anywhere these days. I allowed her to come today because she begged me, and I didn't have the heart to let her sit at home whilst I'm here. Besides, I want her close in case the baby comes." Henry smiled and waved at his wife as the men went back to work.

John stood and headed toward the barn site. He picked up a board and a nail. "If I were you married men, I'd keep your women close to home. You never know who might be lurking around. I'll make a point of stopping in to check on my Elsie each day. I wouldn't want anything to happen to her. She needs a *real* man to take care of her." He glared at Benjamin.

Benjamin's heart pounded as he started working again, having no desire to spout a retort he might later regret.

"You going to let him get away with that?" Mark murmured in his ear.

"For now." Benjamin refused to be baited into a disagreement.

Just then, Elsie rounded the corner of the barn, hands planted on her slim hips. "Benjamin David, just what do you think you're building now? I refuse to have a church built on my property!"

She resembled the snorting, leg-stomping bull he'd seen in a field when he rode the circuit.

His heart pounded in his ears as he considered how to tame the savage beast before him.

"You'd better go talk to her." Mark chuckled. "I reckon you've got some explaining to do. Be gentle with her, and I'm sure she'll come around. She strikes me as more bluster than bark."

Gentle? Benjamin probably needed a shield to ward off the fiery daggers shooting from her eyes.

"I'll take care of this." John laid his hammer down and started in Elsie's direction.

Mark halted John with a hand to his arm. "This is something the preacher needs to face. Let's keep working."

John hesitated, glancing between Elsie and Benjamin. Finally, he picked up his hammer and pounded in another nail.

"Go ahead." Mark gave Benjamin a little push.

At that moment, he had a better understanding of Daniel when he'd been thrown into the lions' den.

Elsie's blood boiled. She fisted her hand, waiting for the conniving scoundrel to make his way toward her. He was sadly mistaken if he thought a little affection and revealing her biggest secret to him meant she'd forgotten about their battle for the property. It was high time she remembered her priorities.

She turned and stomped away, out of hearing of their neighbors. Elsie spun back, only to have Benjamin plow into her. As his hands steadied her, something flickered in his eyes. *How could he betray me like this? I thought he was different than the others.* This was one battle Elsie refused to run from.

"You low-down, two-bit skunk. What do you think you're doing? I thought things were starting to be different between us." She jabbed her finger into his chest, surprised by the taut muscles. "Who gave you permission to build something else on *my* property? How could you construct this without asking me?" She leaned forward until they were practically nose-to-nose, daring him to be the first one to break eye contact.

"You're right, I'm sorry. I should've said something, but I thought you'd understand after reading my letter." Benjamin's scan shifted to her mouth then back to her eyes. Elsie despised the warmth rushing to her face.

"What letter?"

A muscle in his jaw twitched. "You didn't find it after the tornado?"

"No, and I don't see what that has to do with anything." She shoved hard against his chest but couldn't budge him. "You say all these things about coming here to tell others about God and other such nonsense, then you turn around and don't follow your word to me that we'd work on things together. You're like the rest." She growled, and his eyes grew wide, but he didn't shift away from her.

"What do you mean?"

"I don't know what you're building, but I want you and everybody else off my property by sunset." She stomped away.

"Elsie, wait."

She ignored him and kept clomping toward her soddy.

"Elsie."

She cringed as he jogged up beside her. Never mind. She had better things to do than listen to his prattles.

"It's a barn. I'm building a barn."

She stopped in her tracks. "A what?"

"A barn. With winter coming, I figured we needed a barn for the horses."

She glanced in that direction. "Well, why didn't you say so in the first place?"

Not waiting for a response, she stalked into her soddy and swung the door hard. Leaning against the wood, she closed her eyes, wishing she could snatch back her mean words. Elsie dragged the table and settled it against the door. As she did, something fluttered to the floor.

Was this the letter he'd mentioned? Picking it up, she slid a sheet of paper from the envelope.

Dear Elsie, please forgive me for my poor handling of things this morning. It has never been my intent to cause you embarrassment or harm. I'm afraid I made a mess of what I had hoped would be a meaningful sermon.

Forgive me for being sharp with you when you showed kindness in regard to my injured hands. You could have made a comment about the poor job I had done with plowing, but you didn't. Instead, you were gracious and compassionate. You're an incredible woman, Elsie. One I'm blessed to call a friend.

I pray you can forgive my bumbling efforts to seek your forgiveness. I am forever indebted to you for all the assistance you've given me.

I will find a way to make things up to you, and I'll try my best not to hurt you again. I pray God will guide me to a way to seek restitution. Until then, I am your faithful servant, Benjamin.

Elsie dropped the letter. What had she done?

Benjamin traipsed along the creek, struggling to rein in his churning thoughts before he returned to the men. He hadn't figured out what he'd tell them, but he might as well face the inevitable. He headed to the barn.

"Where's Elsie? We do all the work while you go off chatting with my gal." John scowled at him. "You didn't hurt her, did you?"

As if he'd do such a thing. "She's fine."

"I think I'll go see for myself." John clambered down the ladder and strutted toward Elsie's soddy.

"I reckon she's a bit sore with you, eh, Preacher?" A smile darted across Henry's face. "Don't let it get you down. Women spout off, but eventually, they come around. You'll see."

"Let's get back to work, gents." Mark handed Benjamin a sack of nails.

The pounding did little to soothe Benjamin's frayed nerves. He couldn't stop from peeking as John knocked on Elsie's door with no luck.

A short time later, Beatrice shaded her eyes from the sun. "Time to eat, fellas. Should I go ask Elsie to join us?"

"Henry …" Mildred doubled over.

Henry hurried around the side of the building. "What is it, sweetie?" He put his arm around her waist.

"My time." Her breathing came in short bursts.

"We best get you home right away, although, I don't know how much help I'll be." Henry's face paled.

"The roof isn't finished. It's no place to birth a baby. Besides, I need a woman's help. I thought I'd have time to ask Elsie or Beatrice to assist me when the time came but—" She squeezed Henry's arm, her face contorting. "There's no time. I think the baby's almost here. I didn't want to tell you earlier, but I've been having pains since the wee hours. Weren't sure if they were early pains or not."

"Land's sake, woman. Maybe we could've made it to town and found a real doc."

"We don't know if Enid even has a doc, and it'd take us all day to have reached town. There's no way I'm giving birth in the wagon. That's no place for a baby to be born. I hoped Beatrice could help."

Beatrice's face paled.

Mildred sucked in a breath, and her face twisted again.

"C-could we use your house, Preacher?" Henry glanced at Benjamin.

Mildred grunted. "No, it's unseemly for me to give birth in a single fella's place. It's just not done. Take me to Elsie's."

"But—"

"Now, Henry!"

Benjamin couldn't pull himself away as the couple's conversation volleyed back and forth.

Henry supported his wife as they made slow progress toward Elsie's soddy.

Benjamin trotted ahead of them and pounded on Elsie's door. "Elsie, it's Benjamin."

He glanced over his shoulder to see Mark dishing out food. Beatrice sat off to the side looking a little green.

Mildred groaned. It appeared she'd break Henry's arm the way she held it. Benjamin turned back toward the door and pounded again.

Something thudded against the door before it swung open. "What's going on?" A frown puckered Elsie's face. "Mildred?"

"It's her time." Beads of perspiration dotted Henry's forehead. "She doesn't want to go home since we don't have a roof. Can you help her."

Elsie froze. "I don't have any experience, other than helping a mare drop a foal."

Benjamin refrained from reaching out to touch her arm. "Come on, Elsie, you need to do something. Henry and Mildred have no one else."

Elsie stiffened her shoulders. "Benjamin, fetch as many fresh sheets and towels as you've got. I'll probably need some hot water too."

"Thata girl." He smiled and ran, calling out, "John, put on a pot of water to boil!" Inside his home, he gathered the items Elsie had mentioned as well as a rain slicker. *Dear Lord, keep Mildred and the baby safe.*

He sprinted back. His heart stampeded as he dropped the items on Elsie's table. She tossed her quilt at him. He folded the cover and set it on a chair, handing her the oil-skin cloth.

She draped it across the bed and spread the sheet on top.

"What else do you need me to do?" he asked.

Panic lined Elsie's face.

"There you go, Mildred." Henry laid his wife on the bed. "I'll check on the water." He turned tail and ran.

Mildred moaned.

"I'm not sure I'll know what to do." Elsie wrung her hands.

"You'll manage fine. I've never seen a more capable woman."

Elsie gave a short nod. "Beatrice?"

"Last I saw her, she was getting sick. I doubt she'll be much help." Benjamin's finger itched to tuck the stray curl behind Elsie's ear. "I've every confidence in your abilities."

"Oh … oh … I think the baby's coming, Elsie." Mildred flopped back against the pillow.

Elsie's face paled. "You better go."

He hesitated at the doorway as Elsie crossed the short distance to the bed. "Benjamin?"

In two strides, he stood beside her, squeezing her hand. "Yes?"

"Pray for me. I mean for us." Elsie met his gaze. "In case I don't get a chance to say it again, I'm sorry about earlier."

He lifted her chin with his index finger. "You're already forgiven, and I've been praying for you both, Elsie, dear."

CHAPTER TWENTY

Discussion of married life and the nature of the two species is unsuitable for the hearing of a single lady. She is too fragile and gentle to be able to handle the complexities of wedded bliss and what results from such a union.

Mrs. Wigglesworth's Essential Guide to Proper Etiquette and Manners of Refined Society

Elsie's mouth went dry. A cry from Mildred snagged her back to the task at hand instead of mulling over Benjamin's words. "Do you have any information about birthing, Mildred?"

The woman blew air through her teeth, gripping the sheet tight in her fists. After a minute, she relaxed. "More than most. I'm the oldest of twelve children. By the time I was ten, I'd helped Ma with the birthing of my siblings. We lived too far for the midwife to get there in time, and Pa wasn't ever any use, other than keeping the little ones out of the way." Mildred paused when her face contorted with the next pain.

When her body relaxed, she continued, "You'll have to help me remove my clothes, and you'll want to spread that slicker over top of the sheets instead of under them."

Elsie scurried to a crate and yanked out a nightgown. She helped the woman change, then get back into bed. Mildred hiked the gown to her knees. "Henry and I didn't think we'd ever have a child. We've been married over twenty years."

That explained why the couple both had gray hair.

"Check and see if you can see the head yet." She panted between pains. "It's gotta be soon because I feel the need to push."

With a quick gulp of air, Elsie grabbed a chair and set it at the end of the bed. "I can see a dark head of hair."

"Good." The woman panted and reached for Elsie's hand. "You're doing great. I'm glad you're with me."

Mildred's face turned an alarming shade of red as she bore down with each pain.

Elsie couldn't tell how much time had passed, but it sure seemed like a lifetime.

She wanted to ask how the woman could put up with such pain but bit back the words. It didn't seem natural for a body to undergo such agony.

Several pushes later, a squirming baby boy dropped into Elsie's extended hands. She stared down at the wriggling newborn, speechless. Her arms longed to be filled with a child of her own.

The baby let out a scream. Startled out of her musings, Elsie wrapped the child in one of Benjamin's towels.

Mildred strained to see before collapsing back against the bed. "What is it?" Perspiration glistened on her round face.

"It's a boy. What do I do now?" Her arms shook as she examined the newborn.

"You'll need to clear the mucus from his nose and mouth, and get a string to tie around the cord before you cut it." Mildred's whispered words were difficult to hear.

A knock startled Elsie.

She settled the infant on Mildred's stomach and opened the door a crack. Henry stood with the hot water.

He set the pot down. "She … is she, uh …"

Elsie smiled. "Mother and son are doing well. Can you heat a knife in the fire? I need to cut the cord. I'll let you see them once I get them both cleaned up." Henry handed her the pan and took off. She chuckled and turned back toward Mildred. "I'd say you got one proud papa there."

Mildred smiled.

The tired woman instructed Elsie through the final stages of birthing and cleanup before her eyes fluttered shut.

Elsie bathed the child, then let the new father in to see his baby.

Mildred and Henry's faces radiated joy as they stared in adoration at their tiny son, touching his miniscule hands.

Elsie stepped outside and closed the door behind the trio, allowing them time alone. She yawned and glanced at the starlit sky, surprised to see how much time had passed.

It took a huge effort to put one foot in front of the other as she made her way to the little group assembled around the fire. They glanced up, expectation lining each face.

John stepped forward. "Elsie, my dear, have a seat here beside me. I'll dish you up some grub. You must be starved. We've already eaten."

Movement to her left drew her attention. Benjamin stared at her. Did he remember that he'd called her dear? She shifted her gaze away from his.

"How're they?" Beatrice leaned against Mark. "I-I'm sorry I couldn't help you."

"It's fine. Mildred and her son are doing well. He's a healthy young'un. Got a good pair of lungs." Elsie accepted the plate of food and started shoveling it in.

"How about we give a word of thanks to God for this new life and for helping you deliver the baby?" Benjamin bowed his head.

Her fork clattered as shame washed over Elsie. She *had* asked him to pray for her, and here she'd been thinking about what a great job she'd done on her own. Elsie dipped her head.

"We thank You, Lord, for the new life You brought into the world today. Thank You for being with Elsie and guiding her as she assisted Mildred. I ask You to be with the little family. May they raise their son with a desire to follow You. Thank You for the food You provided. May it bring strength and nourishment to Elsie. In Jesus' name, amen."

"It's getting late. I best get on home." John stood. "I'll see you tomorrow, Elsie." He brushed his hand across her shoulder. "Perhaps then we'll have an opportunity to talk. Alone."

He clapped his hat on his head, strolling to his horse. In one motion, he mounted and kicked the horse into action.

Elsie concentrated on forking food into her mouth and chewing. It took all her effort.

"We should be heading home too." Mark rose. "It's getting late."

"Can we just wait a few more moments?" Beatrice's gaze darted between Elsie and her husband. "I was hoping to speak to Elsie about, eh, something personal."

Elsie's gaze narrowed.

Mark sighed. "Can't it wait till we come back to finish the roof?"

Beatrice shook her head. "Please."

Her husband let out another sigh but nodded.

"I guess that's our hint to make ourselves scarce." Benjamin stood and clapped Mark on the back. "What do you say we go to my place for a bit and give the women some privacy?"

Beatrice's hands twisted as she watched the men leave. Once they were gone, she turned to Elsie. "I owe you an apology."

Elsie set her plate aside. "Whatever for?"

"I should've helped you with Mildred and the baby." Her face paled. "You'll think I'm a dolt. Fact is, I probably am."

Elsie patted her friend's arm. "I don't know what's got you all twisted in knots, but I have no reason to be upset with you. Now, what's going on?"

"I got sick when they suggested I help with the birthing. I've always been squeamish. Get sick at the littlest bit." Her chin quivered. "I don't know what I'm going to do when it's my time. Was it awful?"

"Awful? You mean the delivery?"

Beatrice nodded.

"No. In fact, it wasn't a whole lot different than an animal giving birth. Have you ever seen a birth before?"

She didn't think it possible, but Beatrice turned another shade paler. Elsie hid her smile by swiping her sleeve across her mouth. "I take it, that's a no."

"Whatever am I going to do when I get near the end of my time?" Beatrice reached over and grasped Elsie's arm. "Promise me."

"Promise what?"

"Promise me that when my time comes in February, you'll assist me like you did for Mildred."

February. That would be well after the courts decided who was awarded the property. She'd be here if they ruled in her favor, but what if they didn't? She couldn't make a promise that she maybe couldn't keep.

"Please." Beatrice squeezed tighter.

Elsie glanced at her friend and smiled. "If I'm in the area, yes, I'll come help you."

Beatrice yanked her into a hug. "Thank you. I don't know what I'd do without you, and of course you'll be in the area. Why wouldn't you?"

"If I'm not, Mildred's the woman you'll want with you. She has more experience with birthings than me. Apparently, she assisted her ma since she was little."

Beatrice shook her head. "No, it's you I want. You're my very best friend, besides Mark of course." She giggled.

Mark poked his head out of Benjamin's house. "Are we able to come out yet?"

"Yes," Beatrice called.

Elsie chuckled as the men sauntered toward them.

Mark stepped up beside his wife and ran a hand along her jaw. The motion brought to mind how Benjamin had touched Elsie's face. She looked away.

Beatrice yawned. "We best get on home, husband."

Mark rolled his eyes. "That's what I've been telling you. G'night folks. See you in the morning." He led his wife toward their wagon. They soon waved as they headed out into the moonlit night.

The sound of the wheels rolling across the buffalo grass dulled until only the whir of insects and the occasional snorting of a horse could be heard.

Benjamin hadn't said a word as he stared off in the direction the Sawyers had gone. Finally, he turned toward her. "You must be exhausted. You're welcome to sleep at my place. I'll stay in the barn."

Warmth soared to her neck. "No. Don't think that's appropriate for me to stay there. I can bed down in the barn."

"There's no roof."

"It won't be the first time I've slept out under the stars. I'll be fine."

He shook his head. "I don't like that idea."

"You worry too much." She yawned. "I think it's best if I turn in."

"Hold up there. I'll get you a bedroll and pillow." He didn't wait for her to respond but took off toward his place.

He returned a minute later. His hand grazed hers as he handed her the bedding.

She longed to let his hand wrap around hers and take comfort from his strength, because right now, she didn't have much left.

"Elsie?"

"Yeah?"

"There's so many things we need to discuss." He rubbed circles along the back of her hand with his fingertip. "Things I need to make right."

A door creaked open, and both their heads swung in the direction of Elsie's place.

Henry stepped out. "Hey, Preacher, you want to come see my boy?"

Elsie shifted her gaze back to Benjamin, and he turned agonized eyes toward her.

"Preacher?"

Benjamin gave a soft moan. "I'm sorry. It looks like our conversation will have to wait a few moments. I'll be back."

He trotted toward her soddy.

She headed into the barn, spread the blankets in a corner, and sank to the ground, hugging the pillow tight in her arms. Elsie buried her nose in it. It smelled like Benjamin. She leaned her back against the wall, and her head drooped as she tried to figure out what things he needed to make right.

Benjamin chafed with the delay in speaking with Elsie but shoved his frustrations aside as he stepped into the soddy.

Mildred sat on the bed, her back against the sod wall. Henry was near to bursting as he settled a wriggling bundle in Benjamin's outstretched arms. The baby's bright blue eyes stared wide at him. A tuft of brown hair brushed the babe's ears on either side. A small hand poked out of the blanket. Benjamin couldn't resist reaching out and touching it. It felt smooth like satin. "What did you name him?"

"Henry James, although we'll just call him James so he doesn't get confused with his pa," Mildred said.

"It's a right fine name. Congratulations to both of you."

The couple beamed.

Benjamin snuggled the child close. A heavy weight settled on his chest as the desire to have a son of his own filled him. He could picture a little boy with blond hair and blue eyes like his mother. Somehow the image of Elsie as wife material no longer seemed objectionable.

The baby nuzzled against his finger, latching onto Benjamin's knuckle. A suckling sound filled the room.

Henry laughed. "My boy's an eater."

Mildred smiled. "I just fed him a little bit ago, but I guess he didn't get his fill."

The little face puckered and a louder squawk than Benjamin thought possible came from the infant. He handed the child to his mother. "I'll let you three be."

He stepped outside and started to close the door only to find Henry had followed. The man glanced around. "Do you know where Elsie got to? I never did get a chance to thank her for all she done for us. I wanted to tell her we'll clear out in the morning, but Mildred's too tuckered out to head home tonight."

"She planned on bedding down in the barn for the evening."

They strolled to the opening of the barn.

"Elsie, you in here?" Henry poked his head inside. "I guess I'll have to thank her in the morning. G'night, Preacher." He turned and left.

Benjamin glanced inside the enclosed barn. Bright moonlight shone through the top. At first, he didn't see anything, but then he spotted her sitting on the bedroll with her arm wrapped around the pillow, her head sagging to the side. She'd likely have a crick in her neck by the time she woke. He'd like to go in and ease her body into a more comfortable position, but it wasn't his place. That was the place of a husband.

He turned away before his thoughts meandered too far along that path. It was high time he took Elsie and their future to the Lord.

CHAPTER TWENTY-ONE

Avoid speaking of your past accomplishments or tales from your youth as it can create boredom or boastfulness. When asked to speak, do so briefly. Don't dwell on the past, making others feel ill at ease.
Mrs. Wigglesworth's Essential Guide to Proper Etiquette and Manners of Refined Society

Elsie woke to raised voices. She shook off the remnants of a perplexing dream. Stretching, she glanced around trying to place where she was. The new barn. As she stood, Elsie rolled her neck back and forth to ease the tight muscles.

"I got here early so I could speak with Elsie. You have no right to tell me I can't." It took a moment to recognize John's muffled voice.

She shrank back against the wall. Maybe he'd figure she was still asleep if she sat back down.

"Just 'cause you're a preacher, don't mean you got first dibs on her. I've already asked her to marry me. You have no claim on her, and I do."

Not if I can help it. Elsie shivered. If only Benjamin would make such a claim. She stumbled. Was that what she really wanted?

"I didn't say you couldn't speak with her, I said just not yet. We should probably move away from here so she can sleep longer."

She warmed at Benjamin's words.

"I guess you're saying we can't start work either." John's tone hardened.

"All I'm asking is that we wait. I'm sure Elsie needs her rest."

A silken cocoon of joy settled around her. Maybe all neighbors couldn't be lumped into the ones she'd had back in Kiowa. At least Benjamin was different. The Sawyers and Larsons were too. Only John was more like the other folks—out for what was best for themselves.

Elsie bent and retrieved the blanket. She'd avoided the confrontation long enough. Her composure firmly in place, she strolled toward the entryway. The men had moved off and were settled by the campfire.

The frown on John's face transformed to a beaming smile as soon as he caught sight of her. "There you are, my dear." He stood and reached for her hand.

She slid it behind her back. "I most definitely am *not* your dear."

A grin spread across Benjamin's face. She handed him the bedding. "Thank you so much for allowing me to borrow these. I hope you weren't without a pillow last night because of me."

"It wasn't any hardship, I assure you."

"I appreciate it, Benjamin. Sorry I couldn't stay awake for that conversation you wanted to have."

"What conversation?" John edged closer, glaring at the two of them.

Elsie winked at Benjamin.

Mirth lit his countenance.

John tugged on her arm. "There's something I've been meaning to speak with you about, Elsie." He glanced at Benjamin with a scowl. "If you'll excuse us."

She allowed him to lead her a short distance away. "Oh look." She pointed at an approaching wagon. "The Sawyers are almost here." Elsie hoped their arrival would discourage a long-winded talk.

"Have you thought more about my proposal?"

She shook her head. "Don't need to. I'm not interested."

Elsie expected some sort of outburst from the man. Instead, his brow lifted. "When Benjamin wins the claim for himself and tosses you out on your ear, I'll be waiting for you with no hard feelings. I've told you before. I'm a patient man when I know what I want."

The man had the tenacity of a badger.

"Hello." Beatrice waved.

Elsie returned the wave and headed in their direction. "Good morning."

Beatrice climbed down and gave her a hug. "I see the Larsons' wagon. They're still here?"

Elsie nodded. "They spent the night at my place. Haven't seen them yet this morning."

"Oh, good, that means we'll see the baby before they head out. I was disappointed we didn't get to yesterday."

Benjamin joined them. "Thanks for coming again. It shouldn't take us that long to get the roof completed." He shook Mark's hand.

"I left my hammer outside the soddy. I can pitch in too." Elsie glanced at Benjamin.

He gave a short nod.

Elsie scurried to get it before he changed his mind, not that she'd have listened if he refused. After all, the barn was on her property, so the least she could do was help with the construction. Not wanting to disturb the new family to retrieve her Stetson from the soddy, Elsie joined the others instead.

They worked until late afternoon, only taking a short break for the midday meal and to see the baby before the Larsons headed home. The sun beat down on Elsie's head as she hammered the last two nails into the final board of the roof. She sat down and scanned the horizon. Two men rode by on horseback in the distance. She squinted. The duo stopped and stared in her direction before they went on their way again. A shiver slithered up her spine.

She flicked away the feeling and clambered down the ladder after the neighbor men.

Benjamin shook each of the fellas' hands, and she followed suit, thanking them for coming and helping. John didn't linger but left immediately.

Beatrice squeezed Elsie's hand as she said farewell, then climbed onto the wagon seat. "You best put some butter on your face. Looks like you have a nasty sunburn."

Elsie could just imagine how she looked. The tight skin pulled as she flexed her face muscles. She bit back a moan.

Benjamin shifted closer and stared at her face. "Hey, Freckles." Mirth twinkled in his eyes.

Elsie slugged him in the arm. "Don't. Ever. Call. Me. That."

Surprise flashed across his face.

She spun on her heel and thundered away, her fingers fisted.

A vise on her arm yanked her to a halt.

"Why do you always respond that way? I was just trying to have fun, and you get all heated up about something, spouting, and stomping off like a three-year-old. When're you going to face things you don't like to hear instead of running from them?"

Her chest heaved as anger surged through her veins. He had no right to talk to her like that.

"I didn't mean to hurt your feelings. If you ask me, I think your freckles are cute." Benjamin snagged her chin and forced her to meet his gaze. She couldn't identify the expression resonating in his eyes. "*Talk* to me, Elsie. Let me in. You can't keep things bottled up all the time. If you do, you'll keep spewing on everybody when they least suspect it, and you'll become a lonely, old woman."

He removed his hand, and the warmth of his touch on her jaw lingered long after.

"I've always hated my freckles."

"Why?" Benjamin lifted her chin again and stared into her eyes.

"Mind if we talk about this while we eat? I'm half starved." Elsie glanced toward the campfire, where the scent of ham-and-bean soup wafted.

"Of course. Let me grab some bowls." Benjamin trotted to his house.

He returned a few minutes later. Elsie dished the soup and handed it to him. After he prayed, she asked, "You really want to know about my freckles?"

He nodded.

"I've always hated the foul things. None of my sisters have them." She motioned at her face. "They get worse whenever I'm out in the sun, and with helping Pa on the farm, they always shone like strawberries in a patch unless I wore my hat."

Benjamin chuckled. "I wouldn't compare them to berries."

"When I was ten, I helped Pa whitewash the fence by our house. The job didn't take more than an hour, but my face burned. We had a little bit of paint left, so I painted my face before I headed off to school."

"You didn't."

"I did. I thought the kids wouldn't tease me anymore about my freckles. Instead, they called me 'Pale Face' all day. My teacher had trouble not laughing too. Even Pa chuckled when he saw me at the end of the day. By then, it had dried, and my face felt as hard as a rock. It took some scrubbing to get it off. It took longer for the kids to stop teasing me."

"What other stories from childhood can you share? I'd like to learn more about you." Benjamin leaned forward.

Lord, give me insight to know how to help Elsie—to encourage her to find her way back to You. Benjamin smiled.

"My ma died giving birth to me. Some say Pa spoiled me since I'm the baby of the family, and it's a good fifteen years betwixt my oldest sister and me."

"How many sisters do you have?" Benjamin watched as she scooped up the last bit of food.

"Four. My sisters are each a year apart. There's Abigail, Bithiah—though we call her Bitty since she's a little thing. Takes after Ma. Then there's Cora. She didn't get a Bible name since the only 'C' name Pa knew …"

"Yes?"

"Was Cozbi. Pa couldn't think of any other, and he didn't want no daughter named after that one since she and her husband ended up with a spear in their guts. Then there's Dorcas and me."

"No, I don't suppose Cozbi would've been a good name." He chuckled. "Do your sisters live nearby?"

"Nah. They all married and moved far away before I turned six. Dorcas and her family live the closest, but it still takes a whole day's train ride to get to them. Pa and I only went to see them once after they left. Couldn't afford to go see the others."

"Does it bother you that your pa gave you a boy's name?"

Elsie shook her head. "I got something my sisters don't—a piece of both my ma and pa. Pa couldn't bear to call me Esther, though, on account of how much he missed Ma, so he mostly called me Elm."

"I imagine you didn't have a chance to really get to know your sisters."

"Nope. Most of my growing up years I spent with Pa, and sometimes Aunt Kate. She tried to put the fear of the Lord in me, but Pa said it never took so well."

She poked the embers with a stick. "Probably gave my teachers chest pains from all the shenanigans I tried in order to keep up with the boys in my class. Aunt Kate said Kiowa couldn't keep a schoolmarm more than a year on account of me. Not sure what she meant by it."

Benjamin smiled. He could well imagine the scrapes Elsie had gotten into as a child.

"Pa and I spent most days together working on the farm. When I was a little tyke, he figured out a harness so I could be on his back while he did the plowing or milking. Pa said I'd nap when he strapped me to him. I gave up naps at the age of three. He had a hard time keeping me out from underfoot after that."

"You mentioned something about your Aunt Kate and the Lord." Benjamin prayed she wouldn't balk at the subject change.

Elsie jumped up. "I've taken enough of your time today. Surely you've got better things to do than listen to my ramblings."

He snagged her wrist and tugged her to sit again. "Truly, I want to hear about your past."

She let out a sigh. "Aunt Kate made sure we attended church each Sunday. Every Saturday, she'd say, 'Elmer, you make sure to have that girl in church tomorrow.' She said it like we were heathens or something, even though we always went." Her voice lowered a notch. "I took the Lord into my heart at age ten."

She fiddled with a stick, pushing it into the fire. "Pa had given me a kitten two weeks prior and told me to keep a sharp eye on him. One day, I took my gaze off him for a second, and he got run over by the wagon."

"I'm so sorry." Benjamin couldn't resist squeezing her hand.

Elsie shrugged. "I couldn't understand how God let it happen. Pa shared with me how God knows when a sparrow falls to the ground and dies. He told me how I could have Jesus in my heart and spend eternity with Him—like Ma had. So, I prayed with Pa."

So she *was* a Christian. "What—"

"What made me stop being on speaking terms with God?" She rose and fisted her hands, fire sparking from her eyes. "Pa wanted to come here, you know."

"What happened?"

"He died before we could make the trip." Her voice turned gravelly.

Benjamin stood and stepped closer, laying his hand on her shoulder. "I'm sorry."

"Pa helped survey this land back in the seventies, during a brief stint with the military." Elsie withdrew a crinkled paper from her shirt pocket. "He drew a map so he'd remember exactly where to come if they ever opened the land for settlement."

No wonder she had such an attachment to this particular piece of property.

"With all the rest of the girls married, Pa had planned to sell the farm and have us come on the run together, and we'd get two plots side by side. Except the bank foreclosed on the farm two months before we could sell it." She shifted away from his grasp. "Pa started fading more and more after we lost it. What little money he had, he gave me, but with the prices of everything so much higher here on the strip, it doesn't go far."

Pain ripped through Benjamin's heart. "What about your aunt? Couldn't you have stayed with her?"

"By then, she no longer lived in the area, and I wouldn't have wanted to move in with her anyway."

"Didn't you have neighbors who could help you?"

"With the drought and financial scares, they had all they could do taking care of their own families."

"You know, not all neighbors are bad. Most can be trusted to help when you have a need, as you've seen with the Sawyers and Larsons." His conscience pinched for not mentioning John Clark as well. "Nobody offered to help you and your pa? Surely the minister—"

She shook her head.

"Oh, Elsie. I'm so sorry." A weight settled on his chest. He wished he could go back and change the past. For both of them. Instead, he provided the only comfort he could think of. Benjamin wrapped his arms around her slim waist. His pulse quickened.

She relaxed in his embrace.

"You may think God let you down, but I want you to know, God never left you. He's been beside you each step along the way, whether you choose to talk to Him or not."

She pulled back. "You have no right—"

"Hear me out. You've had lots of pain and disappointments. I understand that. My life hasn't turned out the way I intended either, but you can't keep holding on to the bitterness, or it'll eat you alive. Don't allow Satan to win. He desires for you to be discouraged, defeated, and unforgiving, but God has better things in store for you if you'll allow Him to work in your life again."

He wanted to mention a possible future for the two of them together, but he doubted she'd be ready to hear such a thing.

She folded her arms across her chest, eyes blazing.

"You can't keep these things bottled inside. God can handle your pain and disappointment. Your anger too. Bring it all to Him, and I'm always here if you need a friend to talk to as well." He tucked a wisp of her hair behind her ear and tugged her close again. "I know He has your good in mind for the future. You can trust Him. And me. I'll be praying for you."

Elsie relaxed. "Thank you." She stepped out of his embrace. "Benjamin?"

"Yes?"

"When're you going to let go of *your* past and see what's already in front of you?"

He snapped his mouth shut as Elsie strolled toward her soddy without a backward glance.

CHAPTER TWENTY-TWO

At all costs, avoid entering a business agreement between an unmarried man and woman, as this can lead to disputes and conflicts which can ruin a friendship. Intermingling business with pleasure is highly discouraged.
Mrs. Wigglesworth's Essential Guide to Proper Etiquette and Manners of Refined Society

Benjamin couldn't move for a good five minutes as Elsie's words rolled over him again and again. Each time, they bowled him over as they had when she'd said them.

He tugged at his shirt collar, frustrated by the surge of emotions surfacing at her questions. He no longer pined for Mary. Didn't Elsie see that? Couldn't she tell he cared for her? He spent time with her, encouraged her to share her past, urging her to let go of the hurts. How much more obvious could he be?

Benjamin paced in front of his place and froze when the realization of what she'd said hit him. Did that mean she might be interested in the idea of courtship?

He shoved back his hat and looked at the sky. "Lord, I can't understand why Elsie's questions have me all out of sorts. Guide me to see Your truth. Open her heart to see what being in a Christlike community is all about. Help me to show her Your unconditional love. Use me in her life."

Benjamin needed something to distract his mind. He glanced at his new barn. Perhaps he should head to town and see about purchasing a cow or two. The money he'd inherited from his grandfather would easily cover the cost and still leave him with plenty. He licked his lip anticipating fresh milk and cheese.

Benjamin would have to ask one of his neighbors if they knew how to make cheese. If they didn't, maybe someone in town would.

Should he invite Elsie along? No. He likely wouldn't make it back home until the morning. Benjamin threw a saddle on Milly.

Besides, maybe he could learn more about the outlaws while in town. He hadn't wanted to alarm Elsie when they were on the roof, but he'd seen two men in the distance. Something about them set him on edge. Maybe someone in town would have more information, and he'd know better what to watch out for.

He'd do whatever he could to keep Elsie safe, but he didn't want her to worry unnecessarily either. Likely the woman could handle the information, but he wanted to get clear details first so they both could be on guard. If he discovered the men had come farther west, he'd be sure to speak up and say something.

Lord, protect her while I'm gone. Keep John away while I'm in town.

The thunder of hooves told Elsie that Benjamin had left. She cracked the door open and peeked, stepping outside as soon as he disappeared from sight. She glanced at the dry, dusty field she and Benjamin had plowed. Elsie hated to plant the winter wheat until there was at least some kind of moisture. She scratched her head. What would Pa do?

Elsie sighed. She didn't feel like trying to figure that out right now. Instead, she peered in the direction of the Sawyers'. For the first time, she craved a woman's viewpoint who had a better understanding of men than she did, especially after her crazy dream that morning. Decision made, she whistled for Buster. She cinched the saddle in place. "How you doing, fella? Ready for some exercise?"

Buster tossed his head as she swung onto his back. She kneed him, and he responded. The hot wind whipped across her cheeks. The Sawyer claim soon came into view, and her chest tightened.

"Hello there." Mark waved. "Didn't think I'd see you for a while. What brings you out here?" He held Buster while she swung off the horse's back. "Beatrice is in the house resting. Feel free to go in. I'll take care of your horse."

"Thanks, Mark." Elsie patted Buster before knocking on the door of the soddy.

It swung open. Her friend's dark hair was messed up and sleep lines stretched across her face. Beatrice crushed Elsie in a hug. "I'm so glad you came. I've been craving woman talk. Earlier you were too busy working on the roof, and Mildred was tied up with the new baby." She chuckled. "I think Mark gets tired of my drivel, but sometimes a woman just needs to chat, you know."

Actually, the experience was new for Elsie. She paced in the small soddy, slapping her fist into her hand a few times, then came to a halt in front of her friend.

Beatrice's eyes narrowed. "What happened to get you all riled?"

How could she tell her that she'd been considering what her future would look if she hitched up with Benjamin? It wasn't like she could just blurt something like that out.

Beatrice patted Elsie's arm. "You want to talk about it?"

She shrugged. "I'm not exactly sure."

Her friend's eyes danced. She motioned toward the table. "I'm guessing it has something to do with Benjamin?"

Elsie slumped onto a chair beside her friend. "I woke up this morning after a troublesome dream."

"Really? What kind of dream?" Beatrice perked right up with the bit of information.

Elsie wished she'd kept it to herself. "I, uh, had a dream about a box supper."

Beatrice's eyes sparkled. "Did a fellow bid on your meal?"

Elsie shook her head. "Not exactly."

"Well?"

Elsie shifted on her seat. Might as well get it over with. "Pa set it up for the fellas to make the meal and for me to bid on one."

Beatrice giggled. "I've never seen that idea done before."

"That's not all. After I finished the meal, Pa made me marry one of them."

"Oh?" A smile spread across Beatrice's face. "Who brought a meal?"

Elsie ran her finger along her shirt collar and took another gulp of water. "There were two ... John and Benjamin." She didn't dare look at her friend.

"Who did you pick?"

She shrugged. "I don't know. I woke up before I found out."

"Who did you hope to win?"

Elsie snuck a peek at her friend and found her leaning toward her. *Benjamin.*

"The preacher, right?" Beatrice's smile widened. "You're in love with him. I can tell. I've seen the way you peek at him. He does the same to you too."

He did? She'd never noticed anything different in his reactions.

"I sensed tension between you and John earlier today." Beatrice rested a hand on her slightly bulging stomach.

Elsie shook her head. "That crazy man keeps pressing to marry me, and I ain't interested, but he won't take no for an answer."

"Most would say he's handsome."

Elsie hadn't detected anything special about the man, other than being a pest.

"Quick, give me your hand. The baby's kicking." Beatrice reached out and snagged Elsie's fingers, pulling them toward her midsection.

Elsie rested the palm of her hand against the small bump. Nothing happened, but then. *There.* A slight fluttering of butterfly wings flitted against her hand.

"Did you feel it?"

Elsie nodded and settled her hand against her own flat stomach. What would it feel like to have a child growing inside? She struggled to rein her thoughts in, blinking rapidly.

"I'm sorry, Elsie, I didn't mean to hurt you." Beatrice leaned forward. Moisture pooled in her dark brown eyes. "What's going on? Did you and Benjamin have another fight?"

"No, I just said something I shouldn't have."

Beatrice gripped Elsie's hand. "I'm here if you want someone to talk to."

Elsie shoved to her feet, and the chair toppled over. "Sorry," she mumbled as she righted it.

"You'll feel better if you confide in someone."

She wasn't so sure. "I told him he needs to let go of his past and see what's in front of him."

Beatrice gaped before a grin spread across her face. "What did he say?"

"Nothing. Of course, I didn't exactly give him a chance to either." Elsie blew a wisp of hair out of her eyes. "What am I going to do, Beatrice? I never counted on fighting a fella for a piece of property, then coming to care for him."

"He kissed you. That's gotta mean something."

The starch drained right out of Elsie's body. "H-how did you hear about it?"

"The preacher mentioned it to Mark and me after service when you went off with John. Well, he didn't mention it, exactly. I guessed it."

Elsie's heart pounded so loud she feared Beatrice would hear it.

Her friend stood and placed her hand on Elsie's arm. "I think he really cares for you, but he hasn't gotten the gumption to say anything about it yet. Give him time. He'll come around. You'll see."

"But come December, he'll be out of my life."

"Are you willing to stay and fight for him?"

Elsie's mind churned like the wind before a storm. For so long, she wanted him gone, but now? What if she stayed and fought for him only to find he didn't return her feelings? She longed to be held in his arms, in his tender embrace again, and have his mouth claim hers without being mistaken for his deceased fiancée.

"Give him a little longer to figure it all out. If he hasn't already, he'll soon notice what's been in front of him this whole time."

Did he really love her? Her face warmed at the thought.

Beatrice snapped her fingers in front of Elsie's face.

"Hmm? What were you saying?"

"Do you think you can come?"

Elsie dragged her attention back to the conversation. "Come? To what?"

Beatrice chuckled. "You're still thinking about the preacher, aren't you?"

"What were you saying?"

"Mark and I are planning to frame a barn in two weeks. I thought maybe Benjamin would help the men, and you and I could take care of the food. I don't suppose Mildred will be up to cooking much, with getting used to the little one's schedule."

"It don't make sense for me to help you with the food when you've handled it yourself this morning. Besides, I do better helping out the menfolk. It's what I'm used to."

Beatrice stood and arched her back. "I think the men can get the barn framed without your help this time. If you get all prettied up, maybe the preacher will think twice about what he's missing. What do you say?"

"I don't think so. Last time I wore a dress, I ripped the hem out, and then it got all filthy with helping the Larsons repair their soddy after the twister tore through."

"You can borrow one of mine. I have plenty."

"What's wrong with what I'm wearing?" Elsie inspected her faded shirt. Stains marred her britches. She'd never cared how she looked, especially while farming. The animals had never complained about her appearance. "Besides, Benjamin sees me like this every day. Wearing a dress won't make no difference."

"Will you indulge me, just this once?" Beatrice batted her eyes like she had a speck of dirt in them.

"Well ..."

"Oh, thank you. I knew I could convince you." Beatrice squealed and yanked Elsie into a tight hug. "You won't be sorry. I have the very dress to bring out the color of your beautiful eyes. The preacher will be sure to notice."

Elsie already regretted her decision, but after witnessing her friend's face, she knew she couldn't disappoint her.

Beatrice crossed the room and lifted the lid of a trunk. She withdrew a blue dress bedecked with ribbons and other things Elsie couldn't identify. The woman's eyes lit as she held it up in front of Elsie.

"It's perfect. Do you think you could make some kind of dessert for us?"

"Well, the one thing I can make is my ma's prune cake. Pa gave me the recipe. He says mine is better than hers. I have some canned ones I got from—" Elsie gulped and dropped the subject, hoping Beatrice hadn't noticed.

"Wonderful. I'll let Mildred and Henry know about the date. It'll be a worry off Mark's mind if we have a shelter for the animals with winter soon coming. We'll need to make sure the Larsons have a shelter figured out before long too."

Elsie opened her mouth to respond, but Beatrice continued to spout like a gush of water from a water pump.

"You'll tell Benjamin, won't you?" Beatrice wrapped the dress in paper and tied it with string. "I have a hat you could wear too."

"No thanks." Elsie could just imagine what kind of frippery bedecked it. "My Stetson will suit me fine."

"If you insist." Beatrice gave Elsie a quick squeeze. "You made my day. Thank you for coming by. I wanted to have a chance to chat with you longer, but Mark won't let me travel alone right now, not with the rumor of outlaws around Enid." She shivered. "I pray they never show up at our doorstop."

"Outlaws? What outlaws?"

"Didn't Benjamin tell you? The men have been abuzz with the news. At first, Mark wouldn't tell me, but I knew something was bothering him. He finally shared in case he's ever away, and I'm here by myself. I'm sure the preacher didn't want to worry you. I had to practically drag it out of Mark. Are you sure Benjamin didn't hint about it?"

Elsie shook her head. "I would've remembered it if he had. What have the outlaws done?"

Beatrice shrugged. "Mark didn't share the particulars with me. You'll be careful when you go back home, won't you? It'll be dark before long. Maybe Mark should ride with you."

"Nonsense. It's best if he stays here. Besides, I'll make it home before twilight. It's not like an outlaw will stroll around in broad daylight."

"I suppose you're right. You can't be too careful, though. You be on the lookout, just in case."

"I will. I guess I'd better head out."

Beatrice hugged her tight and released her. "Will I see you at church again?"

Elsie shrugged and tugged open the door.

"Think about it, won't you? I realize Benjamin botched things at the last service, and he felt horrible about it. I've never seen him so discouraged as when you rode off with John."

What exactly had Benjamin shared with them? Elsie didn't have the gumption to ask. She might not like the answer. "Bye."

Outside, she shoved the dress into her saddlebag, the paper crinkling as she buckled it closed.

Beatrice waved as Elsie swung up onto her horse. "Don't forget to say something to Benjamin."

Elsie returned the gesture. As she left, she couldn't resist a quick glance around to make sure nobody followed her. Her erratic heartbeat slowed.

By the time she drew close to home, dusk draped the area. An unsettledness raced up her backbone. Elsie dared a peek over her shoulder. A coyote howled in the distance. Icy tendrils slithered up her spine. She urged Buster to a faster pace. Elsie couldn't shake the sensation of being watched and had no desire to linger long enough to find out by what or whom.

CHAPTER TWENTY-THREE

Never listen to part of a conversation that doesn't involve you. Such behavior is beneath a lady of means. To take part in this activity leads to abasement and degradation due to misguided assumptions.
Mrs. Wigglesworth's Essential Guide to Proper Etiquette and Manners of Refined Society

"Do you smell that?" Elsie's nose wrinkled as a strong scent of something burning carried its way on a burst of wind from the east. She shielded her eyes from the sun and peered in that direction. Smoke billowed across the field where they were working and rolled across the plains. Her heart lurched. She unhitched Buster from the sod splitter, her fingers fumbling with the harness.

Benjamin sniffed the air, a frown marring his face. "How far away do you think it is?"

"Don't know. We gotta get over there lickety-split. If it's a brushfire, they can easily catch you unawares. Go hitch Milly to the wagon, and bring it here. We'll need to try and divert it from coming this direction."

He took off at a sprint.

Elsie threw the leather rigging over her shoulder and patted Buster. "You stay safe, fella. Don't wander too far."

The horse tossed his head, his eyes wide, nostrils flaring before he took off. Elsie watched him for a second before running toward her soddy. She threw open the door and dumped the harness on the floor. Digging through her saddlebags, she whipped out two of Pa's handkerchiefs, thrusting them into her pants pocket. Elsie secured the door, snatched up a bucket, running toward the creek.

Dipping the bucket into the cool depths, the water sloshed as she drew it up. Her gaze swung back toward the smoke as she hurried toward Benjamin.

"Whoa." He drew the wagon to a halt beside her. "Where's Buster?"

"I let him go. He's too high-strung to get anywhere near a fire." She lifted the bucket into the bed of the wagon. "Where's your bucket? We need to fill every pot we have. Fetch whatever feed sacks you can spare to beat the flames."

"I'll get them." Benjamin vaulted from the high seat and landed with grace. He ran toward the barn.

Elsie jogged back to her place, searching for anything that could hold water. She snagged up a cooking pot and bowl, throwing a towel across her arm in case it was needed.

Benjamin met her at the creek. A pile of various cookware lay in a jumbled mess. "Here, fill these. I'll let the cows out."

Within minutes, Elsie filled the containers and secured them in the wagon. She jumped onto the seat and released the brake. The conveyance hitched forward. She glanced back as the water sloshed onto the floor. "Easy, Milly."

Elsie urged the mare to move slowly until they reached the plow. She dropped to the ground.

Benjamin raced to her. "What're you doing?"

"If it's a brushfire, we'll need the sod splitter."

"What for?" He helped her lift the equipment into the wagon.

She jumped into the back as together they shifted it all the way into the bed. Elsie straddled the wagon seat then settled onto it.

"We'll use the splitter to plow furrows. Hope we have time to make them wide enough so fire won't jump the line and come this way." Elsie squeezed his arm as he settled beside her. "Hurry, but be careful of the water. We'll need every drop of it."

Benjamin joined her, taking the reins. Milly plodded forward.

They didn't speak as Benjamin urged the horse toward the fire. As they got closer, flames sparked and popped. Sure enough—

the dry grass burned, the fire rushing across the plains burning everything in its path. Henry and the Sawyers were already in the middle of a patch of buffalo grass, beating flames.

Benjamin stopped the wagon about two hundred yards away. They vaulted from it. He secured his horse to a scraggly bush. Elsie hefted the plow towards her.

John rode up. "Here, let me help you with that, Elsie." He dismounted and helped lift the plow to the ground. Benjamin unhitched Milly from the wagon and backed her to the plow. John secured the harness.

Elsie coughed as the smoke blew in their direction. She ripped the handkerchiefs out of her pocket and plunged them into the bucket. "Here." She handed one to Benjamin. "Tie it around your face." She secured hers, and he did likewise.

"I'll start the plowing." Benjamin untied Milly.

Elsie and John dipped the feed sacks in water and ran toward the fire.

Her heart quickened. *Please keep Benjamin safe, Lord. Keep all of us safe.*

Benjamin's gut twisted as he and his neighbors battled the roaring dragon. They weren't making any headway. *Please, Father, don't let anything happen to Elsie. Keep us from harm.* He dipped his handkerchief in the water again and secured it around his face. His gaze swung toward Elsie. The flames nipped near her like an angry dog.

He picked up the reins and snapped them across Milly's back. The mare strained against the unyielding soil.

Henry plowed at an angle from him. Mark, Beatrice, and John worked alongside Elsie, beating the hungry fire, intent on devouring everything in its path.

A woman screamed.

Elsie?

He raced toward the women.

Mark blocked his vision as he drew closer.

There on the ground.

Flames licked at Beatrice's skirt. Mark and Elsie slapped at the fire, smothering the flames. Tears streaked Beatrice's face.

"Are you hurt?" Once the flames were out, Mark gathered his wife in his arms.

Her chin wobbled. "I-I don't think so."

"What about you, Elsie? Mark?" Benjamin's heart thundered in his chest. "How're your hands?"

Mark studied his gloves. "These won't be useful anymore, but the skin isn't even singed."

Elsie's hands trembled as she stared at her red skin. "I'll deal with them later. We gotta hurry. I think we're making some headway."

Benjamin caught a glimpse of the blisters marring Elsie's hands. He started to say something, but she rushed away and beat at the burning grasses with another wet feed sack.

"You stay back and watch for sparks reigniting," Mark said as he stroked Beatrice's face. "I want you and the baby safe."

Beatrice nodded. "You best get back to it."

Mark pecked his wife on the cheek before he returned to the blaze.

John had picked up the abandoned plow, so Benjamin dipped his sack in water and headed toward the flames, working beside Mark and Elsie. If they didn't get the fire under control soon, he'd be in danger of losing his homestead. Lord willing, the animals had moved to safety.

Time stood still as he and his neighbors battled together.

John and Henry continued to widen the furrow.

The rest of them beat at the brushfire. They no sooner soaked a feed sack than it needed wetting again. Benjamin lost track of the countless times he repeated the process.

Weariness tugged at his frame.

His eyes watered and burned each time the smoke blew in his face.

The charred ground crackled as he walked across it to wet his handkerchief. Again.

They slowly made progress. Hours later, blackened soil covered a wide patch.

"I think it's working." Mark rubbed his hand across his forehead, leaving a black smudge.

Benjamin guzzled a pitcher of water. He filled it again and handed it to Mark.

His friend accepted it with a shaky hand. "Will you try and rebuild if the fire comes your way?"

Benjamin glanced toward his place. "Depends on how the judge rules ..." *and if I have any chance with Elsie.*

Elsie's sore, singed fingers lost their grip on the feed sack. Did Benjamin really think they could lose their home? What did it have to do with how the judge ruled? Would he really leave her? Her thoughts continued to whirl as she plunged the sack into the bucket of dirty water that sat behind Mark and Benjamin.

Henry and John jogged toward them.

"I think we've done all we can do with the plows." Henry wiped his face with a handkerchief. "Now we pray the fire doesn't jump the furrows."

John gulped some clean water. "I think we have it boxed in. Hopefully, it will burn itself out."

Elsie turned and studied the flames. They'd died down but still dipped and rose, chewing up the vegetation in their path.

Benjamin's gaze pierced her. "How're those hands doing?"

"What hands? Did you injure yourself?" John reached for her wrist.

She whipped away from him and headed toward a patch of burning buffalo grass with her wet feed bag.

Elsie was unsure how much time had passed before she and her neighbors sank to the charred ground. Beatrice groaned as she sat. "Thank God, it's over."

Elsie didn't have the energy to respond.

"Where's Mildred and baby James?" Beatrice shifted the ragged edge of the hem of her skirt.

"Back home. Didn't want either of them breathing in this smoke." Henry hacked. "Little James couldn't handle it, and Mildred's still recovering from childbirth. I left her a horse in case the brushfire switched directions and headed her way. Told her to leave as soon as she caught sight of it."

"I wanted Beatrice to stay home too." Mark settled beside his wife.

"We're a team. We stick together. No matter what. I'd be worried sick if I stayed home and didn't know what was happening to you." Beatrice grasped her husband's hand.

"Speaking of, I should head out and check on my family. Don't want Mildred anxious about me any longer than need be." Henry shifted his hat. "I'll load up my plow, and see you all later."

"I'll help you." John stood and stretched.

They all mumbled a farewell to the man.

Silence settled over the weary group as they watched Henry's wagon trail through the scorched path.

"What do you think started it?" John asked.

"No telling, I suppose," Mark said.

Beatrice coughed. "You think it was a leftover fire from the Sooners?"

"I doubt it," Mark replied. "That was too long ago. It would've died out weeks ago."

Benjamin dropped beside Elsie. "Doesn't matter. We got it out, praise the Good Lord."

"Pa and I helped fight a grass fire once. They're like ferocious beasts, eating everything in their path." Elsie's voice rasped as she studied the scorched earth. “I thought we were going to lose everything today. Don’t know what I would’ve done if that happened.”

“We would all have pitched in and done whatever we could to help you and Benjamin.” Beatrice’s arm snaked around Elsie’s waist. “It’s what neighbors do.”

Benjamin couldn’t keep his eyes off Elsie.

Elsie’s head came up as she studied each of her neighbors, her gaze settling on his.

Did she know how much they all cared for her?

“I told you, Elsie, I’m willing to make you my wife,” John said. “If something happened to your place, you’d always have a home with me.”

Why hadn’t *he* thought to say something like that?

“Oh, Elsie, your hands.” Beatrice gasped.

“It’s nothing. Really.” Elsie started to shift her hands away, but Benjamin saw her wince before she schooled her features.

“We best get you home so we can take care of that.” Benjamin stood and helped Elsie to her feet. *Home.* He liked the sound of that.

CHAPTER TWENTY-FOUR

Dress consistently with your station. Gloves are to be worn when paying a call on someone. A young woman should always aim to look as put together as possible.
Mrs. Wigglesworth's Essential Guide to Proper Etiquette and Manners of Refined Society

Elsie inhaled the sweet scent of prune cake, refraining from opening the cookstove door to check on it. Again. Aunt Kate had told Elsie patience was a virtue, but she hadn't told her how to achieve it.

Needing a distraction, Elsie fingered Beatrice's dress splayed across her bed. A fluttering like moths around a light took up residence in her chest. In a short while, she'd have to don it or disappoint her friend. She should've never agreed to the woman's plan. Elsie didn't need a dress to attract Benjamin. The past few days had proved it.

Elsie smiled as she thought back over the last week and a half. He hadn't allowed her to do much of the hard labor since the fire. He'd babied her, warning her to take care of her healing hands. Still, together they had worked to clear land, plant crops, and take care of the two cows. Thankfully, the pair hadn't wandered far after the fire, and neither had Buster. *All we need are chickens and maybe a pig to make it a real farm.*

We. Since when had she started to think about the farm as we? Elsie sighed.

She didn't regret Benjamin's friendship and no longer thought of him as an enemy, but come December, she'd have a hard time saying goodbye. Was that what he had thought when he mentioned it to Mark while they fought the brushfire?

"Enough! Stop acting like a lovesick heifer. Don't go and ruin a perfectly good friendship by falling for him. Things will only end in heartbreak." If only she could convince her heart with those words.

She huffed and turned back toward the stove. Her nose wrinkled at the tangy, burnt scent. "Oh, no." Elsie snagged a towel and yanked the door open. "Thank goodness." The cake had browned to perfection. After the dessert cooled for a few minutes, she moved it to a plate and added the gooey topping.

Then, before she could change her mind, Elsie slipped the beautiful dress over her head. She settled it into place, securing the long line of buttons. The squared neckline exposed her collarbone. Her hand rested there. Would Benjamin think the dress too low? Elsie snorted. All this feminine stuff made her mind go to mush. Never before had she cared so much about her appearance.

She dragged a brush through her tangled hair, trying to bring some semblance of order to it. Her fingers shook as she braided and fastened it with pins. She twirled about her soddy like a moonstruck schoolgirl. She wished she owned a mirror to see her reflection.

A thump hit the door, and her heart did a funny hiccup. She placed a hand over her chest again, willing the erratic beating to slow.

Wiping her hands on the side of the dress, Elsie flung the door open.

Benjamin handed her a bouquet of wildflowers. She buried her nose in the fragrant blossoms. "Thank you." She crossed the room, poured water into a mug, arranging them in it. When she spun around, Benjamin stood in the doorway, staring at her.

"Do I look that bad?" Elsie glanced down at her worn cowboy boots.

"On the contrary. You're as beautiful as an exquisite flower."

Her pulse skittered as she studied him. Elsie's tongue darted across her lips, and his stare settled there. Her lips quivered in anticipation.

He cleared his throat. "I have the wagon outside since you're bringing the cake along. Didn't figure you wanted to try and balance it on your lap while riding Buster."

"Thank you. That's very thoughtful." Elsie jammed her Stetson onto her head. "I'm ready. Do you think I should bring my hammer along in case you fellas need an extra hand?"

"Leave it behind. You won't want to stain your dress. Besides, I'm sure Beatrice will be grateful for your help." Benjamin offered his arm.

"Actually, the dress is Beatrice's." Elsie pinched a piece of fabric between two fingers. "I'm not exactly sure why she wanted me to wear it. It's a real nuisance."

"I'm glad you agreed to it. You should wear dresses more often." A smile crinkled the skin at the corner of his eyes. "Are you ready?"

"I need to grab the cake." Elsie turned toward the table.

Benjamin brushed past her and picked up the dessert.

"Allow me." He looped her arm through his and balanced the cake with the other.

Elsie closed the door behind them.

She squinted in the bright light, tipping her hat forward to shade her eyes from the sun.

Benjamin set the cake on the wagon seat then placed his hands on her waist. He swooped her onto the high bench in one fluid motion.

Her pulse raced when his hands lingered at her waist.

Elsie shifted the cake to her lap as Benjamin jumped onto the seat. She peeked at him, her bright eyes sparkling. He longed to touch her cheeks to see if they were as soft as they appeared. He glanced away and released the brake. "Get along, Milly."

The scent of honeysuckles tickled his nostrils. He'd come to love the smell that emanated from Elsie. He leaned a little closer and lightly breathed in, hoping she wouldn't notice.

She peered at the surrounding fields. "Do you think we'll get rain anytime soon? I'm afraid we, I mean I—" She swallowed. "I won't get any winter wheat if we don't get some moisture soon."

He'd noticed her slip. He'd started thinking of *we* when it came to their claim too. Maybe it was a sign that she'd consider his suit if he ever got up the nerve to do something about it.

She swung her gaze back toward him. "Benjamin?" Her brow wrinkled.

"What? Sorry, I'm afraid you caught me woolgathering. I pray we'll get some rain before long. Maybe we should start carting buckets of water to the fields." Benjamin swiveled his gaze to straight ahead, not trusting himself to stare into her dark blue eyes again.

"Great idea." She chuckled. "I'll make a farmer out of you yet."

Silence fell between them. Elsie had grown better at sharing things with him of late, but today she seemed reserved for some reason. He couldn't pinpoint what had caused it.

"Do you think Mildred and the baby will be there? I imagine little James has grown these past two weeks." Elsie shifted her hat. "D-did you and Mary ever talk about children?"

He frowned and darted a glance at her. His conscience pricked. Benjamin never had told Elsie that when he kissed her, he hadn't been comparing her to Mary, but merely feeling guilty for enjoying it. How did one bring something like that into everyday conversation?

"We hadn't discussed children much. Mary's health wavered from time to time, and I questioned whether she'd be physically up to the task of carrying a child."

"I guess she didn't come from sturdy stock like me." Elsie cleared her throat. "I mean, my sisters, they all have young ones of their own. Even Bitty, despite being small like Ma." Elsie twisted her hands in her lap.

Benjamin held back a smile. She'd come a long way in being able to talk to him about almost anything. He'd like to tease her, but he kept his thoughts to himself. Instead, he snuck another peek as she struggled to compose herself. "Have *you* ever thought of having children?"

She blushed a deeper shade of red, making the freckles on her nose stick out a little more.

This time he couldn't help smiling.

"I ain't never thought of children much since I never had a fella court me." She dipped her head.

"Surely you had some young man who fell prey to your charms."

She snorted. "Nope. A man would only agree to marrying me if Pa done like he did in my dream." Elsie clamped a hand over her mouth.

"Dream? What dream?"

She shook her head. "N-never mind. Let's just say nobody is clamoring at my door to get married."

"What about John?"

"He's made himself scarce as of late, and you haven't heard me complaining."

Pleasure rippled through Benjamin. "Would you ever consider marriage if the right man came along?"

Her gaze snapped toward his, and her eyes narrowed. "I won't marry because folks think I need a man to take care of me. I've done plenty good taking care of myself."

He held up a hand. "That's not what I meant."

She scowled. "If I ever did get hitched, I'd want a man willing to have me work alongside of him on the farm, instead of thinking cooking and cleaning is the only work a woman is capable of."

"What would it take for you to marry?"

Elsie took a deep breath and blew it out slowly. "I guess it would take finding a man who loved me for me, with no desire to make me into something or someone else. A fella willing to go through the good and bad times together."

"Would faith play into your decision?"

She shrugged. "I suppose so, even though God and I aren't exactly on speaking terms yet. Having a husband with a faith wouldn't hurt none. He'd be less likely to be gambling or drinking away our earnings. I wouldn't want a man who did those things." She peered at him. "Why all the questions?"

"Just passing the time." He clawed at his suddenly too-tight shirt collar. "Would you consider John?" His heart stampeded as he waited for her response.

"No, there ain't no spark between me and John, no matter how much he wants there to be one. Besides, he's got his own property and ideas for improvements. I think I'd be too much for him to handle."

Benjamin bit back the laughter that longed to be let free. He sat up taller, thrusting his chest out a smidgen. She couldn't have stated more clearly that she might consider him whenever he got around to asking her. He wanted to question her more, but the Sawyer place came into view.

"Looks like most the folks are here already." Elsie waved. "I see Mildred and the baby. I can't wait to hold the little one again. It's been a long time since I've seen my nieces and nephews. Of course, none of them are babies anymore. Some are just a little bit younger than me."

Benjamin pulled the wagon under a cedar tree and set the brake. He vaulted from the seat and rounded the conveyance to assist Elsie, but she'd already jumped to the ground and run toward the new mother. He scooped up the cake and followed.

A minute later, he spotted Elsie holding the tiny infant, her face lit up like a child on Christmas morning. He couldn't help but imagine how she'd look holding a child of her own.

Benjamin cleared his throat and forced himself to look anywhere other than at Elsie.

"Thank you, Benjamin." Beatrice took the cake from his hands. "I see Elsie forgot it." She chuckled. "Never witnessed anyone make a beeline toward a baby like she did. She's a natural with him, don't you think?"

He nodded. "I better get to work."

Beatrice's quiet laughter trailed after him.

Elsie's gaze followed Benjamin as he headed toward the menfolk. She snuggled the babe closer, enjoying the sweet smell of his skin. The infant was a welcome distraction from her wandering thoughts. "He's such a doll baby."

"He's not such a doll in the wee hours when he has a dirty diaper or he's starving and can't wait for me to get him settled." Mildred yawned, covering her mouth with a hand. "James is a blessing, though. Thank you again for helping me, Elsie. I couldn't have done it without you."

"Fiddlesticks. You're the one who told me what to do. I'm glad I could help."

"You look ravishing today, Elsie." Beatrice waggled her eyebrows. "Did anyone in particular notice?"

Elsie stroked the baby's fine, silky hair, ignoring her best friend.

"What're you saying?" Mildred glanced around. "Whose attention is she trying to snag?"

"Hello, ladies." John lifted his hat. "I came for a glass of water."

"Certainly." Beatrice dipped water from a bucket into a mug. "You all must be hot and thirsty after working for a couple hours already."

"Elsie, dear, you look as fresh as dew on the mountains on a hot summer morning. Such a vision." He touched the side of her face. "If you weren't holding the baby, I'd sneak a kiss."

She turned away and snuggled James closer.

Mildred stiffened much like a mother hen, ready to gather her young. "You best keep your distance, Mr. Clark. It isn't proper to make advances like that unless you have plans to marry the woman." Her tone filled with warning.

John cozied up closer to Elsie and winked. "The proposal's already been made, I'm just waiting for her to see what a fine idea it is and agree. She'll give in one of these days."

He reached toward her again, but Elsie shifted away from his grasp.

John puffed out a breath. "I see I've offended you."

"That's right, you've offended her." Mildred planted her hands on her hips and glared at John. "You best leave Elsie alone, or you'll have me to contend with."

"Me too," Beatrice chimed in.

"Forgive me, my dear." He swept his hat back onto his head and sauntered away.

Elsie didn't know what to say. She'd never had friends who defended her before. She could get used to their concern.

Baby James let out a squawk, and she handed him to his mother.

Mildred shifted the baby to her shoulder and patted his tiny back. "That man isn't good enough for the likes of you. I know you've said before that you don't plan to marry, but what're you going to do if you don't get awarded the claim? You'll need a man to care for you. Lord knows I'd be lost without my Henry caring for us. You can't make it out here on your own. Maybe you should consider marrying the preacher. We all can see he cares for you."

Elsie hoped the ground would open and swallow her alive, yet at the same time pleasure coursed through her.

Mildred chuckled as the infant rooted against her neck. "Beatrice, do you mind if I use your soddy? I think James here is hungry."

"Go ahead. The two of us will start the fire for the noon meal." Beatrice looped her arm through Elsie's.

Beatrice guided Elsie to a charred spot in the grass, lighting the wood that had already been teepeed in preparation for a fire. The flames rose and dipped.

"What Mildred said is true, Elsie. We all care for you," Beatrice said. "Don't let John get to you. Maybe the preacher will notice you as more than a farmer if you keep wearing a dress."

She frowned. "I don't know about that. Sure got John all riled up. That man just won't take no for an answer, no matter how many times I've told him."

"Don't get discouraged." Beatrice hung a pot of water over the flames. "Did the preacher say anything when he saw you in the dress?"

Elsie nodded.

"I knew it." Beatrice's eyes twinkled. "What happened?"

Elsie repeated their conversation from earlier. "What am I going to do, Beatrice? He sounded interested in having a wife and children, but how do I get him interested in pursuing *me*?"

CHAPTER TWENTY-FIVE

Be open to having others assist you when needed, and don't be afraid to lend a helping hand whenever the opportunity arises. Blessed are those who put others above themselves.
Mrs. Wigglesworth's Essential Guide to Proper Etiquette and Manners of Refined Society

"What are you looking at, Benjamin?"

At John's question, Benjamin turned back to the task, swinging the hammer hard, narrowly missing his thumb. He concentrated on hitting nail after nail into the side of the barn.

Beside him, muscles bulged under John's cotton shirt as he positioned a nail and drove it in with one mighty swing. The man had a knack for getting under Benjamin's skin. John appeared to have a prowess with every task he performed, but Elsie said she wasn't interested in him. Benjamin stood a little taller and bit back a grin.

The sun baked them as the barn took shape.

"I've brought water if anyone's thirsty." Elsie's voice interrupted their work.

John dropped the board he held, and it landed on Benjamin's foot. "Oh, sorry, Preacher. I didn't see you standing there."

Elsie smiled as Benjamin limped towards her. He allowed the other men to line up before him. Maybe he'd manage a few private words with her.

"You're as sweet and refreshing as this water, Elsie." John swept his hat from his brow and took a long drink, his gaze lingering on her.

Her fingers tightened on the bucket handle, but she didn't say anything.

John reached over and tucked a piece of hair behind Elsie's ear. She took a step backward.

Benjamin's fingers curled at his side.

"I don't think the lady's interested," Henry said. "You best keep your hands to yourself, John." He crowded closer to the man.

John scowled. "You aren't her keeper. Besides, you don't hear her complaining. She recognizes a strong, strapping man when she sees one, and she knows it takes a man like that to work a claim. If she's as smart as I think she is, she'll make the right choice." He turned and glared at Benjamin before he stalked away.

Henry awkwardly patted Elsie's shoulder. "Don't you worry none about him. We'll take care of you."

"That's right," Mark said. "He's all bluster and a braggart. Nobody expects you to choose the man just 'cause he keeps pressing you to marry him."

Benjamin glanced around at the neighbors who'd become his close friends, and he couldn't be prouder of them. Surely after the fire, Elsie could see that these folks would be with her no matter what came her way. "We all care for you, Elsie."

Her blue eyes met his. "Thank you." Her gaze then swung to encompass each of them. "I don't know what to say."

Benjamin smiled. It was one of the first times he'd seen her faced with an uncomfortable situation she hadn't run from. This Elsie was so different than the one he'd met months prior. A peace settled over him. He couldn't help but think what his life would be like with her as a daily part of it.

Elsie's heart throbbed with the outpouring of concern from her neighbors. Pa would've loved this place. These people. She snuck a peek at Benjamin. What would Pa have thought of the preacher?

Benjamin dipped the ladle into the bucket and brought the utensil to his mouth. He took a long guzzle then wiped the moisture droplets with the back of his sleeve. She couldn't help staring at his full lips. Would he ever kiss her without thinking of another woman?

He took another sip and then offered the dipper to her. "You thirsty?"

Only for you to take notice of me.

"Elsie?"

Good heavens. How could she speak to him after those thoughts? What had he asked again? *Water.* Something to do with water. She nodded, hoping her response made sense.

Her fingers grazed Benjamin's as she gripped the ladle, nearly losing her grasp. She fumbled with the utensil before she managed to bring it to her mouth. Only a swallow remained, which was fine with her. Any more and she would've choked on it.

Heat shot through her body as she realized her mouth touched the dipper in the same place Benjamin's had.

She gave herself a mental shake. "You best get back to work with the rest of the fellas." She didn't wait for his response, but turned and scurried back to the safety of the soddy.

The folds of fabric twisted around her ankles as she ran. With her luck, she'd fall and stain Beatrice's dress. Aunt Kate had said Elsie and grace weren't acquainted, but she knew clumsiness far too well.

Elsie threw the soddy door open and stepped inside.

"What's the hurry?" Mildred stared at her. "Was John pestering you again?"

Elsie shook her head. Her heart pounded as she closed the door behind her, half afraid Benjamin had followed her and partially wishing he had.

A soft mewling came from the bed in the corner. Setting the bucket on the table, Elsie wandered over and scooped up the squirming James.

"I can't believe he's hungry again. I fed him not more than an hour ago. If he's like most men, he's hungry all the time." Mildred and Beatrice shared a laugh while Elsie planted a kiss on the baby's forehead.

"Don't you listen to them." Elsie snuggled her nose against the baby's cheek. Little James rewarded her with a smile. She half listened as the two women chattered about quilt patterns.

"Elsie, what do you think?" Mildred asked.

Elsie rocked the baby when he started to wiggle. "I'm afraid I never learned to be handy with a needle. I can sew a button on or mend a hole in a shirt or pants, but that's the extent of my sewing abilities."

Mildred halted in the midst of peeling an apple. "You have such a beautiful quilt on your bed, though. I saw it the day you helped with James' delivery. I've never seen such a lovely pattern before. You didn't make it?"

"My ma did. Pa told me that she wanted it to go to her youngest daughter and to have it passed down through the generations—always to the youngest daughter. That way, she'd leave a legacy of sorts." Elsie shifted James to her shoulder and patted his back. "It's one of my most prized possessions."

"What a beautiful story." Beatrice wiped her hands on a cloth. "I guess you never got a chance to learn to sew from your ma. Didn't you say she died giving birth to you?"

Elsie nodded. "Aunt Kate didn't have patience with me when it came to domestic tasks."

"What a shame." Mildred started peeling apples again. "Ma always said every woman needs to learn the finer things in life. Cooking, cleaning, quilting, sewing, pickling … and the ways to snare a man."

Elsie gulped, almost wishing she hadn't come back to the house.

"Beatrice and I've been trying to figure out a way you can catch the preacher's eye." A smile spread across Mildred's wide face. "We have it all planned out."

"I think I'd better go check on the stew." Elsie handed James off to Beatrice before scurrying outside. Her body had a mind of its own as her head swung in Benjamin's direction.

He glanced up at her.

She high-tailed it toward the cooking pot.

With her back to the men, Elsie stirred the soup. Some of it boiled up and spat onto her hand. Elsie bit her lip to keep from crying. The "woman talk" and the kindness from these folks were making her soft. She best remember to stay strong. Next time, she wouldn't be caught wearing a dress and thinking about female drivel. It did odd things to her innards.

Benjamin arched his back, trying to loosen the taut muscles. He flexed his arms, tightening and unfurling his fingers. His body welcomed the noon daybreak. The scent of the stew had been tickling his nostrils for a while.

John and Henry scampered over to where the women had set out the food. Benjamin's steps slowed as Mark caught up to him.

His friend clapped him on the back. "You need to tell her the way you feel."

Benjamin stopped and turned toward Mark. "Is it that obvious? Do you think she's noticed? I've been biding my time until she's more open to the idea of marriage."

Mark chuckled. "I know a woman can be blind and not always see what's in front of her nose, but you best figure it out soon 'cause if you don't, John's going to keep pressing until he wears her down, and she eventually gives in to his proposal."

"But she can't stand him."

Mark shook his head. "She wouldn't be the first gal to crush under pressure, no matter how strong she is. My guess is her boasting about not needing a man and how she can do things on her own is just a bluff. You ask me, she's like any other gal—she wants a good man who'll love her and treat her special. I think *you* are the man she needs and desires, even if she hasn't said anything to you."

Was Elsie really waiting for him to make a move? Benjamin cleared his throat and ran a hand across his jaw. *Guide me, Lord.*

"Come on, Preacher," Henry called. "We're waiting on you to say the blessing."

He scurried over and mumbled a prayer, not exactly sure what he said as his thoughts were elsewhere. The men settled down to the makeshift table. Despite his earlier hunger, the food was tasteless as he shoveled in each bite. Conversation flowed around him, but he didn't join in.

Elsie leaned around him and refilled his glass. "Do you need me to get you another bowlful?"

John rubbed his belly. "Elsie, this is the best prune cake I've ever tasted. Any man would consider himself blessed to be married to such a fine cook."

Benjamin stabbed a piece of chicken as if it were alive and needed to be killed.

"Thank you." Elsie moved down the line, refilling glasses.

Beatrice shielded her eyes as she looked at the barn. "Looks like you fellas have made great progress. I can't begin to tell you how grateful we are for your help."

Mark stood and put an arm around his wife's shoulders. "Thank the Lord we'll be starting the roof after we finish here. This is what a church family does for one another. Help in the time of need."

Elsie's chin came up, but she didn't respond.

"Yep, takes some strong men to get the job accomplished." John flexed his arms. "Well, at least some of us are strong." He shifted his attention toward Benjamin.

Benjamin refused to respond to the obvious insult.

"Hold up there." Mark frowned. "There's no call for insulting our preacher. He's pulled his weight, just like everyone else."

"That's right," Henry said. "I think it's time you learned how to work as a team and think about someone other than yourself,

John. Why don't we have a little contest this afternoon?" He forked a piece of cake into his mouth and spoke around it. "You single men against me and Mark to see who gets their side of the roof finished first."

Benjamin caught Elsie staring at him, her eyes wide. Would she root for him? He surged to his feet. "Let's do it."

Elsie peered at the men as the roof took shape.

"Which side do you think will win?" Beatrice stepped beside her.

Elsie shrugged. "What do you think?"

A laugh bubbled out of her friend. "I have to vote for Mark and Henry, but the other team might do better since John has building experience. I saw him drive in a nail earlier. He did it in one fell swoop. That has to give his team an advantage."

Mildred yawned. "Beatrice, do you mind if I feed James again and lay down for a short nap? Land's sake. I never knew having a young one would wear me so. If I'm this tired when he's a little scrap of a thing, what am I gonna do when's he running around everywhere?"

Beatrice chuckled. "Ma used to say it was the being up through the night feedings that did a woman in. I'm sure you'll get your strength back once he's not getting you up so much in the wee hours."

Mildred yawned again. "I suppose you're right. Funny, I remember Ma giving birth to most of my siblings, but I don't recall how she kept up with all of us." She waved and headed inside.

"I guess that'll be me in a few months." Beatrice's eyes twinkled. "I find I tire out quicker these days too. Right about now, a nap sounds pretty good. Maybe I'll grab a blanket before Mildred settles down and spread it under the tree over there."

As her friends napped, Elsie cleaned up the midday meal, prepared for the next, and watched the men as they worked. She was rooting for Benjamin's team, but her feelings had nothing to do with John.

Once she set up everything to her standards, Elsie strolled away from the house, past the barn construction, and kept on walking for some time. Insects whirled and flew out from the grass as she disturbed their hiding places. A small grove of trees stood in the distance. Movement snagged her attention. Her pulse jumped. A man stepped out and gawked at her before turning his back and disappearing.

A chill rippled up Elsie's arms. The man had been too far away to recognize any of his features, but Beatrice's words about outlaws whispered in her mind, as well as the conversation she'd shared with Benjamin. Elsie shuddered. Maybe lingering here wasn't such a great idea. She hiked her skirt and ran toward the Sawyer homestead.

The barn loomed in her vision a few minutes later. She could see figures on the roof. Elsie turned and scanned the hills behind her, but the man wasn't to be seen. She blew out a relieved breath. Despite not seeing anything, she had the distinct feeling someone still watched her.

CHAPTER TWENTY-SIX

Allow a gentleman to lead in the relationship. Never should a lady drive a conveyance when a man is present. Don't make known your affections toward a man until he first shares his desires.
Mrs. Wigglesworth's Essential Guide to Proper Etiquette and Manners of Refined Society

Sweat poured from Benjamin's body as he struggled to keep pace with the other men. He lifted another board into place and hammered in the nails. He glanced over to check the progress of the married men. So far, the teams were tied. A sliver bit through his glove and into the palm of his hand as he settled the next board in place. He'd lost count of the number of times it'd happened.

Benjamin clambered down the ladder and picked up another stack of boards. As he reached the ladder, Elsie ran into view as if hounds were chasing her. He glanced behind her but didn't spot anything at first. *There.* Movement off to the left. He blinked, and it disappeared. Perhaps the heat was playing tricks with his mind.

Elsie slowed and threw another glance over her shoulder. Her face relaxed.

Assured she wasn't injured, he gripped the load tighter and scampered up the ladder. Back on the roof, he set the stack down and started working again. He refused to be the reason his team lost. John didn't need another reason to think ill of him.

He and John made steady progress as the afternoon wore on. Benjamin hated to think of the sore muscles he'd feel the next few days, but to have the building finished for the Sawyers was well worth any aches and pains.

As he positioned another board, he glanced over his shoulder, trying to catch a glimpse of Elsie. A whoosh of air blew past, followed by a resounding crack to the side of his head. His arms flew wide. Benjamin staggered and fell.

A scream ripped through the air.

The ground flew towards him. Before he could think of anything, he came to a bone-crunching halt. Pain shot through his head before everything went black.

"No!" *Dear God, be with him. Please don't take him away from me.*

Elsie's heart vaulted like a frenzied stallion as she ran to Benjamin's still form. "B-Benjamin?" The men sped down the ladder and huddled around her.

"I didn't notice him there," John said with a strained voice.

"Is he d-dead?" Beatrice scurried over and grasped Mark's hand.

Elsie lifted Benjamin's wrist and felt a pulse. *Thank God.* She shook her head. "No, but why isn't he waking?" She touched his face. "Benjamin?" Her throat tightened.

He stirred. His eyes flickered open.

"How're you feeling?" Mark leaned closer.

Benjamin squinted and focused on Elsie. His hand shook when he reached out to touch the side of her face. "My head hurts."

"Sorry, Preacher." John whipped his hat off and curled his fingers around the brim. "I didn't see you standing. Honest."

Benjamin nodded. Pain dulled his eyes.

"I think I need to get you home. Can you move?" Elsie scanned the length of him. Nothing appeared at an awkward angle.

"Nonsense. A little fall from a roof isn't reason to leave yet. We haven't finished." Benjamin moaned, trying to sit.

Elsie and Mark slipped their arms behind him as they helped him sit up. She couldn't resist running her hand through his sweaty curls to examine his head. Thankfully, no blood soaked his scalp, but she did note a knot the size of a bird egg at the back.

He winced when she touched it, shrugging off her hands. "I don't need your help."

An arrow pierced her heart as she watched him struggle to stand. He swayed, and Mark steadied him.

"Let's get back to work, fellas. Mark has a barn that needs completing."

"No, we can take care of things here." Mark squeezed his friend's shoulder. "I appreciate your work today, but I won't allow you to get on the roof again. We'll manage. Any man would need a rest after the fall you've had."

Benjamin's face paled, but he didn't say anything.

"I'll get my cake plate, then I'll hitch up the wagon." Elsie turned away.

Benjamin clenched his jaw to try and get his mind off the branding iron searing through his head. He hadn't meant to be so abrupt with Elsie, but her concern had been his undoing. He wobbled and concentrated on staying on his feet.

"Maybe you should sit down while Elsie gathers everything." Mark eased him to the ground again.

"I'll help her hitch your horse." John headed toward Elsie.

"Please don't let me keep you from working." Benjamin gritted his teeth as his head pounded.

"There's plenty of time for work, my friend. We first need to make sure you aren't hurt bad." Mark sank down beside him.

Henry clapped his hat on his head. "We'll be praying you feel better soon. Watch out for head injuries, Preacher. Don't overdo it. Take things nice and easy the remainder of the day, and tomorrow too. Wouldn't want to see something happen to you."

Beatrice and Mildred wandered back to the soddy.

"She's trying to help you." Mark nodded toward Elsie. "You must've given her a terrible fright. Lord knows you did me. Please make sure you take care of yourself and don't be afraid to accept Elsie's help. Maybe allowing her to nurse you back to health will give her the chance to see what she's missing."

Benjamin's gut swirled and swelled into his throat. He couldn't tell if it had to do with his throbbing head or Mark's words.

Elsie hurried over and hovered like a mother hen. When he stood, her pale face floated before his eyes. He closed them and slumped back to the ground.

"I think we'd better lay him down in the back of the wagon." Mark's voice cut through the fog clogging his thoughts.

Benjamin didn't have the strength to open his eyes or protest.

"Hey, John, can you help us get him into the back of the wagon?" Mark yelled.

Benjamin cringed. "No need." He croaked the words.

They either ignored him or didn't hear him because his body was lifted like a sack of flour and set in the wagon. When he and Elsie got further away from the property, he'd insist she stop and let him drive the rest of the way home. One bump to his noggin sure didn't need this much babying.

"Be sure to make him take it easy." Mark cleared his throat. "I can't leave Beatrice alone, otherwise, I'd come along. You probably should keep an eye on him, and make sure he hasn't had more damage than we realize. Especially be on the lookout for him getting sick all of a sudden like."

"I could ride along and keep a watch on him." John's voice grated.

"I'm sure I'll be able to take care of him."

Benjamin wanted to cheer at Elsie's answer, but he kept quiet. The wagon swayed beneath him. She must have climbed onto the seat.

"It won't be any trouble, honest." John edged closer from the sound of it.

"Nope. We'll be fine. Besides, the men need you to finish the roof. G'yup."

What a girl, standing up to the persistent man. Benjamin grinned. He prayed neither of the other men witnessed it.

A slight moan squeezed from Elsie's mouth along with a prayer. "Dear Lord, heal him, and why did it have to be ..." Her shoulders shook as tears blurred her eyes. She struggled to keep a grip on the reins. She glanced back at Benjamin. He lay completely still with a smile on his face. *Odd.* When he didn't move, she faced forward again.

"Pull over, Elsie."

She jumped, swiveling in her seat. The reins slipped from her fingers, and his horse came to a halt.

"What is it? Are you going to be sick?" Elsie hated the tremor in her voice.

Benjamin struggled to sit. "Would you mind helping me to the wagon seat?"

"I most certainly will not." Elsie grabbed the reins and snapped them across the horse's back. She heard a thump and glanced back.

Benjamin lay sprawled with a scowl on his face.

"Please, Elsie. Each time the wagon hits a rut, the floorboards hammer against my head something fierce."

She nibbled her lip for a moment before bringing the vehicle to a halt. Elsie clambered from the seat, hoisting her skirt as she cleared the wheel. By the time she came around the back, Benjamin had scooted toward the edge. He leaned heavily on her shoulder as he eased from the bed. His face grew chalky white.

"You ain't going to pass out again, are you?" Elsie slipped her arm around his waist. Her heart fluttered at his nearness.

He shook his head and then grimaced. His knuckles turned white when he gripped the side of the wagon. "Give me a minute."

A waft of his hair tonic mixed with sweat accosted her nostrils. Slowly color flooded back into his face. His gaze shifted back in her direction, holding her captive.

Elsie peered at his lips as they lowered.

His mouth caressed hers once. Twice. Like the wings of a butterfly flitting. The third time, his mouth lingered on hers, causing her pulse to skitter. Pure bliss shot through every fiber of her being. Her arms snaked around his body, closing the gap between them. She couldn't refrain from deepening the kiss. Elsie expected him to pull back and break the bond between them, but he didn't. His fingertips traced the side of her face, drawing her closer. *Lord, let him be thinking of me this time.*

Benjamin stroked the length of Elsie's neck, enraptured by her sweetness. Her pulse thudded under his fingertips for a crazy moment or two … or five. As he broke the kiss, his head throbbed, or perhaps it was his heart.

A tiny sigh escaped as her eyes fluttered open, and a blush flooded her cheeks. "I'm sorry. I shouldn't have done that." Elsie looked away.

Benjamin refrained from kissing the tip of her nose. He tapped under her chin until her eyes sought his again. "You've nothing to be sorry for. Besides, you don't hear me complaining any, do you?"

Moisture trickled down her freckled cheeks, and she averted her eyes again. She buried her face in his chest as sobs racked her frame. Benjamin prayed for her as he held her, knowing she'd soon share what was on her mind.

Several minutes passed while her shuddering gasps filled the sweltering air. He handed her his handkerchief, and she blew her nose. Benjamin couldn't resist wiping her tears with his fingertips. She trembled under his touch, as her honeysuckle scent filled his nostrils. His pulse escalated, and he longed to taste her sweetness again. He dipped his head.

Elsie pulled away, taking a small step away from him. "We best be on our way. We need to get home before dark." She glanced over her shoulder before slipping her arm around his waist and tugging him toward the wagon.

"Why?" He leaned heavily on her as she helped him walk around to the side of the wagon. Too bad he didn't feel up to a gallant move like swinging her on the seat, but he didn't trust himself not to fall over if she didn't help to support him.

Elsie shrugged and glanced over his shoulder. "Nothing for you to worry about. We can talk more about it when you're feeling up to it. For now, we need to get you home."

He started to turn to see what she kept looking at, but the throbbing in his head caused him to stop.

"Here, grasp my shoulders, and I'll shove you up."

His world tilted at an awkward angle as Elsie thrust him onto the seat. Her strength surprised him. It was all he could do to maintain his balance. Once he was up, Benjamin closed his eyes, praying it would help to stop the endless swimming and rushing in his ears.

"Benjamin? You feeling poorly?" Elsie's voice whispered beside him.

He opened his eyes and gave the slightest nod, not trusting himself to speak. He regretted the motion when additional pain swelled.

"I'll get you home in no time." Elsie smacked the reins.

"Don't go too fast." He spoke the words through gritted teeth.

Things finally stopped moving before his eyes, and he settled against the back of the seat. "I think I can drive now." He placed his hands over hers.

Her cheeks flushed, but she didn't loosen her hold on the reins. "I can handle a wagon. Just because you're a man doesn't mean you have to be the one in charge all the time. Besides, you look as green as the dress Beatrice wore today."

Benjamin huffed and withdrew his hands, supporting his aching head as each jut and bump jarred him.

"I still say you'd be better off lying down in the back."

"No, this is better. Just get me home." He forced his mind off the dull throbbing in his head, and instead, thought about the kiss. He smiled. Easing Elsie's pain had been the first thing he desired until a teardrop had glistened on her lips. Then all that consumed his thoughts was showing her how much he cared for her. When she'd deepened their kiss … he hadn't experienced such joy and peace in a long time.

Elsie squirmed on the seat and risked a peek at Benjamin. Did he regret kissing her? She should have never thrown herself at him the way she had. Now the man had planted crazy notions in her head and heart but—truth be told—she didn't regret one second of it. Especially since he hadn't mentioned Mary once.

She smiled and snuck another peek at him.

Elsie kept thinking about that kiss, startling when Benjamin's horse halted in front of his house. Good thing Milly could find her way home. If they had been dependent upon Elsie, who knew where they'd have ended up?

"We're here. Let me help you down." She set the brake and scurried around to his side of the wagon.

Benjamin eased himself to the ground and stood, gripping the wooden side panel for a few seconds. "Thank you, Elsie. I'll see you tomorrow. Would you mind taking care of Milly for me?"

"I'll help you get inside the house." Elsie went to put her arm around him, but he shrugged away from her touch.

"No thank you."

A muscle flickered in her jaw.

"I'm sure I won't need you any further." Benjamin swayed, righting himself when he staggered against the doorframe. "Thanks again."

I won't need you. The words echoed in Elsie's heart.

CHAPTER TWENTY-SEVEN

Violence is never the answer to a problem. A gentleman should always convey deepest respect and honor to a lady, never speaking in a gruff tone of voice.
Mrs. Wigglesworth's Essential Guide to Proper Etiquette and Manners of Refined Society

Elsie paced her tiny home. She hadn't slept a wink. In fact, she'd crept over to Benjamin's home in the wee hours and knocked. When he didn't answer, she'd imagined the worst. Come sunup, she'd see with her own eyes how he fared.

She creaked her door open and was greeted by darkness. Elsie blew out a breath and checked Pa's pocket watch again. She still had an hour before the sun rose.

Elsie sank to her bed, weariness tugging at her frame. Not willing to risk falling asleep, she stood and scooped up her saddlebags. Flipping open the leather flap, she withdrew Pa's last gift to her—his worn leather Bible.

His words were just as vivid now as they were then.

"Elm, promise me you'll take this and read it. It's my greatest possession, besides you and your sisters. Always treasure God's Word. What's in here is most important." He'd tapped the book with his thumb, then had her read from the book of Ecclesiastes about there being a time to be born, to die, to plant, to harvest, to weep, and to laugh.

Elsie flipped open the heavy book. An underlined passage drew her attention, and she traced her fingers across the page. *"Lord, are You ever going to make something beautiful out of my life?"*

Perhaps too much time had passed, and God didn't want her anymore. She closed the book and glanced at the watch again.

Only a few minutes until sunup. Her experience with Pa told her that sometimes a man needed his distance. Hopefully, by now, Benjamin had worked through whatever had been stuck in his craw.

Elsie flung open the door, strolling across the short distance to his home, pounding on his house. She waited several seconds before repeating the action. No response.

"You might as well open up, Benjamin, because I'm not going away until you do."

The door opened a crack. "What?" His voice rasped like horseshoes on gravel.

"Let me in. I want to check and make sure you're improving." Elsie managed to get the crack wide enough to see his rumpled clothes and hair standing on end. Had he slept in them?

"You've seen me, now go away."

"Why are you being so cantankerous?" Elsie planted her hands on her hips. "I'm trying to help you. How's your head doing?"

"If you'd quit all the hollering, my head would be fine. Let me be so I can sleep. As I said before, I don't need you, and you shouldn't be here." He shoved the door closed, hitting her nose in the process.

She refrained from kicking the doorframe by stomping toward the creek instead. The merrily trickling water did little to assuage her foul mood. Crazy man. Probably regretted that he kissed her. Or more appropriately, that she'd kissed him. She picked up a pebble and tossed it into the water. The tiny splash did little to ease the tension building inside her. What she needed was action.

Crossing the property, she snagged a bucket and carried it to the creek, dipping it into the water. Droplets of moisture dripped on the dry ground as she carried it to Benjamin's place. She rapped on the door. "Open up."

It swung open.

"Here." She shoved the bucket into his arms. "Dip a rag in this and hold it on your goose egg. It'll help with the swelling."

His hands fumbled as he gathered it close to his chest. "Thank you."

"Hopefully, it'll help your headache to subside. Not sure what'll fix your orneriness, though." She turned and clomped back to her place.

After the shock wore off, a smile broke across Benjamin's face. His orneriness didn't compare to Elsie's all-fired stubbornness. He chuckled. They were a pair. He'd have loved nothing more than her help, but sharing those kisses had left him weaker than the knock upside the head. Had he allowed her inside to assist, well … there's no telling where things might have led. His willpower couldn't take the temptation with her so close and his desire so strong.

He grabbed a cloth, dipped it into the bucket of water, and gently held it against the lump on the back of his head.

The coolness brought immediate soothing and helped to ease the throbbing. He dropped the cloth back into the bucket and repeated the process a couple more times.

A half hour later, the rumble of a wagon drew his attention. He jammed his feet into his boots and stepped outside.

Mark waved. "Howdy, Preacher. Hope you don't mind some company. We decided to stop by for a visit to see how you're faring."

The two wagon seats were crammed full with the Sawyers and the Larsons. John trailed behind on his horse.

When the wagon stopped, Henry hopped down and guided his wife as she scooted to the edge. He reached for his son and then offered his elbow to Mildred.

Elsie meandered over but kept at a distance from everyone.

John swung down from his horse and gazed at her before he came over to Benjamin. "I'm really sorry about yesterday,

Preacher. I didn't see you when I swung the board around. I know better and should've checked first. Can you forgive me?"

"Of course. Accidents happen. No hard feelings." Benjamin shook hands with the man. "I appreciate that you all came here to see how I'm doing. Elsie brought over cold water earlier, and that helped." He glanced at her. She edged closer.

Beatrice smiled at him. "We're so glad to hear you're better. Mildred and I brought you some stew and fried chicken. If you don't mind, we'll put the food inside." Mildred and Beatrice headed toward his home.

John strolled over to Elsie.

Benjamin shifted closer to the married men.

"You're awful quiet this morning, sweet pea. Something bothering you?" John's finger grazed Elsie's cheek.

Benjamin's fingers curled into a fist.

She swatted John. "Nothing worth mentioning."

"You sure?" He inched closer.

"Now, son …" Henry raised his voice.

The blatant man ignored them, snagging Elsie's hand. "What do you say we go for a walk?"

She tugged her hand free.

"Please, Elsie. If you'd just give me a chance, I think you'll fall in love with me." John leaned in and skimmed his lips across her cheek.

Her eyes widened.

The scoundrel took advantage of the situation and covered her mouth with his.

She stepped back and raised her hand.

Benjamin yanked John's shoulder and spun the man around, slugging him in the jaw. John stumbled before righting himself, scowling and holding his mouth. A tiny drop of blood trickled down his chin from his lower lip.

Henry shoved forward, his arms folded across his barrel of a chest. "I think it's best if you leave now, son, before something worse happens."

John scrambled to his horse without a backward glance.

Benjamin took a step toward Elsie, but she ran toward the soddy. He shoved his fingers through his hair. "I should've controlled my temper."

Mark slapped him on the back. "If you hadn't slugged him, I would've."

"Me too," Henry said. "The man ought to know better than to take liberties like that with a lady. Especially when she's told him numerous times she wasn't interested." Henry shook his head.

Benjamin coughed. He'd taken the same liberty with Elsie yesterday, but she hadn't complained any. She'd even pulled him back in when he'd drawn back. And hadn't she also said the same thing to him? Perhaps he was no different than John. "As a preacher, I should've done better. Been better."

"Phshaw. Just 'cause you're a preacher don't mean you aren't a man too. A fella takes it personally when another man moves in on his territory." Henry shifted his hat.

"Except I punched him. I shouldn't have given in to violence."

"I don't know about that, Preacher. The Old Testament is full of fighting. It's not wrong to protect the people you care about," Mark said. "Maybe it's time you let Elsie know how much you love her."

Love? Something stirred in Benjamin. He'd become accustomed to seeing her every day. Talking with her. Working on the farm together. Planting their first crop of winter wheat. She was the one he thought of when he learned something new. Could it be love?

The women stepped outside. "Where's Elsie?" Beatrice glanced around. "She didn't go off with John, did she?"

"No, honey. John, uh, left."

"Where's Elsie then?" Her brow wrinkled.

"She had a run-in with John."

"Oh, no." Mildred handed the baby to Henry. Beatrice and Mildred looped arms and hurried toward the soddy.

Mark adjusted his hat. "Well, fellas, looks like we'll be a while. What can we help you with while we wait?"

Benjamin's gaze followed the women. If only Elsie would freely talk to him as she would them.

The door to Elsie's soddy burst open. She jerked to a seated position, ready to yell at Benjamin. Her shoulders sagged as Mildred and Beatrice shoved into the room, stumbling over one another. Beatrice pulled Elsie to her feet, the young woman's arms engulfing her.

Mildred touched Elsie's arm. "What happened? The men said you and John had some sort of altercation."

Elsie's chin wobbled. "They didn't tell you?"

Both women shook their heads.

"He …" She touched her mouth. "He kissed me."

"Wait. John kissed you or Benjamin?" Mildred asked.

Elsie shoved her hands in her pockets and avoided eye contact. She cleared her throat. "They." She cleared her throat again. "They both did."

"What?" Beatrice squeezed her side. "Benjamin finally got up the nerve to kiss you again?"

"Why would John kiss you?" Mildred frowned. "What do you mean again?"

Elsie wished she'd kept her mouth shut.

"You'd better start from the beginning." Mildred sank onto a chair.

Beatrice flopped down on the bed.

Elsie flipped a chair around and straddled it.

"If you don't want to tell us, we understand." Mildred patted her hand. "But if you care to share what's on your heart, we're here for you."

Elsie glanced at both women, folded her hand over the top curve of the chair, resting her forehead against it. *What do I do, Lord?* She gathered her courage, sat up straight, and told them about her encounter with Benjamin the day before.

Beatrice giggled. "He's so romantic."

"Except you still haven't told us what happened with John." Mildred leaned forward.

Elsie sighed. She already told them this much, she might as well continue. "He first stroked my cheek then kissed it. Before I could do anything, he kissed me square on the lips. Would've slugged him but good, except Benjamin got to him before me." She wiped her lips, wishing the memory would fade.

"No wonder the preacher punched him," Beatrice said. "It's obvious he cares for you or he wouldn't have."

"It doesn't prove anything." Elsie stood up fast, and the chair clattered to the dirt floor. "All I know is that I'm miserable. What if he thinks I initiated John's kiss?"

Beatrice snagged her wrist. "You mustn't think that way."

"You've made it clear you don't care for John and didn't welcome his pursuit. We've all seen that. Benjamin knows it too. You have nothing to fear." Mildred stood. "All it takes is for you and the preacher to sit down and clear all this up, and you'll see that the man loves you."

"How do I know if it's love or he's just worming his way into my heart so he can take over the property?" A heavy weight settled on Elsie's heart.

"Nonsense. You two were meant for each other. It's just going to take one of you giving up being mulish and waiting for the other person to say something first." Mildred gripped her hand.

"Well, it's not going to be me starting anything." Elsie shook off the woman's touch and crossed her arms. "I tell you, it's not my place."

Beatrice nodded. "You can take that stance, but are you willing to let your pride stand in the way of happiness? Is it worth that?"

Elsie didn't have an answer, but she knew who did. "Thanks for coming, ladies. If you'll excuse me, I need to do something."

No sooner had the two left when she sank to her knees and folded her hands. Taking a deep breath, she exhaled slowly, speaking in a shaky voice. "I don't know why You let Pa die and had folks stand by and do nothing while I lost everything, but I'm sorry for blaming You for so long, Lord. Thank You for the good people I have here. For Benjamin. I don't want that shawl of bitterness to rule my life any longer. I desire for You to make things right in me, Lord."

Elsie glanced up at the cedar pole and sod ceiling. "The ladies seem to think that Benjamin cares for me. I don't know if You plan to have him as part of my future or not, but I choose to leave that in Your hands. Guide me, Lord, and forgive me for taking so long to come back to You. Amen."

She rose and ran a hand across Pa's Bible. Might be the toughest thing she'd ever done … leaving things to someone she couldn't see.

CHAPTER TWENTY-EIGHT

When courting, be sure to first ask permission of the father and then the young woman. If she answers in the affirmative, don't pour out a rush of emotions as this may scare her away.
Mrs. Wigglesworth's Essential Guide to Proper Etiquette and Manners of Refined Society

Benjamin paced his two-room house then plopped onto the chair. "Things are shifting between us, Lord, and I'm not sure where You want me to go with this. How do I tell her I'm interested in courting without making it seem like all I care about is the property?" Benjamin stabbed his fingers through his hair. Ever since he'd seen Elsie helping to fight the brushfire, he knew she was the woman for him, but he sensed if he pressed her too soon, she might run like she did in most uncomfortable situations.

After his neighbors had left yesterday, he'd made it a point of staying inside. Courtship was the only answer. He wanted Elsie to be that vital part of his life. The question was, how to convey it so she didn't turn tail again.

He shoved to his feet and cracked open the door. A cold wind blew through the crack. They'd gone from blistering temperatures to cold weather almost overnight. He shivered and closed the door behind him.

The cold gave him an idea. He loaded his arms with firewood and carted it toward the front of Elsie's soddy. As he plunked the last log in place, her door opened.

"Benjamin? What're you doing up so early?" She yawned and shivered, her bare toes peeping out from the blanket wrapped around her torso. "We finally get a break from the heat, and it turns bitter cold." Elsie shook her head. "It probably won't last long and will be warm by midday."

"Good morning." His heart pounded. "I thought you might like extra wood for your stove."

Her brow rose. "Why, thank you. I'd invite you in, but I haven't dressed yet." She wouldn't quite meet his gaze.

He tipped his hat. "See you later." His breath frosted out in front of him. The cold air nipped against his cheeks and nose. His pulse hadn't calmed by the time he made it back to his house. *Lord, help me find the right way to let her know I care.*

Too bad her family members weren't here for Benjamin to ask permission to court Elsie. He'd have to come up with another way of asking her.

Elsie shivered and closed the door. The one time she'd chosen to sleep in a nightgown, the man decided to make an early appearance. Of course, greeting him in her long johns wouldn't have been any better. She waited until Benjamin headed back to his place before she stepped out onto the frosty grass to snag a log or two. She stoked the embers and blew on them, soon adding a couple of pieces of wood. Her toes were near frozen by the time she got the fire lit. She stood in front of the stove, willing it to warm up faster.

She yawned as she pulled on her clothes. Not bothering with a comb, she whisked her hair under her Stetson and shoved her arms through her coat, pulling on gloves as she closed the door behind her.

As she traipsed to the barn, Elsie peered at the field. After her neighbors had left yesterday, she'd watered the entire thing. Tiny spots of green were beginning to poke their heads above the dry, cracked ground. Once she thought she'd spotted a man watching her in the distance, but when she checked again, he was gone.

After Benjamin had come back from Enid two weeks ago with the new cattle, Elsie had shared her concerns with him about the man she kept seeing. He'd cautioned her to not leave the property without him. Since then, she'd been watchful.

A minute later, she cracked open the barn door, breathing in the welcoming scents. It reminded her of home. *Of Pa.* A thump sounded in the corner. She cocked her ear and listened. There it came again. She wished she'd thought to bring her rifle. Maybe she should start carrying it wherever she went, just in case. The noise came again, and this time she recognized it as a horse stomping its hoof.

She moved further into the barn. If she hurried, she'd be able to milk the cows, muck the stalls, and feed all the livestock before Benjamin came out.

Elsie crept to the last stall and poked her head around the corner. Nobody. She breathed a sigh of relief. Her overactive imagination had her seeing outlaws around every corner.

She entered the stall and patted the cow on the rump. "How're you doing this morning, girl?" The cow flicked her tail and turned big, brown eyes toward Elsie.

After setting the three-legged stool by the cow's side, she sat and started milking, enjoying the ping as milk splattered against the side of the pail. The cow chewed its cud as Elsie worked, resting her head on its side. When she finished, Elsie moved to the next cow before she shifted the bucket out of kicking range and forked hay into the trough. As she mucked out the stall, she grew warm and stripped her jacket.

The normal activities of farm life soothed her soul. Pa had known she did her best thinking in the barn. Either there or outside in nature.

She smiled, brushing Buster's coat until it shone. "I wonder what Benjamin would do if I went over to his place and asked him if he wanted to court me? He'd probably think I'd gone loco."

Elsie chucked the brush into a box of supplies and shuffled back to where she'd set the buckets of milk. "You girls have the easy life. Everything is taken care of for you. Meals, a fresh, clean bed. Sure would love for things to be easier. I wish I had a man to take care of me and treat me special.

"I keep thinking about how lonesome Pa used to get for Ma. He must've loved her something fierce. Don't know if I'll ever have a man love me like that." She snorted. "Can't understand why I'm telling you this." Elsie patted the cows one more time and glanced around the empty barn, checking to make sure nobody had joined her. Dropping her voice a notch she added, "Between you and me, Bessie, if I had to choose a man ... I'd choose Benjamin."

Benjamin's heart soared. Had she really said what he thought he'd heard? She wouldn't refuse his court when she'd mentioned it herself. Now to find a special way to tell her that he desired to marry her. He took a step backward, opened the door quietly, then thudded it shut behind him. Whistling as he worked his way down the aisle, he patted Milly's nose. "Good morning, girl. How're you doing?"

Out of the corner of his eye, he saw Elsie's head poke above the stall. He kept his eyes trained on his horse, pretending he hadn't seen her. "Looks to be a cold one today. I bet you're glad I brought you inside last night." The horse snorted.

"Milking and mucking are done." Elsie stepped into view and set down two brimming buckets. "Here's the milk."

"Why don't you keep it? You mentioned a few days ago about wanting to make some butter."

"You sure? I wouldn't want to put you out any." Elsie didn't quite meet his gaze.

"I'm sure. Besides, what're neighbors for?" Benjamin closed the gap between them, hoping she'd look at him. "I'm counting on you sharing some of your delicious rolls along with the butter."

She nodded, keeping her head down. "I best get working on it. Thank you for bringing the butter churn back from Enid last week." Elsie picked up the buckets.

"Here, allow me." He reached for the pails, his fingers brushing against hers. He jutted his elbow out, praying she'd thread her arm through his.

"No, thank you. I can tote it myself." She pulled the buckets towards her.

Benjamin bit down his frustration. Elsie always had to do things on her own. He wanted to be able to help her whenever a need arose. Wanted more time with her too.

He'd given up thinking she'd budge on the matter when suddenly she handed the pails to him and slipped her arm through his. His heart swelled as he led the way. One step in the right direction. He didn't want to think about how many more steps he still had to go.

"Did you wear a jacket? You might want to get it first. It hasn't gotten any warmer."

"Um, yes, it's back there. Wait a minute, and I'll get it." She ran back down the narrow corridor between the stalls.

He grinned as she strolled toward him. "My lady." Benjamin dipped his head and offered his elbow again.

She chuckled and looped one hand through his arm and opened the barn door with the other.

Outside stood a tall man wearing a badge. A dark mustache covered a good portion of his face. The man's horse nickered.

Elsie pulled her hand from Benjamin's arm.

Benjamin set down the milk and closed the barn door. "Can I help you?"

The man nodded. "I'm the county sheriff. I came to warn you and the missus that several outlaw bands have been creating a ruckus in the area. Before now they've been a good twenty miles from here, but we just got word from a man a few miles away that he's had a few things stolen."

"We aren't married," Elsie interrupted.

The man glanced at her, then back to Benjamin.

"We both claimed the same land and are waiting for the courts to decide our fate," Benjamin said.

"Humph. As I was saying, the one group is the Yeager gang. My deputy and I haven't figured out yet if they're all working together or separate." He jutted his chin toward Elsie. "You best keep your woman close to home. A beauty like her could be a mighty temptation to a man who's on the run from the law."

"I'm not his woman."

"That may be, but he'd do best to keep an eye on you and make sure you're protected."

Benjamin shifted in front of Elsie.

She shoved her way around him.

"No need to worry about me. I can take care of myself." Elsie threw her shoulders back. "I have a rifle, and I ain't afraid to use it."

"Well, little lady, it don't hurt to be careful. Have either of you seen anything suspicious lately?"

"We've both spotted men watching us from time to time. They never got close enough to catch a good look at their features and never made an effort to speak to us," Benjamin said.

Elsie nodded. "A couple months ago, I overheard some men out at the Glass Mountains. The way they talked, I could tell they were up to no good. Figured they'd move on and not bother folks. Haven't thought about it since that night. Maybe they're some of those fellas you talked about."

Benjamin cleared his throat. "What else can you tell us, Sheriff?"

"If you've visited Enid, no doubt you heard all about them. Folks have been gossiping like crazy. Makes it hard for a man to root out the truth." The tall man tipped his hat back on his forehead. "The one is beating up landowners, demanding their deeds, and then giving them a week or two to clear out. Figured the fellow didn't get land in the run and is trying to snatch up some of the prime homesteads. Either that or he isn't happy with only having one claim." The man nodded and swung up onto his horse. "As for a couple of the others, they've been stealing from folks. Keep your eyes peeled." He tipped his hat and rode away.

Neither of them spoke a word as they trekked the short distance to Elsie's soddy, but Benjamin noticed she kept glancing over her shoulder. He wished he knew the words that would give her comfort and help her not to worry. "We'll keep a watch out for those bandits."

Elsie nodded.

"God will protect us. Of course, that doesn't mean bad things can't happen, but we can trust Him to have our good in mind."

She opened the door and stepped back as he placed the buckets on her table. Elsie's gaze bounced around the room, stopping everywhere but on him.

Benjamin rested his hand on hers, and she jumped. "Elsie, look at me."

She shook her head and surveyed the dirt floor.

He chucked under her chin, and slowly she lifted her face but not her eyes.

"Elsie, there's something I've been meaning to talk to you about." He held his breath trying to gain the courage to continue.

Her eyes flitted toward his, widening.

A knock thudded against the door.

Really, Lord? You had to send someone now when I've finally got my gumption up?

Elsie swung the door open.

"Howdy. I weren't sure whether to try here or at the other house. Figured I'd start here first. I'm trying to find a" —the man consulted the paper in his hand— "a Benjamin Hays David. Do you know where can I find him?"

Benjamin inched forward. "That's me."

"I'm a clerk for Matthew Montrose. He wanted me to tell you he'll be able to deal with your land dispute a little earlier than he'd anticipated. You'll need to be in Enid three weeks from Monday."

Dear Lord, can't I get a break here?

Blood pounded in Elsie's ears. She'd known better than to get attached to Benjamin. She tried to stop the buzzing in her head as the man continued.

"The lawyer said it'd be best if you both come since you're contesting the same property, providing this is the other person you mentioned when you stopped by the office." The man's face puckered. "Hopefully, we'll be able to handle the decision peaceably." He glanced between Elsie and Benjamin. "Either way, the deputy will be there, just in case."

"What's going on here, Elsie?"

She gasped. Only one person had a condescending tone like that. *Aunt Kate.*

"Er, I best be on my way." The clerk's face turned red as he ran toward his buggy.

"Humph." Aunt Kate waved a hanky in front of her nose. "The nerve of him." She scowled at the departing man. "He didn't even have the decency to carry my baggage inside after giving me a ride out here."

"Allow me to get that for you, ma'am." Benjamin squeezed past Elsie. His long legs covered the distance in no time. He lifted the two overstuffed bags and carted them back to the soddy.

"Well, aren't you going to introduce us?" The older woman plunked her hands on her ample waist.

Elsie swallowed past the lump in her throat. "Aunt Kate, this is Benjamin David. Benjamin, this is Kathryn Tyers."

He set the bags on the floor and dipped his hat. "I'm pleased to meet you, Mrs. Tyers. Elsie has told me a lot about you."

Aunt Kate pierced Elsie with a look that made her want to squirm. She resisted the urge, throwing her shoulders back instead.

"I'm afraid I haven't had that pleasure since my niece hasn't sent any word to her family since she left Kiowa." Aunt Kate lifted an eyebrow. "No matter. We'll soon be leaving this godforsaken place and moving back to civilization." She waved her hand in dismissal.

"I ain't leaving." Elsie crossed her arms, glowering at her aunt.

"We'll discuss this once your company leaves. Although why you'd entertain a man unchaperoned in your home, I'll never know. Apparently, all my lessons in deportment have fallen on deaf ears."

"I best leave you two be for now." Benjamin hung his head and left.

A deep sadness settled over Elsie. Just when she'd let go and trusted God with her future, He yanked the carpet out from under her. According to the clerk, it looked like there was no possible future with Benjamin because soon one of them would be leaving. Not that she harbored any desire to depart with her aunt. Her heart ached. Falling in love with Benjamin had been a mistake. Biggest one she'd ever made.

CHAPTER TWENTY-NINE

Family priorities take precedence over all other matters.
It is one's responsibility to see to the needs of loved ones
even if it conflicts with an individual's desires.
*Mrs. Wigglesworth's Essential Guide to Proper Etiquette
and Manners of Refined Society*

The woman hadn't let up since she arrived. Elsie longed for Benjamin to rescue her from her aunt's constant barrages.

"At least you kept the quilt your ma made you instead of selling it like you did everything else. Lord knows why my sister insisted the bedding went to you instead of her oldest daughter." Aunt Kate sniffed. "If you ask me, it's a waste passing it on to the likes of you."

Elsie fingered a raised flower on the quilt.

"This place is disgraceful. I'll never understand why you've chosen to live in a *dirt* home. You've had enough of this little adventure. It's time to—"

A knock cut Aunt Kate's words short.

Elsie crossed the crowded soddy and threw the door open. Beatrice grinned at her. She'd never been so happy to see her friend.

"Mark needed to borrow the plow from the preacher again. Thought I'd ride along so we could visit a little." Beatrice's gaze swung toward Elsie's aunt. "Oh, hello. I didn't realize you had company."

Aunt Kate snorted. "Family isn't company."

"I'm Beatrice Sawyer, and you are?"

Aunt Kate squeezed around Elsie and shook Beatrice's hand. "You'll have to forgive my niece. I tried my best to teach her manners, but unfortunately, she takes after her pa instead of my dear sweet sister. God rest her soul."

"This is my Aunt Kate—Kathryn Tyers." Elsie mumbled the words, yearning for the opportunity to secret Beatrice and herself away from her aunt's stifling personality.

"I didn't realize you were expecting family to join you." Beatrice let herself into the soddy, settling on one of the two straight-back chairs.

Aunt Kate perched on the other, so Elsie slumped onto the bed. She opened her mouth to reply but didn't get the chance.

"It took some doing to track down Elmer's youngest." Aunt Kate stared at Elsie before turning to Beatrice with a smile. "The girl's too much like her pa. Why the man didn't ever rein her in and make her behave like a lady is beyond me."

Elsie's cheeks flamed. "You never did say how you managed to find me."

"Believe me, it was quite an undertaking. If it weren't for your pa's constant chattering about this land, I wouldn't have known the first place to start. Especially since you didn't bother to tell any of us about your plans." Aunt Kate pulled a fan out of her skirt pocket and started it fluttering.

"The strip is vast. I still don't see how you tracked me down." Elsie glanced at Beatrice. Beatrice's gaze kept straying to the door. Her friend looked uncomfortable.

"I rode into the territory with a freighter." Aunt Kate shuddered. "Never saw such an uncouth man, and my sore backside from traveling in such a primitive conveyance … Well, let's just say that we won't leave with that manner of transportation. We'll find some sort of cushioned seats, even if I have to make them myself."

"Told you, I'm not leaving my land."

Aunt Kate sniffed. "We'll just see about that."

Beatrice cleared her throat. "Mrs. Tyers, you still haven't said how you found Elsie."

"Oh, yes. The freighter took me as far as Enid. How the locals can call that a town is a puzzlement. It's nothing more than a tangle of tents and ill-bred men."

"Actually, it's a marvel considering everything sprung up overnight." Elsie scooted forward on the edge of the bed. "It's come a long way in a short time. Someday, I'll wager the town will be a sight to behold."

"You always were a dreamer, like your pa. Grasping at fantasies you have no business going after. I tell you, your place is in a real house, surrounded by fine things like your sisters have."

Elsie wanted to slug her aunt. Instead, she bit her tongue.

Beatrice reached for Elsie's hand and squeezed it. "I don't know, Mrs. Tyers, Elsie's managed to do quite well, as you can see."

Aunt Kate glanced around the room and scowled. "How did you accumulate all these things? From what I heard, your pa lost everything else he owned. The man never had more than a few coins to rub together. Where did you get the money to purchase all this?"

Heat flooded Elsie's cheeks again. "A friend bought them for me." Her gaze darted to Beatrice who gave a tiny shrug.

"You never had friends your whole life." The woman's eyes pierced. "You didn't break the law by stealing did you?"

"Of course not!" Elsie barely kept a lid on her seething temper.

"Elsie would never do something like that. She's the most honorable woman I know." Beatrice's nostrils flared.

"It wasn't bought by a young man, was it?" Aunt Kate's gaze narrowed. "Surely you know better than to accept gifts from someone of the male persuasion. It's inappropriate. I trust you didn't do anything unsavory to garner his attention."

Elsie swallowed. There was no way she was sharing that Benjamin was her benefactor.

"The gift was anonymous." Beatrice darted a glance at Elsie, then back to Aunt Kate.

Her aunt let out a puff of air. "No gift like this comes without strings. If you ask me, the *donor* has a hidden agenda. Mark my words, one day he's going to come calling and will have expectations. You best get out of here before that happens, Elsie. We'll find a way to sell all this, or track down whoever gave it to you and return it. It's what you should've done from the start."

"I said it before, and I'll keep telling you until you get it through your head. I'm not leaving." Weariness settled over her. Would this day ever end?

"I understand you helped to raise Elsie, Mrs. Tyers." Beatrice moved her chair closer to the bed.

"Believe me, I've tried for years to gentle her and all her numerous rough edges, but as you can see"—she motioned toward Elsie—"there's only so much I've been able to do. The girl fought me with every lesson I tried to teach her. Her mother would be ashamed."

"I don't know about that. Elsie's one of the most capable women I know. She's built herself a home, planted fields, and helped her neighbors as well. I haven't found anything she isn't capable of doing."

"All man's work."

Elsie's fingers tightened. "I've worked like any other landowner around here."

"Disgraceful, I say. It's a man's job to take care of the land. Your place is with your sisters. With family. I'll be visiting Dorcas and her sweet family next. They expect me to bring you along. You've had enough of this nonsense. It's time you grew up and found a man who will settle down near one of your loved ones. Dorcas has told me all about a young man who'll be perfect for you, Elsie. She's shared with him your redeeming qualities, few that they are. He can't wait to meet you. Of course, we'll need to get you a proper wardrobe before then. Why you insist on wearing your pa's old clothes is beyond me. It's scandalous."

Elsie growled. "I didn't ask you."

"Family *is* important." Beatrice's hands settled onto her stomach as she spoke. "Sometimes, though, I think friends can become like family too."

Elsie wanted to hug the woman.

"Does Benjamin know about the possibility of you leaving?" Beatrice turned toward her.

"Benjamin? Are you talking about her neighbor? What does he have to do with anything?"

"You haven't told her about sharing the land or …" Beatrice's face colored.

"What's this?" Aunt Kate rose to her feet so fast the chair upended and clattered to the floor.

"I don't know what I'm going to do." Benjamin shoved his fingers through his hair, hefting a sigh.

"How long is her aunt staying? She's not here for good, is she?" Mark took a slurp of coffee then set the mug on the table.

"That's just it. She's talking about taking Elsie away." Benjamin paced. "I was just getting ready to ask Elsie to court me, then her aunt showed up."

"You don't think Elsie'd pull up stakes, do you?" Mark ran his thumb along the mug handle. "I can't imagine she'd be willing to just leave. Not with all the hard work and sweat she's put into building the claim with you."

"I would've thought the same thing too, but this is her family."

"She's had her reasons for wanting to stay here, though."

Benjamin massaged his tight neck muscles. "Her pa was why she came and claimed the land, but without him here, maybe she'll listen to her aunt and move near family instead. Elsie's told us she's never been around her sisters much. I may be wrong, but her aunt is pretty intimidating and might be able to force Elsie to go with her."

"You got all that just from a brief introduction?"

"Believe me, it was enough." Benjamin pulled out a chair and sank onto it. "I wouldn't want to get on her bad side."

Mark chuckled. "You gotta be overreacting, don't you think?"

Benjamin shook his head. "I don't believe so. I have a bad feeling about this whole situation." He puffed out a breath. "Would you join me in praying? I sure could use some godly direction right now."

"Of course." Mark leaned forward and closed his eyes. "Father, we come to You asking for Your wisdom in this situation …"

Benjamin nodded in agreement as his friend prayed. *I need to know beyond any doubt concerning how You're leading me, Lord. Did you send Elsie's aunt as a test? Is it wrong for me to pray You take her away? Give me peace.* Despite his prayer, Benjamin couldn't shake his feeling of unease.

"What do you mean you're sharing property with *that* man?" Aunt Kate spat out the words. She looked like a kettle about to let out a big burst of steam.

Elsie winced. "That man happens to be a preacher and is more than honorable."

"No self-respecting preacher would allow himself to be placed in such a compromising situation. How do you know he really is who he says he is?" Aunt Kate's face turned a mottled purple.

"He used to be a circuit preacher before moving here," Beatrice said. "Elsie's right. He's been nothing but a gentleman. There's been several times when Elsie was sick, and he took care of her."

Elsie closed her eyes. *Lord, guide my words … and Beatrice's too.* Her eyes flew open as her aunt's voice went up about ten notches.

"Do you mean they've been alone on this property since September?" The purple deepened in her aunt's face. Would she have a fit of apoplexy?

"Here, Aunt Kate." Elsie jumped from the bed and righted the toppled chair. "Why don't you sit down, and we can talk about this calmly."

"Calmly?" She sputtered. "How do you expect me to be calm when you've been running around acting like a hussy. Outrageous! I tell you, I should've followed my instincts and never left you alone with your pa. I see his teachings have brought you nothing good."

"Now you just wait a minute." Elsie waggled her finger in front of the older woman's face. "I won't stand for you speaking ill of Pa in my own home. He was the best thing in my life."

Beatrice stood and crossed the small room, wrapping her arm around Elsie's shoulders. "That was unkind, Mrs. Tyers. If you truly knew Elsie, you wouldn't say such horrible things to her."

"I see she has you duped too." Aunt Kate flicked a speck of lint from her sleeve. "Perhaps you're as foolish as my niece."

Elsie curled her hand into a fist.

Beatrice grabbed a hold of it and tugged her toward the door.

The cool air rushed across Elsie's hot face as she allowed her friend to lead her to the barn.

"I would've chosen the creek for us to talk, but I was afraid she might follow us there." Beatrice tugged the barn door open. "I figured she wouldn't want to set foot in here." She giggled.

Elsie snorted. "You sure got her pegged. I doubt the woman has ever set foot in one before. She and Uncle Hiram lived in town, and he kept his horses at the livery."

Beatrice sank onto a hay mound and patted the spot beside her. "You poor thing. Has she always been like that?"

"As long as I've known her. Pa mentioned one time that she and my ma were as close as two bees on a blossom. He said Aunt Kate was heartbroken when Ma died, and I lived."

"What's she been doing the past year? Where's your uncle?"

"Uncle Hiram died about five years before Pa."

"Where did she go?"

"Pa didn't like how she treated me. He finally convinced her to go see one of my sisters. Even paid for the train fare. It took all he could to scrape up the funds since our crops failed that year. Aunt Kate liked it at Bitty's so much, she stayed on with her and her husband. Maybe Bitty got tired of her and sent her packing."

Beatrice chuckled. "I could see how she would've worn out her welcome. Has she always been so bitter?"

"No way of telling for sure, I reckon. She's always been meaner than a rattler far as I can tell." Elsie plucked a piece of hay and ran it back and forth between her thumb and fingers. "Most times it's just aimed at me, though. Don't know what got in her to start treating other folks nasty too."

"I'm sorry I said what I did." Beatrice sighed. "I didn't mean to get you in trouble."

Elsie dropped the piece of hay and dusted her hands off. "No need to fret about it. Believe me, it doesn't take much for Aunt Kate to find fault with me. I never understood how the woman could call herself a follower of God and still be so mean."

Beatrice's brow wrinkled. "I can't figure that one out either. It definitely isn't the way we're supposed to act. Did she say when she anticipates traveling to your sister's place?"

Elsie shook her head. "She's traveling light, so my guess is she sent her trunk on ahead. Hopefully, she'll follow soon afterward. I imagine she'll travel back to Kiowa and catch the train from there. Aunt Kate has a lot of friends she might want to visit before she heads west." Elsie huffed. "When I was growing up, she used to brag about all her great-nieces and great-nephews. Whenever she could, she'd include a dig about me. I've never measured up in her eyes. I may have gotten my looks from Ma, but in every other way, I'm like my pa. And you heard what she thinks of him."

"You don't plan to go with your aunt, do you?"

A burst of laughter gurgled out. "There's *no* way I'm leaving with her. My place is here. I won't be persuaded to do so no matter how much someone offers me."

CHAPTER THIRTY

Show restraint when dealing with people who tend to find fault with all whom they come in contact with. Patience is a virtue that few obtain without trials.
Mrs. Wigglesworth's Essential Guide to Proper Etiquette and Manners of Refined Society

A sharp knock interrupted Benjamin's sermon preparation. He opened the door and bit back a gasp when a disheveled, gray-haired Mrs. Tyers greeted him. The woman's beefy arms wound around Elsie's bucket. *Dear God, help me know how to deal with this woman.*

"I'm in need of your assistance, young man." Her voice held a no-nonsense tone.

"What can I do for you?" He held the door wider. "Did you want to come in?"

She stamped her foot. "Isn't it obvious that I need water? That fool niece of mine ran off this morning without leaving me any instructions on where to find the well."

"We don't have a well. We use the creek." He motioned toward it. "I can fill your bucket for you."

Mrs. Tyers lifted her nose in the air. "How primitive." She stepped aside, handing him the pail.

He slipped his fingers around the handle and closed the door behind him. "You said Elsie left this morning?"

The woman fell into step alongside him as they strolled toward the rippling creek. "That girl can never be trusted. She's just like her father."

"I don't know. I've found Elsie to be extremely trustworthy and—"

"You have no business calling my niece by her given name. It's inappropriate. If you truly are a man of the cloth, I would expect you to know better." She drew to a halt.

Benjamin stopped, turning toward her while taking a deep breath. "Actually, I've been praying about being able to speak to one of Elsie's family members. Your visit is fortuitous."

She scowled at him. "What did she do now?"

He swallowed and gathered his courage. "She's stolen my heart. I'd like to ask your permission to court her."

Mrs. Tyers reared back. "Most certainly not!"

His mouth gaped before he snapped it shut. That hadn't gone the way he'd hoped. He cleared his throat. "May I inquire as to why?"

"I plan to take her away from this godforsaken place at the earliest possible convenience. Don't you dare plant any ideas into her head that will make her reconsider staying in this *place*." She shuddered.

"I believe Elsie loves me as well."

"Love. Bah. What good is that? It's sentimental tripe. People who're ruled by their emotions can't be trusted. Hiram and I never fell into such nonsense. We were merely two people who had a mutual ambition in life."

"From my understanding, you share a Christian faith with your niece?" Although the woman certainly wasn't showing any evidence of it right now. He shoved down the uncharitable thought.

"Lord knows I tried to teach her Christian principles. Never did seem to take with her, though." Mrs. Tyers crossed her arms. "She and her pa went to church each week. I saw to that, but just going to church doesn't make one a Christian."

No wonder Elsie struggled with her faith when she'd had this woman as an example in her life. "Yes, I'm well acquainted with spiritual truths. Not only am I the pastor of my tiny congregation here, but my father is also a preacher."

Her eyes narrowed. "Humph."

"Will you at least pray about considering my suit to your niece?"

"There's no need. I already know what the answer will be." She poked her pointy finger into his chest. "It's an N-O."

Benjamin understood now why Elsie had slipped away this morning. He wished he could've joined her instead of listening to her aunt's constant tongue-whipping as they continued to the creek. His father would've given quite the sermon if a member of his congregation acted in such a manner. Benjamin forced himself not to further anger the woman. If he had any hopes of winning her approval, he suspected it wouldn't be because of his verbal ability. Perhaps actions would speak louder to the difficult aunt.

He turned toward the creek and dipped the bucket into the sparkling stream. Benjamin switched the pail to his other hand so it wouldn't splash Mrs. Tyers as he led the way back to Elsie's soddy. They walked in silence until they reached the door. Mrs. Tyers opened it and motioned him inside.

"Just set it there on the table. How that girl stands living in all this filth, I'll never know." She rubbed her hands along the side of her skirt.

He set the bucket where she instructed. "Is there any other way I can assist you?"

Her brow furrowed as she studied him. He forced himself to stand still and not fidget although the temptation to move was killing him.

"You wouldn't happen to know who purchased these things for Elsie, would you?"

He coughed. Of all things, why did she have to ask that? He couldn't very well lie to her. "Y-yes."

The woman's gaze bore down on him like a hot poker. "Well?"

"If there's nothing further, I should get back to preparing my sermon. I hope you'll make a point of coming to our service."

He waited for her dismissal, but instead, she just stared at him.

Again, he refrained from squirming like a schoolboy in front of his teacher after he'd been caught doing something naughty. Benjamin started to turn toward home when her words halted him.

"I didn't see any church nearby. How far away are the services?"

"We don't have a building yet. One day, hopefully. For now, we meet by the creek."

"How archaic."

"We'll need to figure out a more permanent place with winter coming. Maybe we'll be able to take turns having it at each of the parishioner's homes. Although, most of them are small." He shrugged. "I'm sure we'll manage one way or another."

"If we're still around on Sunday, I'll make sure Elsie attends with me."

"She's been coming on her own."

Mrs. Tyers' eyebrows rose. "That surprises me."

"You may find there're a lot of things that have changed with your niece since you've last seen her. I think you'll be happy to find she's quite a remarkable young lady."

She snorted. "That's *yet* to be seen. Elsie can't be trusted to be on her own. She needs to be near family so we can keep her under control. The girl's no good. Like her father."

"I must insist that you not speak about Elsie that way." He wanted to shake the woman.

Mrs. Tyers ushered him toward the door. "The answer still is no, and you won't be changing my mind about it either so don't bother trying. Once my mind is made up, I don't falter. Do you understand me?"

Benjamin didn't answer as he took his leave. Somehow, he'd find a way to wear down the disgruntled woman. He didn't know how, but one thing he knew. It would take God's intervention to chip away the shield around the woman's heart. Benjamin wouldn't give up until God got through.

Elsie sighted her rifle and aimed at the prairie chicken. The shot rang out, finding its target. It made the third bird she'd killed since she'd left before dawn. She'd been avoiding turning back toward home—to Aunt Kate. In fact, she'd been delaying it for the past eight hours.

She retrieved the game, tying the legs of the chicken together. Good thing it was a cool day or she wouldn't have been able to stay out so long and risk the meat turning before she got it home.

Elsie let out a sigh. Something she'd been doing a lot of since Aunt Kate arrived the afternoon before. After many hours of hunting, Elsie still had no plan on how to get her aunt to leave without her.

A movement to her right caught her eye. Elsie turned but didn't see anything. She'd been gone long enough. Benjamin wouldn't be happy when he found out she'd left, but she'd been extra careful and on the lookout for the outlaws. Until then, she hadn't spotted anything suspicious. There it was again. She squinted then puffed a sigh of relief. Merely a baby bunny. Her shoulders relaxed. No use killing the little fella.

Elsie strolled to Buster. He tossed his head as she drew closer. "We best be on our way, boy." She patted him as she swung onto the saddle. "We got a stop to make on the way back."

The terrain rose and fell as she traveled the short distance to the Larsons' place. She knocked on their door moments later.

Henry poked his head out. "Hello, there, Elsie. Come in. Wasn't expecting you. Everything all right? Didn't think you'd be out on your own, what with the outlaws."

"I needed some fresh meat. Had a successful hunt and thought maybe you and Mildred could use a prairie chicken. It's too much for me and my aunt." She held out two of the birds.

He held the door wider for her to enter, then closed it behind her.

"Why, Elsie. What a pleasant surprise." Mildred rocked James. "Did I hear you say your aunt?"

"Yep. Somehow she managed to track me down."

"How nice for you."

She shook her head. "I wouldn't say that."

"Oh. Is she *that* aunt?" Mildred stopped rocking James and shifted him to her shoulder.

"Unfortunately, yes. I'm hoping she'll leave soon, but she's determined to take me with her."

"I should let you ladies talk. I'll be outside if you need me." Henry grabbed his hat from a hook on the wall.

"There's no need to leave on my account. I have to get back." Elsie tried to hand the birds to Henry again. "I know you aren't partial to charity. I ain't either, but the Lord blessed me by providing way more than my aunt and I can eat. You'd help me out if you take these two."

"Well …"

"Don't insult the girl, Henry." Mildred smiled. "We welcome your gift."

"I best be on my way." Elsie chucked the baby under the chin. "You take care of this little fella."

"You be careful." Henry stepped closer to Mildred and wrapped his arm around his wife's waist. "I think I spotted one of those outlaws. It only happened once. I was halfway to your place when it happened."

"Sounds like the pattern Benjamin and I've noticed too."

"I'll feel so much better when those ruffians are caught." Mildred shivered. "Please take care of yourself. Henry, maybe you should ride along with her."

Worry lined Henry's face.

"I'll be fine. Buster can outrace any horse we've ever come in contact with. You stay here, Henry, and make sure your family's safe. I'd feel terrible if something happened to them while you saw me home." Elsie tipped her Stetson. "I'll see you two on Sunday."

"Thanks again." Mildred smiled.

A minute later, Elsie turned Buster toward her claim. It was the first time she'd dreaded going home. *Please, Lord, make Aunt Kate leave soon. Help me know how to deal with her until then.*

CHAPTER THIRTY-ONE

Show hospitality to strangers. Be compassionate in all your words and deeds while still maintaining a proper standing in the community.
Mrs. Wigglesworth's Essential Guide to Proper Etiquette and Manners of Refined Society

Two long days had passed since Elsie last saw Benjamin. She wanted to flop onto her bed in frustration, but Aunt Kate perched on the edge watching Elsie's every movement. *If I don't get out of here—or she doesn't—I'm gonna scream.*

Her thoughts strayed to Benjamin. *Again.* Was he as worried about meeting the lawyer as she was? A rap at the door mercifully interrupted her ponderings.

Benjamin. He's decided to tell me what he wanted to say before Aunt Kate showed up. Elsie smiled and swept the door open. A tall man wearing a rumpled, dusty suit stood with hat in hand. A glint from the weapon strapped to his side flashed in the late afternoon sunlight. He unbuckled the gun belt and let it dangle from his fingertips.

She reined in her disappointment—*not* Benjamin. Her gaze strayed to the gun belt again.

"Howdy, ma'am. I wonder if I could trouble you for something to eat. You see, I've been traveling for days, and my horse came up lame about two miles back. Had to shoot him. I'm parched and near starving since I've been walking since then." He smiled, his teeth gleaming in his tanned face. "If you'd be willing to part with some food, I'd be much obliged."

She hesitated.

"What's the matter with you, Elsie. I thought I taught you better than that." Aunt Kate bustled over and threw the door wide open. "You'll have to excuse my niece. She can be a bit dense at times. I taught her better than this." Her aunt ushered him inside and motioned toward a chair. "Come in, come in. I can tell by the cut of your coat that you're a man of means. My niece will fetch you some water from the stream so your clothes won't get soiled. This is an awful dusty place. My niece doesn't do a good job of taking care of her home." She glared at Elsie. "Get a move on, girl."

"But—"

"Now no back talk from you. Git." Aunt Kate swatted at Elsie's arm.

The man smirked as he nudged past her. "Thank you kindly, ma'am." He tipped his hat to Aunt Kate and slung his gun belt over the back of the chair. "I'll wait here."

"Let me take your hat. You look exhausted." Her aunt took the man's hat and hung it on a peg Elsie had shoved into the sod.

Elsie snagged the bucket, not bothering to put on her coat, and raced toward the creek. *Lord, tell me what to do here. I can't let Aunt Kate know about the outlaws, or she'll never let me stay. Keep us safe.*

As she dipped the pail into the water, Elsie squinted toward Benjamin's place. A sharp pain shot through her. What was he doing right now? Did he miss her? What would it be like to be here alone on the claim? In just a short time, either she or Benjamin would find out. She shook off the melancholy that threatened to overwhelm her.

Careful not to spill the liquid, Elsie hurried back to her soddy and shoved open the door.

The man sat at the table while her aunt chatted with him. With unsteady hands, Elsie held a glass out to him. She glanced at her rifle propped in the corner.

"Land's sake, child. What's the matter with you? You're acting more nervous than a jackrabbit." Aunt Kate plopped her hands on her waist. "Get a move on, and fix the man something to eat."

Elsie cleared her throat and kept an eye on the man. *Calm down.* Just because he had a gun belt didn't mean he was an outlaw. Practically everyone on the strip carried a weapon of some sort when they moved throughout the territory.

"Thank you, miss." He gulped the water and set the cup down. "Exactly what I needed. Despite this cold air, a man can build up a powerful thirst."

A prickle of uneasiness raced up her spine when his stare settled on her with his last words. That voice sounded familiar … like she'd heard it before. Wishing she could place it, she swallowed. "You didn't mention your name."

"Neither did either of you ladies." His brown eyes twinkled.

"I'm Mrs. Tyers." Aunt Kate tittered like a schoolgirl.

"What a pleasure to meet you, Mrs. Tyers." He reached over and snagged her aunt's hand, planting a kiss on the back of it.

"Oh my." Aunt Kate's face turned beet red. "Miss Smith is my rude niece's name."

"Hello, Miss Smith." He grabbed her hand and kissed it as well. "I'm Herbert Santos."

The tiny hairs on the back of her neck stood on end as Elsie stole her hand away from his grip and hastily turned to light the cook stove. The frying pan clunked as she set it on top. "I have fresh eggs and a slab of bacon." She glanced over her shoulder.

"Mmm. Sounds wonderful." He grinned. "You ladies are a sight for sore eyes. I can't tell you how much it means to see a friendly face."

"You poor thing. I can't imagine someone of your refinement wandering around in such a barren land. It must be quite taxing. That's why I want to take my niece back to family, where she belongs."

Aunt Kate kept up the small talk as Elsie made the meal. The food wasn't cooking fast enough to suit her. The sooner she fed the man, the sooner he'd be on his way. *Please, Lord, make it so.*

Her hands were ice cold as she placed the steaming plate of food in front of him a few minutes later. She went to stand by the stove while he ate. She could be neighborly while still keeping her distance.

"My partner's been scouting out the place for a while. You say you're planning on leaving?" Mr. Santos shoveled food into his gaping mouth.

Burning coals lodged in Elsie's chest.

His eyes had taken on a certain gleam she didn't like.

She gulped. "N-no."

"I can't imagine you beautiful ladies enjoy being here all alone. Surely there's a man around to take care of you."

Elsie refused to answer.

Aunt Kate shook her head. "Oh no, we're not married. My Hiram's been gone for five years, God rest his soul. I plan to take my niece back to civilization where she can find a man of culture like yourself."

"I'm sorry for your loss, ma'am."

He took the final bite, then stood, strapping his gun belt in place. "Thank you for your hospitality ladies." His hand snaked out, snagged Elsie's again, and he planted another slobbery kiss on it.

As the door closed behind the disturbing man, Elsie had the sudden urge to wash. With a vengeance. Anything to remove the unsettledness creeping over her skin.

Benjamin rubbed his tight neck muscles. He'd paced for hours and had yet to come up with an answer. "What do I do with this mess, Lord? I thought I'd have more time to figure all this out." He sank into the chair, waiting. Listening. *Why aren't You answering, Lord?*

The door flew open, smacking against the wall.

Benjamin jumped, as a large man filled the doorway. Herbert, from the dining tent. Benjamin darted a rapid glance toward his rife in the corner.

"Where's your deed?" Herbert whipped out a gun and pointed it at him.

"My deed?" Benjamin cleared his throat, rising to his full height. "What business is it of yours?"

Herbert sneered. "Because I'm expanding my holdings, and your plot is part of it. Go get it."

Had the man visited Elsie's soddy? Had he hurt her? Benjamin would do whatever he could to protect her and their claim. "Sorry, I can't."

Laughter split the air. "Can't?" His eyes narrowed. "Or won't? Maybe I need to make a visit to the ladies in the soddy again. The young one fixes a fine meal. Perhaps I'll go back and help myself to something else as well."

Anger flared in Benjamin's chest.

Herbert stepped into the house, closing the door behind him. "Not so sure of yourself now, are you?" He took a step closer, all humor gone. The gun barrel slammed against Benjamin's head. "Now get me the deed, or I'll have to pay *another* visit to Miss Smith and her aunt. The old lady was practically swooning over me."

Ice coursed through Benjamin's veins. Just how long had Herbert been with the two? As ornery as Elsie's aunt was, she wouldn't have stood for any tomfoolery. *Dear God, please be with her. I'll do anything to keep Elsie safe.*

He crossed the room and lifted the mattress. The paper crinkled as he gripped it tight.

Herbert snatched the deed from him and studied it. "You have two weeks to clear off my property. You and your lady friends."

"But—"

"Here's a little warning, in case you think about going to the authorities."

Herbert plowed a hand into Benjamin's gut, knocking the air from his lungs. The force bent him in two, as he struggled to catch his breath. The next punch sent him reeling to the floor. Benjamin held up his hands to ward off the continual blows. *Dear Lord, don't let it end this way.*

Herbert continued to pummel, kick, and punch Benjamin's body until he hovered on the brim of consciousness. The acrid taste of blood filled his mouth as he ran his tongue over his split lip. One eye had completely swelled shut, and the other had become too blurry to see.

Herbert leaned close, his hot breath washing over Benjamin's face. "I think you've got my message now." He grabbed a hold of Benjamin's shirt and slammed his head hard against the edge of the table. Pain shot through his temple like a bullet.

A crack split the air, then everything went black.

A sliver of moon swept the land in soft light. It'd been hours since the stranger had left. Elsie had to tell Benjamin about the man. With Aunt Kate finally asleep, Elsie took the lantern outside and lit it. She peered over her shoulder before sprinting the short distance to Benjamin's. Standing before his door, Elsie hesitated. *Aunt Kate would tie me to the chair if she knew I was coming to talk to Benjamin.* She rapped twice and tapped her foot as she waited. No noises came from inside. Maybe she should've tried the barn first.

Elsie debated going there, but intuition prompted her to stay at the house. She breathed a prayer and opened the door a crack. "Benjamin, are you here? Benjamin?"

She edged the door open a little further. With a swallow, she stepped into the room and lifted the lantern high. A dark form lay on the floor beside the table, leaning at an awkward angle. Her body went hot then cold.

Rushing into the house, she set her lantern next to his, her fingers shaking as she lit the second. Was he dead? Her heart floundered as she took in Benjamin's sprawled frame. Dropping beside him, Elsie checked his pulse, thankful to feel its slow, steady beating beneath her fingertips. Her breath puffed out in relief.

"Oh, Benjamin." Dark bruises covered his face and eyes. Blood pooled beneath his head and near his temple.

Who had done this? Mr. Santos had left her house hours ago. Had Benjamin been lying here, that long, needing help, and she'd been too scared of her aunt to check on him earlier? A lump lodged in her throat. *I should've warned him right after the stranger left. This is all my fault.*

"Benjamin, please wake up." She gripped his hand and squeezed.

Not a single muscle flickered.

What should she do? He'd made her promise not to leave the property without him, especially with the outlaws on the loose. A shiver ran up Elsie's arms. Not knowing who had done this, she didn't feel safe riding around by herself. She couldn't leave her aunt undefended either. No. Traveling in the dark to the Larsons' wasn't an option. She sighed and closed the door.

This is something I'll have to figure out myself. It was the least she could do after all Benjamin had done for her.

Elsie ran her hands along his limbs. She didn't feel any broken bones, and no pools of blood darkened the floorboards other than by his head. She should be thankful for that, but the fact that he hadn't awakened concerned her. Elsie slipped her arms under his shoulders and tried to scoot him closer to the bed. She only managed to move him a few inches. Digging her heels in, she tried again. His body slid a foot further. Five more feet to go.

Sweat soaked her clothes as she continued to move him inch by inch. She couldn't tell how long it took to get him to the side of the bed. Taking a moment to catch her breath, Elsie latched her arms around his chest and hoisted him to a seated position.

Give me strength, Lord. With a grunt, she stood, yanking his body backward. She fell onto the bed with his body on top of hers.

Warmth rushed to her cheeks as she slid out from under him and lifted his legs onto the bed as well. Good thing no one could see her now. They'd surely have something to say about her being in a man's bed. Of course, it'd only been for a few seconds.

Shoving those thoughts aside, Elsie removed Benjamin's boots. She twisted her hands together, trying to figure out what to do next. Maybe she should boil some water. Elsie spotted his bucket in the corner of the room, pleased to find it full. She poured a small amount into a kettle. Elsie stoked the almost burned out embers, blew on them, and, as soon as the flame came to life, she set a log in the stove.

A chill whispered over her skin as her body cooled from the exertion of moving Benjamin's deadweight. Elsie rubbed her hands up and down her arms trying to warm them. She could see her breath. She hadn't noticed the cold in the house until then.

Looking about, Elsie found a crate in the corner near the bed. She yanked out a blanket and secured it around Benjamin's frame. He still hadn't moved. Wanting to somehow provide comfort, she ran a light finger across the narrow, unbruised portion of his face.

Dear God, save him. A hiccupping sob burst out.

Spotting a small rag, Elsie dipped it into the bucket and gently ran it across his face, cleaning away the dried blood.

Wake up, Benjamin.

I need you.

The land doesn't matter. You do.

I care about you.

Dear Lord, please don't take him.

The mantras echoed in her heart as she bathed his face in cool water, running the rag across the bruises she could see.

How many were hidden under his clothes, she didn't know. She prayed he'd awaken.

Elsie dragged a chair beside the bed and perched on the edge of the seat. Her fingers stroked through his curls, checking his head for any lumps. Her heart faltered when she felt an egg-sized bump at the side of his head. Elsie swallowed, a tumbleweed settling into her throat.

The last time Benjamin had a knock to his noggin, he'd been out for less than a minute. Would he ever awaken?

Elsie grabbed his wrist to reassure herself his heart still had a strong beat. A relieved sigh escaped when she felt the steady pulsing. Her throat constricted as she kept vigil.

"Dear God, I'm not sure what to do to help him. Please show me. Make him wake up soon and be with his head." Fresh tears sprang to her cheeks.

"Benjamin." Elsie patted his arm.

She held her breath, waiting for him to stir.

"Benjamin?"

Still nothing.

Shoving to her feet, Elsie crossed to the stove. Rifling through his belongings, she found what she needed to make a cup of coffee. Maybe preparing a strong brew would help to settle her nerves and perhaps keep her awake through the long hours ahead.

I love him, Lord. Please help him to come back to me. Even if he doesn't want me, I can't stand to see something happen to him.

Elsie alternated between drinking coffee, sitting by his side, praying, pacing, then going back to his side again. She couldn't tell how many hours passed before his eyes flickered.

"Benjamin?" Elsie hovered beside the bed.

One hazel eye peeped open. A moan escaped through his split lip. "W-wat-er."

She poured a glass and supported his head to help him drink, careful not to rub against the bump.

Some of the moisture trickled down his chin. She wiped it away with the back of her hand. "I've been worried sick, fearing you'd never awaken." Elsie set the glass on the floor. "How're you doing?"

"Hurt. All over." He turned a pain-filled eye toward her.

"Who did this to you?"

His forehead wrinkled. "I ... uh ... don't remember. Where am I?"

Dear God, how hard had he hit his head?

Benjamin groaned as he shifted on the bed. A searing pain in his temple made it difficult to think or remember what happened. He strained to recall but came up with nothing. His whole body felt like it'd been trampled by a stagecoach.

"What do you remember?" The woman peered at him.

He glanced around the room. It wasn't familiar. A flaxen beauty stood before him, lines of worry etched across her face. Benjamin stared at her intently. *Nope.* She didn't remind him of anyone.

He strained to recall how he ended up in bed, hurting all over, but came up with nothing. "I don't know. Everything's fuzzy."

He scrunched his blurry eye shut, then opened it again as he surveyed the woman beside the bed. He'd never seen a nurse wearing britches before. Didn't they wear uniforms? "Where did you say I am?"

She cleared her throat and fiddled with the cuff of her sleeve. "You're here on the Cherokee Strip, in your home."

Benjamin had no idea what she was talking about. "I need to rest, Nurse." His eye slid shut once more, and he heard her suck in her breath. He opened his eye, studying her pale face.

"Don't you know who I am?"

"My nurse. Who else would you be?" You'd think the woman would notice he didn't have strength to discuss it further. Maybe she was new to the profession. Pa must've hired her straight from her training. Hadn't he read in the newspaper about a school in New York that was based on Florence Nightingale's principles?

Her brow puckered. "Nurse? How did you come up with that?"

He tried to concentrate on the conversation, but sleep tried to claim him. His eye drifted shut and then back open again. He couldn't think clearly with the constant thudding in his brain.

She shook her head, and something flashed across her face. "Don't you remember, Benjamin? I'm Elsie, your … neighbor."

He started to shake his head but stopped when the pain intensified. "Nurse Elsie, if you don't mind, we can talk about this later." He struggled to speak again, but with no energy left to argue, his blurry eye flickered shut.

Benjamin awoke to find the nurse dozing, sprawled part on the chair that sat beside the bed, and part across his chest. Her face turned toward him. He smiled, lifted a hand, and stroked her blonde hair before he could stop himself. Something about his nurse put his mind at ease. Made him feel secure.

He strained to remember. Hadn't she said her name was Elsie? Yes, that was it. Benjamin smiled. "Good morning, Nurse Elsie." His voice croaked. He cleared his throat and tried again. "I don't think I've ever awakened to find a woman spread across me before. I've read that patients fall in love with their nurses, and not the other way around."

Her long eyelashes fluttered against her cheeks before her eyes snapped open. Color rushed to her face. She sat up and adjusted her shirt. "Y-you're awake."

He started to laugh but held his aching abdomen. "Never been gored by a bull before, but I sure feel like the horns of one jabbed me in the side." His arm shook as he pinched the bridge of his nose. "Must be a cowboy, but that doesn't seem quite right."

Nurse Elsie shook her head. "No, you aren't a cowboy."

"What am I then?"

She licked her lips. "You're a preacher."

"Preacher? You must have me mixed up, that's who my Pa is." He scrunched his eye shut. "My head hurts something fierce. What happened?"

"I'd hoped you could tell me. You were sprawled on the floor when I found you. I'm guessing that Santos fellow must've done this to you. Can you remember anything?"

"Santos? What're you talking about? Maybe you have things mixed up." Benjamin ran his hand across his forehead and reopened his eye. He had no memory of any incident. He strained to recall anything other than hurting, but couldn't.

"Benjamin?" A tremor shook her voice.

"You don't need to worry." He patted her hand. "I'm sure I'll be fine in a few days, and you can move on to your next patient, once I can get my head to stop all this pounding."

"Would you like a cool cloth?" She stood.

"Thank you. That might help, Nurse."

She swallowed and studied him. "I don't know why you keep thinking I'm a nurse. I'm not who you think I am."

Benjamin ran a hand along his jawline. She didn't have to make things so difficult.

A loud hammering pulsated in his head. Or maybe the noise came from someone knocking at the door. He couldn't be sure.

The woman who refused to be called his nurse crossed the room and pulled the door open. A group of people stood there, worry lining each face.

"Elsie? What happened?" One man elbowed his way to the front.

Benjamin struggled to place who they were, but couldn't.

A woman with a baby in her arms gasped. "Oh, my. You poor thing. I hope it wasn't the outlaws."

"What's this about an outlaw? Who are these folks, and why are they all het up all of a sudden?" He twisted on the bed, his legs jerking beneath the sheet.

One man shoved past the nurse and stepped into the room. "We'll do whatever we can to help you, Preacher."

Benjamin glanced around. "I don't know why you keep talking about preachers. Pa's not here. You'll have to look for a preacher elsewhere."

CHAPTER THIRTY-TWO

The woman never proposes to a man but waits for him to take the lead. To be the first to initiate in such situations is considered crass and uncouth.

Mrs. Wigglesworth's Essential Guide to Proper Etiquette and Manners of Refined Society

A collective gasp reverberated. Elsie braced herself for their words of condemnation for spending the night caring for Benjamin unchaperoned. Instead, confusion and concern spread across each of their faces.

Beatrice and Mark elbowed their way past Henry and Mildred. "What's up with the preacher, Elsie? Why's he talking strange?"

Elsie scrubbed at her heavy eyelids. "I don't know." Her gaze flicked to Benjamin and then back to her friends. "He's been talking out of his head ever since he woke up. Can't seem to remember anything about what happened to him either. When I found him last night, after Aunt Kate fell asleep, he was knocked out."

Benjamin propped himself on an elbow. "I don't know who you all are, or why you're asking about my pa."

Elsie fluffed his pillow then gently pushed his shoulders back on the bed. "Whoa there, Benjamin. You need to settle back and rest. Best lie still until your body has time to heal."

"If you say so." His fingers picked at the sheets, and he frowned at their neighbors. "Didn't know you planned on inviting visitors. Maybe you can ask them to leave since I'm not feeling up to company." He yawned and snuggled against the pillow. His good eye fluttered shut a moment later.

Elsie turned, holding a finger to her mouth. "I think he'll sleep now. Why don't we go outdoors and discuss this so he can rest?"

The group traipsed outside, and Elsie lightly pulled the door closed. She strolled toward the bank of the creek where the Sawyers and Larsons had gathered in the shade.

Mark leaned against the trunk of a tree but shoved to a standing position as she got closer. "How did our preacher get so beat up?"

"A stranger showed up yesterday wanting food and water. He left right afterward. I didn't see which direction he went." Elsie sighed. "I should've warned Benjamin."

Beatrice sidled up to her. "This is *not* your fault."

Henry rubbed his chin. "When's the last time you spoke to the sheriff? He stopped by our place and said there might be two groups of outlaws."

"We saw him too, and he said the same thing." Elsie bit back a yawn.

"We didn't spot anything unusual on our way over," Mark said.

"Us neither," Henry replied. "Did the stranger give any indication he was working with another outlaw?"

Elsie wrapped her arms around her body. "Come to think of it, the man did mention something about his partner watching us, or at least the claim. Aunt Kate kept chatting with him like he was a respectable gentleman, but something didn't sit right with me." She glanced over her neighbor's shoulders across the land but didn't see anyone. "Benjamin and I've seen men at a distance, observing or following us."

Henry nodded. "Happened to us a couple times now as well."

"Me too." Mark rubbed the back of his neck.

Beatrice wrapped an arm around Elsie. "It's a shame you weren't able to come and get one of us sooner to help you."

Elsie fidgeted. "Figured it wouldn't be safe, and I'd promised Benjamin not to leave on my own. Besides, if the fellas had been watching us, I didn't want to risk bringing trouble to any of your doorsteps, especially with my aunt here. I'd rather not tell her about the outlaws just yet. She's already chomping to get me to leave."

"Stuff and nonsense." Mildred shifted James to her shoulder and patted Elsie's arm with her free hand. "The Good Lord has us here to help each other out. Don't you fret about your aunt. It'll all work out, you'll see."

"Why did he call you his nurse?" Henry's brow wrinkled.

Elsie shrugged. "He couldn't remember where he was or nothing. He has a huge knot under his hairline. Near as I can tell, whoever beat him up hit him hard on the noggin. No telling how many hours he was out cold before I found him."

Mark rubbed his hand along his chin. "I heard tell of a man who got hit hard on his head after being thrown from a horse. He lost his memory for a while afterward. It eventually came back, but until then, all he could recall was things from his past and not memories from the present. I think they called it amnesia. Wonder if that's what happened to Benjamin." Mark glanced toward the house.

"You think?" Henry stared at Mark. "You feel his recollections will come back then?"

"I pray so," Mark said.

"How do we get him to remember?" Elsie wrung her hands.

"We don't, at least from what happened to this other fella. I think the more we press Benjamin, the more frustrated he'll get. Allow his recollections to flow back on their own. If you agitate him with remembering, it will slow up the process. Try to keep things even-keeled. The man I heard about had his memory come back in snatches. It likely won't happen all at once."

"Even if it means that he doesn't know who we are?" Moisture pricked Elsie's eyes.

Mark nodded. "Afraid so. Hopefully, it won't last long, and we'll be able to figure out who did this to him."

"What do we do now? Elsie's plumb wore out." Beatrice placed an arm around her shoulders.

Mark's face darkened. "I don't like how things are going. If Benjamin got injured in broad daylight, it's not safe for any of us to be alone, especially the womenfolk." He glanced at his wife. "One of us needs to head into Enid to tell the sheriff what happened."

"You willing to go, Mark?" Henry chucked the baby under the chin. "It might be a hard ride for this little guy."

Beatrice's face crumpled as she reached out to her husband.

Mark nodded. "If Henry stays here with the women, I'll ride to Enid and warn the sheriff."

Baby James let out a squawk.

Henry rubbed his jaw. "I reckon that's best. Elsie, do you mind if Mildred feeds the baby at your place? She won't bother your aunt. I'll stay out here and keep an eye on things."

"Feel free, Mildred. Tell Aunt Kate I sent you over. I best see to Benjamin." Elsie turned back toward the house. She crossed the short distance and closed the door, figuring she'd only have a moment of privacy before Beatrice joined her.

Once inside, she knelt beside the bed and placed a hand on Benjamin's. His strong, calloused hand. It'd been a long while since she'd questioned Benjamin's abilities to work the claim. What if he grew fearful and left? Elsie bent her head, a tear slipping down her cheek. *Please, God, help him to wake up and remember who I am. Help his body to heal quickly. Lord, protect us. Give me wisdom to know what to do after our fates are decided. My life won't be the same without him in it.*

Benjamin's eyes fluttered open, and he squinted, trying to get his bearings. A blonde-haired woman stood by the stove with her back toward him. Another with black hair sat in a chair with her feet propped up on a stool. Her eyes were closed.

The one at the stove turned. *Elsie*. That's the name she'd told him. His breathing ratcheted up a notch. Why was he in bed?

"You're awake." She crossed the room and placed a hand on his forehead. "How're you feeling?"

"I hurt all over." He closed his eyes and struggled to concentrate. Why was everything so jumbled in his brain? He glanced again at the woman in the chair and studied her. No name came to mind.

Elsie lifted a jerky hand and smoothed her hair. "You must be parched. I'll get you a glass of water."

"Come here." He held his hand out to her.

She came forward, surveying the floor in front of her, still seeming to avoid eye contact.

Why was she acting so strange? Had he done something to hurt her? If only he could remember. "Are you upset with me, Elsie?"

Her head snapped up, and her face paled. "Y-you recognize me?"

"Of course, I know you. You told me your name before and said we're neighbors. Why wouldn't I recall that?"

She shoved her hands into the pockets of her pants. "I … that is … you. Never mind. Where're you hurting? Henry figures you maybe broke a rib or two, but there's no telling for sure."

"My head and side are the worst. What happened to me? Who's Henry?"

Elsie wobbled and gripped the back of a chair. "We don't know how you were injured. I found you out cold on the floor last night. Henry's one of our neighbors."

He squinted as he concentrated, but he couldn't place the name. He shrugged. "Sorry, that doesn't sound familiar. What's the day and time?"

She pulled out a pocket watch. "A little after four in the afternoon on Sunday."

He nodded. "Pa won't be happy with me missing services." He groaned as he stretched. "The way I feel, I doubt I'll be out of bed at all today." He glanced toward the woman apparently asleep. "Who's that over there?"

"You don't recognize her?"

He shook his head. "No. Should I?"

"She's also one of our neighbors."

"Is she married to—"

Someone knocked on the door.

Elsie reached for a rifle he hadn't noticed and tiptoed to the door. She opened it a crack and peered out. A few seconds later, she swung it wide.

A couple stepped into the room. The woman held a squirming baby. Another angry-looking woman moved around the small family. She thrust her hands on her hips and glared at him.

"How're you doing?" the man asked.

"Fine. You?" Benjamin held out a hand. "I don't think we've met before."

The couple's gaze darted toward Elsie then back to his.

The fella shook his hand. "I'm Henry, and this is Mildred and our son, James. Mind if we sit with you for a while so Elsie can take a break?"

He glanced at Elsie. Dark circles smudged beneath her eyes. From the looks of it, she'd been up all night, or longer. "I don't know. I think I'd feel better if Elsie stayed, especially since you and I just met."

"We'd like to get to know you better Preach … Benjamin. I'll only stay a few moments, then I'll go back out and keep watch." The man carried a rifle too.

"Are we in danger?" He glanced around the room for some way to help protect the strangers.

"Don't you worry about that." The woman with the baby pulled a chair from the table and set it beside the bed. She plopped down onto it. "James here likes to see new folks."

She shifted the baby so Benjamin could see him. The infant's blue eyes lit up, and a smile played across his tiny face. A sweet gurgle made Benjamin smile.

"I demand to know what's going on here." The older woman strode toward the bed, waving a finger in his face. "I woke up to find my niece gone and all these folks descending. You said you're a preacher, why're you lying in bed instead of doing your duty?"

"I don't understand." Benjamin's heart rate ratcheted up a notch.

"Aunt Kate, please. Leave him be. Can't you see he's been hurt?" Elsie tugged the woman away from him.

The black-haired woman in the chair awoke and stretched. She stood and crossed over to him.

He squinted. She looked vaguely familiar.

"We were just telling Benjamin here that Mildred and the baby will stay with him while Elsie gets some rest," the man said, looking at the black-haired woman.

Hadn't that man said his name was Henry?

"I'm going to keep watch outside but thought maybe you could take Elsie to her place."

"Of course." The woman placed her arm around his nurse's shoulders and led her toward the door.

"I can take my niece back to her soddy."

"No," the man shifted his rifle. "You best stay here in case you're needed, Mrs. Tyers."

"Humph." The woman slumped into a chair.

"Wait, Elsie." Benjamin lifted a hand toward her. "I don't know these people. Promise you'll come back."

"I'll meet you outside," the dark-haired woman said as she left with the armed protector.

Elsie's tired gaze swung toward Benjamin's. "I promise. These folks will take good care of you. They're your neighbors. They care about you." She turned and was out the door before he could respond.

He wanted to cry out, to ask her if she cared about him too, but that made no sense. Being a nearby neighbor didn't mean Elsie had special feelings for him. He shook the thought aside.

Elsie leaned her head against the outside of Benjamin's door. Needing time alone before speaking with her friend, she wandered toward the field dotted with green shoots. Henry watched from a short distance away, keeping his gaze on the surrounding country. Once Elsie had collected herself, she headed in the direction of the creek where Beatrice stood waiting.

"What you must've been through last night." Beatrice fell into step beside her. At the soddy, she opened the door, and they stepped inside. "I'm sure having your aunt here isn't helping matters. Why don't you sit down, and I'll make you a cup of tea and some toast?" She led Elsie to a chair.

She sank onto it, folded her arms on the table, and rested her chin against them, watching her friend as she poked around the soddy looking for supplies.

Beatrice removed the cloth from a loaf of bread. She sawed off two huge slices, plopped them on a small tray, placing them in the oven. "Sorry I ended up falling asleep." Her hand rested on the small swell of her abdomen. "This little one sure tuckers me out."

A few minutes later, Beatrice plunked the buttered toast on the table along with a steaming cup of tea in front of her.

Elsie bowed her head and prayed before nibbling on a piece of toast and taking a sip of tea. The hot beverage soothed down to her toes.

"Did I hear right, that Benjamin called you by name?"

She nodded. "Apparently, mine's the only one he can remember. He said it's only because I told him, though."

"Maybe he recalls more since you two have spent a lot of time working on the claim."

"Could be." Elsie shrugged. "We may never know." She chewed another bite of toast. "I don't know what I'm going to do, Beatrice. Benjamin acted funny the other day. He brought a load of firewood and said he had something to talk to me about, but then Aunt Kate showed up, and he's made himself scarce since then."

"I bet he plans to pop the question." Beatrice squealed and bounced in her seat.

"What question?" Elsie's hand halted halfway to her mouth as she raised the cup. "You can't possibly think he planned to ask me to marry him. He hasn't ever said that he cares for me."

"He does, I tell you. What stopped him from talking to you?"

"The sheriff showed up, followed by the clerk from the lawyer's office in Enid—the one Benjamin hired to represent his case for getting awarded the deed. We only have three weeks until one of us must leave. And then Aunt Kate showed up in the middle of the mayhem. What am I going to do?"

"Swallow your pride, and tell the man you love him."

"I don't even know what he remembers, and I can't exactly say anything right now when his memory's not complete. Mark said he needs to remember on his own."

"But what if it helps him remember you? What're you afraid of?"

Elsie's chest constricted. "His saying that he's not interested in me. I'm afraid I'm not good enough for him, that I'll never measure up to Mary. She would've made the perfect preacher's wife, not me. I'm too rough and uncultured. Besides, it ain't right for the gal to tell the fella that she wants to be married."

Married? Could I be happy as Benjamin's wife? Elsie's stomach pitched like a toy boat in a flood-stage river. She fiddled with her shirt sleeve. She most definitely could picture herself married to him, but only if he truly cared for her. If she asked him, he'd feel pressured, put on the spot. There was no way she'd do it and risk rejection. She'd had enough of *that* to last a lifetime.

No. She'd wait for him to come to her. No matter how long, no matter if he never did.

That might just kill her.

CHAPTER THIRTY-THREE

It is important to keep lines of communication open and flowing. Do not allow things to fester between each other, especially those you are closest to.
Mrs. Wigglesworth's Essential Guide to Proper Etiquette and Manners of Refined Society

Benjamin pounded his fist on the table. It'd been nearly two weeks since he woke to pain and no memory of those who'd claimed to be close friends. All their names had come back, or was that because he'd been seeing them so often? Most frustrating of all was the looming sense of doom and having no idea what it could be.

When the door creaked open, he glanced up.

Elsie poked her head inside. "Benjamin? How're you feeling? You look a little flushed." She stepped closer, and he got a whiff of honeysuckles.

She placed her hand on his brow.

A tremor ran through him at her touch. He'd teased her about falling for her patient, but honestly, his feelings for Elsie had stirred instead. She'd been a true professional in every way. Not once had she said or done anything inappropriate. Of course, most times her steps were hounded by that aunt of hers.

Elsie had said he'd lived here, on the strip, for over two months already—he wished he could remember what had transpired during that time.

"Benjamin?" A "V" formed between her eyes.

"Sorry. You caught me woolgathering again. I'm fine. Just wishing I remembered more."

"Give it time." Her voice was a soothing balm. "Maybe if you don't try so hard, it'll come back faster."

"Maybe." He watched as she dished food onto a plate and set it before him.

"I-is there anything else I can do for you?" She fiddled with the placement of a fork on the table.

He ran his hand through his hair and blew out a huge breath. "Do you have a husband?"

"N-no." Her gaze darted to his before she crossed the room and poured a glass of water.

"Really? I'm surprised. I thought for sure you'd be taken."

She shook her head.

"How about a beau?"

Again, she shook her head.

The more time Benjamin spent in her presence, the more he'd have liked to capture her hand in his, kiss the palm, working his way up her arm, to her slender neck and alluring lips. He'd refrained, clearing his throat and attempting to get his clamoring emotions under control. There'd been no opportunity to act upon his urges when her aunt was an alert watchdog.

Not that Elsie'd given any indication she cared for him other than a friend. Benjamin puffed out a breath. Oh, what could it hurt? It was now or never since the disapproving aunt hadn't come along this time. Benjamin snagged Elsie's hand and planted a chaste kiss near the inside of her wrist.

Her pulse skittered beneath his fingertips. He longed to tug her closer, closing the gap between them. Instead, he asked a final question. "Is there anyone you have in mind to be your beau?"

Her face tightened, and her eyes flashed. She pulled her hand back. "T-there might be."

Hens' feathers. Apparently, he had competition. Who wouldn't fall in love with a beautiful, caring woman like Elsie?

"Were you needing anything else?"

For you to have an interest in me.

"No, that's all for now." He watched as she shrugged back into her coat and wrapped a scarf around her head.

"Enjoy your chicken and biscuits." Elsie whisked the door open, glancing back at him.

Benjamin forced a smile and a wave before she closed the door. *Feels like she just took my heart with her. How is that possible?*

Elsie whipped open the barn door and stepped inside. The one place Aunt Kate wouldn't follow. Usually, being with the animals helped calm Elsie, but not so today. She rubbed between Buster's ears and then rested her cheek against the horse's warm head, wrapping her arms around her faithful friend's neck. "What am I going to do, Buster?"

The horse snorted.

Time's getting short, Lord. We only have a little over a week before we meet that lawyer fella. I can't bear to ask Benjamin to leave if I win the claim, not with him forgetting everything. She clenched her jaw. *I thought before the sheriff showed up that we might be able to build a life here, but if he doesn't remember me as more than a neighbor, I don't see that happening. I don't want to leave with Aunt Kate but … maybe her coming is a sign that Benjamin and I aren't ever supposed to be more than friends.*

Elsie huffed. She'd turned into one of the things she despised most—a sappy female. It'd taken all she had to hide her feelings from Benjamin when they were together. She didn't dare let Aunt Kate see. The daily visits to check on him were wearing her thin, though. She'd tried to stay away, but each time she returned like a bee to a flower. *Lord, give me the reserves for another week. Don't let me turn into a woman who cries at the drop of a hat.*

She picked up a brush and curried Buster's coat, trying not to think about the feel of Benjamin's mouth pressed against her wrist, or how she'd longed for it to be pressed against her lips instead. Warmth coursed through her body, but she forced herself to concentrate on the task at hand. The monotonous activity helped clear her roiling thoughts.

After mucking out the stalls, she groomed Milly. Elsie startled when something bumped against the corner of the barn. She cocked her head but heard nothing more. Had the noise came from inside or outside? She reached for her rifle and realized she'd left it at the soddy. She'd planned on going straight home, not taking up refuge in the barn. That kiss had her all off-kilter.

Quiet descended, except for the sound of the cows chewing their cud. Elsie shrugged and went back to brushing Milly. Both horses needed some exercise, but that would have to wait until Benjamin was well enough to ride with her. Icy tendrils trailed up and down her spine whenever she thought about the man she'd spotted weeks ago. Was he the one who'd visited her and her aunt?

The barn door creaked. Surely Aunt Kate hadn't decided to track her down. Elsie peeked over her shoulder, afraid to leave the stall. Maybe she'd forgotten to latch the door, and the wind had blown it open.

A shuffle in the corner sent prickles dancing up her arm.

John Clark stepped out of the shadows. "Thought I'd check and see if you needed anything and see how the preacher is doing." He crumpled the rim of his hat.

"You near scared me to death."

John lowered his gaze. "I'm sorry. When I didn't find you at your soddy, your aunt mentioned you might be here. I wanted to tell you how bad I feel about, well, you know. I hope you'll forgive me." He glanced up. "I've done a lot of thinking lately, and I know now that I was wrong. I shouldn't have taken such liberties with you, especially when you kept telling me you weren't interested. Ma would be ashamed of me."

Elsie sucked in her lip, unsure what to say.

"I want you to know you won't see me for a while. Figured it's best if I attend church in Enid."

"Oh?"

He nodded. "Before I do, I wanted to check in. I heard the preacher ran into some trouble. Is it true that he can't recall much since his accident?"

"Yes. He was roughed up pretty bad."

He frowned. "I'm sorry for him. I know he and I didn't always see eye-to-eye when it came to things, particularly you, but I've never wished ill to come to him."

She didn't know how to respond.

"I've taken enough of your time. I just wanted to apologize before I see the preacher. Again, I hope you can forgive me."

"I do."

John turned and strolled away, securing the door behind him.

Darkness would be settling in soon. Elsie'd best get to her soddy. Aunt Kate would nag her all the more if she stayed away longer. Elsie chucked the currying brush into a box. The rest of the chores could wait until morning. She shouldered her coat on, fumbling with the buttons. When she stepped outside, snow flurries scurried across the worn path to her place. Shivering, Elsie flipped the collar up, trying to prevent the wind from whisking down her neck.

By the time she entered the soddy and stood before the stove to warm herself, a chill had settled over her. Elsie couldn't tell if it came from the elements outside or her cold, lonesome heart.

Lord, I need to remember what happened. Benjamin rubbed his hand across his forehead. *Please.*

A knock at the door made his heart quicken. He prayed it wasn't Aunt Kate. His heart constricted. Maybe Elsie'd decided to come back. Perhaps if she helped him talk things through, they'd be able to clear up his fuzzy memories. They hadn't had the chance to do so when her aunt interrupted at every opportunity.

When he whisked the door open, Elsie wasn't hovering in his doorway. A man he'd seen before stood there, but a name didn't register.

"Hello, Preacher. Do you mind if I come in?" A tempest flickered across the man's face.

Benjamin hesitated. "I think I know you." He studied the man's features. "John something." He waved his hand. "Don't tell me. I almost have it."

The man studied him.

"John. John Clark, right?"

The man smiled. "How're you doing? The Larsons told me about your run-in. I'm sorry to hear it. I was hoping you'd be open to my talking with you about something."

Benjamin swung the door wider. "Come in. Please, excuse my manners."

They moved into the room. He motioned to a seat, but John declined.

John twirled his hat. "The Larsons mentioned you've lost some of your memories?"

He nodded. "At least most of the recent ones."

"Do you remember," John cleared his throat, "your tussle with me?"

Benjamin half-closed his eyes in concentration. It took him a minute, but he eventually retrieved the memory. "I recall a fight of some sort between us, but nothing more than that. Sorry."

John's face stiffened. "I just spoke with Elsie in the barn."

"Oh?" Benjamin tightened his grip. John must be the beau she spoke of earlier. What did the couple remember that Benjamin didn't? Why had he punched the man, and why could he recall that incident but not the myriad of other details from the past months? The constant barrage of questions did little to ease his mind.

John grinned. "We've made up, and she's forgiven me. I told her I was sorry for my actions. Wanted to tell you too. I think we'll be able to move forward in our relationship now, and I was hoping you and I could too."

"Huh?"

"What I'm trying to say, Preacher, is that I hope you can forgive me for how I've acted in the past. My ma would be ashamed of me." John gulped.

"No hard feelings." Benjamin was at a loss of what else to say.

"Thank you. That means a lot to me." He turned to leave then shifted around again. "I wanted you to know that I plan on taking Elsie's advice."

"What advice is that?" Benjamin cringed, not really wanting to know.

"I'm going to take things slow, and get to know my girl really well. Should've done that first-off, but my impatience got in the way."

"I don't know what to say." *Literally.*

"Thanks again for forgiving me. I told Elsie I won't be coming to services here anymore. I've been attending over in Enid. Figured it's best for all of us."

John clapped him on the back. "Take care, Preacher. I'll be seeing you. Make sure you get this sharing-the-land thing taken care of before time goes on any longer." He left without another word.

Benjamin sagged into a chair. What had the man meant by sharing the land? It niggled at the edge of Benjamin's consciousness. He strode across the floor, flinging the door open. Snow swirled around him as he stepped outside. He hadn't been outside since—

As he stared toward Elsie's soddy, uneasiness settled over him. Benjamin closed the door, hurried over to the bed, searching beneath the mattress. He felt underneath it, but he couldn't find it. Sinking to his knees, he lifted the pallet higher, but no slip of paper could be seen.

What exactly had happened to *his deed*?

He rubbed his temples, willing his memories to come back. The recollections slowly seeped into his mind.

Herbert threatening Elsie if Benjamin didn't give him the deed to the property. How would the man have known about Elsie? That part was still fuzzy.

Two weeks before the man returned.

Fists colliding with his body.

The thud of his head against the edge of the table and then …

Nothing.

Dear God. How could Benjamin have forgotten about the man who'd robbed and beaten him? Herbert must be one of the outlaws the neighbors kept talking about. With shaking fingers, Benjamin counted how many days he'd been healing. Fourteen days.

He had to get word to the sheriff and tell him what he knew. Would he be able to prove the land was his? Didn't claim offices have that kind of information on file? Maybe he should stop there after seeing the sheriff.

He threw the door open again. A soft snow fell as darkness shrouded the land. Too dark to make it to Enid tonight, providing he remembered how to get there. Most of his memory had returned as far as he could tell, although something still niggled at the edge of his consciousness concerning Elsie. That's what he wanted to recall the most, but it remained elusive. He sighed. Pulling out a piece of paper, Benjamin started making a list of what needed to be done.

Snow crunched beneath Elsie's boots. A coyote howled in the distance. She increased her pace as she hurried to Benjamin's. Aunt Kate puffed along beside her. This would be the last meal she'd fix him. Truth be told, he probably could've fixed his own meals the past week now that he was up and moving, but she hadn't been able to keep from visiting him.

"I don't see why you make food for the man. He's on his feet. It's not proper for you to keep swarming after him like a moth to a light. It's shameful." Her aunt scowled.

She ignored the woman as they reached the house.

After a short rap, Benjamin's door swung open. A taut expression clouded his face. *Something* had happened since she'd last seen him. Maybe his visit with John hadn't gone so well.

He motioned them inside.

She'd planned to hand the food to him and take her leave, but she yearned to be near him—something she'd always scorned her schoolmates for doing.

"Thank you. You've taken such wonderful care of me. I can't begin to thank you enough." He took the basket from her and set it on the table.

"Ain't no need for a thank you."

"You've taken advantage of my niece's generosity far too long now. She won't be coming back." Aunt Kate crossed her arms.

"I kind of hoped you'd join me this evening." He glanced at Elsie.

Something *had* changed, but what? She opened her mouth to refuse but found herself nodding.

"Here, let me help you with your coat." He reached to assist her.

"No need." She shrugged out of it before he got closer. Elsie couldn't think straight when he stood beside her.

He took both of their coats and slung them over one arm. With his other hand, he lifted the towel covering the basket. "Mmm. Smells good. You're an incredible cook. You'll make a man happy one day."

"It certainly won't be a frontiersman like you." Aunt Kate lifted her nose a smidgen. "She'll be marrying someone with money who can take care of her and help keep her in line. Lord knows the man will have a huge undertaking ahead of him."

Elsie ignored her aunt. "Ain't nothing fancy. Plain fare like I fed my pa." She scooted onto a chair, far from him. *Dear Lord, let him sit on his side of the table and not beside me.* He pulled out tin plates and set them down before sitting across from her. Aunt Kate settled to her left.

Elsie reached into the basket, withdrawing the big bowl of chicken stew that she'd started earlier, dishing it onto their plates.

He bowed his head and prayed.

"At least your ma taught you manners." Aunt Kate smiled at Benjamin. "It's more than I can say for my niece."

Elsie ignored her aunt's comment. While Benjamin and her aunt ate, she shoved the food back and forth across her plate, hoping he wouldn't notice her lack of appetite. "There's something different about you. John didn't threaten you, did he? He said he'd changed."

Aunt Kate's head lifted. "John who?"

"Nobody important." Elsie darted a glance at Benjamin.

He frowned. "No. My conversation with John was nothing like that."

She studied him. Was it her imagination or did he squirm?

Her eyes narrowed. "What're you keeping from me, Benjamin?"

Benjamin watched Elsie's knuckles turn white as her fingers curled around the handle of the fork. "I saw it snowing again earlier. Is it the first time?"

She shook her head. "Second snowfall. Had one a couple days ago, but it was only a light dusting." Her right eyebrow lifted.

He couldn't help taking a sudden interest in the food on his plate.

"You were outside?"

He peeked at her from beneath his eyelashes as he took another spoonful of food.

Her face paled. She glanced at her aunt then dropped her gaze.

"Yep, but only for a minute or so."

"It's stopped now, although I think we've a couple inches." She stared out the window before meeting his gaze. "Benjamin? You don't seem to be yourself tonight." Her eyes darkened.

"The man's been crazier than a loon the past couple weeks." Her aunt wiped her mouth. "What makes you think he's acting any differently?"

"Aunt Kate! Honestly. Don't you ever have anything nice to say?" Color filled Elsie's cheeks.

"Humph." The older woman went back to eating.

Benjamin cleared his throat. "I'm much better today. In fact, I'd like to visit Mark tomorrow and was hoping you'd drive me. Your aunt is welcome too."

"She's not going anywhere without a chaperone." The older woman's eyes narrowed as she glared at him.

"Yes, well, I'm not sure if I'll be capable of getting to the Sawyers on my own. Besides, I thought you might enjoy visiting with … Beatrice, right?"

A small smile crossed Elsie's face but didn't shine in her eyes. "You figured that out on your own this time. That's good."

"The Sawyers are the ones who don't have a baby yet?"

She nodded. "See, you're starting to recall things."

He snorted. "I don't know that I'd say that. When you weren't watching, I took notes and have been trying to memorize them so I wouldn't forget."

"Oh." Elsie deflated at his words. "You sure you're up to the trip?" She went back to pushing the food across her plate.

He reached out, stilling the movement of her fork with his hand. "My ribs are mostly healed, and I've been penned up in this house for too long."

Her aunt rapped her knife against the top of his knuckles. “Keep your hands to yourself, young man.”

A stricken expression crossed Elsie’s face. She dropped her hands to her lap. Well out of his reach.

Benjamin cringed. He *needed* to convince Elsie and her aunt to drive him to the Sawyers. “I could use some male company.”

Her cheeks paled. “Perhaps you should go there on your own, and I’ll work in the field.” She pushed her chair backward.

“You and I both know there’s nothing to do in the fields when they’re covered in snow.”

She stood and tugged her coat and Stetson on, settling the brim over her eyes. “Come along, Aunt Kate.”

“Elsie, I didn’t mean to imply that I want to get away from you. I appreciate your friendship. From what I can tell these past weeks, you’ve been a good neighbor to me.”

“She won’t be that much longer.” Her aunt stood and tucked her chair under the table.

He blew out a breath and tried again. “There’re some things I need to discuss with Mark. I’d appreciate you taking me there in case I tire.”

Her shoulders drooped. Benjamin thrust his hand through his hair. He couldn’t seem to say anything right tonight. If only her aunt weren’t here, he could talk freely. It took all his willpower to keep from going to Elsie, swooping her into his arms, and never letting go—except he refused to steal another man’s woman. Too bad he hadn’t recognized his feelings for her before John had. *Had I even stood a chance?*

CHAPTER THIRTY-FOUR

Allow the male to lead in the relationship. Trust his headship in all matters.
Mrs. Wigglesworth's Essential Guide to Proper Etiquette and Manners of Refined Society

Elsie couldn't find Aunt Kate anywhere. Elsie'd gone to the barn to hitch the wagon and returned to find the soddy empty. She squelched the momentary pleasure that rippled through her. *Forgive me, Lord.* That pleasure quickly turned to panic.

"Benjamin!" Elsie ran toward his place.

His door flew open. "What is it?"

"It's Aunt Kate. I think something's happened to her."

She ran up the steps, and he gripped her arms. "What do you mean?"

"She's not in the soddy, but she wouldn't just wander off on her own."

"Are you sure?"

Elsie nodded. "My aunt is not one to go for a stroll across the plains by herself."

"Right." He pinched the bridge of his nose. "Was anything disturbed at your place?"

"I didn't really look other than to see if Aunt Kate was ready to go." Elsie glanced back toward her soddy.

"We best double check. Maybe Herbert returned." Benjamin held his side as they jogged in that direction.

"W-what did you say? Where did you hear that name?"

"My memory of that day returned. The man who beat me up was the one I saw the day before the run."

"The man who came into my house said his name was Herbert Santos."

Elsie shoved the door with her hip and quickly lit the lantern. Benjamin lingered in the doorway. Items were strewn across the floor. Her gut twisted. "Somebody was here. There hasn't been a single item out of place since Aunt Kate arrived."

"What's that scrap of paper on the table?" Benjamin pointed.

Shoved underneath the edge of her Bible was a crumpled note. Elsie's hand shook as she picked it up.

If you want to see your aunt alive, bring your deed to the Glass Mountains.

She handed it to Benjamin before rustling through items in a crate.

"Don't do it." He crossed the room and touched her shoulder.

"I *have* to do something." Elsie found the deed and shoved it in her shirt pocket. "I can't let him hurt her like he did you. Even as cantankerous as Aunt Kate is, she doesn't deserve this. Don't try and stop me, Benjamin."

"We really should fetch the sheriff."

"There's no time to ride all the way to Enid and back. By then, Herbert might have hurt her …" She snagged her rifle and motioned him out of her house.

"I'm not letting you go by yourself."

"I don't think you're up to riding Milly." She didn't wait for his response as she sprinted to the barn.

Benjamin caught up as she unharnessed the horses from the wagon. He worked alongside her cinching his saddle in place.

Minutes later, they both were ready.

"Give me a second." He trotted to his house and returned with his rifle and a rope.

They didn't speak as they rode toward the Glass Mountains. Elsie led the way, angling toward the opposite side of the range from where she'd first heard the probable outlaws, praying they could find cover before anyone started shooting.

Minutes later, they crouched behind a cedar tree.

"Do you see anything?" Benjamin knelt beside her, whispering.

She studied the terrain above them. *There*. The glint of sunlight on the barrel of a gun. Or was it reflecting from the bright stones that covered the mountains? It flashed again in the same position. No. Definitely a gun. Elsie put her finger to her lips before pointing it out to Benjamin.

"What do you want to do?"

"We need to get a lay of the situation first. We can't rush in there and risk getting either us or Aunt Kate hurt."

Elsie couldn't tell how much time passed as they kept watch. She was glad to have Benjamin beside her, lending his moral support, but she had to keep him safe. She couldn't bear to see anything happen to him, especially on her or her aunt's account.

Benjamin wiped his slick hand against the side of his pants and gripped his rifle tighter. He'd do whatever it took to keep Elsie safe. His gaze narrowed as he watched a slight movement where they'd seen the glint of a rifle earlier.

A muffled voice echoed off the wall of the rocky terrain.

Elsie's eyes widened. "Didn't that sound like Aunt Kate?"

He shifted and cupped his ear. "I think she must be gagged, otherwise, I'm sure we'd hear her."

"At least she's alive."

He nodded and squinted. "Looks like it's just Herbert. If someone else is with him, they would've made an appearance by now. He hasn't shifted position."

The lines on Elsie's face tightened. "We need a plan. We can't wait much longer."

"You cover me while I sneak around that way." He motioned. "I'll come up on the side there and take him by surprise." He grabbed the coil of rope at their feet and slung it over his shoulder.

The color drained from her cheeks. "No, Benjamin, that will leave you in the open. You could get hurt worse." She started to grab his arm, but he shook free of her grip.

"Trust me."

Elsie watched Benjamin until he disappeared behind a pile of rocks. She then turned, keeping an eye on her aunt and Herbert, partially blocked behind a rock outcropping. She caught glimpses of Benjamin creeping along the side of the mountain. *Please be with him, Lord. Don't let anything happen to him. I …*

She couldn't finish the prayer, but the Lord knew what her heart wanted to say.

If only Aunt Kate would distract Herbert, perhaps they'd have a chance at capturing him.

A bullet ricocheted at Elsie's feet. The no-good varmint. Raising her rifle, she took aim, but there was no clear shot. Not without possibly hitting Aunt Kate.

Another bullet narrowly missed Elsie.

Her heart pounded as she pressed tighter against the tree. Its slender trunk did little to protect her. She searched around for better cover but didn't see any. If she ran for a different hiding spot, she'd likely get shot.

A third bullet whizzed and thunked into the trunk just above her head. She swallowed. Her hands shook as she sighted the rifle again.

Peeking around the side of the tree, something moved only a few yards from Herbert. *Benjamin*. The outlaw'd been so busy shooting at her, Benjamin had managed to get close.

Her heart skipped a beat as he lunged toward the outlaw. At the same moment, a shot rang out.

"No!" She screamed, running toward the mountain.

Dear God, please don't let him be hurt.

CHAPTER THIRTY-FIVE

When met with an impasse, it is important for one to admit defeat and be willing to give up their desire to be right in order to bring harmony and peace to the relationship.

Mrs. Wigglesworth's Essential Guide to Proper Etiquette and Manners of Refined Society

Benjamin's arm burned as he wrapped the thick rope around the unconscious outlaw's wrists. A bruise was already appearing where Herbert had hit his head against the rock when Benjamin had tackled him—to stop him from shooting at Elsie.

Once he was satisfied the bandit couldn't break free, he ungagged Aunt Kate and loosened the twine binding her arms and legs.

A single tear trickled down her cheek. Her blouse was dirty, and there was a ragged rip on the hem of her skirt. The woman's gray hair sagged on one side as a long wisp escaped the tight bun at the nape of her neck. "Y-you saved me. Why? I haven't been anything but mean to you. I don't understand why you'd care enough to rescue me."

"How people treat us shouldn't determine whether or not we do the right thing. My faith commands me to forgive, even when I'm placed in difficult situations."

"You really are a preacher, aren't you?" She wobbled as he helped her to stand.

"Yes, ma'am. I remember that now and lots of other things too. Except there's one thing that keeps nagging at me that I can't recall. It's been driving me near loco." Benjamin watched as Elsie scurried up the mountain toward them, climbing over jagged rocks. "Be careful."

She lifted her head, her face paling. "Benjamin? You're bleeding!"

He glanced at the blood oozing from his right shoulder. "Just a graze."

The older woman reached over and grasped his left hand. "You asked me a question a few weeks ago. I've changed my mind. The answer is yes."

He pinched the bridge of his nose as he struggled to recall what the lady was talking about. "I'm sorry. I don't have any idea what you're saying. Perhaps—"

Elsie vaulted the last few steps, right into his arms.

Tears streaked her face. She squeezed him tight, released him, and backed away. Her gaze searched his. "You've been hit. Is the bullet still in?"

He shifted his arm. "I don't think so. It's not bleeding much."

She extended her hand to him but then let it fall by her side. He wished she'd return to his arms. He shoved the thought aside. It wasn't right to pine after a girl who was already attached to another man.

After finding no other wounds on Benjamin, Elsie hugged her aunt. "Did Herbert hurt you?"

"No, dear. Although his shins will be bruised for a while." A crooked smile broke forth like it'd been a long time since her facial muscles had been used for such an activity. "Uncouth man. I should've noticed it from the start." She straightened but still held her niece's hands. "*You* did, though."

Elsie's brow furrowed as she glanced at Benjamin.

He shrugged his shoulders, then wished he hadn't.

Elsie's gaze swung back to her aunt. "Are you sure he didn't hit you or something?"

"I'm positive."

Elsie kicked Herbert's boot. "What're we going to do with him?"

"Maybe between the three of us we can get him down the mountain," Benjamin said.

"You're not up to carting him into Enid with your bad shoulder and still recovering from broken ribs." Elsie bent to help lift the unconscious outlaw.

He hefted as Aunt Kate came around and shoved until they had the man standing between Benjamin and Elsie.

"Is that his horse there?" The older woman pointed to a clump of cedars not too far from where they had tied their horses.

"Looks like it." Elsie grunted as they moved the bandit past a jagged rock.

By the time they made it down the mountain and to the horse, sweat soaked Benjamin's shirt. They slung Herbert over the rump of his own horse, fettering him securely. Blood seeped from his head wound, trailing down his neck.

Aunt Kate puffed, her face turning red. "He must've hit his head hard when you knocked into him."

Elsie tugged on the horse's reins as they strolled toward their mounts. "I say we stop at the Sawyers' since they're on the way to Enid. We can see if Mark will help take this guy in. You aren't strong enough yet to make the hard ride to town."

"I can make it." He gritted his teeth, his shoulder throbbing with each footfall.

Aunt Kate snorted. "Young man, I thought you were smart. My niece has a valid plan. You wouldn't make it all the way there without causing more pain and possibly opening yourself to infection, and there's no way I'll allow Elsie to travel with the bandit herself. Ask your friends to help out."

He sighed. "Yes, ma'am."

It took every ounce of his strength to hold the reins as they headed toward the Sawyers'. Fire blazed from the wound. He blinked, trying to focus on Elsie and her aunt ahead of him on

Buster, with Herbert's horse trailing. Asking Mark for help was suddenly a welcome idea. Benjamin breathed a sigh of relief when he spotted his friend's homestead.

Elsie slowed her horse until he'd come alongside her. "Looks like they got company."

He squinted. "Can't tell from here whose horse that is."

"Me neither."

As they drew closer, the soddy door opened, and a man stepped out.

"Isn't that the sheriff," Benjamin said. "Maybe we won't have to ride to Enid after all."

"Wonder why he's here?" Elsie shifted on the saddle. Her aunt wobbled behind her. "We're almost there, Aunt Kate."

"Good. I'm not used to this mode of transportation." The older woman sat at an odd angle.

As they rode into the Sawyers' yard, Benjamin swung down from his horse, gripping the saddle to steady himself. The sheriff walked toward them, his gaze shifting between all of them.

"What do we have here?" The sheriff stood with his arms folded across his barrel chest.

Elsie jumped down from Buster and turned to assist her aunt.

"We found one of those outlaws," Benjamin said. "Or at least the one who beat me up."

The lawman's brows rose. "Is he dead?"

Benjamin shook his head, leaning heavily against Milly.

"Herbert was shooting at me when Benjamin lunged at him. Knocked him out cold." Elsie's heart constricted as she remembered the scene. She'd thought for sure Benjamin'd been killed.

They quickly brought the sheriff up to date with what had transpired.

He nodded. "I arrested the other fella yesterday who we believe has been working in cahoots with this Herbert Santos. The man started talking when he realized he was facing a long jail time. He's the fella that mentioned watching a single woman's place." The sheriff motioned to Elsie. "Figured it had to be you. I'm doing my best to return the stolen deeds to folks, but it might take some time since most of them moved from the area after being scared off by Santos."

The soddy door opened, and Mark stepped out, followed by his wife.

"Did you all want to come in?"

Aunt Kate hugged Elsie, then made her way to the soddy. "I'll see you inside, dear."

Beatrice's brows rose as she held the door open. "Make yourself at home, Mrs. Tyers. I'll be right in." She closed the door and joined them, drawing Elsie into a hug.

The bulge of her friend's belly shoved into Elsie's gut. Her throat constricted as she shifted out of her friend's embrace and away from the reminder of something she might never experience.

Benjamin glanced at the sheriff. "This Santos we think is the outlaw who beat up landowners and took their deeds."

"He's the man who stopped by my soddy before going over to Benjamin's place and roughing him up," Elsie said.

"I can't believe you fed an outlaw." Beatrice twisted her hands together. "Oh, Elsie, you could've been hurt."

"It wasn't my idea." Elsie glanced toward the soddy, then back at the lawman. "What were you saying about the deeds, Sheriff? You mean some of the people won't be able to claim their land after having it stolen?" She kicked at the dirt. "What'll happen then? Will their land become available for purchase?"

The lawman shrugged. "I don't know for sure. The land office can probably give you better answers to that than I can. I'm just trying to find the folks who had their deeds stolen so I can return them."

"Why're you asking, Elsie?" Beatrice touched Elsie's arm. "You looking to buy more land?"

She shook her head. "What? No. I don't have money for it right now. Maybe one day, before long."

"Well, I best get this outlaw back to town. By the way, we got word the Yeager gang has left the area." The sheriff mounted his horse and took the reins from Elsie. "When you're both up to it, I'd like you to stop in town so I can get a written statement. You'll probably want to bring your aunt along too."

"A statement?" Mark stared after the departing lawman before his gaze swung back to Benjamin. "Sounds like you have a lot to tell us. We best see to your wound."

The men entered the soddy first, and Beatrice scurried after them. Elsie followed more slowly, needing a moment to compose herself. When she entered, Aunt Kate was sound asleep, curled up on the bed in the corner.

"She's had a rough morning," Elsie whispered as Beatrice draped a blanket across her aunt.

Benjamin sat on a chair, his pale face shimmering beneath his blond waves.

Elsie refrained from rushing to his side and checking on him. It took sheer willpower to stay put. Digging her fingernails into the palm of her hand helped.

He removed his jacket and shirt while Mark pulled out medical supplies.

Elsie's face flooded with warmth as she forced herself to look away from the corded muscles on Benjamin's chest.

As she sat across the table from the doctoring, her thoughts returned to what the sheriff had said about the unidentified claims. Perhaps God planned to provide a way out for her after all. The more she thought about it, the more she realized the unlikelihood of her getting awarded ownership of the property in an all-male world. She wasn't sure she wanted it either. Without

Benjamin there to work beside her, it would never be the same. If only he'd be completely healed from his amnesia.

She puffed out a breath. Maybe if she sold some of the things Benjamin had bought for her, she'd have enough money to purchase another plot of land. She should've thought of the idea months ago instead of hoping that her troubles would go away. A different property wouldn't be the same one Pa had wanted her to have, but she'd at least be able to stay in the area, in case Benjamin ever came to his senses.

"Elsie?"

Beatrice's voice snapped her out of her wandering thoughts.

Benjamin's gaze found hers as he buttoned up his shirt. "I think I'll stretch my legs."

Mark reached for his coat. "I'll join you."

The men left the soddy, and still, Aunt Kate softly snored.

Elsie's friend stood with a hand covering her round belly and spoke in low tones. "Do you still think you'll be around when this little one makes an appearance in a few months?"

"I want to be, but you know you can always have Mildred help you like I said before."

"I know, but I pray it'll be you who's here to help me. Mildred has her hands full with James. I think she still hasn't adjusted to having to get up through the night so often. We spoke a couple days ago, and she had trouble concentrating on what we were talking about because she was so tired."

"Maybe James will be sleeping more by the time the birth of your baby rolls around. Like you said, that's still a few months away."

"Do you want to see some of the things I've made already?" Beatrice arched her back, making her stomach bulge out more.

"Sure." Elsie averted her eyes.

Her friend crossed the room and opened a chest that stood in the corner. She lifted out a small bundle and brought it back to the table.

Elsie fingered the hand-stitched little gowns. A pair of knit booties drew her attention. She picked them up and held them in the palm of her hand. "Seems hard to believe how tiny a newborn's feet can be. When James was born, I was reminded of the size of the doll one of my sisters left behind when she moved away."

"Mildred let me use a pattern she had so I'd know how little to make them." Beatrice chuckled. "I think we have about everything we need. I'm knitting a blanket yet, and Mark's working on building a cradle."

"You're about ready then." Elsie placed the booties back in the pile.

Beatrice fingered them. "You know, this baby"—she rubbed her stomach—"and Mark are two of the things I've always longed for. What about you, Elsie? If you had to pick one thing to have with you in this life, besides the Lord, what would you choose?"

Benjamin. Elsie shook her head. If only she could have him.

"I've been thinking about it a lot lately. I'm not sure why, maybe because I'm increasing. What're you most wanting in life, Elsie?"

To be loved and accepted for who I am. To have someone love me so deeply nothing else matters. To have Benjamin go back to the way he was before the outlaw came. Elsie didn't trust herself to put it into words.

"You've always made it known how much the land means to you, but if I had to hazard a guess, it's not so much the claim you care about, but the man who's shared it with you all these months." Beatrice snagged Elsie's hand and gripped it hard. "Am I right?"

Elsie snatched her hand back. "None of it matters since I'm going to lose both of them."

"Then *say* something to him. Tell him how you *really* feel."

"You know I can't. Even if he did feel something for me before, he doesn't remember it now. I can't expect him to tie himself to me when he can't even remember all the experiences we've shared." Elsie strode a few paces away, not trusting herself to say more.

"I still say you should tell Benjamin how you feel. If you win his heart, you'll get to keep your land too."

Elsie's shoulders stiffened. "Please don't press me on this. I'm not hitching myself with any man just so I can keep my property. He'd have to love me for *me*, not the land." She balled her hands into fists.

A blast of cold air chilled her. Elsie turned and saw Benjamin standing beside Mark.

"Why don't you leave Aunt Kate here, and when she awakens, we'll bring her back to you?" Beatrice winked at Elsie.

"Fine by me." She shoved past Benjamin and Mark. "I'll be outside when you're ready to go." She threw the words over her shoulder and closed the door behind her.

Elsie wanted to get on Buster and leave, but with the fatigue she'd seen etched on Benjamin's face, she needed to make sure he made it home without a hitch. A quick walk would afford her plenty of time to think, or at least to pray.

A verse Pa used to quote zinged across her mind. *"The wicked flee when no man pursueth: but the righteous are bold as a lion."* Pa had told her to be bold and to face her troubles instead of running from them.

Elsie glanced toward the Sawyer place. She didn't think she had it in her to stay and fight this time.

Lord, I'm not strong enough to go to Benjamin on my own. He's too fragile right now, and ... I'm afraid of being rejected. I can't bear to lay my feelings out only to have him not feel the same way. Can You make him remember?

I know the time is short, but I've read in the Bible that You perform miracles. Is it too much to ask for one? I've spent too long away from Your presence. Maybe You aren't interested in answering my prayers until You see that I'm not going to turn away from You again.

Elsie's breath puffed out, and a tiny cloud rose before her face. At least one good thing came from this whole experience. Benjamin had brought her back into a relationship with the Lord. Well, make that two things. She'd found friends in Beatrice and Mildred too. The first ones she'd ever had.

Elsie set her chin, knowing what she needed to do. Somehow, she'd find a way to get through it.

Horses' hooves crunched in the snow behind her. She turned on her heel and realized how far away from the house she'd traveled.

"You left without me." Benjamin stepped down from his horse, keeping a tight hold on his ribs as he came to stand in front of her. "How come?" He handed Buster's reins to her.

"I, uh, didn't intend to. Needed time to think I suppose." Elsie turned away from him as she mounted Buster.

"What about?" A soft umph escaped him as he settled back onto his horse.

"Oh, just things." She didn't dare tell him what she'd decided, not when she'd have to explain why.

He didn't say anything on the trip home, so she kept silent until they rode up in front of Benjamin's house.

Elsie swung down from Buster as Benjamin dismounted. "Go on into your house and get warm. I'll take care of Milly."

"You sure?" He rubbed a hand across the back of his neck.

She smiled, her throat tightening. "I'm sure."

As he turned toward his house, she halted him by touching his arm. Benjamin swung back toward her. "Yes?"

She leaned over and pecked him on the cheek. Heat surged to her face. "Get some rest, Benjamin."

He stepped toward her. "I wish—"

Elsie tugged the horses toward the barn, not waiting around to hear what else he wanted to say.

Once inside, Benjamin placed his hand over the spot where Elsie'd kissed him. "If only John hadn't staked his claim on her." He sank to his bed, kicked off his boots, dropping his hat to the floor. Between the ache in his side and the pain in his arm, his energy was gone. Maybe if he lay down and rested his body, he'd have the energy to figure out what to do about her.

His eyes drifted shut, and by the time he opened them, darkness filled the room. He blinked. Just how long had he slept?

Benjamin tripped over his boots as he searched through the blackness for the lamp. Striking a match, light washed over the room. The wick caught, and the flame sent shadows melding into the corners.

Funny. Elsie hadn't come to check on him or brought him food. It wasn't like her—at least from what he knew of her since his altercation with the outlaw.

He rubbed his face. What had caused her to kiss him on the cheek? He rubbed the spot again and smiled. Maybe she'd be open to talk to him more tomorrow. For whatever reason, she'd been closed-mouthed on the way home.

He scrounged up a couple biscuits Elsie had baked yesterday and spread them with sand plum jam. His stomach rumbled as he prayed over his simple meal.

Benjamin traced his finger along the rim of his plate. Should he have told her about his stolen deed? It wasn't like it would make a difference to her. She was his neighbor and had her own plot of land.

Hadn't she been talking about her land to Beatrice when he entered the Sawyer house? He closed his eyes trying to recall it. Something about marrying a man for property. Was John pressing her to give up her land to marry him?

Something niggled at the edge of his memory. If only he could pinpoint what exactly he'd forgotten.

He stood and started pacing, jamming his fingers through his hair. *Is this one of those times when I'm to wait and see Your salvation, Lord? Right now, I can't see anything positive coming out of this mess. I need You to do some unraveling for me.*

Spotting a small box beside his bed, Benjamin crossed the room. He sat on the bed and opened it. The memory flooded back as his fingers wrapped around the cool metal of the compass his father had given him before … Pa had given Benjamin the gift before he left on his journey to try and claim land. He hadn't thought about it since the day of the race. He withdrew it now and rubbed his thumb across the lid. Flipping it open, he read the inscription. *"And whatsoever ye do, do it heartily, as to the Lord, and not unto men."*

Benjamin sank to his knees beside the bed. "Forgive me, Lord, for not trusting You to bring my memories back in Your timing. I give this land up to You, Lord, to do with as You see fit. When the time is right, show me why You brought me here. If it isn't against Your will, I'd love to have all my recollections return, especially about Elsie."

He glanced at the inscription again. "I trust You, Lord. My life is Yours to use as You see fit. In Jesus' name, amen."

Peace settled over his heart. He stood and crossed to the door, throwing it open, and glancing toward Elsie's soddy. Was she still up? Darkness filled the space between them. He looked up at the clear night sky, stars twinkling.

Benjamin smiled as he shut the door.

When he crawled into bed for the night, sleep didn't come. A myriad of images of Elsie flooded his brain. How she looked when blazing mad at him, her tender care when he'd fallen off the roof, and also when she'd found him after being beaten—his plan to ask her to court him. As he lay there, everything came back in a swirl of memories.

So did the revelation, like a blow between the eyes. She'd been showing her interest in him, she merely hadn't used any words.

John had come to say farewell—*not* claim his right to Elsie.

Benjamin's heart ached to think of the hurt he'd caused her by not remembering who she truly was to him. He wanted to tell her now—to run to her and explain everything—but he wouldn't risk her reputation with a late-night visit. Come tomorrow, though, he'd use as many words as possible to convince her he wanted her as his wife. Maybe a kiss or two would help to persuade her as well. He chuckled in anticipation.

That's what Aunt Kate was trying to tell him on the mountain! Benjamin let out a hoot. She was giving her consent for him to pursue her niece.

Benjamin smiled as he shifted, trying to sleep, but Elsie continued to invade his thoughts. He punched his pillow and settled his head against it, blowing out a breath.

"Lord, I sure wish You'd bring morning about a little quicker this time."

CHAPTER THIRTY-SIX

Sometimes the answer to your problem is where you least expect to find it.
Mrs. Wigglesworth's Essential Guide to Proper Etiquette and Manners of Refined Society

Benjamin shoved his arms through the sleeves of his coat and trekked the short distance to Elsie's soddy, not bothering to grab his hat or gloves though his breaths came out in little clouds. He'd been up for hours, and still the sun hadn't peeked above the horizon. When he finally stood before her door, he sent another quick prayer heavenward.

Gaining his courage, Benjamin knocked. His heart hammered against his ribcage as he waited for the door to swing open. A minute passed before he tried again, pounding. Surely she'd forgive him for waking her at this hour because what he had to say couldn't wait any longer.

Still no noises came from her home. "Elsie?"

The barn. Of course, why hadn't he thought of it sooner?

He raced to the structure, throwing the door wide. "Elsie!"

The cows mooed, and Milly snorted out a greeting. He rushed down the small corridor, glancing in each stall, but no Elsie. Where could she be? As he retraced his steps, an empty stall snagged his attention. Buster. The horse should've been near Milly.

There was no reason for Elsie to be out before daylight unless she was running from something again.

Dear God, where has she run to now? Don't let me be too late.

Benjamin ran, slipping on the straw littered across the barn floor. Outside he sprinted back toward her soddy, ignoring the pain in his ribs. His chest heaved as he cracked her door open.

"Elsie?"

As he stepped inside, he knew she wouldn't be there. Benjamin surveyed the small room. The rose quilt was gone. Her saddlebags too.

He sank to a chair. "I need direction, Lord."

A gust of cold air swept through the open doorway, fluttering two pieces of paper nearly hidden behind the lamp. Lighting it carefully, his hand shook as he stared at the pages. He flipped the documents over. No. She hadn't done it. Ice wove its way through his veins and into his heart.

He scrunched the papers into his pocket and trotted back to the barn. Throwing a saddle on Milly, his fingers fumbled as he cinched it in place. "Come on, girl."

Benjamin urged his horse toward town.

Lord, don't let me be too late.

Elsie spotted the first glimpses of Enid by early afternoon. It seemed as if it had doubled in size since she'd last been there. More false storefronts had been erected, and fewer tents dotted the horizon. She shivered, thinking about what it would be like to spend winter in one of the canvas shelters. Elsie prayed it wouldn't be her fate.

Once they located the store she'd visited before, Elsie swung her leg over the saddle and jumped to the ground. She reached up to help her aunt.

"I appreciate you bringing me to town, Elsie." Aunt Kate grunted as she climbed down from the horse's wide back. "Do you think we'll be able to find a way for me to head north?"

"Won't know until we try. It's not like a stagecoach will be starting up anytime soon." Elsie held back the tent flap so her aunt could duck through the opening. She waved the owner over. "Howdy. Have you heard about any folks heading to Kansas?"

The clerk grinned. "As a matter a fact, that family over there are just purchasing some last-minute supplies before they head back from where they came from. I think they mentioned going thataway." He pointed to them. "They're pulling up stakes. Said it's too hard to get things going out here."

Aunt Kate strolled over to the young couple. "Excuse me. The store owner mentioned that you'll soon be departing and going north. Is there any chance you'll be passing by Kiowa on your travels?"

"Yep. We'll be goin' right through there." A tall, lean man glanced at his wife and then back at Aunt Kate. "There somethin' we can do for you?"

"I'm in need of a ride and am willing to pay."

The woman waved a hand of dismissal. "No need for that. We's just glad to help out where we's can. You don't have much baggage, do you? You'd have to ride in the back with the young'uns."

"I only have two small bags." Aunt Kate smiled. "I can't thank you enough."

"As long as you can be ready to leave in the next ten minutes, you're welcome to ride with us." The man dipped his hat, then went to settle his account with the store owner.

Elsie and Aunt Kate trooped outside to retrieve her carpetbags.

"I guess this is goodbye." Aunt Kate pulled Elsie into a hug. "I owe you an apology."

"What do you mean?"

"I've allowed my bitterness to flow and spill all over you." Aunt Kate dabbed her eyes. "I blamed you for your mother's death. I miss my sweet sister, but it was wrong of me to take it out on you.

"And I owe you an apology for the way I treated your pa. It wasn't so much Elmer that I disliked, but what he represented.

You know your ma and I were poor growing up. When I was of age, my pa decided to pair me with a lucrative partner. It didn't matter that I didn't love the man he'd picked out for me."

"Uncle Hiram?"

Her aunt nodded. "I've been miserable my entire life because of it, and I allowed bitterness to take root and splash onto others. I didn't see it until that ruffian pointed it out." She pulled out a handkerchief and dabbed at her tears. "When I was on that mountain, I realized how like that evil man I'd become. Not caring who I hurt in the process of my selfishness. I knew then that I didn't want to die without first asking you to forgive me and telling you I truly love you."

It took a few moments for Elsie to process all her aunt said. "I forgive you, Aunt Kate."

"We need to be leavin', ma'am." The man shifted his hat. "If you want to go with us, you best finish your good-byin'."

"One more moment." Aunt Kate smiled at Elsie. "Promise me you'll listen to what that young man wants to say to you."

"What young man?"

"Your preacher."

"What does Benjamin have to say?"

"Ma'am, it's time to go." The man took Aunt Kate's arm and ushered her to his wagon.

"Just listen to him." Aunt Kate waved as the man helped her to the back of the vehicle. She squeezed in between a small boy and girl who immediately started chatting to her.

"But what were you saying about Benjamin?"

"What?" Aunt Kate leaned toward Elsie, but the children kept talking. As the family drove away, Aunt Kate smiled and waved.

Elsie waved back. "Goodbye, Aunt Kate. I promise I'll write to you. Give my love to Dorcas and the others."

Her aunt fluttered a handkerchief until the conveyance turned north and disappeared.

Elsie sucked in a deep breath and patted Buster. "Never figured I'd see the day when Aunt Kate would apologize." With her aunt safely on her way home, Elsie headed toward the small building on her left. Shoving open the door, she stepped inside the office. A man glanced up from his desk. "How can I help you, young fella?"

"I understand there might be some land still available in the area."

"There might be, but you'd have to be twenty-one." He flipped his visor up and studied her.

Elsie walked toward the map of land plats on the wall. "Are these the ones standing vacant?"

The man picked up a pair of spectacles and settled them on his nose before joining her. He squinted. "Yep, those are the ones. Might be more, according to the sheriff, if he can't get a hold of some folks. Did you hear about the outlaw who stole them? It's all they're talking about in town."

"Are the plots the same price as the day of the run?" Elsie belted the words out, hoping to conduct her business and be on her way. She had no desire to hear about how the land had become available.

"Let me see. I just got an update on that." He crossed back to his desk and rifled through a stack of papers. "I have it here somewhere." He stooped to sort through a pile on the floor. "Give me a minute."

Elsie sighed and turned back to the wall. The door opened and closed, but she kept her gaze on the map, searching for an area she might like. The chart blurred, and her throat clogged. *This isn't the way I wanted things to turn out, Lord.*

"Elsie?"

She stilled, not needing to turn around to know Benjamin had entered the building. Her heart hiccupped, then vaulted like a stallion at the start of a race. Why did he have to come here and make it more difficult? She'd already said goodbye in the note. What else could he want?

Before Elsie could look for a way to escape, his arms wrapped around her shoulders. She longed to lean against his chest but stepped out of his grasp instead. She fisted her hands and took several steps away from him before turning.

The clerk stared at her. "You're a girl?"

"Woman." Benjamin corrected. "She's mine, so don't get any ideas."

Her eyes widened. Had he remembered more? About her? *No*. It couldn't be that.

Elsie shoved past him.

"Elsie, wait." Benjamin continued to call her name as she wove through folks strolling on the boarded walkway.

A few seconds later, he yanked her to a halt. His grip didn't loosen when she turned to face him.

"Here." He shoved a paper into her hand. "I refuse to keep your deed."

"My decision's already made, and there's no changing my mind."

"Please, Elsie, let's go somewhere quiet where we can talk about it." His eyes pleaded. "I promise I won't take much of your time. Please hear me out."

Despite her hesitancy, she found herself nodding.

He threaded his fingers through hers and led her down a quiet street until they stood on the outskirts of town. Nobody lingered around them. She willed her pulse to cease the hammering in her head.

"I have something to say to you." Benjamin released her hand.

Elsie tucked it beneath her arms, not sure she wanted to hear what came next from his mouth. "I—"

"Please." He held up a hand to halt her words. "Let me get this out, then you can tell me whatever you want."

Elsie chewed on the inside of her cheek, warily watching him.

He tipped her chin up, his eyes boring into hers.

"Right before I settled down last night, the Lord restored *all* of my memories. I know how much it must've hurt these past weeks when I didn't realize who you were and what you mean to me." He swallowed, his Adam's apple jumping in his neck. "I'm sorry I put you through that pain."

Could it be? Her pulse skittered as she waited for his next words.

"There's something else, though. Herbert paid me a visit the day he saw you, and he threatened to hurt you if I didn't do as he said."

A shudder rippled the length of her spine.

"He wanted my deed. I gave it to him so he wouldn't come after you."

Elsie gasped. "You don't have your deed anymore?"

He shook his head. "No, and I don't want your deed either." Benjamin motioned toward the paper clutched in her hand. He took a step closer, his breath tickling her cheek. "What I want is *you*, Elsie Smith."

Tears sprang to her eyes, but she shook her head. He'd finally said the words she'd longed to hear, but her heart ached. Could she believe him? She broke free of his grasp and stepped a short distance away before he swung her back around by the waist.

"Now, woman, will you stop running off on me when I'm trying to propose to you?"

Moisture dripped from her chin. "Why? I'll never be like Mary."

"Nor would I want you to. I want you to be just who you are, Elsie. It's *you* I've fallen in love with."

She shook her head, and a tear trickled down her cheek. "I won't marry because you want the land."

"Will you listen to me? I don't care about the land. It's you who's captured my heart." He ran a fingertip along her neck. She trembled at his touch.

"Is this fella bothering you, miss?"

Benjamin scrubbed a hand across his face. The sheriff had lousy timing. Elsie edged away from him, but he snagged her wrist. He refused to let her go until he could make her understand how much he loved her. *Help me, Lord. Give me the words to say that will break through to her, and the patience to deal with this man.*

"Miss?" The sheriff's brow wrinkled.

"I'm fine," she mumbled.

The sheriff looked between Elsie and Benjamin before recognition brightened his face. "I'm glad I spotted you. I've got some news."

"What's that?" Elsie tried to pry his fingers from her arm. He held tight, never planning to let go of her again.

"If you stop over at my office, I have the deed to your place. That scoundrel Santos finally told where he hid the rest of the stolen deeds. He came clean when he heard all the evidence stacked against him and that folks were willing to testify." The sheriff chuckled. "Guess he wasn't counting on that. Don't forget to come on over so I can get your written statement, if your memories have returned, that is."

"They have," Benjamin said as he continued to keep a hold of Elsie.

The lawman glanced at Benjamin's grip on her. "You sure you don't need help, little lady?"

When the sheriff's gaze returned to Benjamin's, his eagle eyes seemed to pierce through him.

"I know things look bad, but I'm just trying to let Elsie know how much I love her. Honestly, we're fine, Sheriff. I'll be at your office in a bit. Now, if you'll excuse us."

A hard boot slammed into Benjamin's shins. He howled as Elsie scampered away from him and stood beside the sheriff.

"Please, Elsie." Ignoring his throbbing shin, Benjamin bent down on one knee before her. "I'm trying to ask you to marry me. It's you I want—nobody else. Nothing else."

The sheriff chuckled. "I try not to get in the middle of matters that have to deal with the heart. If I were you, little lady, I'd listen to what the fella has to say." He tipped his hat. "Excuse me, folks."

Elsie stared at Benjamin, her eyes unblinking. He wished she'd say something, anything. He whisked his hat off and stood. "It's you I want. Not the claim. Just you."

He inched closer, and she didn't move a muscle. Benjamin took it as a good sign. At least she hadn't hauled off and slugged him. He scooted closer still until a mere inch separated them. Her breaths came in short bursts. A tear slid down her cheek. He thumbed it away, and she rested her face against the palm of his hand.

"I didn't want to run away this time, but I thought God wanted me to give you the land, and I couldn't exactly stay on it without ..." Her cheeks turned a delightful shade of pink.

"Your running days are over, my dear." He leaned his forehead against hers.

"That means I'll have to learn to stay and fight my battles, and you may not like me when—"

"I already love you, and nothing will change that. We'll face our struggles together." His mouth grazed her cheek. "With the Lord."

Elsie slipped her hand into his and grinned. "You won't hear me complaining."

"I'll even make sure we have room for your aunt. Is she still with the Sawyers?"

"She just left—and after this trip—I don't think she'll be back."

Thank you, Father.

He dipped his head.

Her dark-blue eyes stayed focused on him.

She nuzzled her nose against his neck. "You sure you won't change your mind about us?"

"Never." He pulled her into his embrace.

His kiss started out gentle, but Elsie pressed closer, wrapping one arm around his back and threading the fingers of her other hand through his hair.

Her heart drummed so hard she feared it would burst from her chest. She deepened the kiss, her thoughts whirling. When he broke free, she stood breathless.

Elsie had no idea how much time had passed while they stood smooching in the middle of the street.

Though her cheeks had warmed, she couldn't resist the urge to look over her shoulder to see if anybody had observed them.

Benjamin chuckled. "Never fear, my dear Elsie. Nobody saw us."

She swung her attention back toward him, and her heart sang. *Lord, thank You for answering my prayers.*

"I love you, Elsie, and I want to marry you today."

"B-but—"

He placed a finger over her mouth before planting a quick peck on her cheek. "I don't want to wait any longer. You're the woman God has for me, and I love you. Will you marry me? Now?"

A giggle bubbled out of her, making her sound more like a young schoolgirl than a grown woman. Heat rushed to her cheeks. "Yes. Whenever you like."

He let out a whoop and twirled her around.

"Careful, you'll hurt your ribs."

Instead of heeding her warning, he kissed her, sending her soaring above the clouds.

When she finally caught her breath, she smiled at him. "Why don't you go round up a preacher and somewhere for us to get married while I do a little shopping? Providing you don't mind parting with some of your money." Elsie stood on tiptoe to kiss his cheek. She sent him a mischievous grin.

"You want to go shopping now?" His brows puckered, but he pressed a few bills into her hand.

Elsie laughed. "Trust me. I'll meet you in an hour."

EPILOGUE

A bride should be properly attired for a wedding, taking careful planning with her habiliment.
Mrs. Wigglesworth's Essential Guide to Proper Etiquette and Manners of Refined Society

Ripples of pleasure skidded up Elsie's spine as she settled the white, shimmering fabric over her hips. She smiled as her cowboy boots poked out from the hem of the dress. Her fingers trembled as she brushed her hair, swooped it up, and pinned it in place.

"You look lovely, dear." The pastor's wife smiled. "I've never seen such a beautiful gown before. Where did you say you purchased it?"

Elsie fingered the fabric. "From the storekeeper in town. He said some wealthy woman sold it to him after her wedding didn't work out. She didn't want to be reminded of it."

The woman clucked. "It looks like it's tailor-made for you. My, what a beautiful veil. Here, allow me." The pastor's wife pinned the sheer fabric in place and draped it around Elsie's shoulders. A twinkle sparkled in the woman's eyes. "Your mother would be so proud of you, and your young man will be quite surprised when he sees you come down the aisle."

Elsie's heart raced. She sure hoped Benjamin would be pleased with the purchase she'd made.

She blinked away the threatening moisture. "I'm ready."

The little old lady scurried ahead of her. She motioned for Elsie to halt in the doorway while she took her place at the piano. Soon music filled the small sanctuary.

Benjamin stood at the front, his mouth dropping open before a huge smile spread across his handsome face, his love for her clearly shining in his eyes. Dressed in a new suit, he looked more handsome than ever. He winked at her as she started down the aisle.

He's claimed my heart in a way I never imagined, Lord. Thank You.

AUTHOR'S NOTE

Twenty years ago I was first introduced to the history of the Cherokee Strip Land Run of 1893 by my dear mother-in-law, Merrietta Jo (Randolph) Wolfe. She shared tales of her family members who had staked claims during this great land race in the Oklahoma Territory. In the summer of 1997, Mom took me to see the original homestead where a modest sod house had been built into the hillside, near a creek. It was in a state of disrepair, but I could already picture characters living in the area. The Glass Mountains, sometimes referred to as the Gloss Mountains, are only about a mile from there. My mother-in-law recounted stories of when she was a kid, and the shimmery stones that were still prevalent.

I made brief mention of the Dick Yeager Gang. Dick Yeager (known by several different aliases during his lifetime, but born as Nathaniel Ellsworth Wyatt) and Ike Black teamed up, and were actual outlaws who terrorized the area in those days. On one occasion, the local men formed a posse and rode out to apprehend the notorious outlaws. My husband's great-great-grandmother was left alone with her children. There was a knock at the door. She answered it, and the outlaws stood in the doorway wanting food. She recognized their faces, but still invited them in and provided a meal. They hung their gun belts on the back of their chairs, ate, said thank you and then left.

The Rose of Sharon quilt is one that has been in my husband's family since the 1850s when it was stitched. It's a beautiful appliqued quilt passed down to the oldest daughter in the family.

The prune cake recipe is one that my mother-in-law treasured and fiercely guarded.

95629818R00190

Made in the USA
Columbia, SC
12 May 2018